Anne Rivers Siddons is a major American bestselling writer.
Both HILL TOWNS and her previous novel, COLONY,
spent three months on the *New York Times* and *Publishers
Weekly* bestseller lists. She has written eight other novels and
lives in Atlanta, Georgia.

Praise for HILL TOWNS:

'An outstanding multigenerational novel' *New York Times*

'Anne Rivers Siddons' vibrant, compassionate tone captures
Italy's powerful effect on the timid, and even the frightened
Catherine becomes compelling' *Entertainment Weekly*

HILL TOWNS

ANNE RIVERS SIDDONS

WARNER BOOKS

A *Warner* Book

First published in Great Britain in 1994
by Little, Brown and Company
This edition published in 1994 by Warner Books

Published by arrangement with HarperCollins Publishers, Inc.
New York, New York, USA

A CIP catalogue record for this book is
available from the British Library.

ISBN 0 7515 0891 8

Printed in England by Clays Ltd, St Ives plc

Warner Books
A Division of
Little, Brown and Company (UK) Limited
Brettenham House
Lancaster Place
London WC2E 7EN

This book is in memory of my father,
MARVIN RIVERS,
who would have loved a Tuscan odyssey;
and for Cliff and Cynthia, who did.

"Only the very young can live in Eden.
Innocence prolonged ignores experience; knowledge
denied becomes a stone in the head."

ANDREW LYTLE

"I remember Rome chiefly as the place where Zelda
and I had an appalling squabble."

SCOTT FITZGERALD, LETTER, 1922

HILL
TOWNS

CHAPTER ONE

WHEN I WAS FIVE YEARS OLD I made a coldly desperate decision to live forever in a town on a hill, and so I have, from that terrible night in June until this one, thirty-seven years and one month later. If it has been bad for me, as many people these days seem to be telling me, I can only consider that anything else at all would have been worse.

"They never saw it coming; they didn't know what hit them," everybody said after my parents were struck and killed by a speeding truck on the old chain bridge over Tolliver's Creek. After that, I knew as simply and unalterably as a child knows anything that staying alive meant always being able to see what was coming. Always knowing what might hit you. So when my father's parents, kind and substantial Virginians from the Tidewater who might have given me every advantage, made to take me home with them after the funeral, I simply screamed and screamed until, in despair, they left me behind with my mother's eccentric people, who lived on the top of the mountain where my parents had died. I had great affection for my Virginia grandparents and little for the erratic, reclusive Cashes, who were strange even in that hill country, where strangeness is king, but the ramshackle, overgrown Cash house commanded the Blue Ridge foothills in all directions. From there I would always know what was coming. From there I would see it long before it saw me.

I could not have explained this at age five, of course; I have only recently become fully aware of it. Then, I only knew that on the mountain I was safe and off it I was not. Everything in my small being strained after my grandmother and grandfather Compton as they drove away from the sly, sunless home of my Cash grandparents in their sedate old Chrysler that sunny afternoon; I felt as if sunlight and laughter and gentleness and childhood itself were rolling away with them. But the new flatland fear was stronger. When I turned my face into the sagging lap of my grandmother Cash, she thought I wept in sorrow for my parents and said for the first of a thousand times, "That's all right. You done right. You stay here with your own kind. Your mama wouldn't be lyin' there in her grave if she'd of stayed with her own kind."

But I'm not your kind, I remember thinking as clearly as spring water. I don't need you. It's your house I need. It's this mountain.

It was, I realize, an extraordinary insight for a small child. And it did not surface again for more than thirty years. Still, the power of it served. It held me on the Mountain through everything that came afterward, all those years that seem in retrospect to have been lived in a kind of green darkness, until I met Joe Gaillard in my senior year at Trinity College and the last lingering darkness took fire into light.

When I told him about my parents' death—and I remember it was long after I met him, only days before he proposed to me—he cried. I stared at him doubtfully; no one had ever cried upon hearing the manner of their deaths, and some few laughed outright, nervous, swiftly stifled laughter. Even I had not cried after that first obliterating grief. I was not too young to perceive that they had somehow simply died of ludicrousness. I learned early to parrot laughter along with the children at Montview Day School, where my Compton grandparents' absentee largesse sent me, when they taunted me with it: "Cat's mama and daddy fucked themselves to death!" "Hey, Cat! Wanna go out and hump on the bridge?"

Later, when I began to perceive the dim shape of their meaning, I stopped laughing and began fighting. By the time I was ten, I was on the brink of being expelled for aggression. Time and Cora Pierce's influence put a stop to that, but I still hear the laughter sometimes, in the long nights on the Mountain.

"I'm lucky you weren't a serial murderer or a Republican," I told Joe later. "I'd have married you anyway. It's pretty obvious I would have married the first man who didn't wince and grin a shit-faced grin and say, 'Well, at least they died happy.'"

"I wasn't crying for them; they probably did die happy, at that," he said. "I was crying for you. Nobody should laugh at a child's grief. Nobody. Ever."

"Well, it wasn't at my grief, exactly," I said. "It's just—you can see why it's funny, in an awful sort of way, can't you? I mean, there they were out on that bridge, just going to town, and here comes this chicken truck—"

"Nobody," Joe said fiercely. "Never. Not under any circumstance. Jesus Christ, when I think what that laughter must have taught you about the world—"

"It taught me never to screw on bridges," I said, and he did laugh then, the exuberant, froggy laugh that always made people's lips tug up involuntarily at the corners. I knew he was laughing largely because I wanted him to. Joe was a lovely man then, in the supple greenness of his twenties.

My father was a tall fair boy who came to Trinity College because his father and grandfather had come before him; and before them his great-grandfather Cornelius Compton, an Episcopal bishop of modest fame in the South, had helped to found the university. There had been Comptons at Trinity since the beginning. The theological seminary, Compton Hall, bore their name, and young Corny Compton IV from the Tidewater was destined to take his place in the southern Episcopal hierarchy of the last half of the twentieth century. He had, everyone assured his proud parents, a real passion for the ministry.

Instead he met my mother in the village at the start of his senior year, in our lone dry cleaning establishment. She had come down from the Cashes' old home, hidden away on the very top of Morgan's Mountain, to make a little money and see a little life, and all his fine passion fled the church in a rush and poured into her. Literally, probably. They were married by the New Year, and I appeared in the earliest days of May. I was a quiet child who absorbed a great deal of grown-up talk, and while I was still small I came to know that my mother and father had done it practically the day they met and whenever afterward they could, and I was lucky they stopped doing it long enough to marry and give me a name. I knew what "it" was, too, vaguely; I heard them so often in the night and sometimes in the daytime, whispering and laughing and then breathing in that sharp, short way, and finally moaning and shouting aloud, that I ceased to be curious about what actually transpired and never even bothered to spy on them. I suppose I assumed that everybody's parents were the same. It did not bother me at all; I truly believe they loved each other profoundly as well as lusted after each other, and much of that love overflowed onto me. We were a happy little family, even though both sets of my grandparents predicted nothing for us but ruin.

If they had lived there probably would have been more children. Despite my mother's assiduous use of the pill, the law of averages would have undoubtedly caught up with them sooner or later. My father barely managed to graduate from Trinity between bouts in bed; as one of my Cash aunts observed, "His brains must of leaked out, his fly was unzipped so often." His grades were flaccid and his ambition flown, and after commencement he simply stayed on in Montview and got a job at the hardware store. The same aunt said he took it because it was the only thing he could find where he could come home and bang my mother at lunchtime. I don't believe that aunt ever married.

By the time I was five my parents had still not let up much and were becoming adventurous in their choices of arenas. I was now old enough to lift from sleep and bundle into the back seat of their old Nash, and they would range the mountain on moonlit nights, laughing and fondling each other, my mother reaching back to check on my blankets and send me back into sleep with a pat, and when they found a spot that was inviting, and later one that demanded a certain amount of daring, they simply stopped the Nash, made sure I was asleep, and got out and did it under the cold smile of the moon. I think they were probably becoming a little jaded, a little flown with the sheer audacity of the spots they chose, by the time they died. The old chain-hung bridge over Tolliver's Creek was daunting even in daylight; it hung a good fifty feet in midair over the white-rushing water below, with space above and below and all around it. I hated it even before that night.

But it must have swayed gently and irresistibly before them in its frail emptiness that June night, because they parked the Nash on the far side, off on the ferny verge, and left me sleeping in it, and went onto the middle of the bridge and took off their clothes and began to make love, and it was during their final blinded and deafened transports of that love that Leon Crouch, drunk in his father's chicken truck, caromed onto the bridge and smashed them off it and onto the granite rapids below. If they weren't dead when they went off, they most surely were as soon as they hit. It was a closed-casket funeral, a disgrace nearly tantamount to the manner of their death in the Cash family.

I did not hear the truck coming. I did not hear it hit them. I only heard, an instant later, the squall of brakes and Leon Crouch shouting over and over, "Holy shit! Oh, holy shitfire Jesus *Lord!*"

And then, when he found me in the back seat of the Nash, "God*damn* those trashy fuckers! Right in front of their baby!"

It was as good an epitaph as any for Rosellen and Cornelius Compton in the eyes of the Mountain, and it was most assuredly the start of a consensus. After that, most of the tears shed for them were, at least in part, tears of embarrassed laughter. Only mine and perhaps my grandparents' were pure, and even mine were inward.

Trinity College crowns the flat summit of Morgan's Mountain in south Tennessee like a mortarboard or a forage cap, or perhaps a bishop's miter, apt similes all. It was born just after the Civil War (referred to on the Mountain as the War for Southern Independence) expressly to serve the southern dioceses of the Episcopal Church in the Christian education of its young gentlemen. It was modeled, as perfectly as human frailty allowed, after the venerable Anglican colleges of England and held together during its hardscrabble early years by the unspent passion of a great many unemployed Confederate officers. Many southern bishops blessed it, and not a few came to teach there. Several still do. Widows of Confederate officers or Episcopal clergymen were its first housemothers. Early on, it became an indulgent little joke that "Trinity" in the college's case referred to God the Father, God the Son, and General Robert E. Lee.

Succeeding generations of Trinitarians have found no cause to scuttle the joke. God the Father and God the Son are still manifestly present in the mellow gray dimness of All Souls Chapel and Compton Seminary, and General Lee's portrait, flanked by draped Confederate flags and crossed dress sabers, still hangs in Commons.

The education presided over by these eminences is unalterably classical liberal arts and generally first rate in spite of it, and for that reason many undergraduates are now drawn from all parts of the country and even the world. Very few these days come to be molded by God and Robert E. Lee for life and service in the vanished world of the Christian gentlemen's South, and many new students come up the Mountain for the first time prepared to jeer. Even those of us whose permanent world it is often laugh at Trinity's sheer hubris of intent and tradition; the "Trinity experience" no longer fits one to live anywhere but Trinity, it's often said at faculty doings on the Mountain.

But those who remain do not wish to leave. And the young who enter laughing and stay to graduate almost always go out into the world off the Mountain taking with them the swish of invisible academic gowns and a set of near-chivalric values. There is enormous power in these old gray stones, cloistered away up here on Morgan's Mountain. They bend reality and stop time. I do not wonder that Trinity produces so few successful junk bond salesmen and politicians. The daily subliminal infusions of honor are an effective lifelong purgative for a great many contemporary ambitions. I sometimes imagine that the last sound new graduates hear as they roll out under the stone arch that marks the southernmost boundary of the Domain, as we call it, is the triumphant laughter of long-dead bishops and generals.

Much of Trinity's power lies in its sheer beauty. The Mountain and the village of Montview are almost phantasmagorical in their loveliness. There are to me no mountains on earth so beautiful as these. They are among the oldest in the world, smoothed now to the curves of a sleeping woman's body. They roll across the middle South in symmetrical soft, misted waves. Morgan's Mountain sits a little apart from the rest, a last convulsion that marks the dying of the Appalachian chain. And green: green everywhere, always, all the greens of the entire earth, each to its own season. The top of Morgan's Mountain is a globe of pure green swimming suspended in the thin, clear blue air of the southern highlands. It comes eventually to be the only air where permanent Trinitarians can thrive. We are unfit, I have always thought, to breathe other richer, ranker air for long.

That dreaming old beauty is the snare, of course. Those who

do not need it do not stay. A high percentage of freshmen and
sophomores do not return. Some flunk out, but many simply bolt
back to the rich, comforting stench of the world. Those who stay
need bells in their ears, and plainsong, and countless angels
dancing always on the heads of pins. And after all, the world is
lucky that relatively few do stay; what would we do with all
those elite young philosopher princelings if their numbers were
legion? Where would we fit all those languorous, learned young
Anglophiles?

But the ones who do stay . . . ah the old mossy stones and
the flying dark gowns and the ranked pennons in chapel looking
for all the world like medieval banners, and the slow turn of the
burnished seasons in the great hardwood forest, and the mists of
autumn and the white snowfall of spring dogwoods and the
world spread out at one's feet all around off the Mountain, and
the bittersweet smoke of wood fires and the drunkenness of
poetry and mathematics and the flow of bourbon and the night
music of concerts and dances through new green leaves, and the
delicately bawdy laughter of young girls and the sheen of their
flesh and hair, and the special trembling awareness of cold dew
and dawn breaking on monumental hangovers after you have
talked all night of wonderful or terrible things and sung many
songs and perhaps made out by the lake or on the Steep: these
things are golden barbs in the flesh and will hold always. Trinity
is eccentric and elitist and chauvinistic and innocent and arrogant and very, very particular, and it claims its own like a great
gray raptor.

My grandfather Cash was a janitor there.

"What did that feel like?" Joe asked me when he learned
that one grandfather used to clean the structure that bore the
other's name. Not for long; Papaw Cash refused to enter Compton Seminary with his mops and brooms once the Compton of it
entered his family. Everyone at Trinity understood.

Joe was powerfully attracted to my family's bizarre history.

He found none of it amusing and all of it profound. Joe was a born teacher of literature.

"It's pure American tragedy," he said, over and over. "It's all of folklore and literature, really: the Montagues and the Capulets, the Medicis, most of Faulkner—"

"And the Hatfields and the McCoys, maybe?" I said. "Or the Jukes and the Kallikaks?"

I was in his senior Southern Literature seminar that winter. It was how we met. I knew he knew the story of my provenance on the Mountain before he knew me; everyone at Trinity did. I had stopped minding long before. Such was Trinity's ecclesiastical, liberal-arts predilection for wounded birds and fascination with its own redolently Gothic milieu that I was a campus favorite from the days I used to come to work with my grandfather Cash and sit docilely on the steps of whatever structure he was cleaning, Mamaw Cash being practically certifiable by then. Somehow I never felt an outsider in the Domain. Everyone knew and felt sorry for me, the strange little hybrid of gown and town. And I suppose I was an appealing child; I heard it often. I was slight and grave and long-limbed, with a cap of curls like a little Greek boy's, only fair, and fine thin features. I looked for all the world like my father and still do, save for the very dark eyes that were my mother's. Except for the fine dry lines around my eyes and mouth, I could pass now for a rather androgynous late teen. My father had the same look in the photographs taken just before he died, and it is there in the portrait of my great-grandfather Compton, in the seminary. Unworldly and dreaming, patrician as an overbred collie. It has, I think, served all us Comptons well, even my poor father. It both enabled and excused him a great deal.

"What did it feel like?" I answered Joe when he first asked. "To tell you the truth, it made me feel rather special. Everybody bent over backward to make me feel accepted, not to feel . . . singled out because my grandfather was a campus janitor, and not even the head honcho at that. I think I was pretty much Trinity's poster child for a long time. Papaw wouldn't even speak my father's name by then, but I knew the name on the seminary was mine, and somehow I knew that half of me, anyway, was connected to the college in an important way. After a while Mrs. Pierce, the provost's wife, put her foot down and said it was a disgrace for Bishop Compton's great-granddaughter to sit on the steps with the mops and brooms all day, and she took me into her own house with her housekeeper. I pretty much grew up there weekdays; I went to the little Trinity kindergarten, and the faculty children came to play with me, and it got so I went to all the right little Mountain birthday parties and play groups and then to Montview Day. I know my Compton grandparents paid my tuition and probably kicked in a good bit more in those earliest days, but I think they must have sent it straight to the Pierces, or maybe there was a discreet little fund established at the school. The bequest came much later, after they died. I know if they'd sent money to my Cash grandparents' house, Mamaw Cash would have given it all to her church. She was practically handling snakes by that time."

Joe's eyes shone behind his rimless round glasses. More Faulkner; this was beyond his wildest dreams. I could practically see a monograph taking shape inside his long, elegant skull: "The Survival of the Gothic Tradition in the American Southern Highlands."

"Too bad it all had such an ordinary happy ending," I said.

He wouldn't surrender so easily.

"That's not the way I heard it," he said. "I heard you went through a god-awful time with your Cash grandparents before they died. Christ, no wonder you don't want to leave this place. It must seem like the only refuge you ever had."

I didn't bother to ask who had told him about the other side of my childhood, the side that prevailed when I went home each afternoon with Papaw Cash. Anyone could have. It was part of the cherished Legend of Catherine Compton. I heard much later

that another professor, a pale young man in the music school
who much admired the ballads of John Jacob Niles, had made up
a folk song about me once while drunk on jug wine at a faculty
party: "The Ballad of Cat Compton." It amused me when I
finally heard it, in my early thirties and safe in my stone house
on the Steep overlooking the entire valley, with Joe and our
daughter Lacey. But it would have embarrassed me no end if I
had learned about it at the time. Back then I wanted only to put
every vestige of my life in the dark vine-strangled shack on the
other side of the Mountain behind me and melt into the body of
Trinity.

Dark . . . dear Lord, the darkness around that house and in
it! Not only the darkness of the enshrouding kudzu and creeper
vines that finally came to hold the black weathered boards
together; not only the darkness of the encircling pines and the
wet gray lip of pure mountain granite that beetled over it, so that
between trees and rock you never saw the sun or the blue of the
sky unless you went outside and stood in the front yard. No, the
darkness in the house of Burrell and Mattie Cash seeped from
the very walls and canted floors; from the stained rag rugs and
cracked linoleum and the few pieces of scarred old dark fumed
oak furniture; from the black iron stove and the wash pot in the
kitchen and the listing moss-slick outhouse in the pines behind;
from the mean small fireplaces in the four rooms that lay cold
and dank and empty except in the very dead of winter; from, it
seemed to me, the very stuff of my grandparents' shapeless lye-
boiled clothing, to which my own clothing was nearly identical;
from their dark closed faces and shuttered, black Cash eyes.

I never knew why my grandparents were so cold and
angry; it was not entirely at my father, and at my mother's
shameful death with him on the chain bridge, for they were
silent and angry even before that. I remember distinctly that I
really feared going to their house when my parents were alive,
and was always cold there, and finally my mother did not take
me anymore. None of Rosellen Cash's older brothers and sisters

lived in their parents' house that I can remember. All of them
had fled it as soon as they could find sustenance for themselves
elsewhere. Three Cash aunts had married when they were sixteen and could legally do so and moved to the flatlands, where
they raised what seemed to me entire phalanxes of dark, jeering
Cash cousins. Two Cash uncles had also fled to the flats but did
not marry and seemed to spend most of their time raising hell.
They were said by Papaw to be sorry and by Mamaw to be
damned, and I did not see them at all, even after I went to live in
their childhood home.

I think now that the darkness in that house—the metaphori-
cal darkness, not the physical, which was entirely corporeal—
had its genesis in the madness of my grandmother Mattie Cash. I
believe it was that madness that I smelt when I was small, like a
young animal smells hidden blood, and feared her house as if it
had been a charnel house. And I think it is an apt measure of the
terrible fear of randomness, of murdering chance, that was born
in me when my parents died that I chose that house rather than
the benign house of my Compton kin. Mattie Cash was obliquely
mad then; an outlander might mistake it for simple mountain
reclusiveness, the queerness of old ways, and perhaps a long
skein of inbreeding in the blood. There was more than a little of
that in those hills then, born of proximity and inaccessibility and
sheer xenophobia. But the skewedness that poured from the old
house like invisible smoke was madness pure and simple, and in
my grandmother's case it chose, as its object, God.

My grandmother was a religious fanatic from the day she
was converted by a hellfire-screaming, circuit-riding preacher in
her sixteenth year on the other side of the Mountain from Trinity
College. By the time her daughter died naked in her lust and I
came to her, she was drunk on God. By the time my grandfather
began taking me to work with him, she was so deeply possessed
by the Holy Ghost that even he, stone-cold man that he was himself, feared she would harm me if I were left alone with her.

Mamaw never ceased trying, with cries and threats and apocalyptic quotes from the Old Testament or Revelation, to convert anyone who came within range of her terrible God.

And he *was* terrible. He was a God of fire and blood and vengeance, who demanded of his followers flesh and fealty and money and whatever else they had. He took and he judged and he damned. In my grandmother's ruined mind, he left it up to her to save and instructed her to do it with her tongue and her hands and her broom and even the occasional kitchen knife, if the occasion for that arose. She murdered one of Papaw's two prized heifers, destined to fatten and thrive and keep us all in milk and butter for winters to come, because her God demanded of her, one steaming July day, the sacrifice of a fatted calf. She went after the social worker from the county, who heard about the calf and came to see how I was faring, with the same knife. Only the intervention of the pastor of the church to which my grandmother was indentured, and my grandfather's promise to keep me away from her, saved her from being committed then and there to the state mental facility in Knoxville.

Papaw wasn't stupid or mean, only frozen in his bitterness. He could see the trouble my slender fairness and the betraying chocolate eyes of my mother portended for me. As for Pastor Elkins, he was indeed a snake handler and half mad himself, but he was a consummate fund raiser. His ramshackle prophecy-haunted tabernacle in a tangled hollow at the base of the Mountain owed half its provenance to the money Mamaw appropriated from Papaw's wages, money kept aside to feed and clothe us. Even more largesse flowed from the sums my Compton grandparents sent regularly for my schooling and general well-being. I don't doubt that those gentle, cultivated Anglicans financed the upkeep of more than one thick, sluggish, deadly Mountain rattlesnake or water moccasin. Pastor Elkins looked upon his handmaiden's rapt, mad face and saw there many more years of affluence from the Tidewater before I attained my majority. He smiled his bleached feral smile at the county folks and promised there would not be any more unpleasantness from Sister Cash.

"She is God's daughter in her heart," he said. "She's only just got so full of the Holy Spirit that it runs over sometimes."

"Holy Spirit, my behind. That old bat is as crazy as a bedbug," I heard the young woman from the county say to her supervisor as they got back into the battered county sedan and bumped out of our yard.

The next morning I went for the first time up the winding road to Trinity College with my grandfather in his old truck and passed for the first time under the arch and into the Domain.

"Yes," the small part of me deep inside that knew about such things whispered. "This is right. This is the place."

And when the first of the faculty members passed me, sitting quietly, as my grandfather had bidden me, on the gray stone steps of Lawler Hall, where the college's administrative offices were, I raised my head and looked straight at them and smiled.

"It's a pretty morning, isn't it?" I said, and when they invariably stopped and asked me my name and whose little girl I was, I said my name was Catherine Rose Compton, and my mama and daddy were dead, and I lived now with Papaw, who made the college clean. And smiled again.

I was six years old, then, and on that day saved myself.

"And the rest, as they say, is history," I told Joe soon after I met him. I told Joe everything about me soon after we met, except the manner of my parents' death. And that came just a little later, for it was only months after we met that I knew we would marry and I might, with luck, stay forever on the Mountain. Only then did I feel I could trust Joe with the thing at the heart of my fear of leaving the Mountain, though I knew from the beginning I would have to explain.

I told him, finally, on a day when he had asked me to go with him down off the Mountain and over to Chattanooga, to hear an organ concert in one of the big Episcopal churches there.

Like many other new converts to Trinity's Oxbridgian magic, Joe had fallen in love with all things Anglican and wanted passionately for me to go with him and hear Bach and Palestrina played on the new organ at St. Anselm's. I simply could not do it, but no excuse would serve. I was abundantly healthy, lived in one of the dormitories and would have been warmly encouraged by my housemother to attend the concert, and by that time was seeing no one but him.

"I have all the God up here I need," I said finally. "I don't need a dose of anybody else's."

He looked at me in thinly veiled alarm. Joe was a good Congregationalist boy from a poor, rocky little village in rural Vermont; he was both beguiled by and still a bit wary of the lush half-mystic eccentricities of the Domain. I think some buried puritan part of him expected me suddenly to forsake the orderly, dreaming gray and green spell of Trinity and start handling serpents myself.

"I've often wondered what you must have made of God, after those early years," he said. "I mean, your grandmother's fanaticism, and then up here, all this, your great-grandfather and Compton Hall. God must have confused you terribly. Nothing about him was consistent for you."

"I don't think I was confused, exactly," I said. "What did I know about consistency? I just concluded there were two of him. One for up here and another one for ... you know. Out there. Down there."

"Cat," Joe said. "What is this out-there down-there business? Why won't you leave this mountain? What are you afraid of?"

And so I told him. And he wept. And I knew I would marry him if he asked me, and he probably would. And he did, not long after that day.

I fell in love with him on the first day of his seminar, in the winter of my senior year, when he came into class wearing a gray flat-topped Confederate officer's forage cap. Atop his thick fair hair, with his silky, full mustache and short golden beard, the cap looked wonderfully easy and contemporary; it was like meeting Jeb Stuart himself, or someone equally mythic and dashing. His academic gown was flung carelessly over a worn Harris tweed jacket, his blue oxford-cloth collar was unbuttoned, and his tie was jammed into a hip pocket. His eyes were blue and full of a kind of swimming light behind the round wire glasses, and his features were narrow and sharp and tanned by whatever he had been doing the previous summer, before he had come to Trinity. We heard he had been snatched away from somewhere like Yale or Williams and was considered a great asset to Trinity. He was the first of the influx of young Ivy-League-educated faculty Trinity managed to lure south at the start of the seventies, that decade of greatest change, and those of us who had qualified for his elite senior seminar sat silently and stared at him. He did not speak, only stood still, hipshot, in the forage cap and looked back at us. He was tall and very thin.

"Hey, y'all," he said, in a truly terrible parody of a southern drawl. His voice was flat, nasal, and harsh, with two hundred years of New England in it. He fairly honked. We burst into laughter and he grinned, and I caught my breath sharply.

He was the image of my father when he smiled, of my young father as he smiled down at my mother and me on a long-ago sunny day on the edge of the Steep, in the only photograph I had of him. Mamaw had searched out and burned all the others.

"My name is Joe Gaillard," he said. "Josiah Peabody Gaillard. The Josiah and the Peabody are Vermont Yankee from back to Adam, but the Gaillard is a Cajun merchant marine who met my mother in Boston on her high school class trip and married her three hours before I was born. I just figured I'd get things off on the right foot and let you guys know you didn't have the lock on Gothic down here."

We laughed again, and I was lost.

CHAPTER TWO

❦

I MARRIED HIM ON THE AFTERNOON OF MY GRADUATION from Trinity, in austere little St. Rhoda's Chapel, in the sacristy wing of All Souls. I think we could have filled the great pennon-hung main chapel if we had chosen; the entire college was infatuated with our marriage. Fads pop up like mushrooms after rain on the Mountain, and we were that season's craze. Relatively little creeps in from off the Mountain to divert Trinity even now, and it was doubly so twenty years ago. Even the firestorm of unrest and change that consumed the country in the early seventies reached the Mountain only as an echo.

Oh, there were nods to the times. Women students came to Trinity. A good proportion of the faculty was recruited off the Mountain, from other parts of the country and abroad. Male and female hair alike brushed the shoulders of the black academic gowns, blue jeans belled at ankles and tie-dye was everywhere, and the sweet smell of another kind of smoke curled into the air of both student and faculty parties. The music that flowed from lit windows was as much protest as plainsong, as much rock as Respighi. But the Mountain held its own. The Domain prevailed. The dream at the top of the world that is Trinity has never been completely breached by the present. The Age of Aquarius drifted over the Mountain like smoke and did not settle.

The few people we had chosen to see us married were so quintessentially *of* Trinity that in the dim light it might have been a twilight in the forties, the twenties, or even the closing of the last century. Flowered hats bloomed, and white gloves, and the ubiquitous seersucker suit. I wore a simple white eyelet dress that Cora Pierce had married in, with wildflowers from the Steep in my hair, and Joe wore his Dartmouth doctoral hood over his Trinity gown. We had to ask official ecclesiastical permission for him to do that, but the Reverend Dr. Scofield had offered no objection. It was very much Trinity's own wedding, ours was, and somehow the hoods and gowns of academia were right.

Dr. Scofield had known both of us since we came to Trinity. He was, to me, as much a part of All Souls as its famous rose window. I knew it was largely his good offices that had prevailed upon the college not to interfere with Joe's courtship of me. Student-faculty relationships were forbidden then and are frowned upon even now. But, as I said, Joe was Trinity's first golden boy from the Ivy League, and I was their poster child. Joe had melted any incipient resistance by simply going to Dr. Pierce, still our provost and my unofficial guardian since the death of both sets of my grandparents, and formally declaring his honorable intentions toward me. I think he may even have asked for my hand, though he insists that he did not.

Dr. Pierce conferred with Dr. Scofield, who said, in the lovely Anglican rumble that had propelled him straight up the Mountain to All Souls decades earlier, "If exceptions to rules cannot be made in this, the very bastion of the thinking man, we should cease calling ourselves a liberal arts institution."

"And besides," Mrs. Pierce told me later that he said, "it

solves the problem of Catherine's future very nicely. I have often worried that she would choose a husband not of Trinity."

"Or not choose one at all," I said to Joe later, laughing. "This way you get to support me, and the Compton stash can go into the general fund. What if the school had had to dish out for me until I was ninety-five?"

When they died, five years before, quietly and peacefully within four months of each other, my Compton grandparents had left to the theology school a much larger bequest than had been anticipated, but with the stipulation that my full tuition, room, and board be paid from it, plus a generous living allowance, until I either married or died. When one of those eventualities occurred, the balance would revert to the school to use in any way they saw fit. Dr. and Mrs. Pierce were asked to administer the fund and oversee my welfare as long as I stayed on the Mountain, and since I had been living with them ever since my Cash grandparents died when I was thirteen, in the final fire set in the old house by mad Mattie Cash, they agreed—I think, happily—to do so.

It was an unusual arrangement, but Trinity was used to unusual arrangements when it came to me. Exceptions for Catherine Compton were made with regularity. Old Bishop Compton's largesse, all those years before, had been great indeed. And I truly loved the gentle, childless old couple who had plucked me off a stone doorstep all those years ago, and I knew they loved me in return. They had become the grandparents the Comptons might have been to me, if I could have made myself leave the Mountain. But even at thirteen, the fear of the outside world that was born by Tolliver's Creek was too vivid, too real for that. I had made one visit to their home just after Papaw and Mamaw died, and my anxiety was so overwhelming that I trembled and vomited for three days, only stopping when I passed once more under the arch into the Domain.

It was then the suggestion was first made, by Grandmother Compton, that perhaps a discreet stint of psychiatric therapy would not be amiss. But by the time she made it I was radiant and restored in my relief, and so happy to be back at Trinity that I fairly shimmered with it.

"It's not you," I said into my grandmother's lilac-smelling neck. "You know I love you and Grandpa. It's just that . . . I have to be up here. I have to be."

"Then, my dear Cat, you shall be," she said, and hugged me hard, and went into the Pierces' house with Grandpa Compton to talk with Dr. and Mrs. Pierce about the matter. I did not realize until she had driven away again that the tears on my face had been hers and not my own.

After that, I saw my Compton grandparents regularly, and always on celebratory occasions such as birthdays, graduations, and the bestowing of academic honors. But always it was at Trinity. After I enrolled and moved into the freshmen women's hall, upon graduating from Montview Day, I left the Mountain only for infrequent, reluctant shopping and academic field trips to nearby Chattanooga or Knoxville or Nashville and very rarely Atlanta, and I left under the serene kiss of a tranquilizer administered by the college physician, an old friend of the Pierces, with no questions asked. Even then, anxiety curled like a snake in the pit of my stomach, dormant but sentient. By the time I met Joe I had not been off the Mountain in over a year. I was planning, after graduation, to take a position at Trinity as a graduate assistant in the Art Department, where I was taking my degree in Art History. It was already arranged; fortunately, I was a good student and sought after as a teaching assistant. Someone would probably have had to take me anyway if I had not been. It neither escaped me nor pleased me that I was, by that time, a campus icon.

It was a beautiful little wedding, if I do say so, with a spare sweetness to it. The few contemporaries of mine who attended often speak of it. My senior-year roommate, Francesca Leatherberry from Louisville, who is a vice president of a large Richmond bank now and comes back often to the Mountain, says it couldn't have happened anywhere but in the Domain, nor with anyone but Joe and me.

"So medieval, somehow," she has said more than once. "All that gray stone and green light, and you in the wildflowers like Juliet, and Joe in his gorgeous hood. And only the candles, and the Purcell on the recorder, and of course you and he look exactly like effigies on some old tomb in Westminster Abbey, one that goes back to the Crusades. Are you sure you aren't brother and sister, separated at birth?"

"God, I hope not," Joe said the first time she said it. "If we are we're surely damned, the way we've been carrying on. Our issue will be albino idiots with cloven feet."

I have thought often of what she said, and what he replied. I know he has, too.

Even his friend Corinne Parker, then a cynical, foul-mouthed, and thoroughly engaging graduate assistant in the Psych Department and now a successful psychologist with a practice in Montview drawn largely from Trinitarians, was touched by the ceremony.

"It almost made me wish I was straight," she said not long after the wedding, at the first party we gave in our tiny rented guest cottage behind a big stone house in the village. "The sheer innocence of it could have choked a mastodon. I yearned for white eyelet for a week afterward."

Corinne was a lesbian and lived openly with another gay woman in a garage apartment out near the Inn. Nobody particularly cared. One's sexuality has never been of much concern at Trinity; sensuality is as much an element up here as the thin pure air and the cold sweet spring water. How could it not be, with all this closeness, this raptness, this sheer youngness? Same-sex relationships have always flourished here, usually as those all-consuming first friendships that seem peculiar to small colleges, but lines of demarcation blur on the Mountain. The church had an unofficial stance against homosexuality in my time at Trinity, of course, but could hardly afford to make a thing about it, given the ardency of the friendships born in seminary, and generally didn't bother anyway. Far better to save the salvos for the real sins of venality, materialism, and general worldly tackiness.

"You could have white eyelet if you wanted it," Joe said, ruffling her short copper thatch. "Who said it's strictly for girls? Ol' Cat here is built like a fourteen-year-old basketball center."

"I'd look like a fireplug with a tea napkin slung over it," Corinne snarled. "Cat looked like Ophelia on her best day. Nope. Amy and I are going to tie the knot in black leather on Harleys, with Three Dog Night for a processional. Y'all can come if you'll behave."

Amy left the garage apartment and the Mountain the following year, but Corinne has stayed on, good therapist and good friend that she is. She has another friend now, but when she comes to our house it is usually alone. She said to me once, a few years after Lacey was born, "I know it isn't any of my business, Cat, but if you ever feel like talking to somebody about this agoraphobic stuff, I think I could help you. I've had some real successes with it. . . ."

I hugged her. "Rinnie, I'm not agoraphobic. I'm just exactly where I want to be. But thanks anyway," and she smiled and hugged me back. She seldom mentioned it again, but sometimes, at parties at our house, she looked at me thoughtfully, and I knew what she was thinking.

She and 'Cesca Leatherberry were the only two Trinity students at our wedding. Dr. and Mrs. Pierce were there, of course, and the professor whose assistant I would become in the fall, and the head of Joe's department and his wife, and two or three other faculty couples to whom I had grown close in my years with the Pierces. Joe's mother was bedridden with emphysema and his father had been dead for some years, but his older brother and sister, Caleb and Sarah, came, taciturn and solid and swarthy, the living legacy of the dead Cajun seaman, but without, apparently, his dark fire. I liked them, but we had little to say to each other, and I think they found Trinity and the Mountain somehow effete, a bit rarefied and precious, after the rocky harshness of their Vermont farm. They stayed overnight at the inn and left early the next day, with their invitations to come and stay with them in Vermont ringing in my ears and my assurances that I couldn't wait ringing in theirs.

Somehow I knew I'd never go. I don't think Joe did, though; not then.

"Give them a little time," he said, watching their rental car set off down the road toward the airport in Chattanooga. "The Mountain would be pretty esoteric doings to most Vermonters. 'Sheep May Safely Graze' is a Four-H slogan to them. Towers belong on TV stations. They've never even met a Southerner, and the first one they do meet is marrying their little brother. You'll get to know them better when we go up for you to meet Ma. On their own turf they'll be a lot easier with you."

"I wish she could have been here," I said, the old familiar fear starting up in the pit of my stomach. We had not spoken before of leaving the Mountain to go and visit his mother. We had not spoken of leaving it at all.

"I wish your parents could have too," he said softly.

"Yes," I said, my eyes stinging suddenly. I saw them again as they were in the picture I kept on my dresser, only slightly older than I was now, smiling down at me. "This wedding was for my mother, as well as for me. Nobody was laughing at this wedding."

He pulled me to him and held me against him, my face feeling the warmth of his body through the T-shirt he'd pulled on hastily to come and see his brother and sister off. Only an hour before my cheek had rested there against his bare skin. I closed my eyes and burrowed my face fiercely into his chest, to scourge away the stinging tears, to feel the sheer heat and solidity of him, miraculously mine now.

"Come on," he said. "Let's go home. Bed's still warm."

And we did.

We had made love for the first time the night before. It was the first time ever for me: remarkable, Joe said, in that age of mandatory egalitarian sexuality among the young. Everywhere in those days, even on the Mountain or perhaps especially there, love was being made, in car seats and dorm rooms and thickets and behind darkened buildings. On the Steep, you had to step carefully to avoid treading on lovers. Sex hung in the air as thickly as smoke.

"I can see why you never have, with your parents and all," he said, the first time we talked about it, which was not very long after we met. From the very first, it was hard for us to keep our hands off each other, and we both sensed that some sort of policy about sex had to be arrived at.

"What do you mean?" I replied. "They loved it. They did it all the time. I heard them, even if I never saw them. They sounded like a couple of wildcats. Practically everybody on the Mountain knew about them; they were famous."

"I mean the way they died," he said hesitantly. "It would scare anybody." Joe was still awed and reverential about the Faulknerian manner of my parents' demise.

"I'm not scared," I said and believed it. "I don't even think about it anymore. The reason I don't do it is because I never met anybody I wanted to do it with until you. And can you imagine trying to screw in the Pierces' house? We'd turn into pillars of salt the second the tire hit the road."

He laughed and pulled me close, and we resumed the hypnotic, infinitely slow touching of each other's faces and bodies that served us, then, as the prelude to what we both knew would come soon. How could I be afraid after those afternoons and nights spent learning his long, knobbed body by heart and fingertip, inch by inch? There was no part of either of us unknown to, untouched by, the other. When we finally broke apart I would be limp and stunned with wanting him, almost unable to stand. And he would be mute and sweating.

"Can you get cancer from stored-up sperm?" he would say, grimacing.

But we did not consummate it. We agreed. It would be even sweeter for the waiting. And it was the right thing for us.

It was his decision. "Somehow, jumping your bones before the ceremony would be like screwing Trinity's mascot or something," he said. "Until we get married you belong to Trinity. But oh, baby, watch out afterward. Afterward, you're mine."

And so we gasped and burned and fumbled along until our wedding day, and the instant we went upstairs to our room in the inn, to which the Pierces had treated us, we slammed and locked our door, and looked at each other, and then skinned out of our wedding clothes and ran into each other's arms, and did there on the rag rug that had doubtless been hooked in another century by a blameless bishop's wife the thing we had been waiting for. We did not even make it to the bed. After the first time, we did it twice more before we even got up off the floor. It was well past midnight before we finally lay together in the first of the beds we would share throughout our life. Since then I have slept alone very few times.

I loved it. I always have. Making love with Joe is one of the very few totally absolute things I know; it is pure sensation and transport, unleavened by any external element. At the beginning of our marriage it was a kind of warm red earthquake, shaking me until my senses literally left me. Later it became sweeter, longer, deeper, and even later a slow, sliding roller-coaster ride whose course I knew as I knew my way from my bed to my bathroom at night in the dark, familiar in every inch and degree but no less transcendent in the last white burst than it had been the first time. I knew it was so for Joe, too. I knew by the moves he made, the words he whispered, the sounds he made at the climax, the way he laughed aloud, a whoop like a boy's, after it was done.

For myself, I found I could make no sound. Not that first time, and never since, could I so much as whisper, whimper, cry out, laugh. I could feel the sound welling up in me as he filled and rocked me, feel the long, ululating cry of abandon and completion spilling from my lungs and climbing my throat; I could even feel my mouth open with it, and my lips draw back and contort with the long cry of love, and the tendons in my throat strain, but I could force no sound out.

At first it puzzled Joe, and then alarmed him slightly, and finally became a challenge, a matter of honor, a slight. There were times, until we both made peace with my inability to make a sound during love, that he went at me so fiercely I thought he was trying literally to pound a sound from me, ream from me an affirmation. Sometimes afterward, he would fall silent and turn away from me, and I would feel tears of something like guilt in my eyes, and I would roll over on him and tease him with my hands and mouth until we could do it again, hoping that this time the dam in my throat would burst or he would forgive me my muteness. The latter happened always, but the former never did. I was as unable to shout my love as a stone.

We finally made a small joke of it and were able to move past.

"Why does it matter? It's just noise," I would say. "You should be able to tell by now that I sort of like it."

And he would laugh—would have to, because there was no mistaking how I felt about the act of love with my husband. A blind man could have read it from my thrashing body, from the great, silent rictus of passion that arched my neck and blurred my face. "The silent death," Joe came to call it.

"It's just"—I laughed one summer afternoon as we lay on the grass in the shady lee of our garden wall—"that I want to be able to hear you coming."

Neither of us said anything for a long moment. I knew I had gone to the literal heart of my silence. In that last, lost moment I needed more than anything on earth to be able to hear whatever was coming. So I would not, like my parents, die of my love.

"Exactly," Joe said quietly. "Exactly, my poor Cat."

After that he seemed content with my silence. In an odd way it seemed even to please him, to become erotic in and of itself. After that day we did things we had not done before; he moved in new ways, cried out new things. I was pleased and relieved but in some obscure way disturbed, too. It was as though he read in that strange, sad little inability of mine confirmation of that first seductive Gothic strangeness that had drawn him to me. I felt he was fucking a woman in an Appalachian ballad, the Cat Compton of the silly folk song, instead of the living, breathing, particular woman who was his wife. But I did not mention this to him. By then I had made my Eden and drawn him into it with me. I was not about to poke at its stones and mortar.

For all my life with him, I have wondered about Joe's fascination with the South, particularly with the dark and secret veins of the bizarre that run everywhere through this old tapestry. I have come to no firm conclusion, even all these years later. But I think it had its genesis in that stark, rock-spined farm outside St. Albans, in Franklin County, in the northwest corner of Vermont.

Even in the light, Joe said, there was a kind of darkness on the land, not the rich, fecund green darkness of the Mountain and the South in general, but a shallow, flinty murkiness that did not nourish. The farm was not near a town of any size; his mother and her cousins and children tended their few placid New England cattle and raised some stunted New England potatoes wild miles from the cultivated coasts of Massachusetts, New Hampshire, and Maine. It was not much of a farm ever, and his father's early defection and death, added to his mother's chronic illness and the advanced age of the two cousins, bled it into near poverty. Joe worked the farm before and after school and in the summers. There was enough to eat and hand-me-down clothes from Caleb to clothe, if badly, his weedy frame, but there was nothing in the long silences of the house and the rasping of his mother's sick lungs and the dying crossroads villages to feed a soul. Joe worked in silence and studied with furious, focused concentration and remembered that the only music and laughter and dancing he had ever known had come from the South, with his dimly remembered father. His grades were awesome, despite his schedule of farmwork. His SATs struck his teachers into silence. A young guidance counselor, herself an outlander, had the wit to help him apply early to several Ivy League schools, and by the time he was a junior he had received acceptances from all of them.

He chose Dartmouth, partly because it was essentially a village, and therefore within his limited ken, and partly because he had seen a cloyingly romantic movie long before about Winter Carnival that had enchanted him. When he said goodbye to his mother and Caleb and Sarah, everyone understood that it would be a long goodbye.

His first year at Dartmouth he had drifted into a southern literature course and found there such nourishing richness and romantic grotesquerie and indolent beauty that his heart, suckled on granite and silence, flowered like wild honeysuckle, and he was lost. He brought his new degree and his hunger for dark Faulknerian loam south, found the Mountain, and began to sink grateful roots almost before he cut off the motor of his old Volvo station wagon. By the time he met me, he was a perfect medium for such specialized cultivars as we produce here. He would have fallen in love with me, I think, if I had been built like Brünhilde and had a mustache and the mind of an Easter chick. The extravagant personae of my parents and Cash grandparents, plus the whole seductive and beautiful Mountain-church-philosopher business, would have seen to that. The fact that I was bright enough, funny, vulnerable, and matched him almost inch for inch in height, slenderness, and exaggerated Victorian-valentine purity of feature was merely a plus.

After a few bad days and weeks following his promise at the train station to Caleb and Sarah to bring me north to meet his mother, I did not really fear that Joe would try to move off the Mountain and take me with him. That first summer in the little stone guesthouse we rented behind the larger home of the Dean of Graduate Studies, in a hardwood grove bordering the Steep, was a magical one. I started the first of the gardens for which I have become modestly renowned, began the series of small evenings of food and drink and talk that have become Trinity traditions, and began to lay down, with perfect intent and to the best of my abilities, a life for Joe that was so ordered and fulfilling and rich in substance that he would not miss the benison of scope. If he knew what I was about, he gave no sign. He must have known; from the very first Joe and I were able to read each other's minds and hearts. I concluded from his silence and the contentment with which he let me wrap him in a web of beautiful days that he was saying to me, Yes. All right. Make me a life here that I could have nowhere else, and I will not ask you to leave. I will let you build me a world, and the larger one will come to us.

But just for insurance, just for good measure, I covertly threw into the college incinerator, on the second day of my marriage, the little round cardboard wheel of Enovids the college physician had given me. I said nothing to Joe and made love to him, and cooked and entertained for him, and laughed with him, and talked long into the summer nights with him, and waited. And I knew past all doubt the exact moment, on an August night of long, slow rain and sweet fresh flower breath from my new garden, that I got pregnant. And knew that for a few months, at the very least, I was safe.

The next April, when our daughter Lacey was born blind, I knew I was safe forever. We would not leave the Mountain now. If Lacey was to live without sight, she would live at least in Eden. The world that kept me safe would keep her too.

Only decades later did I come to know that Joe occasionally fancied I had somehow literally blinded her with my terrible fear, bought my safety with her sight. But I honestly think he had thought it only a very long time ago, and not often even then. And by that time there were none of those terrible thoughts that had not visited me in the dark still nights when I could not sleep.

* * *

On an evening nearly twenty-one years later we sat in a garden identical save in scope to that first one, having our drinks in the cool spring twilight and reading a letter from our daughter, in college a continent away. She had written to tell us she was going to Europe with friends that summer, to backpack through Spain and Italy and the south of France, and hoped we might join her afterward and travel in Yugoslavia. Her friends had to leave her in Rome, but she was on fire to go farther, into that strange, hybrid old country across the Adriatic from Italy.

I hear that Dubrovnik is the most beautiful city in the world, she wrote in her dark, angular letters, on the paper with the raised lined grids that she used. *I wish you'd come be my eyes. There doesn't seem any reason you can't, now. I'm well out of the nest. I've always wanted to see Dubrovnik.*

Joe put the letter down and looked out over the stone wall, spilling white clematis now, into empty blue air above the lip of the Steep. Our house commanded the whole valley like a fortress. He did not speak, but I knew he was thinking what I was thinking: Lacey for all her blindness would probably see Dubrovnik sooner, and more clearly, than either of us. My throat tightened at my daughter's cheerful valor and my own crippling cowardice. And for my husband, who would not say what I knew: that he wanted with all his heart to stand on the sea wall of that old city with his daughter, and be her eyes, and let her be his.

"We should go," I said, around a great geyser of fear, in a voice that was not mine. "She's right, there just isn't any reason not to. This is silly. Enough is enough."

"I wouldn't do that to you, Cat," Joe said, and there was nothing in his voice but the old love. Old, a long love. . . .

"Joe. . . ."

"No. I wouldn't. It would be like holding a gun to your head and pulling the trigger. What do you think I am?"

"A fifty-year-old man who's never been to Europe," I said, and got up and went into the house and called Corinne Parker.

CHAPTER THREE

❧❧❧❧❧

THERE ARE THESE BANDS OF GYPSY CHILDREN, really small kids, who roam the streets like packs of orphan puppies; they dress in rags and come up to you in tears, begging for money, and while your heart is breaking and you're fishing for your wallet, one of them slips around behind you and picks your pocket. Or else they swoop down on you from behind, so quietly you don't even hear them coming, and just snatch your purse and are two blocks away before you realize what hit you. They're all over Rome. Nobody seems able to stop them. Of course, in Rome, nobody tries very hard."

Hays Bennett, who was president of the Faculty Council that year and Joe's number-two man in the department, took a deep swallow of his gin and tonic and grinned his vulpine grin around the room. He had a sharp face and a brush of red hair and looked like a fox. Of all our friends, I was least comfortable with Hays. He always looked as though he halfway meant the sly barbs with which he larded his conversation. Probably he did not; Joe always said he didn't. But he was the only one of our usual party crowd who teased me about never leaving the Mountain, and he did it so often I did not think it was casual or coincidental. He was looking at me now. I knew the story of the gypsy children was aimed like an arrow at me. Colin and Maria had just asked Joe and me to meet them in Rome in July, where they were to be married, and everyone at our party had been babbling in excitement over the proposed trip. My silence had not escaped Hays.

"They sound awful," I said truthfully. They did; the notion of that silent swarming pack bursting around me without warning, snatching, grabbing, was repellent to me, appalling. But I spoke lightly.

"Oh, they never hurt anybody, except accidentally," Hays said. "They're after your money, not your life. Not like on the San Diego Freeway or even Atlanta. Italians are not really into bodily harm. Would you rather be mugged or murdered than surprised?"

"Cat would," Joe said lazily from the sofa, where he was sprawled with his bourbon and soda. I turned to look at him in surprise and the sort of swift, small shock of hurt you feel when a beloved child or a pet lashes out at you. Joe knew how I felt about Hays's needling.

"Almost, I would," I said, smiling. "Death before stealth." The small group in the living room laughed; Joe and Hays laughed with them.

"Who wouldn't? There's no redeeming social value in being scared to death," Corinne Parker said, grinning briefly and looking closely at me, and everyone laughed again, and the moment and the party flowed on.

It was a pretty party, a good one. Ours almost always were. I knew that I had a knack for bringing people together in easy groups, and I had honed it by determination and repetition into an art. I liked the deep sense it gave me of nurturing, of caring for and making happy the people whose lives were intertwined with ours. After twenty-three years, most Trinitarians and much of the village and the Mountain were among that number. A party at the Gaillards' had come to be, almost, Trinity's official sanction; over the years I had given them to celebrate graduations, appointments, promotions, publications, new arrivals, retirements, grants received, degrees awarded, and every other ritual of academic life imaginable. I also celebrated with food and drink and flowers and candlelight and laughter the countless engagements, marriages, births, anniversaries, and once or twice even divorces of my fellow Mountain dwellers and raised enough funds in our stone house on the Steep to keep Trinity solvent well into the next century, or so Joe said.

Joe loved our parties too. He loved being a host. It pleased him to please people, and he was as house-proud as only someone who has lived meanly in childhood can be. He was an absolute monarch of his small rich kingdom at the parties, a graceful and charming and benevolent monarch. It was for him I had them. I had sensed from the very beginning that deep inside Joe was a chasm that hungered for ritual and celebration, for extravagance. I felt that hunger too. Over the years, the parties had fed it for both of us. More glue, they were, more mortar for the perfect world that held us in its bowl on the Mountain. Like my beautiful garden. Like the music. Like the books and paintings and the food. I had taught myself to be a very good cook over the years. I wanted none of Joe's hungers to go unfed. I wanted his needs met entirely in the house on the Steep and the school on the Mountain.

I thought I had succeeded. But his lazy words tonight shocked me. Two words only, but they spoke from some unfilled emptiness I had not suspected, and I was frightened.

I looked at him again. He sat in a circle of warm light from one of the two tall copper lamps that sat on the library table behind the big sofa in the living room, his long legs in chinos flung over the sofa's arm, his head thrown back into piled pil-

lows. He was tanned from early tennis in the thin, clear spring
air, and his hair was in his blue eyes; he needed a haircut. I loved
the thick flaxen tumble of it when it was too long. Over the years
it had lightened with strands of silver to the shade of old ver-
meil, and it and his mustache were lighter than his skin, so that
his teeth flashed very white. His eyes seemed bluer tonight,
darker. It was probably because of the fairly recent contact
lenses, and the lamplight, and the bourbon. He had had rather a
lot of that. Behind him, dogwood branches in a crystal vase
glowed like snowflakes in the room's dimness, and I thought
their whiteness darkened his eyes too. He was still very handsome. Still as lean and sinewy, thin-featured, thick-haired, still as
knobbily graceful as the day I first saw him. The only change
over all the years had been a kind of ashiness that settled on his
skin, a web of infinitesimal dry lines, a small thickening of grain
and pore, a deepening of creases, a sharpening of bone. He was
still Joe, just a bit hardened.

It was not unbecoming. He had aged, I realized, like many
men on the Mountain. He had hardened into age, not slackened.
Up here, men do not often get fat or go to seed. They desiccate.
Something in the thin air preserves them almost like mummies,
both literally and metaphorically. For that matter, there are few
fat women at Trinity, either. We might be a lost race found a mil-
lennium later in some fabulous, airless tomb.

Suddenly I did not want to take the metaphor any further. I
knew what happened to the beautiful, dried dead when the
tombs were opened at last and the air of the world rushed in.

I looked at my husband in the light of the copper lamps and
for a moment did not know him.

I looked around my living room at the people who had
come to my party and did not know them, either.

"Dinner in fifteen minutes," I said, and got up and went
into the kitchen and through it into the downstairs bathroom
and stood at the mirror over the washbasin, eyes closed.

"That better be you," I said, and opened my eyes. It was,

but there was something different. I was still me, but more so. Or maybe me, but less. . . .

I had been in therapy with Corinne Parker for almost exactly two years. I started the week after the letter from Lacey we had read together in the garden, asking us to go to Yugoslavia with her. We had not gone; Lacey did not really expect us to. She had known since early childhood that I did not go off the Mountain, though I had insisted, finally, that she do so. She had seemed as incurious about it as our friends in the village and at Trinity; it was simply a given. Mother did not leave the Mountain. I suppose it did not seem strange to her. Lacey was raised among a thousand strangenesses, great and small. Trinity has always been proud of its myriad graceful eccentricities. Lacey's world was full of people who did nor did not do things that were common fodder to those unfortunates off the Mountain. I think that fact helped her live as easily with her blindness as she did. In the end she had persuaded one of her companions to stay on in Europe and go across the Adriatic with her, and Joe and I stayed at home and read her letters with joy for her and no more overt regret for ourselves.

But I had been determined never to see in Joe's eyes again a yearning for something I held him back from, and I worked with Corinne as I have never worked at anything else. It cost me a great deal, but the look in his eyes over Lacey's letter had cost me more. I trembled and sweated and gasped with the pounding of my heart, and I wept, and once or twice I threw up in Corinne's neat little bathroom off her office, as she walked me through that long-ago night on the chain bridge and the terrible days and years afterward, in the house of my crazy grandmother and frozen grandfather. I gulped Valiums like candy for a while, and lost sleep and weight, and railed at her, and cried endlessly, when I thought Joe could not hear me; and on the nights in the second year before the short, and then longer, trips I took off the Mountain with Corinne at my side, I paced the house or the garden, sick and weeping, until dawn came. But I never once held anything back from Corinne. And I never once missed a session.

Different? How could I not be different, after all that? I might look the same—for, like Joe, I was still tall and slender and tousle-haired, and still had the small face and soft mouth of a child, and still wore the smattering of freckles across the bridge of my nose and cheekbones that I had always worn—but one profound change had been made. Only one, and that one small and invisible. But it redefined me. Before I had been Cat who could not go off the Mountain. Now I was Cat who could. Haltingly, frightened still, not far, and only after escape routes had been mapped and bolt-holes located . . . but I could go. Even if I never did again, I knew I could. And Joe knew.

I looked in the mirror at Cat who could go and knew I had grown, and Joe feared it and had spoken tonight from that fear. In that instant I wanted to undo it all, take back all the sessions with Corinne, go back to where I had been before Lacey's letter came, run to Joe and fling my arms around him and cry, I'm back, I'm here, this is me, don't feel like that about me, don't ever speak like that to me again! See, I've undone it all. Let us be again like we were.

But I knew I could not. I was doomed one day to be healed, if imperfectly and reluctantly.

I leaned my forehead against the cold surface of the mirror and shut my eyes again. "Oh, God," I whispered aloud. "Why didn't I see what was happening?"

Corinne had seen. Seen, and tried to make me see. But I would not, could not.

"Well then," she said to me in exasperation finally, after nearly a year of arguing with me about Joe's role in my recovery, "we'll just damned well do it without him. But I don't like it, Cat. I don't think you realize how deeply all this is threatening Joe. I don't think he realizes it, come to that. He's capable of sabotaging everything we've worked so hard for, of cutting your legs off under you. He wouldn't think he was doing that, of course; he'd think he was protecting you. I've known him even longer than you have. I've seen him operate in faculty situations. He wouldn't hesitate, and he'd never admit he'd harmed you. It will be up to you to protect yourself."

"I thought you were such a great friend of his; I thought you loved him so much," I cried, furious with her.

"I am. I do," she said. "But I love him like he really is, and there's nothing I need from him. I can see him a lot clearer than you can right now."

"Corinne," I said, still angry, "I think you are probably the best therapist this side of Vienna, but if you say one more word to me about Joe, I'm going to terminate. Right now. I mean it."

She looked at me for a long moment over her horn-rimmed glasses. Corinne was a handsomer woman than she had been a girl, her tanned, lined face alive with intelligence and caring. There was no answering anger in her eyes, only a kind of weariness.

"You're right," she said. "It was the friend talking and not the therapist. It's one of the pitfalls. I'm sorry, Cat. No more about Joe. It was way too soon."

I let it go. In fact, I buried it deep and forgot it. Or thought I had. But now, staring into the mirror, I saw the two of us, Joe and me, over the past two years, as if we had been on a screen in a theater and I was watching from the audience.

He had not objected to my seeing Corinne at the beginning; he had said only, "It seems a pity to go back into all that when you've made your peace with it. But if it's what you want. . . ."

"It is," I said. "I want to do it for both of us."

"No need to, for me," he replied. "I like us just the way we are. I love you just the way you are."

But he said no more, and I began the long journey with Corinne through the debris of my childhood that I had not thought was there at all.

At first when I came home white and depleted, or cried in

the nights, he would hold me and soothe me. But soon the twice-a-week crises of fear and sadness seemed to annoy and then anger him.

"I can't stand seeing what it's doing to you," he would say, smoothing the hair off my face, holding me hard against him. "It's killing you, and it's just so unnecessary. I'm going to talk to Corinne—"

"No," I said. "No, Joe. This *is* necessary. This is work I didn't do back then. I have to go through it; I can't go around it. Don't say anything to Corinne; this is *my* therapy."

After that, I tried to weep when he could not hear me. I think I succeeded. He did not speak of it again.

But he began to tease me, small thrusts that would have been wounding if they had not been so funny. Joe was and is a very funny man. His eye and ear for absurdity are wicked and true. He could mimic Corinne perfectly, and I would find myself laughing in spite of my annoyance when he said things like, "Now, tell me, Catherine, just when did you first notice this terrible fear of fucking on suspension bridges?" and "Today we're going out to the chain bridge and sit there all afternoon, and you'll see, not a single couple will come do the Black Act on it."

But I never repeated these incidents to Corinne. Some small sane part of me, buried deep, knew what she would make of them.

Later on, when I increased my sessions with her to three times a week, seeing for the first time a crack of daylight in the wall of my fear, Joe began to urge new things on me. Added involvement in the affairs of the college, when I already had more committee meetings and teas and coffees than I could say grace over; more evenings spent with old friends in their homes; more parties at ours.

"You just seem to have extra energy," he said, when I finally protested mildly. "I thought you might feel like doing some things with me now."

"Oh, darling, of course!" I cried. "I haven't meant to neglect you. I didn't realize I was. . . ."

"Well," he said, "I know this therapy stuff has been tough on you."

So I joined the extra committees and went to, and gave, the parties. But I did not cut back on the therapy.

Finally, midway in the second year, I began to make trips off the Mountain with Corinne. Tiny ones, at first; really just drives to the base of the Mountain and back up, or a trip in her car over to a nearby shopping mall on the outskirts of Chattanooga, where I sat in the car and waited, eyes closed and heart pounding, while she went to the drugstore. I was wet with sweat and tears when we got back, and so weak I had to go home and lie down, but I could do it. Before, I could not have. Soon I was driving my car and she was in the passenger seat, and we began to go farther and stay longer. The trips were hard—I can never tell anyone how hard—but I knew I could do them and the fear would not kill me. On the day in January that we drove all the way to Atlanta and had lunch at a suburban Wendy's without my taking a single Valium, Corinne announced it was time for me to make a few trips without her.

Instantly the fear was back in all its old, cold weight.

"I can't," I whispered. "I can't do it by myself."

"I didn't say by yourself," she said. "I said without me. You're leaning too heavily on me. Get Joe to go with you. Surely he knows how important this is to you, how hard you've worked."

"I haven't told him about the trips," I said, not meeting her eyes.

She said nothing.

When I asked him, he would not go.

"I just can't, sweetie," he said the first time. "Midterms is the worst possible time for me, what with Carlton and Hank out. Can it wait till early next quarter?"

Early the next quarter he brought a world-famous poet to

campus for three weeks of seminars. and receptions. It was a great coup, and I could see he could not interrupt the royal visit to drive to a Wendy's or a Burger King thirty miles away with me.

In March he sprained his ankle playing tennis.

I took a triple dose of Valium and made the first trip by myself, in a white haze of sedation and terror. I don't know why I didn't kill someone. The second one I made on two Valiums. My third trip alone I only took one, though the fear was truly terrible. I told neither Joe nor Corinne I had gone alone.

I still saw nothing amiss in Joe's refusals to go with me. We truly do see what we need to see, and only that.

In late April, Corinne wanted Joe and me to go away somewhere for a weekend off the Mountain.

"Go to a fancy hotel in Atlanta," she said, grinning wickedly. "Order room service and drink to excess and screw your heads off. I can vouch for the weekend package at the Ritz Carlton in Buckhead myself."

I laughed and made the reservation that afternoon. That night, over drinks, I told Joe about it. I thought he would be pleased with my accomplishment, and I knew he liked the Buckhead Ritz Carlton. He stayed there when he was in Atlanta for fund-raising trips with President Day or at alumni functions or SMLA meetings.

"What about it?" I said, leering over the rim of my vodka and tonic. "I could get a new nightgown for you to rip off. Or something exotic in the way of marital aids. We could rent a porn video."

He did not speak, and he did not look at me.

"I just don't think we should both be away at the same time, Cat," he said finally. "What if . . . oh, what if Lacey wanted to come home all of a sudden? Wouldn't you want to be here for Lacey?"

I told Corinne about it. I couldn't not, not this time. She was silent for a time, and then she sighed, and got up and walked to her window and looked out at the new green that shawled the Mountain.

"I'm only going to make one speech, Cat, and then I'm not going to mention it again. You can do with it what you choose. If you need to terminate because of it, so be it. Will you listen?"

She did not look back at me.

"I'll listen," I said.

"OK. I think this whole thing—the fear, Joe's peculiar reaction to your handling of that fear, and your *extremely* peculiar reaction to his reaction—is all about control. Control. Up here you can control your world . . . and what a world you've made. It's orderly, it's serene, it's beautiful. Very few people on earth can live like you and Joe do, and almost no one can do it except in places like this. In the Domain. The famous Domain. You control your world, and you control Joe, and he controls you. And it's all in the name of some kind of . . . specialness. Who in their right mind would want to give up being wonderful, special? Not Joe. Not you. I know you had an awful shock when you were a kid, and you had a few bad years with your grandparents. But look at the life you've lived since you got into the whole Trinity thing. I don't think it's safety you're so afraid of losing, I think it's this specialness. Up here you're not just a housewife, you're a Domainian. Joe is not just an English professor, he's head of the English Department in the Domain. On the Mountain. You think he wants you to go running down to the flatland and leaving Eden whenever you want to? Hell, no; he'd have to go with you or lose you, and he doesn't want to do either. Go on, Cat. Go by yourself, then. Hole up in the Ritz and read wonderful books and eat gorgeous food and swim and shop and drink champagne and watch TV, and see what the real world is like. If you can call the Ritz Carlton the real world, of course. If you don't go now, I don't think you ever will."

It was a long speech for Corinne, and her square figure was taut with the passion of it. But she never did turn and face me. I literally could think of no words and stood silent.

"What if Lacey did, for some reason, want to come home?" I said in a small voice, knowing as I spoke how ridiculous I sounded.

"Cat, Lacey isn't going to come home again," Corinne said. "You know that, don't you? You worked hard enough to see that she didn't have to, and you succeeded. You know she isn't going to come home. Joe knows."

"Yes," I whispered. "I know she isn't."

And I turned and walked out of Corinne's office.

I did not go back. When I called to tell her I wanted to terminate, she said only, "Well, it's probably time. You've done good work, and you can take it from here. We still friends?"

"Always," I said, meaning it. "Always. I'll never forget what you did for me."

"Then send money," she said, laughing, and I laughed too and hung up. I felt light and limp with relief. All was well between Corinne and me. All was as it used to be. I could still be her friend and have her at our parties, and Joe would still laugh with her at faculty meetings and at the club. And spring had come, the ineffably beautiful green spring on the Mountain. All the Domain bloomed with it.

I did not go to the Ritz Carlton in Atlanta. I let the sweet swirl of social activities that catches us up in spring wash over me and planned for the day in June when Lacey would come home for her short summer break, before going back for the first quarter of her senior year at Berkeley. Come home and then go away again. Corinne was right. Lacey was not ever coming back for good to the Mountain. I had indeed seen to that.

When she was born, her eyes were not the indigo of the newborn but so clear and light a blue they looked almost silver, washed in a sheen of light that might have been tears but was not. She was a happy baby from the very first. I cannot remember a time when Lacey did not crow, or gurgle, or laugh outright. It was Joe's laugh, froggy and enchanting, ridiculous in a tiny baby. Everyone was enthralled with her.

I think I sensed something was wrong from the first instant I held her, something to do with the strange, beautiful eyes, though it was only much later that I let myself know. When I did, long past the time that Joe and the doctor suspected, when even I could not explain her unfocused stare as a baby's undeveloped muscles, I felt a quick, fierce stab of gratitude beneath the pain and grief. I pushed it away, hating it. But the aftersense lingered.

"It could have been so much worse," I said to Joe, trying to comfort him in his anguish. "It could have been something fatal. It could have been something that would hurt her, cause her pain. It could have been something . . . disfiguring."

"Well, she's not going to have to worry about how she looks, is she?" he said, through almost the only tears I had ever seen in his eyes. "Christ, Cat, you think this isn't going to cause her pain? You know how the world treats blind people—like retards!"

"Well then, she just won't go out into the world," I said savagely. "She'll stay on the Mountain with us. It's a wonderful life; she can have everything up here. She'll hardly know she's . . . without sight."

I could not say "blind" for a long time.

"You're glad, aren't you? Now you'll never have to leave. She'll be your anchor to the Mountain."

I merely looked at him, holding my baby.

"I'm sorry, Cat," he whispered, his face crumpling. "I'm sorry. Forgive me. It's just . . . I wish I could exchange my eyes for hers. I . . . she'll never see this beautiful place. She'll never see your beautiful face. . . ."

I reached out for him over the baby's head, and he came into my arms, and for a long moment I held them both, trying with all the force of my being to pump some sort of healing into them. Perhaps I succeeded just a bit with Joe. He did not cry again, not that I saw, at any rate. Not for Lacey.

Lacey needed no healing from me and never has.

We kept her at home. It was Joe's decision as much as mine, perhaps even more so. I never had the impression that he was humoring me. It was not hard to adapt our small house to a blind child, or at least not to one of Lacey's nature. She was fearless and pragmatic to a degree that simply astounded me, who am neither. If she fell, she picked herself up and toddled on. If she bumped something, she fussed a little and went about her business. We padded corners and secured rugs and moved bric-a-brac out of reach and tried our best to treat her as a normal child. She was light-years ahead of us in that respect.

Because she had never known sight, she did not seem to sense dangers she could not see; we had to watch her there. Her other senses were awesome. Even before she received special schooling, she could read her way around her world with her ears and nose and fingertips. She talked early and volubly, and her memory was phenomenal. Corinne told us her IQ—"if that idiocy matters to you"—was probably astonishing.

"She doesn't have to live with limits," Corinne said, early on. "With her intelligence and temperament, she can probably have almost any sort of life she wants. Do almost anything, go almost anywhere. There are special schools to help her live just about as normally as any other child. I've looked into them—"

"She's going to stay here," Joe said. "We're going to teach her. Later on she'll have tutors for the things she needs. I've already been in touch with the National Institute for the Blind; they've sent literature. When the time comes, she'll have everything she needs—"

"She needs the real world, Joe," Corinne said.

"This is her real world," he said. "There's nothing she needs that she can't have here. Who wouldn't love growing up in this place? Nobody's going to think of her as a blind kid here."

"She *is* a blind kid," Corinne said. "She needs to go through and past that. So do you two. You can't keep her locked away in a tower all her life. What happens when she wants something she can't get up here? What happens when she marries and her husband lives somewhere else . . . if you all ever let anyone near enough to marry her? What happens when you die, or do you plan on not doing that? Did you ever read *The Secret Garden*?"

They came as close to quarreling over Lacey as they ever did over anything. After that talk Joe simply would not speak of her to Corinne. And she stopped bringing the matter up. Lacey stayed on the Mountain with us, in our little house and walled garden, and was taught Braille and simple coping skills by a young tutor who came each day from off the Mountain. She managed her schoolwork with ease and joy and played contentedly in her nursery or our garden with the children of friends and faculty, who came each afternoon and weekend, and had toys and pets and her radio and phonograph. She loved listening to television.

Joe and I spent virtually all our free time with her; I remember those early years as the years when the Mountain began to come to us. We did not go out, but we did not lack for companionship, and neither did she. She was a pretty, puckish child, small and rounded, like my mother, but with Joe's thick fair hair. And the beautiful, light-spilling blue eyes were riveting. You literally forgot they saw nothing when she fixed them on you, following the sound of your voice. Her laughter rang like chimes. Everyone who met her fell in love with her. Somehow, we managed not to spoil her. I really think her own sunniness and enormous curiosity saw to that.

"I forget for hours and sometimes days at a time that she can't see," Joe used to say, and I agreed. I was proud and grateful for managing to fashion a world for our child that made sight virtually unnecessary. I was happy in those days, no less happy than I have been in our later ones. It seemed to me that all the value and beauty in the world lay here in microcosm.

I never looked far ahead. For a long time, I saw no need to.

When she was ten, Joe and I began to plan the house we wanted to live in for the rest of our lives. We'd been talking about it for years, and we'd finally bought a lot. It was the back four acres of an old estate on the very lip of the Steep, thick with first-growth hardwoods and dogwood and laurel and rhododendron, sweeping level and sweet up to the granite outcropping that guarded the land from the air. It had belonged to the first patrician general who had retreated to the Mountain after the "late unpleasantness," to lick his wounds and form a mountain fastness where sons of the Confederacy might learn in their turn the precise things that led their fathers into war. The last of his line had died, and Joe had his bid in to the estate lawyers indecently soon after the service at All Souls. There were much higher bids, but they came from off the Mountain, and I suppose the trustees saw their duty clear. We had an architect friend translate our ideas into drawings, and on the night we sat down with him to review them, Lacey sat with us, her head against Joe's knee. We paid little heed to her. She often sat like that when we had friends over. She seldom interrupted. More often than not, she was off in her own world, the one behind her eyes where we could never follow. She stayed there a lot.

Philip talked of how the new rooms would look, and how we might live in them, and how he thought the furniture and artifacts of our lives might fit there. He talked of the air and sun and space and the magnificent panorama of flatland and foothills that the site commanded, of how it would come right into the house to be a part of it as the stones and mortar and oak beams were. He talked of how space and air were a design element, how the walls themselves would seem to open endlessly to sun and rain and the turn of the seasons.

"I see it as a house without boundaries," he said. "As a place where you won't know where you leave off and the woods and sky start. This is a nice starter house, kids, but these little rooms are like living in shoe boxes. Like a little rabbit warren. Tacky. The house I'm going to build for you will be like living in the woods, with the trees for a roof and all the world for a garden."

Lacey began to scream. Within seconds she was hysterical and so near breathlessness we finally had to call the pediatrician. It was only after an injection of sedative and much holding and rocking that we got words out of her.

Lacey was afraid she would fall out of her new house into thin air. And Philip's words about the only house she knew had devastated her.

"That's not how they are!" she said of the rooms he had described as shoe boxes, rabbit warrens. "It's not! This house is beautiful! I hate the new house! I won't live there! I won't leave here!"

It was the first time I realized that the world Lacey had built for herself behind her eyes was far grander, more beautiful, than anything on the earth could be. That when we said "house," Lacey saw something wonderful, splendid, unimaginable to us. How not? What had she for comparison?

And it was the first time I saw clearly what we were doing to her, Joe and I, by keeping her on the Mountain, away from the rest of the world.

I went to see Corinne Parker the next morning. By that fall, Lacey was enrolled in the long-term children's rehabilitation program at the Cleveland Sight Center. When she went away in September to learn to live in the world, Joe went with her, of course, not me. Corinne had said that was best, and so had the people at the center.

"She's already afraid," Corinne said. "It's inevitable, with her intuition, that she'll catch your fear of leaving, and not understand it, and think she's going into danger out there. Let Joe take her alone. She understands he has a job and can't stay with her, and it'll be easier for her to let him go. Don't cry, Cat. This is best and it's high time. Her real life starts now."

But I did cry. Not only for my child, my child of the silver eyes who in her blindness saw palaces and unicorns and wonders and now must learn to see only reality, but for Joe, who lived in an agony of love for her and must now leave her to the ministrations of strangers—and for me. I would miss her as I would miss my hands or the beat of my own heart, and I would fear for her each moment that passed.

I hated knowing that no small part of my tears fell in simple gratitude that it had not, after all, been asked of me to leave the Mountain. But I did know it.

It was the right thing, of course. Lacey learned prodigiously. She ate learning as if it were food and she starving; she embraced the world, with all its stenches and grime and dangers and meannesses and all its simple glories, as she would a lover. She had the tools: the clicker that helped her by its resonances to gauge depths and positions; the white cane; the myriad tricks, such as cooking by sound and positioning food in clock positions around her plate; the computer on which she could access the entire world of words and print out whatever she chose in Braille. And the wonderful dogs, with whom she could walk almost as easily in the world as the sighted. The first, named Luke after Luke Skywalker, lies now in the garden of the new house that she did, after all, come to love, under her favorite red maple. The next, a loving black Lab named Joe after her father, is with her at Berkeley and will go with her through her graduate work in the rehabilitation of other visually impaired people at Western Michigan University, in Kalamazoo.

Joe teased her about Kalamazoo when she told us her plans for grad school.

"Kalamazoo? Why do you want to go to school in Kalamazoo? It sounds like a bad Borscht Belt routine."

I knew he had hoped she would come back to the Mountain and Trinity for grad school, though of course he would not say so to her. But he was proud, too, that she wanted to spend her life working with other blind people. Trinity could not help her there.

"Well, so what?" She grinned. "What do we care, Joe and I? I can't see Kalamazoo and he can't spell it."

Joe had stayed with us in the house on the Steep when Lacey went to Europe, and though he was polite and well-mannered and accommodating to Joe and me, I knew his heart was traveling with Lacey. His big head turned often toward the door she had vanished through when she left him, and when he heard, long before I did, the tap of her cane as she made her way up the front walk with Joe after he met her at the Atlanta airport, he gave a great bark as full of joy as any sound I have ever heard. He had never barked before, not for us.

Yes, it was the right thing I did all those years ago. Lacey was all but out in the world, and it was the world of her choosing, and Joe and I were in the house of our dreams in the world of our choosing, he the department head he wanted to be, with a deanship and who knew what waiting beyond that, I with all I had ever wanted already within my grasp and the world off the Mountain, if I chose, at my fingertips.

I reached up and touched the nose of the woman in the mirror.

"Nothing is different, not really," I said to her. She did not look entirely convinced. Her eyes were shadowy with doubt.

"No, really," I said to her. "It's the same world, yours and Joe's. Absolutely the same one it always has been. Maybe it just doesn't shine quite so much now; maybe the world off the Mountain has tarnished it a little. But it's the same. So are you. So is he."

And I bit my lips to redden them, a trick I had learned reading *Gone With the Wind* when I was eleven, and went back to my party.

Colin Gerard was Joe's protégé. He had been Joe's favorite student through all four years as an undergraduate, the star of Joe's small seminars and survey courses, the chosen one, the heir apparent. Most professors at Trinity have them. Colin was from an old Richmond family, its lineage thick with bishops and generals and academicians, at least three of whom had been at Trinity before him. He slipped as easily into the world on the Mountain as if he had been born there. His specialty was the Fugitives, and Joe still talked about his thesis on Allen Tate now, long after Colin had finished grad school and become Joe's graduate assistant.

I knew Colin planned to·stay at Trinity forever, barring some unimaginable unforeseen calamity. He was the sort of young man who, to me, seemed genetically programmed for the Mountain: handsome in a mussed, fine-boned way, graceful with the kind of shambling indolence that goes well with dusty black academic gowns, funny in the mordant self-deprecating way that is so admired up here, a varsity track man, president of his fraternity and coxswain of his crew, an accomplished drinker of bourbon, bright to near brilliance. He held almost every office for which he ran, and almost every honor Trinity had to offer, and I think there is a lot of money in his family. Old money. When I think of the words "Golden Boy," I think of Colin Gerard. How on earth he had come to be so besotted with Maria Facaros Condon from Newark, New Jersey, was a source of much speculation and enjoyable gossip at Trinity. Colin, the consensus has it, could do better.

Maria came to Trinity on a full scholarship to study political science and met Colin during her freshman year, when he was a junior. There is no explaining chemistry; she is dark and dumpy and short and wild-haired, so large-breasted as to be a campus joke and so quiet that until she began to come to our parties with Colin I had never heard her say a single word. She said few even then. She is awesomely smart; her grades, undiluted with extracurricular activities, outshone even Colin's, and she sailed through graduate school so easily that people still talk of it at the Faculty Club; and she is considered the best of Trinity's young instructors. She cares little for clothes and wears no makeup, and though she has a sweet, rather medieval face and a really beautiful low, rich voice, she is remarkable for very little except her mind and her breasts. Colin absolutely adores her. Steam practically comes off him when he is with her, and off her with him, and they manage somehow always to be touching each other. It is either uncomfortable or amusing to be around them together, depending on your point of view. How can he? the campus says over and over. It would be like keeping your own cow.

No one is crass enough to say she is common, of course, but the word somehow lingers in the air when she is in a group.

I like her, and I like Colin better for loving her. I have never managed to warm up to him all the way. Maria Condon is, I realized finally, me, only in a different skin. An outsider.

"Because she's no competition, basically," I said once to Joe when he asked for the thousandth time why I thought Colin so adored her. "He's a thousand times prettier than she is. Look what he gets: all boobs and food and bed and adoration forever, plus a mind he can show off whenever anybody gets too snotty about her. And best of all, she's a pie in Mama's eye. Can you see Lucy Semmes Gerard introducing her around to the post–Junior League crowd in Richmond? Don't knock Maria, Joe. I like her enormously. She's me, you know."

"What are you talking about?" he protested. "You've always been—elegant, a sprite, really lovely. A little Greek boy, an Athenian at Plato's school. You are, even now. She's an Athens saloonkeeper's daughter."

"Sicilian, maybe. Don't be precious, darling. It doesn't become you. What do you care, as long as Colin is happy? And is he ever happy! I think they'd better get married immediately, before they get any happier. Would you like to ask them if they'd like to be married in our garden? I know he loves it, and it would probably get him off the hook with his mama."

But tonight Colin had announced that he and Maria had decided to be married in Rome, in Michelangelo's beautiful Piazza del Campidoglio, over the coming Fourth of July. And, he said, grinning around the room, there was going to be a dinner the night before in Trastevere to which we were all invited, if we could manage it. Given by Sam Forrest, in his rooftop garden. We were all invited to that, too.

There was a soft explosion of sound, as near to a babble of excitement as we get on the Mountain. Sam Forrest! An American expatriate living in Italy for years, a painter of such renown and charm that hardly a glossy international magazine managed an issue without some mention of him and his beautiful Italian wife, Ada, of their legendary parties and his extravagant showings and openings. His huge canvases, flaming with bawdy color and a kind of elegant savagery, hung in every important museum in the world and most large private collections. The whole world knew about his affairs and his feuds and his brawls and his periods of reclusion, when he locked himself into his studio or retreated to a borrowed one and painted as if possessed by devils for months at a time, seeing no one, emerging thin and depleted with another show's worth of work. Somehow he did not repeat himself and had not, so far, faltered in his trajectory. His talent was immense and real. The life he led with Ada Forrest was exactly, he said over and over in the magazines and newspapers, the sort of life an artist should lead. Neither of them asked anything of the other or minded what the other did. And what they, together and separately, did was as famous as his paintings. Sam Forrest. Sam Forrest with this young graduate assistant and his bovine child from Newark, New Jersey?

"Did you win the wedding in a Top Forty contest?" Hays Bennett said.

"Actually, Hays, he's family," Colin said. His smile was creamy with satisfaction.

"Family. I see," Hays said. "Your mother's or your father's?"

"Well ... Maria's, really. He's her uncle or something. By marriage. He's married to her mother's cousin, I believe. The family who still live in Florence."

"Naples, Colin," Maria said in her smoky voice. She smiled at him indulgently. "The Mezzogiorno. It's not at all the same thing."

"Well, wherever," Colin said. "Isn't that something? Even I didn't know, and then she hands me this letter from him. . . ."

We all looked at Maria. She dropped her eyes.

"It sounds like bragging," she muttered.

"So, anyway, you're all invited," Colin crowed. "And right now, before God and man and this assemblage, Maria and I want to issue a formal invitation to Joe and Cat to come with us and be our attendants and drive with us through Tuscany. Go on our honeymoon with us. Is that tacky, or what? How about it, Joe? Show us the Italy of literature. Be our cicerone."

The group fell silent. Joe did not speak. I felt Hays's eyes on me.

"Let's do it," I said, my heart bucking like a wild thing under my silk shirt. "Let's just . . . do it!"

"Ah, God, I'd love to, but we couldn't," Joe said. "Cat couldn't. . . ."

"Oh, yes," Corinne Parker said. "Cat could."

"Could you?" Joe looked at me. Everything that was unsaid, had always been unsaid, shimmered in the air between us. I could not read his eyes. They were, still, the eyes of the stranger who had spoken earlier.

"Yes," I said.

"Then," Joe said, smiling, "we will. And on your head be it."

CHAPTER FOUR

❧❧❧

EVEN BEFORE WE LEFT—WEEKS BEFORE, IN FACT—the world on the Mountain turned strange. Everything seemed too bright and vivid; I felt, as I went about making preparations for the trip, that the air around me was perpetually lit by unseen strobe lights.

"Do you feel like we're making a movie about getting ready to go to Italy?" I said to Joe.

"Nope," he said. "I feel like we're already there. Nothing has felt this real in a long time as this trip."

He had been listening to Italian language cassettes for several weeks, and studying guidebooks, and reading prodigiously about the cities we would be visiting. Books on the hill towns of Tuscany, on Etruscan history and art, on food and customs and architecture littered his study and the big room overlooking the Steep in which we practically lived. He was already fluent in the idiomatic Italian of the cassettes and peppered his conversation with phrases he liked.

"*Buon giorno, Catti. Ho fame. Quando che colazione? Facciamoci un bicchiere. Dove sono i gabinetto?*"

"Good morning," I would reply. "Breakfast is never unless you feel like cooking it. And it's about twelve hours too early for a drink. And you damn well know where the toilet is. Joe, do you realize that virtually everything you've learned so far has to do with eating and drinking or the elimination of same?"

"I have my priorities," he said. "OK, how about *spogliati?*"

"If it's not about food or shit, I'm game," I said.

"It means, take off your clothes," he said, leering.

"They do that in Italy?" I said, peeling my nightgown off slowly to the rhythm of an imaginary bump and grind.

"Why else do you think they close the shops from noon to four? Ah, Cat, you'll have every man in Italy pinching you. Look at you. Like a little willow tree, and blond all over except for those wicked black eyes—"

"*Basta,*" I said huskily into his neck. "I'll show you priorities."

We made love a great deal in those days just before we left. I still don't know why. It was not the slow, deep, honey-thick love of our settled married life but the intense, fevered, searching love we had made when we were first learning each other's bodies. We did it many places we had forsaken since the first prodigal flush of total license: the kitchen table, the rug before the fire in the big room, the garden, the bath. Joe seemed to me insatiable, and I felt nearly so. It was as if we sought to imprint one another's bodies, inside and out, on our minds and hearts and visceras. It felt as if we had a time limit to do so. It felt as if we were going to be parted and wanted to be sure we did not forget each other. . . .

"We really ought to cut this out for a little while. We'll be jet-lagged before we ever see the jet," I said, a few days before we left. We were lying on the sofa under the window wall that faced the Steep and the blue summer air beyond it. We were stark naked and sheened with sweat, and guests were due sooner than I liked to contemplate. Colin and Maria were coming for a last American supper; they were leaving the next morning, to try and wade through some of the seemingly impenetrable red tape that surrounds foreign marriages in Italy. Corinne was coming too. I had Tuscan bean soup simmering, and as near as I could devise to the crusty dark bread of Italy baking in the oven.

"I just want to make sure that when some strutting Roman stud comes on to you, you'll remember me and sneer in his face," Joe said.

"I can't imagine ever wanting to do this with anyone but you," I said honestly, feeling swift, inexplicable tears sting my eyes. I hugged him hard. I thought once more how totally wonderful his attenuated body felt under my hands, each long, subtly defined muscle sliding beneath the pads of my fingers, oiled with our mutual sweat. I thought that any other body, especially a dark, stubby, tightly packed one, would make me physically ill. I loved all of Joe: mind, heart, soul, spirit, flaws, eccentricities, but it was his body and his beautiful narrow, carved face that weakened my knees and thickened my tongue. I had often wondered what would happen if he were to be altered in some essential way: a bad accident or a wasting, disfiguring illness. Could I still feel this simple, joyous lust for him that had lasted all the years of our marriage? I thought I could now, but it would take effort, and perhaps closed eyes. . . .

"I'm not programmed to run off with Italians, unless they happen to look like Ichabod Crane," I said, running my fingertips down his back to where the cleft in his narrow buttocks started. "No, don't, really. If we don't get dressed Corinne will come in and turn the hose on us."

I think Joe was almost totally happy in those last few days. He whistled, he sang in the shower, he broke into small silly dance steps when he went about his daily business. He filled notebooks with things he wanted us to do and see in each city and kept a separate list of places to eat and drink. Almost everyone we knew on the Mountain had been to Italy at one time or another, and everyone had suggestions. Joe listened avidly, and jotted and noted and culled his lists, and cheerfully ignored the jibes of his more traveled colleagues when they made indulgent references to innocents abroad and ugly Americans. Joe was neither innocent nor ugly and knew it. In his mind, I believe he had already conquered Italy as surely as he had the Mountain, from the moment he knew for sure that we were going. The stranger who had taunted me, however lightly, on the night of our spring party, was gone, and the man I had loved and known for more than twenty years was back, and then some.

It was I who was the stranger.

"I don't feel like myself," I said to Corinne in the kitchen that night. "I don't feel excited, I don't feel connected, I don't even feel frightened. Last year I couldn't even go to Atlanta, and here I am going all over Italy, and I haven't even had to take a pill. I pinch myself a dozen times a day just to see if I'm real, or if this is a movie I'm watching, or a dream. That's how it feels. Just . . . unreal. Is this recovery or some kind of new breakdown I don't even know about yet?"

"You tell me. It's your psyche," Corinne said, tearing off a crust from a warm loaf. "Mmm. Good. Neither one, probably. Probably just a new kind of defense your subconscious sent up, like a flare, when it caught on that you were going about as far off the Mountain as you could get. Go with it. It's the smartest part of you. I brought you a little ammunition, by the way."

She fished in the pocket of her cardigan and brought out several slips of paper and stuck them into my apron pocket, my hands being slicked with olive oil and wine vinegar.

"Thanks. What are they?"

"The names of decent English-speaking shrinks in each city you're going to. And some spare prescriptions for generic tranquilizers. Also my phone number at the Cape. I'll be there most of the time you're in Italy."

I looked at her. She was smiling, but I could see she was serious.

"Joe can take care of me, if it should come to that," I said. "I'm not going to be alone at any point. But thanks anyway."

"You ought to have your own resources, Cat, even if they're pills and shrinks," Corinne said. She was no longer smiling.

"But Joe—"

"So Joe gets hit by a Fiat. What then?"

Through the calm white snowfall of unreality the old panic coiled and struck like a snake, then faded swiftly.

"Then I take the whole bottle of pills and call everybody," I said waspishly. "I can't go through Italy zonked, Rinnie."

"I'd rather you went through it zonked than be frozen to some hotel room," she said. "Take the stuff and don't argue. If you don't need it, fine. Italy's beautiful, Cat. It's really extraordinary; in one way or another, it's where we all came from. Don't miss any of it. It ought to be yours alone, not just yours and Joe's."

"Have you been?"

She smiled and paused.

"I've been," she said. She said it in such a way that I did not ask when or with whom. Italy meant something to Corinne. I thought suddenly how well I knew her—and how little.

"So," I said. "What should I pack?"

"Toilet paper and antiperspirant." She grinned. "And leave all those sweaters and shawls here. I've seen your suitcases. Rome and Florence will be ovens, and Venice will be a steam bath."

"It's funny, but when I think of this trip, I don't even think about Rome and Florence and Venice," I said. "I mean, I know we're going there first, but what I see in my mind is the hill towns. The Tuscan hill villages. Up there in the shadow of those old walls, you'd want sweaters and shawls."

I heard Joe at the living room door greeting Colin and Maria. I dried my hands and Corinne snatched a last bite of bread and we turned toward the living room.

"When you get back, Cat," she said over her shoulder, "we're going to have to talk about those hill towns. We never did, not specifically. I'm hoping once you've been through Tuscany you'll see that a fortress on a hill isn't anything special; it's just a place like any other place."

"I never said it wasn't," I said, the panic nibbling and then fading.

"Yes, you did," she said. "In a thousand different ways."

About an hour into a thick, heavy sleep, after a barely touched steak dinner and an unwatched movie, I woke with the heart-pounding sense of a missed appointment and looked around the silent, darkened cabin of the huge jet. People slept slumped in their seats or twisted against bulkheads and partners' shoulders, as Joe was twisted against mine, his fair head half buried in the little paper pillow the flight attendant had issued us, along with the stale-smelling airline blankets. I believed almost everyone slept. I had the strong feeling that I alone was awake in the plane. It was one of the loneliest feelings I ever remember having, but I did not want to waken Joe. I sat and tasted the sensation, to see what would come.

Not much did. Soon even the chilly loneliness retreated somewhere inside me, and I could feel and hear only the slight elemental buzz in my veins and ears of the double dose of tranquilizer I had swallowed as we left the Mountain. It had been sufficient to see me incredibly through the maze of freeways around Atlanta, the great teeming, echoing maw of Hartsfield International, the endless wait in the International Departures lounge, and finally the boarding of the Delta flight that would deposit us, some nine hours later, on another continent.

"You OK?" Joe would ask me at one juncture or another. He wore chinos and an oxford-cloth shirt the color of his eyes and carried an old blue blazer over his shoulder with a paperback of Dante in the pocket. Unlike almost everyone else on our flight, he carried no hand baggage, not even our camera; I had that. He looked as if he had left for Europe many times before; he looked fifteen years younger; he looked wonderful. I had seen more than one pair of female eyes among our fellow passengers look at him and then look again, longer.

"I'm great," I would say, smiling through the lovely deep surge of my sedated blood.

"You look great," he said. "You look like the prettiest girl in college, on her way to Europe for her senior trip. You certainly don't look like an old married lady who just got humped on the living room sofa not six hours ago and is coked out of her skull on tranquilizers."

"Yeah, well. You want to try the humping again in another six hours? Did you ever hear of the Mile High Club?" I felt one eye blink away from giggling endlessly and insanely.

"Your six hours are up," I whispered now to Joe, but he did not stir. I reached into the pocket on the seat back in front of me and pulled out the itinerary I had stuck there and looked at it again. In the dim greenish light, the printed columns looked suddenly absurd, totally unbelievable. It seemed in that instant such a *huge* thing we were doing, and on the strength of such tenuous bonds. How was it that all those fragile promises made all those weeks ago, between the airline and the hotels and us, could possibly be strong enough to guide and sustain us on this immense journey? A four-thousand-mile bridge of words across an endless sea. . . .

After the movie ended, the flight attendant told us to leave down the shades that had shut out the summer twilight, so the breaking day would not disturb the sleepers among us. We were outrunning the very night on this journey and would meet the dawn just off Land's End, on the coast of Britain. It seemed so strange, just a nod to the darkness, and then the new day. . . .

I tried to sit very still and empty my mind for whatever would come. I knew I had slept very little, and my circadian rhythms were being savaged, and by all rights I would feel the legendary effects of jet lag soon. But at that moment I felt nothing except the purling of the drug past my wrist pulses and a kind of huge, calm waiting. In an hour or so, about 5 A.M. on my reset watch, the cracks beneath the opaque shades began to lighten and I knew that, below us, Cornwall would soon be waking. I lifted a corner of the shade and peered out but saw only clouds, thick and even as whipped cream on a vast pie, beneath us. I had the fancy that if I could see the earth beneath the cloud layer, I would see, far below, the tiny tribal fires of the first dark little Celts to come out of the rock caves into the air of England.

Then all of a sudden everyone was awake and stretching and rubbing grainy eyes and straightening rumpled clothing, and the flight attendants were handing round a hasty breakfast of cold croissants and coffee, and people were queuing up at the lavatories. Hurry, we must all hurry; we were over Germany; we were within tower range of the Munich airport; fasten your seat belts and return your tray tables to the upright position. . . .

The intercom made a frying, crackling sound, and the pilot came on. There was, he said, a line of rather violent thunderstorms coming across the Alps into Munich, and we were going to circle for a bit. Things would, he said, be a little turbulent, but there was nothing to worry about, just a little rough air. Before he finished speaking, we hit it.

Since I had never been on a plane before, I had nothing with which to compare the next ten minutes. But Joe talked of the experience for a very long time afterward. The plane seemed to yaw and stall; it would drop sickeningly, then be tossed horizontally, then drop and buck and yaw again. Some of the drops seemed endless, and people stopped gasping and exclaiming and fell deadly silent. Soon, at each great lurch there would be stifled screams, and I heard sobs of fear all around me. I clutched Joe's arm and shut my eyes and braced my feet against the seat in front. I realized, even in the midst of the worst tossing, that it was not death in a crash I was afraid of—even then, this seemed simply unbelievable—but that the atavistic fear of falling would waken the other primal fear that lay at the pit of my being, which therapy and drugs had driven back, and call it out again.

We fell abruptly out of the clouds into slanting rain, and red earth and small round green hillocks, like women's breasts, rose up rapidly to meet us. Indeed, we seemed almost upon them. The plane roared and rose steeply and then leveled off and began a slower descent. Behind us, the last line of jagged Alps was fast disappearing in the rain, and the earth beneath us looked like a page from a storybook. The wet red fields and black-green forests and foothills of Bavaria were studded with neat round stacks of hay and tiled roofs that should have had storks clustered on them, and on a winding road immediately below us a farmer drove a wagon piled high with hay and pulled by two white oxen. The intercom crackled again, and the unseen pilot told us, laconically, that he had not been able to outrun the storm or get above it and the Munich tower had talked us down.

The entire plane erupted into applause. "Welcome to Munich," Joe said. "From here on, it's downhill all the way."

There is almost no way to prepare a first-time visitor for Rome if he has come via Germany. There is probably no way to prepare a first-timer for Rome anyway, but Germany is the wadding and shot that makes of the trip over the Alps a blast from a cannon. After a cool, gray, rain-washed, and fatigue-smoothed day and night in Munich, landing at Fiumicino was like being spewed out into the maw of a volcano. Soothed by the remote majesty of the Austrian Alps and an excellent bottle of Orvieto Classico on our noon Alitalia flight from Munich, I literally stumbled and half fell into the roaring, jostling airport in Rome. Only Joe's hand on the back of my blazer and the press of passengers ahead saved me.

Maybe it was a good thing, my abrupt initiation into Italy. I think if I had arrived at a normal pace, seeing and smelling and listening as I came, I would have literally drowned in the old fear. Leonardo Da Vinci Airport is an unceasing twenty-four-hour assault on the senses. But I was well into it and heading for the baggage area in a ragged double line of passengers before I got myself together. Joe was firmly at my back, his hand a vise on my elbow, and the tweed back of the man in front of me was as solid and comforting as a mountain. The fear slunk back into its lair. I took a deep breath and looked around.

"Why is it so dark?" I said to Joe. They were the first words I spoke on Italian soil.

The great space of the airport was not only dim, it was stifling hot. Straining to see, I turned in a circle, half sensing and half seeing the shifting masses of people all around us. The murk was nearly impenetrable. Something felt very wrong; the hair on the back of my neck began to tighten at its roots. Others in the crowd were looking around too, and the buzz of uneasy conversation swelled.

"Holy shit," Joe half whispered in my ear. "There are machine guns all over the place. That guy on the balcony has one trained on *us*."

I looked up. On the gallery overlooking the main level where we were a whip-thin young guard in a tightly tailored uniform stood, a sleekly evil machine gun held at waist level in a loose firing position. I stared into his dark face, and it seemed to me that he stared into mine for a long moment. Neither of us moved. I did not want to take a deep breath. Slowly, as if they were figures in a negative bathed in developing fluid, other armed guards materialized on the balcony. All had guns fixed on the crowds below. None moved.

"Joe, what is this?" I said in an airless whisper.

"I don't know. Nothing, probably. The goddamn *nerve* of those guys."

He turned quickly and made to leave the line and approach a guard standing against a pillar not far away from us. I had not seen him, but once I did, I saw many others, all armed and grim and very still. It reminded me, insanely, of those "Can you spot the wild animals in this drawing?" puzzles in children's magazines. Machine guns and guards were suddenly everywhere.

At Joe's movement, the guard nearest us took one step forward and brought the gun to firing position and aimed it at Joe. He said nothing and his face did not change. Joe stopped.

In the murmur of the crowd I caught one word, "*terrorista*," and my heart all but stopped. Dear God, had there been a bomb threat, or was some unspeakable act of political terrorism even now under way? I thought of the newspaper photographs I had seen of slain women and children in Mediterranean banks and railway terminals and other public locations; I thought of Aldo Moro's pitiful bloody body in the trunk of a car on a Roman street; I thought of my blind child, an orphan. . . .

Joe heard it too and pulled his Italian phrase book out of his pocket and began thumbing it rapidly. Wildly, I wondered what the Italian was for "bomb."

Then, up and down the line, we heard a word we did not know but that seemed to put our fellow passengers from Munich at ease: "*Sciopero, sciopero*."

The line relaxed, and we heard snorts of disgust and one or two bursts of weary laughter.

"*Mi scusi*," Joe said to the tweedy man ahead of me. "*Che cosa significa . . . ah, sciopero?*"

Joe has a sort of combined Ivy League and southern drawl. It gives a languid, cultivated elegance to his speech. All at once I seemed to hear it for the first time. It rendered his Italian virtually unintelligible, even to me, who had been listening to it for weeks. The large man turned and stared at him in perplexity.

"Why the guns?" I said slowly, hefting an imaginary one to my waist.

"Oh," he said, in what must be pure Brooklynese, or perhaps New Jersey. "It's another fucking strike. The electricity this time, probably just the substation that controls this part of Rome, or maybe just the airport. It'll be over in an hour at the most; they save the longer ones for weekends. There's one of some kind about every fifteen minutes; last night the buses were out for three hours, and last weekend the air traffic controllers got pissed and quit for a day. We're lucky this is just the electricity. They're on auxiliary now, and at least the taxis and buses will still be running. It's deep shit when the taxis stop. The Uzis are just because the lights are out and you never know when that happens in Italy. I wouldn't make any quick moves, though."

"Thank you," I said, faint with relief.

"Don't mention it," he said, turning away.

Joe crammed his phrase book back in his pocket and said nothing.

By the time we cleared immigration and were handed back our passports the twilit murk still lingered, and we made our way down the stilled escalator to the lowest level, where our baggage was said to be, as if it were a staircase. I could see the parking lot and bus lanes outside, shimmering in a blaze of white sun. It looked as if it should be cool in the dimness of the terminal, but it wasn't. My stockings and underwear were damp with sweat, and my skirt and shirt stuck to me. Joe had his blue blazer draped over his arm. His fair hair and mustache were darkened with sweat, and he kept blinking. Salt drops must be trickling into his eyes and creeping behind his contact lenses.

"A shower is going to feel like heaven," I said.

"Now aren't you sorry about what you called the poor old Cavalieri Hilton?" Joe said, grinning. "At least you can be sure a Hilton will have a shower. And air-conditioning."

"If the *sciopero* hasn't got it," I said, and he grimaced. Then his face cleared.

"There's always the pool."

"Ah, yes, the pool," I said. "The one and only reason we came over four thousand miles to the very heart of Rome to stay in a Hilton Hotel."

The Cavalieri Hilton International Roma had been Maria's idea. Or, rather, her mother's celebrated distant cousin Ada Forrest's idea. Ada had written that perhaps the American friends of Maria and Colin would like to stay at a hotel with a pool; Americans often did, and she was very fond of the Cavalieri Hilton. It was, she said, just above the Forrests' flat in Trastevere, on a lovely hill, and Ada and Sam always enjoyed swimming in its pool when friends stayed there. There was a lovely restaurant too, with a breathtaking view of Rome; she could recommend the restaurant highly. She and Sam had had many memorable meals there. In light of this transatlantic endorsement, and in view of the fact that Joe and I would be accepting the Forrests' hospitality several times, it seemed churlish not to stay at a hotel in whose pool and restaurant we could reciprocate. But ... a Hilton? I had envisioned something small and vine-shaded and ancient, with wooden shutters and peeling plaster walls, over-looking a piazza with a fountain, surrounded by the cobbles and roof gardens and statuary of old Rome.

"We'll have all that in Venice and Florence and Tuscany," Joe said. "Maybe it's a good idea to ease our way into Italy in a Hilton."

Stumbling beside him through the gloom toward the bay for the Alitalia bags, sweat running and mouth foul with heat and tension, I thought he might be right.

When we reached our bay, there were no bags on the motionless carousel. They had been piled to one side, and there were not many of them. We waded into the small pile, along with the other stragglers from our flight, and eventually cap-tured my one large bag and two small totes. Joe reached for his, frowned, and straightened up.

"That's not my bag," he said. "It's just like mine, but it doesn't have my identification tag on it, or that scratch on the side."

We looked again, but his bag was not there.

"Oh, good Christ," he said tiredly. It was obvious what had happened. Someone with a suitcase identical to his had mistaken Joe's for his own and taken it home. Or taken it somewhere, at any rate. Joe poked at the bag, but there were no longer any identifying tags on the outside by which we might trace the owner and reclaim our things. I thought of the rooftop rehearsal dinner at the Forrests' we would be attending in less than four hours, and of my own two best dresses, which I had tucked into Joe's suitcase at the last minute. I did not think we would be going to Colin and Maria's party, or meeting Sam Forrest for the first time, in the clothes we had planned to wear for the occasion.

We dragged the strange bag over to the baggage master's cubicle. He was very cordial and very sorry for our inconvenience, and very anxious to be helpful, and properly annoyed at inconsiderate people who snatched bags without verifying their identification. He spoke very good English. He accepted the American bills Joe pressed into his hand with gratitude and sweetness and said that the minute, the very instant, the other bag was returned, he would personally notify us at the—ah, the Cavalieri Hilton, was it? A fine hotel; many Americans stayed there; the concierge was a friend of his—and we could come and claim it. And ah, he was sorry, he was desolate, but he could not open the bag and see if there was any identification inside. It was against the rules. The owner could sue if his bag was opened without his permission. He, Guido, could lose his job. *Che posso fare?* What could he do?

"But I don't have any other clothes except the ones I have on," Joe said incredulously, as if he was just registering that fact. "I don't even have any clean underwear. And I have to go to a very important party tonight."

The baggage master was stricken. But then his brown simian face brightened. There were very fine shops in the Cavalieri Hilton, he said, shops that were accustomed to American gentlemen and their requirements. He was sure Joe could be fitted with something suitably elegant for an evening party.

"You go to Ortini's, in the lobby, and tell them Guido said to fix you up," he said, beaming, with the air of one who has solved an enormous problem. "I send many Americans to Ortini."

"One for every bag that turns up missing," Joe said under his breath. He gave Guido another dollar.

Guido gave Joe a handful of forms and disappeared.

The two of us, with phrase book and dictionary, spent nearly an hour completing the forms. When we took them back to the baggage master's cubicle, Guido had disappeared and a very thin, bored young blond woman with ebony eyes and roots put down a movie magazine, took the forms, glanced at them, and tossed them in a drawer.

"I'm only going to be in Rome for a few days," Joe said clearly and slowly, his neck swelling and reddening. "I have got to have that bag before I leave. Guido said he would take care of it."

"Then he will," the young woman said in accented English. "Guido gone home, but he take care of it tomorrow or next day, whenever he get back."

"What happens if the guy who took my bag brings it back and Guido's not here? Will you be here?"

The young woman looked at him as if he had lost his mind. It was clear that no one in her experience had ever brought a bag back. I felt a sudden weary certainty that if we fell upon the bag identical to Joe's and ripped it open we would find dreary, ill-made clothes far past their first youth; no one in their right mind would return the good Brooks Brothers slacks and jackets, the Ralph Lauren polos and thick, creamy oxford-cloth shirts Joe had brought. Or the two dresses of mine. They were by far the prettiest and most expensive dresses I had ever owned, or probably ever would.

Of course the bag wouldn't be coming back.

"Tomorrow is my day off," said the young woman. "But if you want to come back here, the bag will be over there." She gestured toward the carousel, which still sat, motionless and barren, in the gloom. "If the guy bring it back, I mean."

"Never mind, I'll get this straightened out at the hotel, or maybe the embassy," Joe said furiously, and whirled and walked away. Behind him, the girl shrugged.

"*Che posso fare?*" she said, and picked up her magazine.

We took my bags through customs without incident. Outside, the sun was slanting lower off the ranks of farting buses and snarled taxis. It seemed that every horn on every vehicle in Rome was there, and blaring. I looked at my watch. Nearly four. The party began at seven, and we had no idea where it was, except somewhere in Trastevere. We were to call Colin and Maria at the Forrests' when we got in, and they would give us directions.

"Joe, wait," I called after him, as he snatched up my baggage and strode toward the cab stand.

"What?" It was a sharp bark. ·

I felt a surge of sharp irritation, followed by a slower, deeper tide of hurt. Joe very seldom snapped at me. And I was just as tired and hot and exasperated as he was, and nibbled ragged by the tiny teeth of the not-quite-quelled fear to boot; he knew that. But the two flushes faded. I might not have a pretty dress to wear to the party, but I had clean clothes, enough of them to last me through Italy. Joe had nothing.

"I'm sorry," I said, catching up to him, "but we're going to have to cash a traveler's check before we can even get a cab. Don't you remember, you said we'd do it here? Your book says there's a booth by the doors to the taxi stand."

We looked. There was indeed a booth for the changing of currency and the cashing of traveler's checks. One booth, with one attendant in it.

As we started over, a massive black-clad nun herding a phalanx of Asian schoolgirls descended upon it and began an involved operation in which each child, giggling, went shyly up to the window in turn and presented a handful of documents and stood back, finger in rosy little mouth, as the attendant examined each document with the steely scrutiny of a Siberian border guard. I felt tears spring into my gritty eyes and heard Joe say something swift and horrible under his breath.

I counted.

There were thirty-two of the Asian children.

When we reached the pavement outside at last, it was five-thirty, and the first fresh breath of the air of the Eternal City smote my face and neck like the belch of a blast furnace. Wordlessly, we crawled into the first cab in the line and Joe said, "Hotel Cavalieri Hilton, *per favore*."

"I don' go up there," the driver said, not looking around, not even looking up from the exquisite buffing he was giving his fingernails.

"Up *where?*"

"Up there. Up the mountain," the driver said, gesturing contemptuously.

Joe fished in his pocket and thrust a handful of bills through the Plexiglas shield that ostensibly protected the driver from the barbarian likes of us. I could not see what they were, but the digits were not single ones.

The driver grunted, pocketed the bills, clashed the taxi into gear, and we roared out into the river of traffic toward Rome.

I remember everything about my first glimpse of it, and nothing. The careening, squealing, honking, shouting, pounding, brake-screeching trip took fully an hour and three-quarters, and I got no single clear vision of Rome in all of it. Later we learned that Leo—the name of our driver, posted on the filthy Plexiglas that separated us; Joe said he was sure it was an alias—had without doubt taken us via as long a route as possible. I don't doubt that. Romans can smell vulnerability on *stranieri* as wolves can blood. And then, of course, we had hit the villainous Roman evening rush hour head on. And Monte Mario is a long way from Fiumicino. About as far, in fact, as it is possible to get and still be in Rome. But still, it is a long time to spend in a car and not remember one clear scene, one heart-stilled vista, one breath-snatching frozen moment.

But impressions were another matter. After all this time, and after all the country we have traveled since that first day, when I think or hear the word "Italy" it is this suicidal ride in a battered, shrieking, evil-smelling cab that floods my mind and heart. Nearly two hours of apocalyptic traffic and stifling heat and exhaust fumes and cursing; of darting motorbikes and massed street corners full of dark, lounging men and vivid women in stiletto heels; of gestures and music and laughter and screams; of balconies and roofs spilling vines and flowers and Cinzano umbrellas in street cafés, and wide tree-lined avenues and dark, narrow cobbled streets leading back into unimaginable caves of shadow; of a flashing view of the dark Tiber between its concrete banks ("But it's a culvert, Joe!"), and grimy pockmarked saints lining a bridge, and a looming apparition that was Castel Sant'Angelo; of beetling walls of brick so ancient they were scarcely recognizable, and medieval piazzas flashing past and giving way to shops and greengrocers and pharmacies and pizzerias; and, finally, of a twisting ascent up a suburban mountain that might have been a hill in California or Oregon, except that when I turned my head to look back, the entire old city lay below me spread out on its hills, brown and umber and copper and alabaster and cream and russet, bathed in a clear gray-gold light that seemed to spring out of the very earth and air. And in the middle of it all rose the great luminous dome of Saint Peter's. I began to cry. Oh, Italy. The first time I ever came down off my mountain, and it was to this!

Joe laid his arm around my shoulder and patted me, and I knew he was praying that I was not beginning some sort of terrible, escalating attack of the panic. His hand was heavy and lethargic, and I knew he was past dealing with hysteria. I reached up and squeezed it, to show him it was not the fear. But I did not know what it was, only that I could not seem to stop crying until the taxi squalled around a final hairpin turn, and shot through an enormous open gate into a vast parking lot, and screeched to a rocking stop under the porte cochere of the Cavalieri Hilton International. I stopped then and began to hiccup and then to giggle.

"Does Donald Trump know about this?" I choked.

"It looks pretty goddamned good to me," Joe said, and jerked himself out of the taxi and began to scrabble furiously in his coat pocket for his wallet. A shower of crumpled bills and a spray of silver coins shot out at the feet of the uniformed doorman who had just that moment materialized. He and the taxi driver pounced on the booty. Joe turned red and then deadly white. I fled into the haven of the huge, ornate, glacial lobby and sank into an amber velvet banquette, trying desperately to force back the insane giggles. I was dirty and hot and jet-lagged and strung tight as a violin bow, with the fear trying to push its way up into my chest and throat past the laughter, and at that moment I was as profoundly grateful to old Conrad Hilton and his dream of air-conditioned grandiosity as I have ever been to anyone in my life.

"If they live just below our hotel, they must live in a tree," Joe muttered half an hour later. "Ada Forrest obviously suffers from depth-perception deficit." We were in another taxi, winding back down the mountain road we had just caromed up, but this time we rode in soft, cold silence. The doorman, obviously impressed with Joe as a source of endless American largesse, had hailed and rejected two or three cabs from the line at the bottom of the parking lot before selecting this new air-conditioned one. Its driver had not cursed or gestured or banged the side of his vehicle once. Indeed, he had not even spoken. When Joe had said, *"Via della Lungara in Trastevere, per favore,"* he had merely looked back impassively. Joe produced the piece of paper on which he had, at Colin's suggestion, written Sam and Ada Forrest's address and their directions, and the driver had stared at it with an equal lack of affect. The doorman strode over and took the paper from the driver and studied it, and then said to Joe, "You are sure? The old city. It is not such a good spot for Americans. Not so much of the night life."

"It's a private home," Joe said. "We are going to a party there. *Un ricevimento.*"

"Ah," said the doorman. "A party." And he nodded wisely. He leaned into the taxi and spat out a rapid command to the driver, who nodded and closed the window. We glided away down the mountain in the lowering dusk as if in a gondola, sealed away from Rome in new vinyl and steel and chill air. For the first time since we had reached the airport in Munich that morning, we relaxed and took deep breaths. At the end of this ride would be lights and festivity and love, and faces we knew, and language we spoke. There would be food and drink and laughter. Colin's voice on the telephone was jubilant and assured, somehow different, somehow very ... Italian. Maria's was vibrant and full of something I had not heard before, a kind of teasing sensuality, a small, very feminine something.

"It's so beautiful you won't believe it, Joe," she said. "Like a fairy tale. And I can't wait for you to meet Sam. He says tell you to tell the driver to look for the lamppost with the wreath of white flowers on it; it's the third door down from that, on the left. The street numbers are all worn off on this block. Oh, I'm going to give you such a hug! Hurry up!"

"I think Maria's been into the vino," Joe said, hanging up the telephone. It sat on a pretty blond wood desk overlooking our balcony, which did not, after all, overlook all of Rome, but instead commanded the back parking lot and a line of low hills and a kind of mesa in the distance, upon which sat what I took to be a hydroelectric plant. The room we had reserved had been "I regret, *occupato*" when we arrived, and rather than wait for another on the front to be made up, a process that would, the contrite little man at the desk said, take three hours, we accepted this one and a reduction in our bill. After buying Joe pajamas and two form-fitting shirts of some silky material in the appallingly priced men's shop off the marble lobby, we showered and left immediately for Trastevere. I wore a flowered cotton sundress more suited to a morning in Florida than an engagement party, but I did not care. Joe, in the stylish Roman shirt, did.

"I feel I should have on a stretch satin Speedo bikini under my pants," he said.

"It will probably come to that. I can't imagine where we're going to find Brooks Brothers oxford boxers," I said, smiling at him. Joe hated the new shirt. He looked as unlike Joe Gaillard as it was possible to look in it, foreign and rakish and showily handsome. I started to say something about gold chains and chest hair but thought better of it.

We could not see much of the panorama of Rome on the ride down the mountain. The sky had deepened to violet, but few lights had come on yet, or perhaps Rome did not light up at night like an American city. Some few pinpricks dotted the plain below, strung like a necklace, and a peppering marked the suburbs we glided through, but the neon signs had not been lit. Only the white ghost of a fingernail moon hung in the sky, far to the west of us. It was impossible to tell where we were in relation to anything at all. Somehow, we did not speak much.

We reached the bottom of the mountain and turned, and passed through a neighborhood I thought I recognized from the trip up, filled with newish apartment buildings and shops and outdoor cafés and teeming crowds on foot and in the stubby little cars that Romans seemed to aim at one another like ballistic weapons. Fiats and Vespas darted everywhere like bright shoals of fish. It all looked gay and friendly and somehow very real, and I wished fleetingly that Sam and Ada lived here or in a neighborhood like this one. The lights bloomed as we passed, and colored signs glowed like Christmas lights, and lamps in windows and candles on rooftop tables shone.

But then we were out of it, and across a bridge that I knew I had not seen before, and very soon into another world entirely. I knew from the narrow twisting streets, and the crumbling plaster houses leaning over them, and the dim piazzas and the tall shuttered windows that we were in a very old part of Rome.

"Trastevere?" I said to Joe. I said it, for some reason, in a whisper.

"I hope so," he replied in the same low tone. "Somehow I don't think we're in Kansas anymore."

I had read of the celebrated piazzas and churches and fountains of Trastevere. I had looked forward to the crowds of working men and women in the *caffès* and bars, the pizzerias and markets, the rich life of the streets in this oldest neighborhood where the descendants of the first Romans were said to live. But the streets we inched through in our big cold car were mostly dark, and the occasional streetlight seemed dim and gray, as if it lacked essential oxygen. I saw few people on the streets and few lights behind the shuttered windows. This was not a place for which I felt any human ken.

The driver swung the car through an arched gate and into an even narrower, darker street paralleled by a footbridge. I knew the Tiber must run just beyond it but could see and hear nothing. Far down, at a crosswalk, there were a few pale lights, and people walking past the intersection, but this street was bordered only by tall old houses, pocked and stained by what must be centuries of weather and shuttered dark. There was literally no one about, not even one of the famous high-hipped feral cats of Rome. The driver slowed and stopped, Joe and I looked at each other.

When we did not get out, he did, and came around and opened the door on my side, and reached in and gave me his hand. I took it and got out into the warm, soft air. I would not have dreamed of refusing. Joe got out on his side too. There was a little ambient sound, but it seemed to come from far away, not from the dark houses around us. I could not believe we were in a place of living people.

"Via della Lungara?" Joe said. His voice echoed thinly in the silence. "Number twenty? *Venti?*"

The driver nodded. We looked. We saw no numbers.

The driver nodded again. Climbing out we saw, on the lamppost at the corner, dimly, a small wreath of white flowers. Well, then, this must be right, Maria had said to look for the wreath. . . .

Joe paid the driver and he rolled silently away down the

ancient street, his tires bumping softly on the cobbles. He still had not said a word. At the corner his brake lights flared red, and then the car was gone. We stood looking after it. It might have been a mirage.

"Well," Joe said briskly. "Third door on the left. Let's go."

He took my hand and we picked our way down the crazed and cobbled old street, peering into doorways. They were all solid wood and looked as old as the earth itself, and all were dark, and all were as inevitably closed as if they had been nailed shut. We came to the third one, as dead and sealed and dark as the rest. Joe raised his hand to knock and then let it fall.

"Was it third," he said, "or fourth?"

I looked at him; in the gloom I could not see him clearly, but he did not look at all like Joe, not at all. Not his silvery hair, or his mustache, or the narrow Italian shirt, or the neat hands— none of him was Joe. I looked around me. The street slept in its darkness, dreamed in its vast, thick oldness, seemed poached in silence. The houses were so close together I could scarcely see any sky, not even the skeletal moon.

"I don't know which one it was," I said, and the old fear and the afternoon's tears surged back up into my throat, cold and thick. I pressed my knuckles hard against my mouth. I knew in a moment I was going to begin to sob with terror.

The third door on the left flew open, and yellow light streamed out into the street and over us, and a man's deep voice, rich with the music of my own South, called, "Come in this house!"

And I ran straight into the outstretched arms of Sam Forrest as a small animal might into its burrow, or a child to home.

CHAPTER FIVE

❧❧❧

T HAT NIGHT I GOT DRUNK WITH SAM FORREST. If it had been any
other night, and any other place, it would have been an
evening I remembered with radiant shame for the rest of my life.
Sam Forrest? The painter whose luminously barbaric early works
had so excited me in my art history classes, the late-century icon
who was now, as Truman Capote once said of himself, famous
for being famous? Drunk, within two hours of meeting him, on
his own supremely beautiful Roman rooftop? Drunk and singing
"Stars Fell on Alabama"? Oh, Cat.

But at the time it seemed entirely the thing to do, the only
thing to do; and it still does. I believe Sam Forrest saved my life
that night. I don't say it lightly. If he had wanted me to sit on a
bench and drink fusel oil with him, I would have done it gratefully. It was that or, perhaps, jump over his balcony into the dark
below, the fear riding me down like a succubus.

The first thing I noticed about him after he drew me

through the old door into the dim courtyard behind it was that he was much larger than he seemed in his photographs and a great deal more vivid. I knew him from all his photos in the media, but I was not prepared for the sheer redness of him. He was a massive man, heavy through the shoulders and belly, with arms and legs like the trunks of small trees and hands that seemed as large and perfectly modeled as Michelangelo's sculptures. He wore a wrinkled white silk shirt open nearly to his waist, and chinos like Joe wore at home, only seemingly made for a giant. He was beltless, and the pants rode low on his hips. Somehow I did not think the open shirt was an affectation like the few I had seen so far in Rome; two of its buttons were missing, and no chain of any kind gleamed in the mat of silver-frosted hair on his chest. I thought, rather, that Sam Forrest was an essentially sloppy man and liked him for it. It made me feel at home; it made bolting through his door into his arms a bit less embarrassing. He smelled of thin raw gin and acrid cigarette smoke and ripe, powerful sweat, three smells I had literally never smelled on a man before. No man I knew on the Mountain smoked cigarettes or drank gin, and if they sweated they washed it off almost before it dried. I realized it was all of a piece with the rest of him and I liked it, even as my nose wrinkled metaphorically. I knew Joe would comment on the smell at some time or another, and the knowledge made me slightly and obscurely annoyed.

"I have your *View of Gahanna;* it was the first signed print I ever bought," I babbled, looking dizzily up at him. "I'm Catherine Compton. God, I mean Gaillard. Did anyone ever tell you you look like Errol Flynn? I mean, if he were bigger. . . ."

My voice trailed off, and I felt heat rising from my chest to my hairline.

"Shit," I said.

Sam Forrest laughed, a great wind of sound.

"As a matter of fact, somebody once wrote I looked like an Errol Flynn balloon in the Macy's Thanksgiving Parade," he said.

It was as thick a drawl as ever I heard at home, almost an affected sound, except you knew instinctively that Sam Forrest would not bother to affect such a small thing. Large things, almost certainly, but not small ones.

"I'm Joe Gaillard, the man who accompanied Cat Compton to Rome, to paraphrase another celebrated redhead," Joe said, holding out his hand. His voice was his "school" one, cool and amused.

"I figured," Sam said. "Maria said to look for a man who was the spittin' image of Ashley Wilkes in seersucker. In this neighborhood that could only be you. Minus the seersucker, of course."

His eyes were small and very bright blue and nearly buried in a network of fine crinkles, as if he laughed a great deal. His shaggy eyebrows were, like his head and chest hair, the red of rusted steel, with gray under it. He was all over freckles, freckles so dense they ran together across the bridge of his thin hawk's nose, as if he were wearing a copper mask. Even his thin lips were bordered with freckles. There were freckles on his hands and arms, too. His hair was thick and grizzled, as if it had once been curly but was now merely frizzed, and he wore it tied back in a ponytail. There was a gold hoop in one ear. What did that mean? Had someone told me it was an ensign of homosexuality or merely a chic thing among the young? He looked like a huge roaring pirate, a modern Barbarossa. There was no way this great red man was gay. Virility boiled off him as thick as the sweat. The blue chips of eyes took in Joe's shirt with good humor and even sympathy, but I heard the stiffness in Joe's voice as he said, "It would be seersucker if I had my choice. Some fool took my bag at the airport. I had to buy what I could find at the hotel."

"Well, you know what they say," Sam Forrest said, turning. "When in Rome. . . . Come on up. The party's just getting going, and Colin and Maria are fairly twitching to see you two. Been twitching ever since they got here, come to that. My God, I think he's finally just going to lose it and sling her down on the table and have at it before the night gets much older. Steam's practically coming off him. What'd you do back in Tennessee, keep a fire hose trained on 'em at all times?"

We followed him through the dimly lit courtyard, where a dry fountain that looked centuries old held a browning palm tree and bicycles leaned in a sweating stone archway. I felt a startling and absurd impulse to step out of my shoes, saunter barefoot and hipshot, smack chewing gum, laugh deep in my throat. I pulled the front of my sundress higher and smoothed back my hair, which had gone frowzily wild in the humid heat. When had it gotten so hot? I did not remember this kind of heat before.

"Well, back home it just somehow never arose," Joe said in the darkness behind me. "If you'll pardon the expression. The steam was mostly off her. I think I recall considerable speculation as to what precisely Colin saw in her. I mean, she's not exactly Gina Lollobrigida. . . ."

I cringed. I actually felt my eyes screw shut and my mouth make a silent grimace. What on earth had gotten into Joe? Did he think Sam Forrest was somehow maligning his protégé? And since when had he thought of Maria in terms of her sexuality? I knew he was as genuinely fond of her as I was, admiring as I did her sweetness and devotion to Colin and her awesome intellect. Gina Lollobrigida indeed. How long had it been since Joe had seen her in a movie, or since she had even made one?

Sam Forrest said, not looking back, "Maria has obviously suffered a sea change into something rich and strange. I think every guy at the party has a pretty clear idea what young Leslie Howard sees in her. Nice young woman on top of that. She obviously does not take after her second cousin once removed, or whatever Ada is to her. Must be the Tuscan side of the family coming out. Ada's from deep in the Mezzogiorno, though she claims Florence. Here's the elevator. Watch your extremities, you two. It'll shut on you. See those X marks on the wall? One for every Roman pecker this sucker has snatched."

I snorted with laughter and Joe said something unintelligible under his breath, and the door shut, and Sam thumbed buttons, and we lurched upward. For what seemed endless minutes we stood pressed close together in the tiny, dingy cell, in the pale-urine light from the single ornate fixture and the complex smells of cooking and sour carpeting and Sam Forrest and generations of other Romans who had risen and fallen here. And then we ground to a stop, and the doors squealed open, and we stepped out into the midst of the party on Sam's rooftop.

I gasped. It was just so beautiful. I have never seen anything so lovely, so exotic, so totally beyond expectation as that candlelit rooftop in Rome on the first night I was there. I don't expect I ever will again. My life at home was rich in beauty, and I was no mean mistress of it, not an unsophisticated woman if a narrowly defined one. But I had no context for this, no standard by which to measure it. It was an enchantment woven of apt, sweetly fitted, uncontrived skeins: the flowers were loose summer bouquets jammed into vases and pottery jars; the candles were set simply in unmatched sticks, saucers, and hurricanes; the small tables were scarred and weathered to a lovely dark-silver patina by their summers on this roof; the night was the deep, soft, midnight blue of a Roman July; the air smelled sweetly of the strange vines that rioted everywhere, and of all the lives lived around and below us, and of fruit and bread and wine; music spilled like liquid from a little radio sitting on the wide parapet: Vivaldi. People laughed and talked quietly. And all around, like the sea seen from its bottom, Rome, floodlit and glowing and pulsing and humming and burning. Saint Peter's dome, and lines of cypress and umbrella pines black against the deep blue. Almost directly above us, columns gleamed on the long crest of a hill, uplit, fantastic among the dark pines.

Sam Forrest turned around and smiled at us. He pointed to the hill.

"Janiculum," he said. "Saint Peter was crucified up there. Beyond it is the Aventine. It's one of the big Seven."

A long shudder ran through the core of me, so profound as

to be almost sexual. What must it be, to live every day of your life in the presence of these monuments to events that divided time for the entire world? How could a life lived here dare be trivial? I reached back and took Joe's hand and pressed it. He pressed back.

A woman detached herself from the crowd and came toward us. At first I thought she was an albino, she was so pale. Her face and hair were almost the same pearled white, and she wore white, too, a pair of wonderfully cut white silk culottes and a silk shirt open to her waist and knotted there. She was not tall, but she was very thin and so she looked somehow long, all of a swallow, a spill of milk. There were big, chunky baroque pearls at her throat and ears, and her mouth was a slash of scarlet in all the gleaming whiteness. My dazzled eyes first registered freakishness, a kind of monstrousness, something out of Fellini. But by the time she reached us I saw she was very beautiful. Her features were perfect, if bleached, and her silky white hair, loose and long on her shoulders, was stunning. Her eyes were the blue of snow light, as far from the live-coal blue of Sam Forrest's as it was possible for the color blue to be. Her hand, when she wrapped my own with it, was long and firm, and so warm as to be almost hot, but dry. How could there be fire in that marble tomb of a body? How did it come about, the union of the snow woman and the fire man?

"I'm Ada Forrest," she said. "Welcome to Rome and to our party. We've been hearing all about you."

There was no trace of any accent in her light voice.

She leaned over and kissed me, first one cheek and then the other in the Roman fashion. Her face was hot; her breath stirred warm against my cheek. She smelled of something clear and dark and slightly bitter, as foreign to me as she herself.

"My dear Joe," she said, and moved past me to Joe and kissed him too.

"It is entirely my pleasure to meet you," Joe said, still in the cool school voice. I knew he was as dazzled by Ada Forrest as I was. The voice Joe uses with women is normally warm and slightly teasing. I think he is as unconscious of it as he is of the air around him.

Ada drew us toward the group on the roof. Before they turned to greet us I looked at them: almost every woman there wore something silken and ankle-brushing, like Ada's pants, or so short as to show leg far up the thigh, and tight, in hectic scarlet or black or white. The men wore elegantly tailored light jackets over open-collared shirts, and pants that were cut narrow or in the deeply pleated European manner. Everybody held stemmed glasses, and many smoked. Shoes were invariably pointed and burnished. No one wore pastel flowered sundresses and sandals, and no one except Sam Forrest wore chinos. And Joe, of course. I, who had never cared what I wore because I had never doubted it was right, felt a crippling callowness, a painfully inappropriate youngness. I felt, I thought, exactly like what I was: a middle-aged woman in a teenager's dress. I wanted to shout at the group, I have grown-up clothes too, but some Roman idiot stole them! Still behind me, Joe muttered, "La dolce vita," and I knew he felt as ill at ease as I did.

Then Maria burst out of the group and ran and threw her arms around us, and Colin was there, pounding indiscriminately on our backs and hugging us over Maria's small body, and the shell of discomfort broke, and warmth and gaiety flowed over us, and we moved into the body of the party.

I still do not have a sense of everyone we met that night. I never saw most of them again. They were, I surmised, Sam and Ada Forrest's closest friends, the ones you would invite to celebrate the rituals of life with you. I knew the Forrests had never met Maria and of course not Colin, but I assumed the Italian sense of family ran deep, and Ada Forrest kept up with her kin in America and had regular news of her cousin's child, the bright one, the one who was marrying the extraordinary young Southerner. It was, I thought, a lovely gesture to invite them to come to Rome and start their life together there—and to pay for most of the trip. I thought perhaps Ada Facaros missed her cousin, Maria's mother, and wanted to renew the old ties of blood and kinship. I was touched that so famous an international couple as she and Sam would want to do something as simple and graceful as introduce their young kinswoman to their friends and ask them to share the celebration of her new life's beginning. It was a sweet, somehow comforting thing to do. We did it at home, on the Mountain.

But the people Joe and I met that night were not like the people back home on the Mountain. They were not, with a few exceptions, like any people I had ever met.

Before I left home I had envisioned this party and seen in my mind a sort of idealized gathering of international artists, the European art community at its best. I anticipated intense talk of works in progress, names I knew from the pages of art magazines, a smattering of austere Italian academics.

But, except for Ada Forrest and one dark, languid young second wife of a documentary film producer, none were Italian. We met Englishmen and one or two Orientals and one Finn, towheaded and long-faced and very funny. And we met many Americans. Of them, almost all were Southerners. That should have put me at ease, as Sam Forrest's accent had when he first spoke, but somehow it did not. They were not of my South; none came out of our academic world. There were two or three other artists in various media, considerably more who worked "in film," seven or eight who did things in television, a few who said they were "in business" and smiled as if I should know what business that might be, a tall man from Mississippi who said he played tennis, journalists, and a scattering of writers whose names and works I did not know. I could tell from Joe's face, intensely interested and composed, that he did not either. I felt shame and a deep disorientation for both of us. It was our business to know writers.

It seemed to me that the people we met who identified themselves with a profession were mostly men. The women either had no outside work or did not speak of it. Some were introduced as so-and-so's wife, but many others were introduced only by their names. They were all ages, from Maria's to perhaps a decade older than Joe and Sam Forrest, whom I knew to be in his early fifties. Not all were beautiful or even pretty, by any standard I knew, but almost all of them were stylish and virtually all were arresting. It was more than dress or bearing. It lay, somehow, in their manner. By no means did all the women on Sam and Ada Forrest's rooftop seem especially happy or animated, but all seemed secure in the knowledge that they belonged, in every atom of their beings, exactly where they were.

The essential gulf between them and me seemed written in neon in the humid air. Rightness seemed to seep out of their very pores, just as otherness did mine. I wondered, feeling with despair the fear start to warm and quicken again, if we on the Mountain ever seemed this way to visitors and newcomers. If we did, we should be ashamed of ourselves. This was as alien and discomforting a feeling as I had ever had. It seemed far deeper, more fundamental than being a stranger at a party. It was plain that few people knew or sensed it, and in my escalating anxiety and self-consciousness I did not believe that any would have cared if they had. Even Maria and Colin, once they had hugged us and introduced us around the group, drifted off, two young people utterly strange to me, twined around each other as though no indulgent eyes followed them. They kissed a great deal, and once I saw Colin lift Maria's damp hair aside to whisper in her ear and put his tongue into it. I turned almost desperately to Joe.

"Let's get a drink," I said, and my voice sounded high and artificial in my own ears.

The bar was set up in a corner of the rooftop garden that overlooked the dark street below. Sam Forrest steered us there and asked us what we would like, but before we could answer the young man who said he played tennis snatched his arm and drew him into a group at the end of the white-clothed table, and a babble of talk and laughter started up. Sam gave us a "be right back" wave of his hand and melted into the group. I looked around brightly. No one was looking at us. I gave Joe a brilliant smile that I could feel in my cheek muscles.

"What can I get you?" the young bartender, who looked like someone's son or nephew, said.

"Bourbon and water," I said, and he looked embarrassed.

"I don't think we've got any," he said. "There's some scotch, though. And some brandy."

"Make it brandy," I said. "Over ice."

"And you, sir?"

"Campari and soda," Joe said.

I simply stared at him. Joe always drinks bourbon. Always.

"When in Rome," he said, looking with a great show of interest around the rooftop. His arm was loosely around my shoulder, and I could feel the sweat in the palm of his hand. I thought it sprang from more than the thick, hot night air. Nothing about Joe was different from what it usually was; he was as tall and stooped-slender and loose-jointed as ever, and his face, in the soft, wavering light from the hurricane lamps on the bar, was still narrow and deeply carved and handsome. But I could feel the unease in him. It was as if, underneath the surface of a placid long-known pool, an unaccountable maelstrom had suddenly started up. I had literally never felt deep uncertainty in Joe before, not even during my therapy; I felt as though a tree or a boulder had suddenly revealed its dense, swarming atoms to the naked eye. Tiny, bright spears of terror spurted up my wrists, and my face tingled numbly.

I swallowed my brandy in a gulp and handed the glass back for a refill.

"Christ, Cat," Joe said under his voice. "Somehow this doesn't seem the perfect place to get drunk."

I drank down the second brandy, and the fear receded a little.

"Just don't leave me," I whispered to Joe, who was still sipping his Campari and soda and scanning the rooftop. "I know we're going to have to go mingle, but please don't leave me."

"I won't," he said, and smiled, and more of the strangeness shrank back. "But go easy on the brandy. I don't want to have to fight Sam Forrest or that tennis player for your honor."

"Since when did you ever have to?" I said, stung.

"Just joking, Cat. Lighten up. I'm not going to leave you."

But he did. In a few minutes the main body of the party, which was clustered around the buffet table at the other end of the roof garden, parted, and Colin Gerard called out of it, "Hey, Joe! Come tell these ignoramuses what Trastevere's greatest poet said about the Trasteverinos!"

Joe smiled, and let his arm drop from around my shoulders, and walked away from me toward the group. I took a step after him and then stopped. I could not seem to make my feet move.

"Would you like another brandy, ma'am?" the young bartender said.

"Yes, thank you."

He poured it and I sipped, grateful for the fire that flowed into my stomach. It was a very empty stomach. Neither Joe nor I had eaten since lunch on the Alitalia flight, eons ago.

From across the roof, and as if from very far away, I heard Joe's lazy school voice saying, "Well, if my memory serves, Carl Alberto Salustri, otherwise known as Trilussa, said:

> "'Don't wanna work, I don't, so what the Hell?
> I'm not cut out for it, and work's a bore.
> Don't wanna work, I don't, need I say more?
> Or can I save my breath and take a spell?'"

Joe paused and looked around at the group, who looked mildly back at him. He laughed, a small dry sound, and Colin laughed too. But no one else did.

Joe said, "Another of your literati, an expatriate like your-selves, said of it, 'It's as good a place as any to wait for the end of the world.' I think that was in Fellini's *Roma*."

Colin laughed again, but no one else did. Joe had found a book at home called *A Literary Companion to Rome* and had mem-orized countless epigrams written by travelers over the centuries about the city. He tossed them off constantly to Colin, who loved them. I did too. I loved knowing what other travelers had found for themselves here. It was like having, instead of one set of senses, many. I had heard the bits that Joe quoted tonight many times before.

"I believe it was Gore Vidal who said it," Joe added into the silence. No one responded.

My heart squeezed with anguish for my husband, my beau-tiful, brilliant husband, drowning in his pedantry like a fish in air on this hateful roof. I thought I would go to him and put my hand in his and say, simply, I believe we'll go home now. And we would do just that. Maybe we would go all the way home, Joe and me together, as we had done before. I would do it as soon as I finished my brandy.

"Did he really say that?" one of the women said, a tall blonde in a short black leather skirt. "It doesn't sound like Gore. I play tennis with him when he's in Rome. I'll ask him."

I stared at her. Sweat beaded her face and ran down her smooth brown legs. Well, really, leather in July, in this furnace of a city. I thought it would be a great pleasure to slap her sweaty, supercilious face. Joe could handle her, though; one soft drawled sentence would cut her down to proper size. I had heard him do it over and over again. I had never known anyone Joe couldn't handle with his wit and his school voice.

"Maybe it wasn't Vidal," Joe said, not in his school voice, and smiled, and shrugged. The smile looked as though it had been cut into his face with broken glass.

"I don't think it could have been," the woman said, and turned back to the group. I banged the glass down on the bar and started toward Joe. At that moment Ada Forrest came as smoothly out of the shadows behind the buffet table as a white shark and took his arm and bore him over to the other side of the roof, where a bank of potted trees with tiny white lights in them made a bower, and low wooden chairs stood. She stood beside him, her white head just level with his chin, her arm linked with his, and pointed to something down below and whispered into his ear. I saw him throw his head back and laugh, and she laughed too, a rich sound, like tawny port. They turned away from the stone parapet and I moved toward them, grateful to Ada Forrest, grateful to hear the all-rightness in my husband's laugh. But they sank into two of the chairs that faced the city and began to talk. I could not hear what they said. They did not look back at me.

I stopped and went back to the bar and picked up my drink and looked around. No one was looking at me. I took my drink over to a carved stone bench that sat against the parapet, in the shadow of a great, gnarled old vine ... wisteria, I thought numbly; it must be a real show in the spring. I leaned my forearms on the parapet. Here I was in deep shadow, from the vine and the warm terra-cotta side of a little rooftop structure that housed, perhaps, a sink and refrigerator and toilet, or maybe garden tools and pots.

The parapet overlooked the back of the house. A great black hill rose behind it, and there was a dark medieval-appearing structure crowning it. Between the backs of the old row houses and the beginning of the hill was a vast ditch or ravine, thick with overgrowth on its lips, inky black in its depths. I stared into it. All of a sudden the blackness looked sweet, seductive, cool, endlessly soft. The fear erupted from the deepest core of me and flooded me like a firestorm, filling me up to the ends of my hair shafts, to the ends of my fingers and toes, to the backs of my tight-pressed lips. I had never felt such sucking terror before, not even in the worst of my times off the Mountain. Not ever. . . .

I closed my eyes. I felt the brandy glass fall from my suddenly dead fingers and tinkle on the edge of the parapet, but I never did hear the shards hit the bottom of the black ravine. Perhaps there was no bottom to it. I felt myself sway; the rooftop rolled greasily beneath my feet.

Someone put a hand on my shoulder. Not Joe, it was not Joe's touch. I could not seem to open my eyes.

"I would be extremely pleased if you would do me the honor of sitting here on this bench with me and getting drunk," Sam Forrest said. I opened my eyes then. He bulked up huge beside me, teeth and eyes gleaming in the green gloom of the vine shadow, smelling rankly and wonderfully of sweat and the earth. He had two glasses in one hand and a bottle of bourbon in the other.

"I keep a bottle in reserve for very special occasions," he said. "Not many people have the innate class to ask for it. I was glad to hear you did. Neat or with water? I don't think there's an ice cube in all of Italy tonight, but I'll look—"

"Neat," I said. My voice sounded normal; how could it? I thought in simple wonder.

He poured two glasses of the bourbon, a lovely, warm, living amber, and gave me one, and clinked his glass to mine. My hand shook only slightly.

"Here's to the start of a beautiful friendship," he said.

He drank his bourbon down quickly and so did I. Without asking he filled both our glasses and sat down heavily on the carved bench and patted the seat beside him. Warmed from throat to stomach with the whiskey, I sat. Neither of us spoke for a small time; I sipped and looked around the rooftop, my lips buzzing numbly, wondering what on earth I would find to say to Sam Forrest that would keep him by my side . . . for my mind was blank and white except for a fierce desire not to be alone on this roof any longer. It occurred to me that Ada Forrest might have seen me standing here and sent him to rescue me; I could imagine the light, languid voice saying, "Oh, for God's sake, Sam, go over there and talk to her. Nobody else is going to, and it's obvious she's not going to mingle. It's what you get, asking people you don't know to these damned parties."

I might have felt embarrassed nearly to death by this image, except by that time the whiskey had done its work and I felt removed from everything around me, as if I stood behind a pane of warm, clean glass. I will say whatever it takes to keep him here, I thought. I will be so cute and clever he'll want to stay all night. Joe will have to come find me sooner or later, and then we can go home. I wonder why I never thought of drinking before. It's better than Valium by a long shot.

In the shadow I could feel Sam Forrest looking at me; I could feel the impress of his eyes on the side of my face. I turned to him and smiled. It was, I fancied, a wise smile, a sophisticated one.

"Tell me what you're working on now," I said.

He laughed.

"Right now I'm working on a hangover," he said. "Aside from that, absolutely nothing. *Nulla. Niente.* I haven't hit a lick at a snake since this time last year. I thought I'd have it in gear by this spring, but I didn't, and now it's summer and nobody can work in Rome in the summer for all the tourists and the visitors dropping in to see what you're working on now."

Even the whiskey did not dim the flame of mortification that burned in my chest and cheeks. I knew he could read its ensigns there. Of course, he must hate the crowds of people who came to his door here; they must, like Joe and me, seem literally to drop in on him from the skies, people drawn by his charisma, his celebrity, his consummate art. . . .

"We should have thought of that," I said formally. "Of course you can't work. Listen, Sam, please don't feel you have to stay here and talk to me. I'm fine; I'm having a lovely time looking at your wonderful view. Joe and I will have to run in a minute; it's going to take years, practically, to get back to our hotel. . . ."

He reached over and covered my hand with his. Only then

did I realize how cold I was, despite the still, thick heat. His hand felt like a fire-warmed mitten.

"I didn't mean you, Cat," he said. "No, come on, look at me. I'm sorry. Christ, somebody should sew my mouth shut. I only growled at you because I haven't been able to work for a year and it's nobody's fault but my own and it scares me and makes me madder than shit. I wouldn't be working if you and everybody else in Rome left me alone for the rest of my life, and I'm here drinking bourbon with you because there's nowhere else on this goddamned roof I'd rather be. You and Joe don't have to run in a minute because Ada isn't going to let go of him till it thunders. Don't you worry about Joe. He's going to be just fine."

I looked across the rooftop to the group around the bar. Everyone fluttered there like luminous moths around the flame that was Ada Forrest in her burning white. On one side of her, Colin and Maria stood arm in arm, laughing. Maria wore a brightly printed cotton skirt to her ankles and a white blouse pulled low on her brown shoulders; even from here I could see the great shelf of her breasts and the cleavage between them. She looked somehow oceanic, an archetypal figure, fecundity written in every line and curve. Her hair was wild on her shoulders and fell over one black eye. I thought of the Willendorf Venus and felt awe and incredulity at the transformation. Colin, beside her, seemed somehow diminished, even in the low-buttoned Italian shirt and narrow pants. It was as if the heat and the thick night had sucked some of the vitality out of his burnished golden hair and blunted, somehow, his fine, narrow English features.

On the other side of Ada, his arm still linked through hers, Joe laughed and lifted his glass and said something to the crowd around them, and everyone laughed in response. Glasses clicked and Maria ran over and kissed Joe on the cheek, and Ada gave his arm a little squeeze.

I thought that Joe was, indeed, going to be just fine.

"We may get home by morning, at the rate he's going," I

said, trying out a little laugh that ended in a hiccup. "Oh, lord. Excuse me."

"Where are you staying?" Sam said.

"At the Cavalieri Hilton. Up there somewhere. I'd never get there by myself."

He laughed too.

"Do I perhaps detect the fine hand of my wife in your accommodations? I'm right, aren't I? Nobody would think to stay there unless Ada put a bug in their ear. I think she's on the payroll."

"It's not a bad hotel," I said. "It's really sort of pretty."

"It's an awful hotel." He grinned. "But it is much beloved of rich Americans, and Ada likes to hang around the pool. She looks fantastic in a bikini, for an old broad, and I think she believes that if we lie around there long enough I'll get lots of commissions from my rich compatriots, maybe to do a mural in a mall in Kansas City or a heroic statue for a state-of-the-art cat-food plant in Scranton."

"Do you take commissions?" I said, uncomfortable with the talk about Ada.

"Hell, yes," he said. "Right now I'd take a commission to do the catfood plant in a minute, if I thought it would get me off dead center."

"Do you work here at home?" I asked.

"No, I've got a studio in a house off the Campo Fiori. It's a long walk, but I like the flowers. I'll take you to see it while you're here, if you'd like to."

"I would," I said, and drank some more bourbon. Sam Forrest was very easy to talk to. I couldn't remember why I had thought he would not be. I thought I could talk to him about anything.

"Do you have children?" I said, startling myself. I had not been thinking of children, not consciously.

"Not with Ada," he said. "But yes, I have a son. Terry. He

lives in Tuscaloosa, Alabama; runs two or three Ford agencies near there. He's around . . . let's see, thirty-two or -three now. Has a pretty little blond wife and two pretty little blond kids. I'm a grandfather. Actually."

"How on earth did he end up in Tuscaloosa, Alabama?" I said.

"Well, I met his mother when I was in graduate school at 'Bama, and then I stayed on and taught in the art department, and we got married and he was born, and one thing led to another and his mother and I divorced and she stayed on, and . . . so has he. It's hard for a certain kind of Southerner to leave home. Like cheerleaders and Ford salesmen."

I turned my head to look at him. The words were tinged with bitterness, but there was nothing in his barbaric red face but lazy humor and a kind of half-lidded enjoyment.

"She was a cheerleader?"

"She was. Prettiest girl at 'Bama that year. Like to dazzled me right out of my mind. Stars fell on Alabama, like the song says."

That amused me. I began to sing, softly, "We lived our little drama, we kissed in a field of white, and stars fell on Alabama . . . last night."

He chimed in on the last line, in a good voice, tenor, smoky with bourbon. The group at the bar turned to look at us, smiled, and turned away.

"But you didn't stay," I said. "May I have some more bourbon?"

"Here you go; hold your glass steady. No. I didn't. I started to grow and change and she didn't, and I just got to where I had painted everything there was to paint around Tuscaloosa, Alabama. So I finally moved on. I think, on the main, she was right relieved."

"And the rest is history."

"The rest, as they say, is history."

From behind us, far up the hill, a voice wailed out of the

darkness, a high, long tremolo. The lament of a lost soul. It died away in a kind of sobbing.

"What was that?" I said, my flesh creeping with chill. I turned and looked up but could only see the dark bulk of the huge building high above us, and above that the sky, full of stars.

"That was one of the good denizens of Regina Coeli," he said, getting up and going to the parapet and leaning his forearms on it. I followed, staggering slightly.

"Every now and then one of them gives voice. It's the Roman version of urban coyotes. The gentleman says he wants a lawyer. It's usually that or a woman. If it weren't dark you could see the guards prowling on the walls with Uzis. Gives a lot of tone to the neighborhood."

I shivered. "That was . . . demonic. Poor people. I hardly even noticed the prison, way up there."

"Well, in a way it's not so much worse than its neighbor," he said. "See that roof over there, just below it? The two-level roof?"

I looked, searching the jumble of tiles and vines and TV antennas that lay below the parapet. I saw the roof he meant. The top level was dark, but the lower one was still lit. Through small, deep old windows I could see figures working at a table in what must be a kitchen.

"It's a retirement home for priests and nuns," Sam said. "The priests get the top level. They sit around all day drinking vino and eating the meals that the poor little retired nuns down on the lower level lug up stairs six or seven times a day. Rear back in their chairs in their long-awaited retirement, while wizened little old women in long black habits wash their holy clothes and cook and clean for them. That's *their* retirement. They'll be up half the night; they are every night. *Spiritus sanctus.*"

"What a . . . strange place this is," I said, feeling the strangeness profoundly but knowing the words were massively inadequate.

"It is," he said. "It is indeed a strange goddamn place. I don't know why I stay. It's impossible for a sane person to live here, and it costs more than anywhere else in Europe, and the inflation rate is out the kazoo, and the unemployment figures are through the ceiling, and they'll steal the fillings out of your back molars if they get a chance, and it's dirty, and it's loud, and the traffic is lethal, and the country is flat broke, and there is an extremely high possibility of getting bombed or kneecapped whenever you go to the corner market."

"But."

"Yeah. But. It's so goddamned beautiful it stops my heart just to stick my head out on the street every morning. Any patch of wall on any street looks like a painting; the layers go back to . . . God, the Renaissance. Medieval times. Every time they dig a hole in the street to build a new hotel or a McDonald's, they hit columns or a ruin out of classical times. The worst hovel in Rome has flowers and filigree and all those wonderful browns and golds. 'Pear-brown Rome,' Keats called it. It's Valhalla for an artist. Even artists who aren't working."

"You'll be working again soon," I said, certain it was so. I felt as if I had known this man for half my life.

"Maybe I will," he said. "Maybe I will."

"I like it that you're a Southerner," I said. "It takes some of the curse off your being so famous. It makes you easy to talk to. Of course, being drunk makes it easy too. I'd be tongue-tied with terror if I weren't drunk and you weren't a Southerner."

He laughed and patted my shoulder.

"Nothing but Southerners here tonight," he said.

"Why is that?" I said. "Why are all your friends Southerners? Where are all the Italian counts and race drivers and French couturiers and international artists? Where are the rich coke dealers?"

"You disappointed? Well, for one thing, Southerners make great expatriates. The very best. Attractive, mannerly, interesting, at home wherever they end up. You know why that is, Cat?"

I thought he must be pretty drunk too. His voice was thick, and his eyes were owlish.

"Because Southerners instinctively sink deep roots wherever they go?" I said.

"Not bad. But the real reason is that Southerners instinctively understand the delicate politics of decadence, and most places you'd really want to go and live are decadent."

"Define decadent," I said ponderously.

"It's that," he said, gesturing up at the dark shape of Regina Coeli.

"Those poor souls?" I felt the southern liberal's mandatory indignance.

"No. That you didn't even hear them. That you didn't even know it was up there."

"I think that's specious," I said, slurring it.

"Well, Cat from Tennessee," Sam Forrest said, "we are all of us nothing if not that. It's the only way to live here."

I said nothing, only looked out over the rooftops of Trastevere and felt the alcohol singing in my blood. It seemed totally unbelievable that I was here, on this rooftop in old Rome, having this conversation with one of the most celebrated artists of my time.

"I don't know which is better," I said. "Being here now or remembering it later."

He laughed, and then he said, "What are you afraid of, Cat?"

I turned to him, the word *nothing* on my lips, and then I said, "I'm afraid of everything. I'm afraid of almost everything in the world that isn't on the Mountain at home, and I've been afraid since I was five years old."

"Tell me," he said. And we sat back down on the bench and drank more bourbon, and I did. I told him all of it. It took quite a long time.

When I stopped talking, he was silent for a space, and then he said, "I would have liked to meet your parents. They had a certain personal style that speaks to me."

"I know it's funny," I said, smiling but feeling obscurely diminished by his words. "You'd have to be a rock or a tree not to find it funny."

"I don't think it's funny," Sam said. "I meant that. Listen, Cat, you mustn't be afraid of Rome. It's just too rich; there's too much you need to *get* here. All that out there . . . all that architecture, that . . . geometry, the sheer physics of it. God . . . it could blow your mind away, if you could really take it in. You must do that. You must take it all in. I'll bet it could heal you."

"All that geometry and physics scares the hell out of me," I said. "Where's the soul and spirit in geometry and physics? Where's the people?"

"Well, there's an awful lot of God sprinkled around out there. All those saints and angels and churches. Saint Peter's. I think God was invented to cut physics down to size, but if you ask me, he hasn't succeeded in Rome."

"No," I said. "God was invented to make physics bearable."

He looked at me for a time in the darkness, a small smile curving the thin bronze lips up. In the vine shadow he looked Etruscan, ancient, mythic. Even the scrofulous ponytail was a part of it.

"I'd like to do two things while you're in Rome, Cat Gaillard," he said. "I'd like to show you *my* Rome. And I'd like to draw you. Your face is all over the city, you know. It's on practically every pagan artifact here and a few select Christian ones. It's amazing, really. Will you let me do that?"

"I don't know about the drawing," I said. "After tonight I'm going to have such a hangover I won't be drawable for ten years. But I'd like to see your Rome. Can Joe come too?"

"Sure," he said. "We'll do it before you leave for . . . where? Where do you go next? Am I right in thinking that you and Joe are going with these randy children on their honeymoon?"

"Yep. Isn't that shameless? From here to Venice, and then to Florence, and then to the hill towns. . . ."

"Ah, yes," he said. "The hill towns. Get Cat back up into her hills, whence cometh her help. Well, we'll do it the day before you go, maybe. I'll let you know. Meanwhile . . . have another drink."

We did. We had several more. At some point in the evening we began to sing again. "Stars fell on Alabama," we wailed into the soft night over Rome, and far above us floated down, as if in reply, *"Vorrei una dama! Vorrei una dama!"*

"Me too, my man," Sam yelled back.

It must have been very late when Joe, still attached to Ada Forrest's arm, came to claim me and take me home. All of a sudden I realized that we were among the last people left on the Forrests' roof. It should have bothered me, but by then nothing did.

"We lived our little drama," I warbled, lurching into Joe and holding on.

"A coach for you, Cinderella," he said, grinning at me with very little humor. We creaked and bumped back down in the little elevator with Sam and Maria and Colin, to hail a taxi. But there were none about, and when we finally phoned, from the Forrests' beautiful white painting-starred living room, it was to be told that there was, alas, a *sciopero* among the taxi drivers of Rome, and so Sam Forrest ended up driving us, badly, all the way up Monte Mario in a disreputable, belching old car of Finnish origin, and I slept all the way.

CHAPTER SIX

ON MY FIRST MORNING IN ROME I SLEPT LATE. It was not good sleep; I tossed and licked dry lips and buried my head deep under the covers to escape the stale chill of the air-conditioning and the spearlike shards of white light from the window wall facing the hydroelectric plant. When I first woke, at dawn, I had a savage headache, one I knew would border on the unendurable if I moved. My stomach roiled. I had never felt anything like this before, but I knew it was a formidable hangover, and my only hope was to lapse again into the heavy unconsciousness that had taken me down the instant I hit the bed the night before. Before I did, I remembered the night on the roof above Trastevere, and the bourbon and Sam Forrest and the tipsy singing, and winced. Even that hurt. I willed myself back into sleep. When I woke again it was 11 A.M., and Joe was shaking me by the shoulder and holding coffee to my nose. I thought for a moment that the dark, thick smell would make me throw up.

"Good morning, Signora Fellini," Joe said, setting the coffee on the bedside table and sitting down on the edge of the bed. He ruffled my hair. I grimaced with the pain of his touch and sat up. My eyelids seemed glued together and my mouth full of flannel. I was profoundly, powerfully thirsty, but not for the caustic Roman coffee.

"Is there any water?" I croaked.

"There's some *acqua minerale* but no ice," he said. I heard sloshing and fizzing, and reached out blindly for the glass, and downed the mineral water in a gulp. It careened around my stomach and threatened for a moment to bounce right back up. I remembered I had eaten none of Ada Forrest's beautiful buffet the evening before.

"Can you die of this?" I said.

"Not in Rome," Joe said. "If last night was any example, half the Eternal City feels this way when they wake up. I've got a tad of hangover myself."

"No wonder they can't balance their budget," I said, and sat up and squinted blearily at him while I waited for the room to stop spinning.

He laughed and took away the glass and brought the coffee back, and with it a small plate with a hard roll and a wedge of soft cheese. He did not look as if he had a hangover. He looked . . . astonishing. He wore white shorts that he might play tennis in except that they were too tight and too short, and a sleeveless T-shirt striped in wide bands of red, green, and white that fit him like an undershirt, and rubber shower clogs. I stared. I had never seen Joe Gaillard in anything remotely resembling this costume, not even his underwear. He never wore undershirts, and his boxer underpants were cut much fuller and longer than those shorts. He looked so utterly alien to the man I had lived with for twenty-three years that I had no idea whether the costume suited him. It probably did. He was still long-muscled and slender, and tanned from tennis, and the hair on his arms and legs was dark gold, untouched by the silver that threaded his hair and mustache. Yes, his new clothes were undoubtedly becoming. But it was still like waking up to a stranger in my bedroom.

He looked down at himself and shrugged.

"Well, it was all they had in the famous Ortini's that fit me; everything over here is cut for tiny little snake-hipped guys. I sent the other stuff to be washed and bought some pants for tonight. The clothes I had on yesterday could stand by themselves. Come on, Cat, stop staring at me as if I had on a dress. Everybody out by the pool is wearing stuff like this, or worse. Had you rather I bought myself a bikini?"

"I'd rather you got your bag back," I said, getting up and walking on wavering legs to the bathroom. "I feel like I've waked up in a strange bedroom with Casanova. I'm glad you're speaking to me, though. I hope everybody else is. Lord, my head. How do drunks stand the next morning? Have you already been down to the pool?"

"Yep. It's nice; it's probably the only relatively cool spot in Italy. Don't worry about last night. You were cute," he said indulgently, and I looked back at him over my shoulder. Joe had never in his entire life called me cute. I would not have thought the word was in his vocabulary. Was he teasing me? Had I behaved so disgracefully he was resorting to sarcasm? He had never done that with me, either. But I saw nothing in his face save amusement and affection. I went into the astounding bathroom, an octagonal cave of tawny marble except for the wall of mirrors over the vanity counter, and crawled under the shower and turned it on as hot and hard as I could bear it. When I came out I felt better.

He was holding out a small handful of cloth, when I came back into the bedroom, and grinning.

"Before you say no, just try it," he said. "You'll look terrific. Everybody at the pool is wearing one. Ada has one on. So does Maria, before God. Sam too, if you can believe it. If Maria and Sam Forrest can wear bikinis, you can too. The signorina who sold it to me swears she sold one just like it to Julia Roberts not long ago."

I took the cloth and held it out before me. It was indeed a bikini, a black one, two scraps of silky cloth that would not have made an adequate dust rag.

"Ada and Sam are here? At the pool? I thought we were on our own till the wedding this afternoon. Did I invite them? Joe, I can*not* wear this thing. I have spider veins. I'm pale as a ghost. All my ribs show. You were sweet to think of it, but I really don't want to swim."

"I invited them last night," he said. "Ada went on and on about how hot it was, and how wonderful it would be to get wet and cool, and I knew we were going to have to reciprocate some-time, and this way we'll get an evening to ourselves tomorrow night. We're going to swim and have drinks and some lunch"— he laughed at my face—"or rather you can have Pellegrino and some lunch and we'll have the drinks, and then everybody's going to go home and change for the wedding, and we'll all meet at the Campidoglio at five. Come on. Put this on and come on down; I've got to get back. We are hosting a very fancy party this morning. You know who else is down there?"

"John Paul the Second?" I said acidly. I did not feel like chatting brightly with Sam and Ada Forrest, and I was not about to put on the ridiculous bikini and parade around the Samuel Goldwyn swimming pool I had seen the evening before, and I liked neither my husband's costume nor his indulgent tone of voice. Least of all I liked myself. I had spent precious hours of my time in Rome in drugged sleep and caused Joe to speak to me as one would to an errant child, and it put our relationship onto a skewed and sliding kind of footing I would not have imagined possible.

"In a manner of speaking," Joe said. "Yolanda Whitney, the pope of the hearthside—or is it popess? In the more than consid-erable flesh, which is spilling out of the smallest bikini I ever saw. You'll make her look like one of her own hand-quilted ottomans. She's in Rome to shoot a show on adapting Italian crafts to the average midwestern home or something. Apparently the Forrests have known her forever. A three-year-old could see she's got the hots for Sam. Apparently it's a rather generic effect among women."

He leered showily at me, and I knew he was not entirely happy with the time I had spent at Sam Forrest's side the night before. Well, tough. I would not have spent any time at all with Sam if Joe had not allowed Ada to tow him away without so much as a backward look.

"Perfect." I groaned. "All this and Yolanda Whitney too. Be still my heart."

Yolanda Whitney was the kind of super-celebrity that only American television can spawn, the sort who celebrates both America and television itself. She had started out with a column on crafts and country decorating in a supermarket women's magazine, hit the talk show circuit, and proved astoundingly popular showing viewers how they could make rustic artifacts and bibelots from materials at hand. She made cornshuck dolls and centerpieces, dried-flower swags and garlands and banners; she painted driftwood and gilded gourds and lacquered autumn leaves and wild berries and turned ordinary ranch houses and condominiums from coast to coast into seasonal wonderlands straight out of nineteenth-century rural Vermont. Because of Yolanda Whitney, every third American home had a quilt stand, a warming pan, whiskey barrels full of herbs, dried flowers hanging all over the kitchen, and paper bags full of sand and candles along the driveway at Christmas. She had her own magazine now, too, but it was her television show that kept her before the eyes of America. I had seen her a number of times, neatly curved and crisply aproned and bubbling with enthusiasm, her cheeks rosy with health, her shining brown hair in a coronet of braids around her pretty head.

"I'll bet she smells like pine cones and salt dough all the time," I had said grumpily to Joe one recent Christmastime, watching her whip up a northern woodland fantasy of a holiday centerpiece.

I thought now I would rather be beaten with wire whisks than go down to that Esther Williams pool and sit and listen to Yolanda Whitney burble about macramé and decoupage. How on earth had the Forrests come to know her?

"You go on," I said. "I'll be down in a little while. Yolanda Whitney. Shit."

"Cheer up. Maybe she'll tell you how to make a centerpiece of gilded squirrel turds," Joe said. He made a face and went out the door, and I let my towel fall to the floor and turned away from the mirror over the desk and put on the bikini. It felt infinitely more naked than nakedness, and I moved into position in front of the mirror and closed my eyes. Then I opened them. In the shadowless light of the white and beige room I saw a tall woman, more thin than slender, skin all over a kind of bluish white in the fluorescence, every bruise and broken capillary and scar and discoloration glowing lividly, double line of ribs looking like an old-fashioned washboard, hipbones and knees and elbows as sharply knobbed as the bole of a young tree. I sucked in my small stomach and threw my shoulders and head back and smiled. The bikini flattened my already small breasts against my rib cage and rode sharply up into my crotch. My hair looked white in the artificial light, a wild cap of short cotton-candy curls atop a narrow face with too many hollows and far too many teeth. I snatched up a lipstick and scrawled red across my mouth.

Like somebody stole the third-year med school skeleton and put lipstick and a bikini on it, I thought furiously, and shucked out of the thing and put on the sundress I had worn last night and sprayed myself all over with Sung and went out, slamming the door behind me. I left the bikini in a wadded ball in the middle of the floor.

Got any more terrific ideas, Joe Gaillard?

The great marble lobby was dim and nearly empty, so that

going out onto the pool terrace beyond was like walking out into the desert from a cave. All I could see at first was the azure lozenge of water, the bright primary colors of the market umbrellas around it, and a great void of radiant white light where the vast panorama of Rome should have been. I pulled sunglasses out of my pocket and put them on and stood for a moment, letting my eyes adapt. Slowly the scene around the pool came into focus, double lines of chaises facing the water on which lay bodies showing a great deal of oiled brown skin and little else, umbrella tables with wrought-iron chairs also full of nearly naked people, tiers of tables being set for luncheon by beautiful young men in hotel livery, pots of cypresses and flowers, several bars with awnings and stools doing a brisk business, the ubiquitous flowering vines everywhere. Beyond, Rome emerged from a haze of white heat, palely, flatly. It looked like a badly faded drop cloth, all dimension bled out of it by the fierce sun. It was still and very hot and seemed no time at all. Even the sound of American rock from several huge boom boxes beside lounges around the pool was muffled and tinny. The weight of the sun on my head was punishing, and I could not seem to get a deep breath. The pool was largely empty, and the water looked wonderful. I thought what it would be like to dive into it and idle along the bottom, how everything would look, sun-shot and wavering and blue, only the silvery spume of my blown-out breath disturbing the deep coolness. For a moment I regretted the crumpled bikini on the floor of my room, but only for a moment.

I heard someone calling my name and turned and saw my group at the far end of the pool, with Maria standing and waving at me, and walked toward them along the scorching concrete apron, feeling as though I were wading through wet cement, feeling on my drooping, reedlike whiteness the scornful dark eyes of every sleek, naked brown person I passed. I got a confused impression of much dark, wet chest hair, tangled gold chains, coconut-smelling oil, green eye shadow, and about a million brown breasts glittering with droplets of pool water or sweat. By the time I reached the umbrella table and the cluster of lounges they had staked out, I was running with sweat myself and pounding with hangover.

"I really don't know how I am going to do this," I said aloud, but very softly. "Morning, everybody," I said in a stronger voice. "Is it always this hot in Rome?"

A babble of voices answered me:

Joe saying, "Ta-*da!* She is risen! But where's your new bathing suit?"

Sam Forrest saying, "Morning, muffin. You look altogether better than you have a right to."

Maria saying, "Come sit and talk to us, we didn't get a chance to last night, I'm so glad you're here, this is divine." Maria Condon saying "divine"? Maria in a bikini?

Colin saying, "Cat! Go back and put your bikini on! It's cruel to get everybody's fleshly hopes up and then back out!" Colin Gerard, talking to me of bikinis and fleshly hopes?

Ada Forrest saying, in her spilled-honey voice, "Pay no attention to this herd of goats. You're smart to stay out of the water. This sun would cook that lovely white skin like pork in half an hour."

Ada Forrest, gleaming like a pearl in her own whiteness as she lay full under the fist of the sun, her mouth and bikini strokes of scarlet, not a drop of sweat on her translucent skin, the white globes of her breasts and her carved waist and stomach untinged by the pink of the cooking pork she predicted for me. Her glorious white mane of hair was wrapped in a scarlet towel, and her ice-blue eyes hidden by huge black sunglasses. She looked unreal, phantasmagoric, almost uncanny, among the fleshy brown bodies around the pool.

I dropped into a chair beside Maria and hugged her as she leaned over to kiss me. A thick smell came off her, of sweat and sun oil and something I thought could only be semen. Joe had been right, Maria in her red-flowered bikini was overpowering:

brown, glistening flesh spilling everywhere, the great bobbling breasts barely contained, all of her the firm, healthy consistency of sun-hot rubber. Her smile was wide and joyous, and she almost laughed aloud in her happiness. I squeezed her hard in a surge of pure love. Maria on this day reduced everything to its simplest and most elemental form; her glowing flesh and barely sated sensuality made nuance and cynicism almost obscene.

"I hope you are always as happy as you are right this minute," I whispered to her, and she hugged me back.

"See Rome and die." She laughed.

"God, I hope not," Colin said from one of the lounge chairs. He wore American swim trunks, faded tartan that hung low on his slim hips. They were what all young Trinitarians wore on the Mountain, but here they looked callow, provincial, wrong. He seemed to know it. He had rolled them as high as they would go on his beautiful brown athlete's legs and sat so that the muscles in the carved torso played whenever he moved. He was thickly oiled and wore black glasses like Ada's. He could not seem to keep his eyes off Maria.

Sam Forrest should have looked obscene in the small blue bikini that was almost hidden under the bulge of his belly, but somehow he did not. He was massive, copper-gold all over with freckles and furred with bronze hair, hard and shining as amber or marble. I thought of some great pagan colossus or, for some reason, of Ozymandias. He wore a towel draped over his head, and sunglasses, and he was drinking a glass of red wine and picking grapes from a plate and popping them into his mouth. All that was missing was the satyr's ears and hooves and the pipes.

Beside him, Joe in his new Italian leisure clothes looked pale and almost fussy, the classic comic Englishman on holiday in the Mediterranean, complaining because they had wine but no tea. I felt shamed and mean-spirited for even thinking such a thing and wished he would move away from Sam and sit somewhere else. But the only other empty place was beside Ada, and I realized I did not want him to sit there, either. Where, I wondered, was the fabled Yolanda Whitney?

As if in answer to the thought a woman heaved herself out of the pool and came over to us and slumped down into the chair next to Ada, snorting and shaking bright drops of water everywhere.

"Damn, Yolie, you're worse than a wet dog," Sam said mildly, and Ada tossed her a towel without comment, and the woman dried herself energetically with it and dropped it on the cement beside the lounge.

"Meet our friend Yolanda Whitney," Ada said, and the woman squinted up at me. "Yolie, this is Catherine Gaillard, Maria and Colin's friend from America. You've already met Joe."

Yolanda Whitney's eyes did not sparkle now. They were flat and dark, like pebbles or marbles. Her hair was not wound around her head in glistening braids but leaped about her face in wet spirals, like Medusa's. She seemed much larger than she did on television, fat, even; her flesh was tanned deep mahogany, but there was an unhealthy bluish tinge under it, and it was slack and peppered with yellowing bruises. The color in her face was hectic: sunburn, not natural rosiness. She did not look at all healthy. She looked wrecked, downright dissipated, years older than I had thought from her television show. The sweet smell of alcohol came off her in waves, and my stomach contracted at it. I could scarcely believe this was the same woman who taught the world to make cornshuck dolls.

"Ah, yes," she said. Her voice was deep and thick, as if she had a cold. "Cat. I've been hearing about you."

"It's a pleasure to meet you," I said. "I've enjoyed your show."

"How nice," she said. "Are you crafty, Cat? I'll just bet you are."

She said it in such an unmistakably spiteful tone that I could think of nothing to reply. What was the matter with this woman? Everyone looked at her, and Ada murmured, "Charming," and Sam said, from behind the sketchbook he had picked up, "Put a lid on it, Yolie. It's way too early."

Her face went white under the sunburn and then dull red, and she turned her back on us elaborately and walked off toward the bar.

"On the contrary, I'd say it was way too late," I heard her say as she went away.

"Has my deodorant failed me?" I said, heat crawling up my neck into my face. I said it as lightly as I could. I sat back down in my chair beside Maria, grateful for the shade of the umbrella and the shelter of my sunglasses, poised for flight. I was not going to sit beside this awful pool and let this awful woman take potshots at me.

"I apologize for her," Sam said. "She's had some very bad news from her agent. The network isn't picking up her show next year, and they're going to have to start scrambling around to find her a new one. They will; she's too good not to. But uncertainty makes her crazy, and she's had too much to drink. She's taking it out on the new gal' on the block. If she does it again I'll swat her."

Ada said, "We've known her since she was the new girl on the block herself. Sam met her at a party at the embassy the first time she was in Rome and brought her home; she'd lost her passport and most of her money, and her hotel had kicked her out. She was a pretty thing then; Sam did her portrait. It's still in our collection. She stayed with us for a while, before she went back and started the column for that silly magazine. I'm sure she's already sorry she snapped at you, Cat. She'll tell you herself when she gets back."

And she did. Yolanda Whitney came back carrying something tall and garnished with fruit in a frosted glass, sipping on it, and put her hand on my shoulder and said, "I'm sorry. I've got a foul temper and a worse mouth. I've been hearing all morning how you look like a Raphael, or was it a Leonardo, Joe? And that kind of makes you mean when you look like a Bosch."

She smiled, but she was looking at Sam Forrest, and I remembered what Joe had said. It was true. Something hungry and hopeless looked out of her opaque eyes when they fell on Sam. I wondered if he knew.

"Not like Bosch. More like Vermeer. Big difference," he said, grinning up at her. I saw, incredulously, that he was beginning a series of pencil studies of me and felt my face flame even hotter. He did not attempt to hide them, but I could not see them upside down and did not want to crane my neck. Yolanda Whitney, herself one of his subjects long ago. What else had she been to him? I wondered. Could she possibly think I was anything to him save a subject for his pencil, or would be? Dear God, I was already so sick of the thick, clotting nuance everywhere I turned in this old city.

"Sam, darling," Ada said. "Why don't you put the sketchbook away? Poor Cat doesn't want to sit there all afternoon with you doing that; you can't have any idea how it makes one feel. Like a bug under a magnifying glass."

"You feel like a bug, Cat?" Sam said, not raising his eyes from the pad. His pencil flew.

"Yes," I said shortly. "Or rather, like Mickey Mouse on one of those 'Draw Me' matchbook covers."

He laughed and threw the sketchbook aside.

"That's enough for now, anyway," he said. "Got a good start. Does anybody want another drink? I'll go."

We sat beside the pool until nearly two o'clock, talking desultorily, sipping drinks, sweating, nibbling at sandwiches. Ada put wet cotton balls over her eyes and slept in the sun, or appeared to. Sam stretched out on his stomach and did sleep; I heard soft snores rising from his hidden face. Yolanda Whitney drank quietly and stared off over the pool down onto Rome, poaching in its heat miasma. Colin and Maria stayed in the pool, bobbling at the edge, holding on to the side with their hands, their bodies pressed closely together. They kissed and nibbled on each other and murmured into one another's ears, and once, when I looked over at them, I could have sworn they were making love underwater. There was little else it could have been. Their faces were blind and emptied out, and their mouths were slightly opened as if they could not get air. No one else seemed to notice.

"Is there some law about that?" I murmured to Joe, who was slumped beside me in a chair reading *USA Today*. He looked over at them and grinned.

"Not in Rome," he said, and went on reading.

Finally, at a little after two, we left the pool to go and dress for Colin and Maria's wedding. Just before we passed under the arch that led back into the hotel lobby, I stopped and looked back. For some reason the heat haze that had lain over the city beyond the pool apron had lifted for a moment, and Rome looked once more like something out of an enchantment, a sorcerer's spell, clear and rich and shining in its own light.

I turned to Sam Forrest, who stood beside me, looking at it too.

"It's all in the light, isn't it?" I said.

"Yep," he said. "Light is everything. It always has been."

They were married at six o'clock in the evening in the Palazzo dei Conservatori on the Campidoglio, on Capitoline Hill, the smallest and to me most resonant of Rome's celebrated Seven. On this ancient outcropping overlooking both the Forum and the great sweep of the Vatican, the religious and political life of the city has been conducted since its birth. The long night of the Middle Ages did not entirely quench that life, and it had its own renascence when Michelangelo designed the exquisite small square that crowns it still. Today, when Romans shrug and say they can't fight city hall ("*Che posso fare?*"), this is where they mean. Sam told me the complex was designed to turn its back on pagan Rome, lying beneath the bulk of the Capitoline to the southeast, and face Saint Peter's, to the northwest. But it did not seem to me, when Joe and I had climbed the Cordonata, and

walked to the back of the square, and looked down on the broken columns and arches and temples of the Forum shimmering
enigmatically in their stillness, that the ecclesiastical shunning
had done much good. The little bowl of antiquity shimmered
and burned with life, no less than the square above it.

"Yow," I said softly. "Eternal is right. It does major things to
your stomach and heart, doesn't it?"

Joe was silent, his arm loosely around my waist. I leaned
my head onto his shoulder.

"What are you thinking?"

"That it was worth everything to come here and see this
with you. Oh, Cat, please don't be afraid to go off the Mountain
anymore. Think what might be ahead of us if you can. I didn't
miss it while you couldn't, but now . . . would you have wanted
never to see this?"

I wouldn't have if I couldn't have, I thought, but to him I
said, "I wouldn't have missed a minute of it. It's like an explosion in your brain. It could change your life. But Joe . . . it's still
hard. It's still hard. Don't leave me alone again. Keep me on the
hills and stay with me."

I said it lightly, but my voice trembled.

"I'm not going to leave you," he said, but his voice was
abstracted, and he was looking around him with a hunger that
seemed almost furious, ravenous. Unease put soft fingers in my
throat. He was only now tasting the world he had abjured for
me, and I did not think he would be content to stay above it
again. He was Joe and he would try, if I asked him, but he would
not be content. Tears stung in my nose and I turned away from
ancient Rome—unlike me, wholly unvanquished still.

"Let's go get some coffee," I said. "I saw a little outdoor
place at the bottom of the steps. We've got some time yet."

We went back across the piazza. It hummed with noise and
life despite the oppressive heat. Families strolled in the fading
light, tourists pointed and posed and snapped their cameras,
dark-suited men and white-bloused women scurried back and

forth carrying sheaves of important-looking *documenti*, children shrieked and laughed and clambered over the fountain and the two granite lions guarding the base of the great staircase. The light, that had been white and flat all afternoon, had by some alchemy turned rich and clear and golden, full of complex depths and planes and slants. I thought of what Sam had said earlier: "Light is everything. It always has been." This light was not like any I had seen on the Mountain, lovely as that often was. You would not mistake this for anything but the light of Rome. I imagined, smiling at the fancy, that it was the light itself that had turned the city to umber, amber, and gold.

Everywhere, young couples were waiting to be married or just had been. Some, in long chaste white and sober black, were toiling up and down the staircase of severe, medieval Santa Maria d'Aracoeli, flanking the Cordonata. They would, I knew, be bound by the iron bonds that only the Roman Catholic Church can forge. The others were destined, like Maria and Colin, for civil services in the Conservatori. Some were as properly gowned and tuxedoed as their counterparts heading for sacraments and sanctity, but others wore costumes of great variety and exuberance. I saw gowns from the chokingly expensive shops around the Piazza di Spagna, silk jackets from Armani and Versace, miniskirts of satin and leather, long dresses obviously made by loving hands and some by indifferent ones, cottons and silks and even one that seemed largely cobbled together of feathers. Each couple moved in a phalanx of laughing, shouting, jostling friends and relatives. The coffee shops and *caffès* around the base of the Campidoglio were clogged with noisy wedding parties drinking everything from *acqua minerale* to raw red wine. Wine predominated. Two couples stand out in my mind still; Joe took photos of both. They are, somehow, simply Rome to me.

One was a pair of a heartbreaking youngness, she dressed in unfashionably cut white with a meager veil and he in a too-large greenish tuxedo that must have seen many such family occasions, standing below the brow of the hill in the Forum, arms around each other, dwarfed by the columns that shone in the evening sunlight, smiling up at their party, who were standing behind Joe and me. It was, I suppose, the juxtaposition of all that hopefulness and sheer youngness, that all-suffusing living love, with the implacable bones of the dead empire, that sent the tears coursing hotly down my cheeks. I wanted terribly, in that moment, to know that nothing would corrode them, change them, diminish them. Poor Roman children, there seemed little in their lives that would not.

The other couple held court in the flyspecked, dusty little *caffè* where we finally found a seat. They were older, but their entourage was no less jubilant, no less loving. The groom wore truly splendid white tie and tails, and his bride, dusky and handsome with her flashing white eyes and teeth and black hair cut modishly short on her neck, wore a skintight, strapless, short gown of scarlet satin with long gloves, high heels, and pillbox to match. She looked to be at least seven months pregnant.

She felt us looking at her and turned, flashed me a smile and lifted her glass of wine to me, and called, *"Voi anche! Congratulizioni!"*

I smiled perplexedly at her and lifted my glass in return, and Joe pulled out his phrase book and thumbed it and began to laugh.

"She either thinks you're pregnant too, or about to be married, or maybe both," he said, and I looked down at myself and grinned.

"She thinks we're a cute little old bride and groom," I said, looking at the great bouquet of lilies and baby's breath I held. I had wanted to give Maria something to wear at her wedding, something borrowed or blue, perhaps, but Ada had outfitted her with a wonderful ecru silk suit from Armani, and she was to wear Colin's martyred mother's pearls. Mrs. Gerard had taken to her bed from prostration and could not attend her son's pagan civil wedding, but sent in her stead the triple strand of matched pearls that had graced the throats of Gerard brides since before the "late unpleasantness." Maria had her own mother's blue garter and her sister's borrowed linen handkerchief.

"Then let me give you your flowers," I said, remembering the elaborate florist shop in the hotel, and she had said she would love that, and I sat cradling them in the *caffè*, masses of luminous small lilies in the colors of the light and earth of Rome.

"*Grazie!*" I called to the scarlet bride, and Joe grinned and nodded and made a gesture I could not see over my head that set the male guests in the party roaring with laughter.

"Whatever that was, you better watch it or you won't be doing it again in your lifetime." I smiled at him. Somehow I felt, just then, like a bride myself, tremulous and breath-held with excitement.

"I plan to be doing it in about seven hours, or sooner if we can slip away from the famous wedding dinner," he said.

I saw them then, Maria in her chic ecru and Colin correct in a dark summer-weight suit, running hand in hand toward the Cordonata, with Sam behind them, still in chinos and a vast, flapping blue blazer and Ada looking like a lit candle in peach silk. Behind everyone, cinched into a smart yellow suit, hair once again shining in its braids, Yolanda Whitney clattered along on very high heels. Even from this distance she looked altogether restored to her twenty-four-inch-screen self, pretty and winsome and celebratory, everyone's favorite young aunt, the good witch come to bless the union.

Everyone's entitled to one bad day, I thought, feeling guilty about my dislike for her that afternoon, which had bordered on disgust. I wasn't any prize myself last night.

Sam caught sight of us and waved a massive arm. He had stuck a white flower in his grizzled red ponytail. The earring flashed in the last light of the sun.

"Let the games begin!" he called, and we all linked arms and ran the rest of the way up the Cordonata to the wedding of Maria and Colin.

Everyone remembers something different about it. I remember the dusty splendor of the old vault-ceilinged gilt-and-red room, spindly gold and red velvet chairs set about the walls except for the four in front of the magistrate's high carved desk where Maria and Colin sat, and with Sam and Ada as witnesses. And I remember the magistrate himself, in his robes, with a face out of *The Garden of the Finzi-Continis*, impassively smoking a malodorous cigarette while we waited for the Italian translator. Mostly, I remember Maria's face as she became Mrs. Colin Gerard, a bonfire of joy. And I remember I thought I would cry but did not.

Joe says he remembers mostly how dim and hot it was; the lights and air-conditioning were not working, whether from simple defect or *sciopero* no one knew. And he remembers that Ada Forrest wept, and he found that strange.

Sam said what he remembered mostly was his own first wedding, in the tiny living room of a justice of the peace in Elkton, Maryland, that smelled of cat urine and throbbed with recorded wedding music and the sobs of his cheerleader bride, who missed her mama and daddy.

"And," he said, "I thought how much I'd like to paint that magistrate, with the cigarette hanging out of his mouth and the Hush Puppies sticking out under his robe. I think I'd call it SPQR."

Maria remembers the surprising liberality of the Italian civil ceremony, with its emphasis on honoring each other, and the unexpected tenderness of the charge to honor each child of their union according to its own talents and identity.

"I remember," Colin said, "that I've never had to pee so badly in my life. I thought I was going to have to run down to the Forum and do it behind a column."

"I remember thinking how wonderful it would be to remember being married in Rome," Yolanda Whitney said. "It would be the one thing you could never lose to the community property laws. Not, of course, that you darling children will ever have to worry about that."

And she smiled her television smile at the new Mr. and Mrs. Gerard.

Afterward, while we milled about in the portico of the Conservatori, waiting while Joe and Ada Forrest snapped pictures of the newlyweds, Sam and Yolanda and I strolled again down toward the parapet that overlooked imperial Rome. He linked his arms with ours and we walked aimlessly, sapped with heat. He stopped and gestured toward a great carved door, closed now, that led into one of the museum rooms.

"There's a bronze tablet in there, a very small one, that says, simply, BRIT. It's the first time in the history of the world, as far as anyone knows, that the word for 'England' or 'English' was written down."

I felt the tears I did not shed for Maria and Colin gather in my eyes and spill over my bottom lashes onto my cheeks. I looked away from Sam and Yolanda.

He saw, though.

"I know," he said. "It just takes the top of your head off for some reason, doesn't it?"

"It doesn't mine," Yolanda Whitney said. "I can't stand the bloody sanctimonious English."

Ada told us that night at dinner, making a little joke of it, that Yolanda's only marriage, failed scarcely a year after the ceremony, had been to an English anchorman of great charm and even greater fecklessness. He had abruptly decided to move back to England and live with his mum in her rambling old house in Padstow and write a book on terns. He had never understood why Yolanda had refused to go with him.

"How many people have asked you if you've left no tern unstoned?" Joe asked Yolanda when Ada told the story. He was obviously pleased with the pun. I thought it was funny too.

"You're the four hundred and twenty-seventh," Yolanda said.

Sam gave the wedding dinner for Colin and Maria at a small trattoria just off the Piazza della Rotonda. We sat at a long table set with pink linen and vases of great salmon daisies and lit with white candles in flickering hurricanes, under a canopy directly on one of the narrow streets that lead into the piazza, separated from the clamoring stream of foot traffic only by a line of small trees in pots. It was the first time, really, that Joe and I had been out in the midst of Rome, swallowed up in its jostling, hooting, honking throngs. It had been crowded up on the Campidoglio, but we had been above the maw of the city there, and later, in the hectic blur of the Piazza Venezia, Sam had miraculously hailed a taxi before there was time for the teeming clot of people and motor scooters and automobiles to close in around me. Now, though, I was awash in Rome, drowning in it. I sat with my back to the narrow street, but every prickling inch of my neck and shoulders and back was aware that, perhaps three feet behind me, a torrent of alien humanity poured by. It was all I could do to keep from constantly swiveling my head from side to side to see what was coming, to keep from bolting out of my chair and dashing inside the dark low-ceilinged confines of the restaurant as a wild animal might into a cave.

There were bottles of red and white wine already on the table, and I gulped mine down and refilled the glass before any-one else had even tasted theirs. Desolately, I wondered, feeling the alcohol's comforting hot track down into my stomach, if I was going to have to get drunk again in order to be able to sit at this table and celebrate the union of Maria and Colin. On my left, Joe turned to look at me, smiling a little, but I read the warning clearly in his eyes: Don't do that again, Cat, for God's sake; enough is enough. He turned back to Ada Forrest. Over the gag-ging fear, hurt and embarrassment flamed. I knew everyone else had read his eyes too.

Across from me, between Maria and Yolanda, Sam studied me for a moment and then said, "Change places with me, Cat. You can't see the Pantheon from where you are, and that's the major reason anybody comes to Rome—or should be."

He got up, shouting to his friend, the waiter Fredo, to bring more wine and some bread. I got out of my seat and moved around the table on legs that threatened to collapse under me. I had put on a white linen shirtwaist in deference to the sacramental nature of the occasion, forgetting that Maria and Colin were being married in a civil ceremony, and it was wet now with the sharp sweat of fear and the thick night, and drying on my body in corrugations. The hair at my nape and forehead was soaked too. I steadied myself against the table and dropped into Sam's chair and murmured, "Thank you." Somehow I could not look into his copper hawk's face.

He laid his hand on the top of my head for a moment and then went around and sat in my abandoned chair. With the wall at my back, solid stone nearly a foot's thickness and perhaps centuries old, the fear shrank back into its kennel and I took a long shuddering breath and let it out and looked around me.

"Now," I whispered. "Now."

And as if in obedience, Rome turned slowly and ponderously, as upon some ancient fulcrum, and settled into place, and the enchantment began.

I will never forget the few hours we sat there in that *caffè* off the Piazza della Rotonda. As bad as the fear had been a few minutes before, and despite everything that came after, that meal has still about it the patina of a perfect thing. The bulk of the Pantheon against the clear green evening sky darkened as full night fell, and the floodlights came on and cast it up for us like the very seat of all the gods that it was. From where I sat I could see only the portico, with its powerful, perfectly proportioned columns and the frieze with the shallow triangle above it; seen above the line of potted trees, it seemed to grow out of a small forest. It was, indeed, very beautiful, profoundly compelling. Was it because it was simply so very old, had stood so long, had seen so much? No, there was more. . . . Real power poured out of it into the night, into the old square. The crowd there, families and drug dealers and prostitutes and pimps and the very young and the very old and the strong and the dying and lovers and pickpockets and tourists from Kansas and Khatmandu and Romans from all neighborhoods, milled and shouted and quarreled and ate and drank and laughed, and each one was touched by the power of Hadrian's great temple to all the gods of his world.

I took another deep breath and closed my eyes. When I opened them Sam was looking at me across the table.

"You OK?"

I smiled and made a circle with my thumb and forefinger: OK. He grinned. Behind me, Fredo, with a platter of antipasti, snorted and then began to laugh aloud, and the waiters following him with plates of pasta and more wine did too. Soon we were all laughing. I did not know what was so funny, but it seemed a lovely thing to do, to sit on a side street in Rome under the benison of the glorious living Pantheon and laugh with joy.

We ate enormously and drank a great deal of wine. Sam and Joe made toasts, and we drank some more. And ate some more. It was the first time I had ever had the wonderful, huge, meaty *porcini* mushrooms, both delicate and as substantial as steaks, simply brushed with oil and roasted. I could have eaten them forever. All the waiters and the owner knew Sam, and everyone came to clap him on the back and to congratulate Maria and Colin, and the owner sent complimentary house grappa when, finally, the meal was over. We lingered on, sipping its sweet, thick fire. I did not want to leave the candlelit table and plunge back into the river of people outside the *caffè*; now, far after midnight, it had swollen to an ocean. No one else seemed to want to leave either.

I looked around the table. In the flickering light of the guttering candles, we all looked . . . Roman. Leaning forward across the table, his fierce face uplit by candlelight, Sam might have been a Barberini. Maria, entwined with Colin and kissing him, dewed with sweat and grappa, could be a Roman girl of any time, celebrating her green young body on a summer night. Ada, still and somehow feline and secret in her beautiful silk, and

Yolanda Whitney, once again dissolved with wine, might have been creatures of Fellini.

"We knew her when she was just a little Irish girl from South Boston on a scholarship tour of Rome," Sam had said. "When she was Annie Laurie O'Reilly." And below the television persona I could see, now, the round little Irish face and snub, sweet nose. But over that . . . oh, yes, definitely Fellini. Exalted by the night and the wine, I thought, Isn't that fitting? How good of Rome, to take us all in and make us hers. . . ."

Only Joe and Colin did not look Roman. Even in the shadow of the Pantheon, even in the light of the candles and kissed with the shine of olive oil, they looked immutably American. Colin looked like an overdressed young expense account traveler who suddenly found himself entwined with a ripe Latin girl, and Joe looked, simply, bored.

How could he? I thought, and remembered it was the face Joe wore when he felt profoundly uncomfortable and out of place, and I had seldom seen it because I could count the times he had felt that way in my presence on the fingers of one hand.

"Should we be getting back?" I said. "We're going to have to get a taxi, and it's awfully late."

That broke the spine of the evening. Colin and Maria, who were staying in a small hotel nearby, hugged everyone and drifted away, their bodies so closely fitted together they seemed glued, all of a piece. They called their goodbyes back to us and melted into the body of the crowd that showed no sign of abating. Sam and Ada went into the kitchen to thank the owner, and Joe and I stood awkwardly on the pavement with Yolanda Whitney, waiting for them. Yolanda had said she would walk to the Hassler, where she was staying, but it was clear to me that she was in no shape to walk anywhere. She lurched and giggled and held on to Joe, and when Sam and Ada came back, Sam and Joe flanked her and took both arms, and we made our way over to the Via del Corso. With the same legerdemain he had displayed earlier in the Piazza Venezia, Sam held up his hand and a taxi cut out of the clamorous pack and veered over to the curb, and he put Joe and me and Yolanda into it.

"Drop her off and take it back to the Hilton," he said. "If we can't get another one we'll just walk. Maybe we'll stop in a neighborhood bar and finish getting drunk."

He leered grandly, and Ada grimaced, but she took his arm and squeezed it. I thought, curiously, that in the hours I had been with them I had never before seen her touch him, or him her.

I looked back, as we shot out into the traffic, and saw that they stood close together, his head bent far down to hers, as she said something into his ear.

"Sweet nothings," Yolanda said in a strange, strangled voice, and I saw she was looking back at them too.

When we got to the Hassler she was so boneless and disoriented that Joe had to walk her to her room. I waited in the back of the cab for what seemed an interminable length of time, smiling stiffly every time the driver caught my eye in his mirror, irrationally afraid he would grow tired of waiting and simply dump me on the pavement and roar away. Well, maybe we could get a room at the Hassler for the night. But he would probably stay, after all. The meter was running; the fare would be astronomical.

It was almost half an hour later that Joe finally came out of the front door, and I was so relieved to see him that it was not until he got into the cab and slammed the door that I noticed he was literally smeared with lipstick, as if he had been drinking blood, and his fair hair hung in his eyes. There was lipstick on the collar of his silk shirt, too.

"Good Lord, Joe," I said, and stopped.

"Don't ask," he said, making a face of deep disgust. "I'll tell you later, but just don't ask right now. I thought that woman was going to rape me in the hall outside her room. Christ, how absolutely and appallingly *sloppy*."

He was silent, except for curt directions to the driver, who did not seem ever to have heard of Monte Mario or the Cavalieri

Hilton Hotel, but in the dark I could sense that some interior motor in him had started up.

For the first time in my entire life I said to Joe, when he turned to me in bed that night, "Sweetie, I have got the mother of all headaches."

And I did.

CHAPTER SEVEN

WE MET SAM THE NEXT MORNING IN THE PIAZZA NAVONA, to start the Sam Forrest Special and Particular Walking Tour of Rome. It was not yet eight, and the great oval square was pearled with soft light. The *caffès* and market stalls were just opening, and only a few people were about: children playing some sort of game with a ball and a stick around the looming Bernini fountain in the center, old men drinking cappuccino at outdoor tables, a handful of people in business clothes coming out of the old houses around the piazza, two or three handsomely dressed women walking dogs. It was quiet except for the liquid purl of the fountain. No automobile or bus traffic marred the cobbled piazza, though the low roar of Rome's morning rush hour was escalating all around us.

Sam was waiting for us at Tre Scalini, where he had said he would be. He was drinking coffee and reading a newspaper, and even in repose, even dwarfed by the heroic scope of the huge

baroque space, he drew the eye. Partly it was because of his costume: he wore blue jeans faded nearly white and cut off at the
knees, strings hanging in fringes around his massive, red-furred
calves, and a denim work shirt faded nearly as pale, open to the
waist and knotted there. His chest looked like the pelt of a great
red bear. A battered straw hat of the sort I associate with southern plantation owners rode low on his forehead, seeming to sit
atop the iron-red hedges of his eyebrows. His ponytail hung
down his back, and a cigarette stuck out of his mouth at the
angle of Winston Churchill's cigar. His bare ankles rose out of
gigantic, dirty running shoes. I burst out laughing with pleasure
at the sight of him. He looked utterly ridiculous and somehow
just right.

"Now don't you feel better about your clothes?" I said to
Joe. He was dressed in the chinos he had worn to Rome, and the
striped sleeveless tank top he had worn around the pool yesterday. His oxford-cloth shirt had not come back from the hotel
laundry as had been promised, and the only other one he had
was wadded up on the floor of our bathroom, scarlet with the
stigmata of Yolanda Whitney's lipstick. He wore dark socks and
polished loafers because he had no other shoes, and was as
unhappy about the whole thing as I have ever seen him. I have
never thought Joe a vain man, but he has always dressed in a
way that seemed as indigenous to Trinity and the Mountain as
the laurel and dogwood in its spring woods, and incongruity is
unthinkable to him. This morning he looked incongruous. Handsome, with his long tanned arms and chest already gleaming
with a light patina of sweat, but incongruous.

He grunted. He had not particularly wanted to come with
me this morning, saying he'd just as soon spend the time seeing
Baedeker's Rome and not Sam Forrest's, but he had come, nevertheless, when I begged him.

"Please," I had said. "I just can't do this without you; it's
too much; there are too many people. And it's too late to back

out, and besides, how many people in the world can say Sam Forrest showed them Rome?"

So he came along. I knew no matter how annoyed he was at me—and I could tell that my headache last night had disturbed and unsettled him—he would not leave me to brave the throngs in the streets of Rome without him. I knew also that the prospect of tossing off the tidbit about Sam in the Faculty Club was not without power.

I squeezed his arm now and said into his ear, "You have better legs," and he smiled reluctantly, and we crossed the piazza toward Sam's table.

He grinned his huge white grin, and kissed me on both cheeks, and gave Joe a hug around his shoulders.

"Coffee first, before anything," he said, and gestured for the waiter. The waiter smiled and called something, ending with Sam's name.

"Do you know every waiter in Rome?" I said.

"Most of them," he said. "I made a concentrated effort when I first got here. People think power is being invited to use the Vatican Library, but the ultimate power is knowing the most waiters. Well, did you get Yolanda home without an international incident?"

"No problem," Joe said, just as I said, "Well, it was more of a domestic incident."

We looked at each other. Sam laughed.

"Put the make on you, did she, Joe? I should have warned you. Past a certain blood alcohol level Yolie gets snuggly. It's not necessarily a problem depending on the snuglee, but I wouldn't have let you in for it if I'd been thinking. Your first day in Rome is tough enough."

"She was fine," Joe said crisply, and I simply stared at him. "But I'd hardly call it hardship duty if she had put the make on me, as you put it."

Sam shrugged, still smiling.

"Definitely not that," he said. "OK, this is going to be a foot tour, and I'm going to walk your asses off. We need to make time. It's going to be hotter than hell by noon. Joe, the top of you is fine, but we might think about stopping and getting you some walking shoes somewhere. Cat, you're just right. That dress will keep the sun off you and reflect heat, and you've got on crepe soles. Good. Y'all about ready?"

We gulped our coffee.

"Am I OK for churches and stuff?" Joe said, studying his bare arms and chest. "This is literally all I had. Cat didn't wash the shirt I had on last night."

"Ain't you got no han's, boy?" Sam grinned at him over his shoulder.

"What?"

"When I was growing up in Demopolis, Alabama, we had a black woman who worked for us, and every time I acted like a little white prince and whined for her to do something for me, she said, 'Ain't you got no han's, boy?' Even now I wash my own underwear if I'm out. Ada thinks I'm a feminist, but it's the early influence of that old martinet in Demopolis."

Joe flushed.

"I'm not blaming Cat," he said. "Of course she doesn't have to wash my shirts. We both just forgot last night."

"Maybe your bag will come today," I said, feeling sorry for him even as I stifled the impulse to grin broadly. I did, in fact, wash Joe's clothes on occasion. I was sure he would wash mine, if I were the one who was out of the house all day. It had always seemed more a matter of logistics than policy.

"I still don't know why you wanted me to wear this," I said to Sam, looking down in distaste. When he had called early that morning, he had asked me to wear the white linen I had had on last night. It was even more wrinkled for the night it had spent on the floor beside the bed, where I had dropped it when I shucked out of it.

"Humor me," he said. "I'll show you before the tour's over."

"It *is* just a trifle worse for wear," Joe said, and I knew he was still smarting over the matter of the unlaundered shirt.

"Well, who cares?" I said, trotting off behind Sam. "I'm sure not apt to run into anybody we know."

He took us first into the interior of the Pantheon. I felt a lump rising in my throat before my eyes even accustomed themselves to the cool dimness. Something about the sweet amplitude of space that swept up to the top of the great dome dropped a deep, abiding sense of calm, of refuge, down on me. I thought I would never be afraid here. The marble of its interior was radiant and lovely.

"It's the color a gypsy's flesh ought to be," I said.

"Yes, it is, isn't it?" Sam said.

He pointed to the aperture in the top of the dome.

"It was to let the smoke from the burnt offerings out, but there's a legend that the devil made it trying to escape when it was consecrated as a Christian church. I've been in here when it was raining; it's a wonderful thing to see, then. Just this column of radiant rain, coming straight down. It looks as if you could climb it."

"The proportions are stunning, aren't they?" Joe said.

"Pure classical geometry," Sam said. "The diameter of the dome is exactly equal to the height of the walls. Who said mathematics wasn't art?"

"God and geometry again." I smiled.

"Like I said. All over Rome."

From there we dogtrotted over to the austere little church that served Rome's French colony. The three great Caravaggios in the Chapel of Saint Matthew bloomed into their rich, deep light when Sam fed a coin into the machine, and Joe and I simply stood mute and stared. I had never seen light like that before. The darkness of light, I thought, the power of dark light. . . . My eyes stung once more.

Sam saw the tears on my face.

"Are you going to cry all over Rome?"

"Looks like it," I said. "Are you going to be embarrassed if I do?"

"No. I'm intrigued. None of the women I know have cried in twenty years."

"I'm embarrassed," Joe said. "Pretty soon you're going to be falling down in a swoon. The Stendhal effect."

But he put his arm around my shoulder.

We walked for what seemed a very long way, through twisted, narrow streets, dodging across wide, traffic-choked thoroughfares. The sun beat down relentlessly. Sam trotted easily over the killing cobblestones. My feet were sore and burning, even in thick crepe soles, and behind me Joe was beginning to limp. I turned back and saw that he was pale and literally drenched in sweat. Joe played tennis four or five times a week, and was perhaps fifty pounds lighter than Sam Forrest, but he was not used to the heat and the cobbles and the constant, hammering noise of Rome.

"We need to slow down," I called to Sam. "You're going to lose two ugly Americans if we don't."

He was contrite. He led us around a corner and onto the Via Condotti.

"We'll make a pit stop at the Café Greco," he said. "I was planning to do it in a little while, anyway. I forget what these streets can do to you if you aren't used to them. You'll like this one, Joe; it's where the foreign literati hung out. Byron and Goethe and that crowd. Buffalo Bill too, if I'm not mistaken. Oldest coffeehouse in Rome. I can recommend the *caffè granita*."

Joe and I both headed for the restrooms. In the dim light of the old mirror I peered at myself. My face looked greenish and wavery, and my hair stood around my head in damp ringlets. The white linen was so wrinkled by this time that it clung to me like a damp, discarded towel. I seemed for a moment a woman drowned. I did what I could with my hair and put on new lipstick and went back to our tiny marble table. Smartly dressed women carrying bags from Gucci and Armani watched me, or I thought they did. Joe was already at the table with Sam, and they were talking intently. Or rather, Joe was talking and Sam was listening. He listened as he did everything else, with his whole person. When Sam Forrest focused on you, you were impaled on his interest, bled yourself for him. I saw gratification in every line of Joe's body. I thought that, on the main, few people except me had paid much attention to Joe on this trip.

"What are you two talking about?" I said, slipping back into my seat and taking a long sip of the *caffè granita*, rich and cold and life-giving.

"Faulkner," Sam said. "I didn't know shit about him until Joe started telling me. You know artists don't read. Now I'm going to go back and read everything he ever wrote. It's probably going to take me the rest of my life. Jesus, nobody ever told me about him before. That's like me. I grew up like that, in places like that, with those people."

"Most of us did, one way or another, even if we're not southern," Joe said. "That's the point. In a way Faulkner's like a painter. Everything's in layers. Everything's impressionistic. Everything comes right out of the felt part of life. Or anyway"— and he looked a little embarrassed—"I've always thought painting must be like that. The most felt of all the arts. The most . . . directly connected to the primal things."

Sam looked at him with interest.

"It is," he said. "Good man. Not that there's not a kind of . . . grid of intellect and form laid over it, but underneath it's all felt. Or what's been seen is translated into felt. Let's get out of here before I discover there's a formal theory behind my work— such as there is of it lately—and get flown with myself."

Joe laughed and they walked out together ahead of me, two men who suddenly liked each other, if only for a small space of time. Two men who met on a common field of expertise. Trudging back out into the whitening heat of midmorning, I felt oddly abandoned. Sam was, by God, *my* discovery.

"Y'all are bonded as hell," I called ahead to them. "You

going to squat in the middle of the street and beat drums?"

Sam laughed and reached an arm back to me, and Joe did too, and we walked together, the three of us, up to a plain brown church on a promontory over the Via Veneto where, Sam said, we were going to see death, Roman-style.

It was a nondescript building, and I could not tell if it was very old. Above the street that I associated with Fellini and fashion and attractive decadence, it was an island of quiet, almost cool in the throbbing white sun. Lord, how much hotter could it get? I pulled my wet linen away from me and fanned myself with my hands. Joe was looking pinched and white again, and there were pink splotches on the tops of his shoulders and along his collarbones. Sam, under the disreputable hat, was no more and no less red than he ever was.

A monk in a plain brown habit sat at a small ticket station in the vestibule and took contributions. There was no fee, but Sam handed him a fistful of paper. I still could not decipher the notes; it seemed to me the smaller the denomination, the larger the note. I found some American dollars and gave them to the monk, who smiled and handed me a pamphlet and nodded but did not speak.

"Thank you, father," I said, and blushed. I knew how, I realized, to address priests and bishops and even archbishops of the Anglican persuasion, but I did not know what you called a Catholic monk. Surely not "brother."

"Brother, can you spare a dime?" I said under my breath, and Sam, who had heard me, threw his ridiculous head back and laughed.

"Not here," he said. "The dimes come from the likes of you, Miss Cat. He's taken a vow of poverty, though like most of the clergy in Rome, he does pretty well despite it. They're Capuchins. Cappuccino is named after the brown of their robes. He could speak to you if he had to, but most of them have taken a vow of silence. It's probably why their order has lasted so long.

Come on. You may hate this, but I don't think so. Children and other savages seem to like it."

"Which am I?"

"Take your pick."

We went inside and passed down into a long dim corridor and down a flight of stairs into the crypt. On one side was a simple, rough plaster wall, striated with the beauty that all old plaster in Rome glows with. On the other side were bones. Cubicle after cubicle, cell after cell, of bones. Human bones. Bones that formed intricate friezes and mosaics, bones that formed the entire walls of cells and small rooms, bones that made chandeliers and furniture and decorative panels. There were patterns to them; Sam said that most of the chandeliers were formed of sacrums and vertebrae, and the pillars of some of the chambers were made of long bones: thighs, arms. A few niches held skeletons, small or large; obviously whole corpses had been interred here.

"If you were particularly rich, you could have yourself or your children's skeletons put here for all eternity," Sam said. "There are a couple of children from the great old families, the devout ones. I bring everybody here. Kids inevitably adore it. But I've known more than one adult to just hit the floor. The monks are used to it. They have a modern first aid station across the piazza there. Look at the plaque."

It was small and easily missed. I did not know what the Italian meant.

"'As we are now, so shall ye be,'" Sam translated.

I stood in that place of bones and laughed. It was too much, it was too awful. Maybe it was wonderful. I could not tell. Part of me was appalled, but a greater part was oddly comforted. This place did not ignore death but put it right in your face. From there you could shudder and go out to lunch.

I turned to Joe and then turned away. I could see that he was profoundly disturbed.

"You going to be OK?" Sam said.

"Yes," I said. "The bones are really very lovely, aren't they? That rich, shining brown. Pear-brown Rome. Boy, it gets into everything, doesn't it?"

Back out in the sunlight again, I unfolded the pamphlet the monk had given me and looked at it. It was a poem, execrably written, from the point of view of an aborted baby to its mother. Death and forgiveness seemed to be the main thrusts of it. I crumpled it up in repugnance.

"It's antiabortion propaganda," I said. "Ugh. How can they, in that place? It's a little Golgotha. They're death engineers themselves, but they still try to lay that trip on women."

"God and physics," Sam said mildly, and we went on out into the heat of noon.

We trudged, sweating, through streets that seemed to me to be devoted largely to couture shopping. I could not imagine who would want to brave this fearsome, living heat to buy clothing, but a great many chic women whose nationalities I could not fathom seemed to be doing so, most with huge Vuitton bags, clicking in and out of small, austere shops with the hip-swaying gait that predominated here, exaggerated by heels so high I could not even imagine walking in them. My own feet, cradled as they were in crepe rubber, were still sore and burning. I seemed to feel the impress of every cobblestone we had trod on their bottoms. Sam, well ahead of us in his steady dogtrot, was running sweat on every bare surface, but his colossal legs ground along as if powered by pistons, and the straw hat still rode at a jaunty angle. At my side I could hear Joe breathing heavily, and I looked at him worriedly. He was not speaking much now—had not, since we left the grisly hospitality of the Capuchins—but I did not know if the malaise was one of flesh or spirit. His silence bothered me. Usually, if Joe was slightly unsettled about something, he made a joke of it. If it was more than a slight discomfort, he simply asked that it be stopped.

We crossed a dingy modern street whose traffic, for sheer

artistry of mayhem, matched that of the Piazza Venezia, and all at once I heard water. Not the plinking splash of the many little fountains we had passed but a deep cool cascade, proper water, running wild. Nothing had ever sounded quite so wonderful to me at that moment. We came into a small, nondescript little piazza and I saw it precisely as I had in innumerable magazine pages, in many technicolor movies: the Fontana di Trevi, the Trevi Fountain, its streamlets bounding joyously over its artfully artless boulders and spuming great Neptune with its exuberance. An extraordinary, playful, baroque, excessive fancy in the middle of one of the most cramped, even banal, little piazzas I had ever seen. I wanted more than anything in my life, just then, to simply step into it and lie down among the glittering coins.

"Oh, Joe, do you remember the song 'Three Coins in the Fountain'? It was popular when I was a little kid. I thought it was the most romantic song in the world. Wasn't it in a movie?"

"The only movie I remember about it was Fellini," Sam said, fishing in his pockets. "When Mastroianni and Ekberg are about to have at it in the fountain and the water goes off and his pecker goes down, not to put too fine a point on it. At least, I've always been sure that's what the symbolism insinuated. Here, turn around, both of you, and throw a coin in over your shoulder. Make sure you come back to Rome."

"Maybe I'll pass," Joe muttered under his breath, as we shouldered our way through the crowds from the tour buses. I smiled at him.

"Just say to yourself, 'Make it October,'" I said, and he smiled back, a stretched ghost of his old full smile, and we tossed our coins.

We made our way along the Corso and back up the Via Condotti to the Spanish Steps, so clogged with people photographing other people and vendors of every imaginable object and teenagers jostling and crowing and lunging that we could hardly see the monumental staircase itself. Sam pointed out the house where Keats lived and died and asked if we'd like to go in.

"Another time," I said, frankly worried about Joe now. He was as pale as a wraith and nearly hobbling. Sam seemed to notice for the first time.

"Christ, I've nearly killed you," he said. "If you don't come down with Roman Foot on top of heat prostration it'll be a miracle. Can you make it to the top? The Hassler has a good bar; we'll get a drink and then we can get you some decent walking shoes and take a cab back to the studio. We'll save the Ghetto and old Aldo Mori for another trip. You should have spoken up. Don't let assholes run you into the ground before you have your second wind."

"I'm fine," Joe said thinly. I wanted to shake him; he was obviously very far from fine. "I think I will get a drink, though, and see if there are any decent men's shops around here. I can't spend the rest of my time in Italy in this getup; I look like a male stripper. I want you all to go on, though. I know there was more you wanted Cat to see, and I know she wants to see it. I'll meet you back at your studio for lunch in . . . what? An hour and a half?"

"No, I'll go shopping with you," I began. "You don't look so good; I'm afraid—"

"Cat, I really want to be by myself for a little while," he said, in a low, fast voice, and I stopped. I could think of nothing to say. Joe had never before told me he did not want my company. My eyes stung.

"But you don't know where the studio is," I said, hating myself for going on.

"I'll bet, if I ask him nicely, Sam will tell me, and I'll tell a taxi driver, and he'll take me there," Joe said, with such soft sarcasm that I turned away and studied the bulk of Trinità dei Monti at the top of the hill, almost black against the furious blue-white of the sky.

"Sounds like a good plan," Sam said, taking my arm. "Come on, Cat. Cut the guy some slack. He can get a cab in a second at the Hassler. There's only one other thing I really wanted you to see, and then we'll all go have lunch. Ada's bringing it from home, and Colin and Maria are coming. Well, as a matter of fact, Joe, so is Yolanda; I forgot. Why don't you buzz her room and see if she's ready when you've finished shopping, and you can ride down together? She knows where it is. That is, if you can stand her, after last night."

"Be glad to," Joe said. "See you guys later."

And he turned away from us and climbed the Spanish Steps without looking back, striding purposefully, as if not to show that his feet were in agony and his legs rubbery with heat. I looked after him.

"He's okay," Sam said, tugging gently on my arm. "Don't hover. He's a big boy. He'll do better by himself for a while: get his bearings and set his own pace. Maybe have an adventure all by himself, one somebody else didn't plan. Let him find his own Rome."

I turned away from the steps and followed Sam back into the piazza. I felt desolate, diminished. How had I offended Joe? It had happened so seldom, this shortness of his, that I literally had no idea. And Yolanda Whitney; I was not sure I liked the idea of that at all.

"I didn't know Colin and Maria and Yolanda were joining us," I said neutrally, climbing into the cab he hailed.

"Yolie called early this morning and asked if we were going to see you; said she wanted me to relay her apologies for being a harlot last night. I told her to come to lunch and tell you herself. Ada said since it was shaping up into a party she'd call Colin and Maria, and we could eat up the rest of the buffet from the other night. Don't worry about Yolanda, Cat. You have no cause to."

"I wasn't," I said, my face hot.

"Yeah, you were."

He gave the driver an address on Via XX Settembre.

"Where are we going?" I asked, profoundly grateful to be off my feet and in a dim, soft interior, even hurtling suicidally through Rome.

"Church," Sam said. "Santa Maria della Vittoria. It's as baroque as a baboon's butt, and what I'm going to show you is a Bernini, not my favorite sculptor. His feet's too big, as the old song says, among other things. But this one is something else. I have a special reason to show it to you. You'll see."

Inside the church, the contrast between the burning day and the rich gray, brown, and mauve marble served to blind me for a moment. I let Sam guide me, sensing people all about me but somehow not feeling the neck-prickling, preliminary seeping of the fear. My eyes gradually accustomed themselves, and when they did we were standing before a little chapel at the back of the church. A small dome just above it let a clear golden light down through an opening; motes danced in it, and I was reminded, by its iridescent solidarity, of the column of light in the Pantheon and of my fancy that I could climb it. The light fell full on a sculpture, and I caught my breath when I looked at it. Then I shut my eyes involuntarily.

"A not uncommon impulse," Sam said, watching me. "The Ecstasy of Saint Teresa. Bernini's ideas of sacred ecstasy and rapture got him into not a little hot water. The head is one of the finest things ever to come from a chisel, I think, and who knows, it may be the most perfect expression of Divine Love ever wrought by man. Eleanor Clark said the smile of the angel who's getting ready to run her through with his arrow is one of the best in all the world's sculpture. Of course, one President de Brosses of France said, that 'If this is Divine Love, I know all about it.'"

I opened my eyes and stared at the saint in her intricately wrought, disheveled robes. There was no doubting the passion; there was so much passion in her blind, naked face, so much transport and abandon, such sheer physical hunger and completion, both at once, that I felt a wave of heat spread slowly through me from the pit of my stomach. The statue was powerfully beautiful and powerfully erotic.

"My God," I whispered. "It's the absolute essence of—"

"Isn't it?" Sam said. "Makes you wonder what the precise

difference between sacred and profane love is. A great conundrum, the one at the very heart of Christianity. I maintain there never has been any difference; that all ecstasy is sensual, and all sensuality ecstatic. It's only our minds that divide it, with not a little help from Mother Church. It's one reason I rank Catholicism right along with Nazism as a source of exquisitely murderous damage."

I did not answer. I continued to stare at the saint, impaled on her passion. There was something, something. . . .

On the other side of Saint Teresa, in the gloom, a little nun knelt. I had not noticed her because she crouched so low, and her robes were almost the precise dark of the chiaroscuro of shadow in the chapel. Now I stared at her. I could tell at once she was not of a Roman order but from one of the rural provinces, perhaps in the Mezzogiorno. I don't quite know how I knew, but I did. It was there in the roughness of the fabric of her habit, the plain shiny-scrubbed face, the raw red hands that were clasped before her, their knuckles swollen with hard work. I thought she was probably quite young, for there were no lines in her face, and her lips, parted, were still soft and formless, almost a child's lips. Her eyes were closed, and tears made silver snails' tracks down her cheeks, and on her face was a flame of such pure yearning and devotion that I averted my head.

I want that, I thought, simply and wholly. I want to feel that.

Sam took my elbow and walked me around the other side of the statue, a little space away from the kneeling nun.

"I damn the church that promises that little girl what she thinks she's being promised," he said. His tone was soft, but he almost spat the words.

"I was just thinking I wanted it for myself," I said. "That certainty. That . . . payoff, which shakes your whole soul. How do you know she isn't going to get it? How do you know she doesn't already have it?"

He made a small sound of contempt.

"I'll take the physics, the geometry," he said. "I think you had it wrong, Cat. I think physics was invented to make God bearable."

We stood in silence for a while, looking at Saint Teresa. Then he said, "What else do you notice about it?"

"I don't know what you want me to see," I said uncertainly. "Something about the technique itself? Something about the marble?"

"Look at the face. Look at the way the light falls on the planes of the cheeks and the forehead; look at the nose; look at the chin. Look at the wrinkles in the robe. Look at the mouth. . . ."

I saw then. In a way more inherent than actual, perhaps, but undeniably: it was my face. My face, over the wrinkled white linen I wore now. My face, my face in ecstasy. . . .

My face as only one person on earth had ever seen it. How had Sam Forrest known?

"I want to go now," I said numbly.

"Don't feel strange about it, Cat," Sam said. "I told you your face was all over Rome. You have that sort of narrow Renaissance look to you; this is just one of several sculptures I could show you right now, this afternoon, that look like you. You'll see a lot more of them in Florence. . . ."

"But you picked this one to show me. Why did you do that, Sam?"

After quite a long time, he said, "I don't know. I really don't. But I do know I meant no innuendo. I hope you'll believe that."

And somehow I did.

We were almost to the Campo Fiori, with the light of midafternoon beginning to slant more gently outside the windows of the taxi, before I remembered that I had not once, in all that long morning on the streets of Rome, been afraid.

* * *

Sam's studio was the top floor of a narrow, flaking russet house in the Via del Pellegrino, just off the Campo Fiori. The produce and market stalls were empty in the Campo as the taxi coasted through it, and the litter and garbage were astonishing; Sam said it was a pity we didn't catch it before one-thirty or so, when it was full of color and life. His own winding street seemed to sleep, too. We made our way up a steep, twisting staircase whose iron railing cascaded with blooming creeper and stopped on a small landing crowded with terra-cotta pots full of flowers. An enormous ginger cat slept in the shade of the largest one. It lifted its scarred thug's head at our footfall, stretched hugely, and reassembled itself back into sleep.

"Is that your cat?" I said. "He looks just like you."

"I guess he is," Sam said. "I never formally acquired him, but so far I haven't evicted him, either. He likes the three squares and the soft bed I provide him, but he hates my work."

"Does he have a name?"

"Brutta," he said. "'Ugly.' For some reason the little old lady downstairs adores him and feeds him lavishly when I'm not here. She calls him *'bel pezzo d'uomo.'* Roughly translated, I think it means hunk. There's no accounting for tastes."

The door opened and Ada Forrest stood there, silvery and translucent, in wide black gauze palazzo pants and a loose gauze top. Her hair was tied off her neck with a black scarf, and the only color about her was the slash of crimson on her mobile mouth and a red-striped-ticking cook's apron. She kissed me on both cheeks, a light swift peck, and touched Sam on his bare chest.

"Perfect timing," she said. "Joe and Colin just got through lugging the last hamper up the stairs. Did you have a good morning? I hope you did; you nearly killed Joe."

I looked past her into the studio, searching for my husband. It was an enormous room, painted white and flooded with light from a wall of casement windows overlooking an inner court-

yard and twin skylights. The floor was so splotched and splat-
tered with paint that it seemed a purposeful stipple. Shelves on
the three other walls held racks of canvases and stacked sup-
plies, and an alcove half sheltered by a magnificent Chinese
screen contained a deep metal sink and a small stove and, I
thought, perhaps a toilet. A small, rusted compact refrigerator
sat on the floor under the sink, and a butcher-block table criss-
crossed with many years of knife hatchings held an array of covered dishes and crockery. There were no paintings on the walls,
and none in evidence anywhere. An easel stood under one of the
windows, but it held nothing. On the deep window ledge a
portable phonograph poured out Palestrina, and a big raffia tray
held glasses and several bottles of wine. Down at the far end of
the studio was a big potbellied iron stove with rump-sprung
chairs and a studio couch ranged around it, and there Joe sat, his
long legs extended out before him, feet propped on a big leather
hassock, drinking wine. He was saying something to Yolanda
Whitney, who sat across from him drinking what looked like
mineral water with a slice of lime, and she was laughing. Colin
and Maria lay tangled on the couch, sipping wine and picking at
each other with languid fingers. Everyone and everything in the
room looked airy, light, lazy, enormously inviting.

"So this is what goes on behind all those shuttered windows from noon to four," I said. "Joe looks as though he's made
a miraculous recovery."

"We've been rubbing his fevered brow"—Maria giggled—
"and dropping grapes in his mouth." She glowed in a red sundress. I had never seen her wear red at home on the Mountain.

"Remarkable restorative powers, grapes," Joe said, smiling
at me over his shoulder. He wore a soft new sage-green shirt
with the little Lauren polo insignia on it and brilliant white running shoes with the Nike swoosh. His golden flush was back,
and his hair had damp comb tracks in it, and he looked carved of
golden ice, cool and remote. Somehow, for the first time, he
seemed to fit into Rome, or at least in this austere Roman room

of light and space. Across from him, Yolanda wore starched blue-and-white striped chambray and sneakers and had pulled her hair into a ponytail and tied it with blue grosgrain. Her face seemed as clean-scrubbed as the little nun's in the church we had just left, except for a touch of pink lipstick, and there were amber horn-rimmed glasses on her short, snub nose. She looked about eighteen, and as crisply clean as Joe, and just as unmistakably American. Or rather, I thought a trifle uncharitably, Irish. I could see Ada Forrest had been right when she said Yolanda was a pretty thing when she first came to Rome. That's what she looked now: an only slightly worn pretty thing.

She got up and came to me and said, in a low, chastened voice, "I want to apologize to you again. I can't drink, and I know it, and I'm not going to, anymore, and that's that. If you'll forgive that ghastly business last night, I promise I'll leave your nice husband alone. I'd like to have you both for friends."

What could one say to that? I said what anyone would—"Please don't think any more about it; friends we shall be"—thinking that perhaps without the liquor she'd make an attractive acquaintance after all, if not a friend. What did I have to lose? We were leaving Rome that night. It was as unlikely that the celebrated Yolanda Whitney would seek us out back in the States as it was that Sam Forrest would, when our time together was over. It seemed likely, rather, that she, like Sam, had a charismatic force of personality that made friends of everyone who came within her orbit. It was, I thought, part of the definition of celebrity.

"So where did you go when you left me?" Joe said, pouring out wine for me.

I hesitated.

"Santa Maria della Vittoria," Sam said, tossing his hat onto a chair. He slicked his thick bush of wiry red-gray hair off his face with both big hands. In the white light of his lair, he looked more than ever like a ruddy falcon, a red raptor poised against white rock. His eyes were bright blue in the wash of light.

"Ah," Yolanda said, looking obliquely up at him. "Saint Teresa."

"Yep."

Ada looked at Sam and then at me, cocking her white head to one side in interest.

"Yes," she said slowly. "I see. A good choice. Sam has good instincts. Well, people, let's eat this fine lunch I lugged over here through that damned furnace outside. And then I have a little surprise for Colin and Maria."

Despite the heat, we ate enormously. Sweet Roman melons, the sort we simply don't have in America; I still do not know what they are called. Tiny, cold grilled chickens with olive oil and rosemary and lemon juice and cracked pepper. Wonderful blood-red tomatoes on fresh arugula, topped with creamy buffalo mozzarella and deep blue-green basil leaves. Cold tortellini with shaved parmigiana. Crusty, chewy bread and more oil. Much wine. I never had another meal in Italy that was as simply and wholly satisfying.

When we had finished, Ada pulled a clean cloth off a platter and held it out for our inspection. We gasped, and then, as one, began to laugh. Two giant yellow onions and a thick, red, rolled column of prosciutto lay on the white platter, forming as perfect a set of testicles and a penis as I had ever thought to see.

"Signora Silvestri from downstairs brought it up when she heard I was hosting newlyweds here." Ada grinned. "She says it's an old custom from her home village, near Siri, in Calabria. The bride and groom must each have a bite of everything on the platter, and then . . . I forget what then. But you get the idea."

"If you don't you're dead from the neck down," Colin said. "What a set. Do you feel shortchanged, 'Ria?"

"Not so far," she said, reaching for his crotch as he twisted away, laughing. "But then I haven't tasted Signora Silvestri's yet."

Red flooded my face and neck and I turned away, angry with myself and yet unwilling to hear any more such talk from Colin or Maria. What was the matter with me? The platter *was* funny, earthily, sweetly funny. It had been offered in good spirits and good faith. I did not think I was a prude. Maybe, after the orgasmic Saint Teresa, it was just too much. Too much sensuality on the one hand, too much God on the other. I was suddenly very tired.

Ada and Yolanda began gathering up the lunch things, and Joe and Colin made reluctant noises about leaving.

"I think," Sam Forrest said lazily into the room at large, "that I would like to paint Cat, and I'm asking your formal permission to do it, Joe. If you'll let her stay and sit for a little while this afternoon, I promise I'll have her back in time for dinner. If she doesn't mind, of course."

"Oh, Cat, how wonderful, a Sam Forrest portrait of you!" Maria cried.

"Darling, that's a splendid idea," Ada Forrest said. "She's just right, isn't she? I thought so when I first saw her. Do say you will, Cat!"

"Well, of course," Yolanda said. "Cat, you're truly blessed among women. He's only done two or three other portraits— that I know of, of course."

Hers, I remembered, had been one of them.

I looked at Joe. He looked at me and then away.

"I don't see how you can do a portrait in one afternoon," he said, "but it's up to Cat. It would be quite an honor, of course."

I knew he hated the idea.

"I don't think—" I began, but Ada cut me off.

"You really must," she said. "Yolanda's right, he's done only a very, very few, and they're enormously valuable, if I do say so. The others are in museums, but I can send you photos of them when you get back home. Trust me, they're lovely, not like anything else he does. Oh, Cat, do! It won't take long; he'll do a few sketches and take some Polaroids for color and lighting and that will be it. I'll take the rest of us somewhere fun while you sit, shall I, and then we'll all have dinner at that marvelous rooftop restaurant at the Cavalieri, our treat. It has the best view in Rome. And we'll drop you at the station by ten. You'll have time to spare."

I looked at Sam.

"I wish you would," he said quietly. "It would please me no end."

I realized that in the short time I had known him and been in his company, I had completely forgotten that he was one of the foremost artists of his time. This was Sam Forrest who was asking, almost pleading, to paint me.

"Of course I will," I said. "I'd be enormously honored."

When the others had left, chattering about where they would spend the rest of the afternoon—except Joe, who said little but "Be good and look pretty"—Sam settled me in a chair in front of the window wall and sat on a stool with a pad of paper and a fistful of oil pastels and began a series of swift sketches. At first I felt stiff and self-conscious, but he kept up a stream of his drawled nonsense, telling scurrilous stories about the various people he had met in Rome, and soon I was laughing and at ease. He made sketch after sketch and tore them off and tossed them into a pile and took several Polaroids from all angles, none that he offered to let me see. And he talked, and I laughed.

"There's none of your work here, and I didn't see any in your apartment," I said. "Why is that?"

"Most of it's in collections or museums or being shown somewhere. I don't know. It doesn't seem important to me to keep it around. When a painting is done, it's over for me. The point of it is the doing, I guess. And like I said, I haven't done anything for . . . a long time."

He told me another story, this one about the Catholic Church, so vitriolically funny that, even though I laughed, I said, "You really do hate the church, don't you?"

"I really do," he said.

"Why? If I may ask?"

"You may. I'm not sure I can answer, but you may ask. Well . . . let's see. I think it's because it asks so impossibly much of its servants. Always, always the one thing that cannot be parted with, that's what the church wants."

"You mean, like giving up your life for it, dying for it?"

"No. I mean giving up what you literally cannot exist without."

He stopped sketching and looked at me.

"Would you give up your sight for your child, Cat?" he asked.

I opened my mouth to say that of course I would, but then I closed it. I looked away from him.

"I know I'm supposed to say yes, I would give up my sight for hers," I said in a small, thin voice. "And I *have* said that, always. But I've always known, deep down, that I wouldn't. I would give my life for her in a second, but I could not give her my sight. Not that. Not a life without sight. And I've always been so ashamed. I've been terribly ashamed."

I felt tears sting my nose and eyes and threw my head back angrily and closed my eyes against them.

"There," Sam said, scribbling furiously. "Hold that. Just that. OK. Now. Listen, Cat. I cannot even imagine what a life without sight would be for you. The worst, worst thing ever, never being able to see what was coming at you, feeling like you do. Worse than death, of course. And that's what the church would ask of you. Don't cry, sweetie. Ah, shit, I'm sorry."

I scrubbed my eyes fiercely, wondering why it was impossible to lie to him. Perhaps because he understood. He knew, and no one else ever had, no one but Joe. How to lie to a man like that?

"I couldn't give up mine either," he said. "And of course, that's what the church would ask of me. Fortunately, my child doesn't need my sight—"

"What does he need from you? What doesn't he have that you could give him?"

"Me," he said.

"And you can't give him that?"

"No. He hates my guts, worse than his mother does, even, and I'm bored to death with him. I can't give him me, and I suppose that's what he has always needed, even if he thinks he doesn't. The fact is, Miss Cat, none of us are willing, in our deepest hearts, to give up the vital, die-without, gut things for our children. Nothing but our lives. That's the easy part."

"That's hard stuff, Sam," I said, but somehow the words comforted me.

"About the only thing I really try very hard not to do is lie," Sam Forrest said.

On the way back to the Cavalieri Hilton in the cab Sam called for me, I had another bad attack of the fear. I was bumping along in relative quiet, having lucked into another of Rome's rare air-conditioned taxis with a marginally sane driver; I was leaning back against the seat and thinking of the past few hours I had spent in Sam's studio while he sketched furiously. My mind was slack, cooled. And then it flew at me like a rattler uncoiling and struck deep into my throat. I shut my eyes and clenched my fists against it, trying to draw fast, shallow breaths through my nose. I clamped my mouth shut lest I cry out, a thing I have always done when the fear strikes suddenly and monstrously, but I need not have bothered. I could not have spoken; the poison had paralyzed my throat.

I think it was so bad because I had not felt it for a day or so, and I had been in circumstances in which I could surely have expected to: on foot in the great open piazzas of Rome, literally drowning in a surf of people. But I had not been alone then. Joe had been with me. And Sam.

When I felt the taxi start up the winding road that led up Monte Mario, some of the paralyzing terror faded, and by the time we reached the gates of the Hilton I was able to open my eyes and wipe the cold sweat off my face and push the clammy hair off my forehead.

"*Grazie*," I croaked to the driver when he opened my door.

Sam had paid him back in the Campo Fiori. All it remained for me to do was flee to the vast, quiet chill of the lobby, and I did. As I went in through the heavy glass doors, the thought stabbed me: I had, because of my tight-shut eyes, missed the incredible panorama of Rome from the mountain. I would not see it again. We would leave by train, at midnight. I was surprised at the desolation I felt at the thought. What had this place meant to me but fear and disorientation?

But I knew there had been more. There had been exaltation, too, and laughter, the beginning of something else. But I could not name that yet.

And then I remembered: Sam and Ada were having us to dinner at the rooftop restaurant before our train left, and I would see Rome again from there. See Sam and Ada once more, and Yolanda Whitney. I felt a small frisson of real pleasure. Strangers they had all been to me two days ago and, essentially, still were; I would not see them again after tonight. But for a small, intense time, they had been my community in this place. My tribe, my pack. Out of all these noisome, alien people, they had been *my* people. The huge and ancient and somehow terrible meaning of the word "community" burst over me, stopping me dead in my flight to the elevator. It was everything; it was life.

I smiled at myself in the elevator's mirrored sides on the soundless rush up. I'm seeing my crowd for dinner tonight, I said silently to the rumpled woman with the too-large eyes who looked back at me.

When I reached the room, Maria Gerard opened the door almost before I got my key into the lock. She was still in the wrinkled red sundress she had worn at lunch, and her round face was pale and worried.

"What is it?" I said, looking past her into the room. It was dim with the kind of hot dimness a room gets when mercilessly white-hot light outside is shuttered out, though the air-conditioning was nearly cold. The room seemed to be full of people. I blinked, to accustom my eyes to the gloom.

Colin lay on the sofa, his foot pillowed on the arm. His ankle was bound in an Ace bandage, and his bare toes looked fish-white in the gloom. A pair of crutches was propped against the desk, and he had a washcloth over his eyes. On one side of the bed Joe was propped up against pillows with his shirt off. There were towels on his bare chest, and another washcloth on his forehead. Ada Forrest sat on the other side of the bed with a bowl of ice on the night table beside her. The television set was on, but the volume was turned off; *Mr. Ed*, insane in this place even without the dubbed Italian, flickered in the gloom. Somehow a talking horse was no stranger than this stricken group in my room in the Cavalieri Hilton.

"Everything's OK, or will be," Maria said hastily, before I could draw breath with which to speak. My face must have been terrible, with the dregs of the ride's sick fear still on it and the new alarm just blooming there.

"My God, what happened to Joe? What's wrong with Colin? Was there an accident?"

I could see it, somehow; the taxi and the other car flying together in a glittering shower of glass and a scream of rent metal; people shrieking and babbling; the blatting klaxon of the European emergency vehicles that I hated so. . . .

"Not unless you call two grown-up little boys showing off and almost killing themselves an accident," Maria said, and I heard the anger in her voice then, below the fading fear. I went across the room and sat down on Joe's side of the bed and simply looked at him. He looked back, tried to smile, and closed his eyes. I thought there was more aversion to meeting my gaze than weakness in it. I looked at Ada Forrest.

"Is somebody going to tell me about it?" I said.

She shook her sleek silver head ruefully and smiled. She was cool and perfectly ordered in her black gauze.

"Everybody wanted to go to the Baths and the Catacombs and the Circus Maximus," she said, "so we got a cab and went to the Circus first. It was terribly hot; I can't remember Rome like this many times. I thought then we probably ought not be doing it. When we got to the Circus, there was practically nobody around, and we went out onto the field, or whatever you call it, and Joe and Colin—they were just teasing, really. . . ." She paused.

"Joe gave a magnificent salute to the crowd and yelled *'Morituri te salutamus!'* and Colin said 'I dare you!' and they looked at each other and took off around the track in a footrace," Maria finished. "Isn't that cute? Isn't it adorable? In a hundred-plus-degree heat? It's a very good thing Colin fell and sprained his ankle; otherwise Joe would be dead of heat stroke or heart failure. I thought he was, for a while. We've just gotten back from the hospital. See Rome and die."

"Oh, honey," I said to Joe, and he just shook his head, eyes still closed.

I touched his cheek. It was cold and clammy. But his chest, under my hand, rose and fell tranquilly. I looked up at Ada.

"How bad is it?"

"Not so very, I don't think," she said, smiling her enigmatic little half smile. "I took them to Salvator Mundi, in the Janiculum. It's the one Sam and I know best. It's staffed by a lovely order of Irish nuns, very kind and matter-of-fact. They got us a doctor straightaway, and he gave Joe some fluids in his arm and X-rayed Colin's ankle. Joe will be fine in a few hours, if he stays quiet and keeps drinking water and juice. Colin has a pretty nasty sprain. He's going to have to stay off it as much as possible for the next day or two. After that, he's to use the crutches and keep the walking to a minimum. No permanent damage, though."

"Well, thank God for that," I said, trying not to think of the days of driving and walking ahead. What would we do now?

"Oh, yes," Maria said, still angry. "He'll be well in time for the summer Olympics. Maybe even in time to sprain the other ankle in Tuscany."

"I've said I was sorry a thousand times," Colin said weakly

from under his washcloth. "I don't know what else you want me to say. Yes, it was stupid. Yes, it fucks up the rest of the trip, unless you and Cat want to carry me through Venice and Florence and Tuscany. No, I don't know yet what we're going to do, but if you'll lay off me until the pain medicine takes effect, I'll try to make some plans. It really hurts like a sonofabitch."

His voice was querulous, like a child in need of adult sympathy but getting none. I saw a quick sheen of tears spring into Maria's eyes. She went over to the windows and pulled the curtains aside and stood looking out at the fading day. I patted Joe's chest and got up and went over to stand beside her.

"Don't worry about it, love," I said. "If worse comes to worst, we'll just stay in Rome until he can get around better. He can rest and you can look after him and you and I and Joe can see all the things we were going to miss—"

"I don't think I could stand another night at that hotel," Maria quavered. "Cat, you simply cannot imagine how hot it is. We've been pulling our mattresses up on the roof and sleeping there. . . ."

"Well, then, we'll move you up here," I said. "It may be Disney World, but one thing it is, is cool. And we can swim."

"We couldn't begin to afford it." She would not be comforted.

"Nice try, but no cigar," Joe said. His voice was thin and bored. "I've already called down about staying on. They can't even accommodate us past tonight, much less Maria and Colin. July, you know. Tourist season. They are desolate, but *che posso fare?*"

"Shit," I said. "Joe, how could you?" I said it softly, but Joe heard.

"I am extremely sorry to have discommoded you, Cat," he said, in the same weary drawl. "Perhaps if you had been with us you might have exercised your well-known restraint and common sense and prevented our schoolboy excesses. But you were having your portrait done, I believe. Or was it your nails?"

I looked at him, speechless, and he flushed.

"I'm sorry," he said. "I've really been feeling awful. It was pretty frightening. I couldn't breathe."

So have I been feeling awful, I thought. So could I not breathe. So have I been pretty frightened. Enough to have just flat died of it, OK, Joe? But you know that, of course. You're the one who promised to look out for me while we were here.

I did not say it, though. Of course I didn't. I don't whine at Joe as a rule. And he must, indeed, have felt awful and been frightened. He could well have died out there under the fist of that terrible sun, died in an ancient white-bleached arena in Rome, all those miles from the Mountain, from me. . . .

"We'll work something out," I said. "We have a late checkout. Let's order something to eat, and something cool to drink, and talk about it."

"Listen," Ada Forrest said. "I've taken an awful liberty, but see what you think about this. I called Sam a minute ago from downstairs, and he thinks it's a splendid idea. We'd like to come with you. We'd really like to do that. He can spell Joe driving, and with another man we can manage Colin with no problem at all, and we both know Venice and Florence and Tuscany; we can show you some things you might miss otherwise and introduce you to some people you'd enjoy. And it would give Sam a chance to work on Cat's portrait in a much fuller, more leisurely way. He's really excited about that. Will you let us do it? He's packing for both of us now, and we'll meet you at the station. You four can order up from room service. It's quite good."

We were all silent for a bit. I could not take it in. . . .

"Of course, we won't be at all offended if you'd rather not," Ada said. "We can put you up at home if need be, though I'm not sure how comfortable you'd be. Just say the word, and I'll call Sam back—"

"Oh, Ada," Maria breathed. "You're every bit the angel Mama said you were."

"It would be the answer to a prayer," I said. My heart lifted.

"It's an awful imposition, I know, but if you really would—"

"It's out of the question," Joe said briskly. His face was pink now. "We couldn't possibly impose on you further. I can handle the driving with no problem; it's an automatic shift. I can read international road signs. Thanks, Ada, but—"

"No buts about it," Colin said. "We accept. Joe, you've never driven the Autostrada. There's no speed limit; you get these huge Lancias and Lamborghinis bombing by you at a hundred and twenty miles an hour. It's horrifying. Not to mention trying to navigate Florence in July, or some of the roads in Tuscany. Or, my God, Siena. We can't go unless it's this way."

"The car won't hold us all," Joe said tightly. "It's a little Opel; it's all I could get on short notice."

"Well, if it will help, Yolanda has said she'd come with us," Ada said. "She's already called Hertz in Venice. They can get her another car; there was a cancellation. She knows the area. She's driven it many times. And she wants to come. CNN picked up her show, and she's celebrating. She's going to be much better company now. We'll go in a caravan; Sam and I used to do it with friends when we were very young. It'll be like that again."

"That might work," Joe said.

"It *will* work," Maria caroled. "And it will be such fun, like . . . like a college trip or something. How can I ever thank you?"

She rushed over to Ada Forrest and hugged her hard. Ada smiled and hugged her back.

"By having a lovely life," she said, and I liked her as much in that instant as I ever have.

Late that night, after a not-so-bad room service dinner, Joe and Maria and Colin and I sat on a baggage cart at the Stazione Termini. It was nearly midnight, but there was no sight of Sam and Ada and none of Yolanda Whitney. Maria had gone back in a taxi and collected their luggage, and it was piled on the wagon with mine. We had, with the help of doormen and taxi drivers and pain pills and lavish tips, gotten Colin to the station and to the proper gate, and he half sat, half lay on the wagon, the bandaged foot elevated, his face white with pain but his spirits high with a forbidden combination of painkiller and wine. There was no sign of our train to Venice. It was to be, a porter said, considerably late. *Che posso fare?*

A station attendant was just posting the train's arrival on the platform board when we saw Sam and Ada sprinting toward us carrying light nylon hand luggage and a huge straw tote. Yolanda was with them, a porter following her with a large handsome Vuitton suitcase and two totes. She wore a long cotton skirt and espadrilles and carried a bottle of mineral water, as did Sam and Ada. Ada wore the same loose, floating black gauze, and Sam wore blue jeans and a shirt knotted at his waist, and the straw plantation hat jammed over his eyes. His ponytail was flying. I could have wept and laughed at the same time, with relief and simple joy at the sight of them. Here they were, my community.

"Here come the marines," I said.

"Everybody ready?" Sam bellowed.

I made an OK sign with my thumb and forefinger again, and Sam grinned hugely, and Joe and Colin collapsed into giggles like children. Behind Yolanda, her porter scowled darkly.

Maria and I looked from Joe to Colin.

"*Will* you tell us what's so funny about that?" I said.

"When we get home," Joe said, almost strangling on laughter, "then, dear Cat, I will tell you. But not before."

Still frowning, Yolanda's porter dumped her bags on the platform, gave me an affronted glare, and marched away. Joe and Sam wrestled the bags aboard the train and then half carried Colin on. They found the Gerards' compartment and settled them in and then found ours for us.

"Sleep well," Ada Forrest said. "I've always loved sleeping on trains. And this is a nice, clean new one."

"We will," I said, and kissed her on both cheeks, as I was learning to do. "There's no way to say thank you, but I intend to find one before this trip is over."

"Letting Sam do the portrait is thanks enough," she said.

Sam hugged me and Joe indiscriminately. He smelled as he had on the first night I met him, of sweat and gin.

"A, don't drink the water," he said. "Get some mineral water from the attendant. Brush your teeth in it, even. The other stuff is just for flushing. B, leave a call for an hour before we get in. It's a madhouse when you come into Venice. The guy will make you some first-rate espresso in the morning if you tip him enormously tonight. It's worth it. C, sleep well. Or whatever. Everything is better on a train."

He winked at Joe and kissed me on the forehead, and he and Ada went off down the corridor toward their own compartment. The train was beginning to move, slowly. By the time we got the luggage wedged into our tiny cubicle and pulled down the overhead bunk, it was swaying and clicking along through the anonymous suburbs northeast of Rome.

We washed our faces, and brushed our teeth with mineral water the smiling, well-tipped porter brought, and struggled out of our clothes. I knew there was no hope of finding my nightgown in the piled-up luggage; we literally had to crawl over it, naked, to get into our bunks. Joe came into the lower one with me, and we lay close together, sandwiched in on both sides, rocking through darkness that was lit in brief, flying intervals as we ghosted through small stations and out into the darkness again. Joe reached over me and pulled down the shade.

"We'd never forgive ourselves if we didn't," he said.

"No," I said, reaching up to pull him down over me. His naked back was smooth and very warm, almost hot. The compartment was cool, though. It was very dark for a long time, and in the dark we might have been anywhere at all, except that the deep rushing-rocking of the train took us with it, deeper and harder and faster than we ever went on the Mountain. If I had not been pressed down so hard by the weight of Joe's body I might have arched completely up off the bunk at the finish. I felt my head snap back, and my mouth open, and I tasted the sweat and salt of the side of his neck, and bit it not so gently. He cried out with more than release when I did, and I think I tasted, along with the salt of his skin, the salt-sweet of his blood.

"A Roman fuck is not your ordinary fuck," he whispered later, when his breathing slowed.

"No," I said, still quivering all over.

Much later, after he had struggled into the top bunk and I knew by the sound of his breathing that he slept, I reached over and let the shade up again and lay washed in moonlight, watching trees and hills and occasional old buildings and the arches of old, old, vine-covered bridges and culverts flash past and over me. The clack and sway of the train got into my blood, and I felt my breathing slide into the rhythm of the train. Just before I slid after it into sleep, I felt a sudden surge of fierce joy, the kind you seldom feel after childhood. Ahead of us lay Venice, safe on its island, safe in its lagoon. After that, Florence, the first of the hill towns. And after Florence, the hill towns themselves, the tall old hill towns of Tuscany. Safe, safe. . . .

And all around me, my people, my community. Joe.

And Sam Forrest.

CHAPTER EIGHT

WE CAME INTO VENICE AT DAWN, but as Sam had said, it was all of a frenzied hour before we had gotten ourselves off the train—Colin in a fireman's carry made by Joe and Sam's crossed arms, furious and hurting—and found our luggage. The morning was still and thick and gray. Even before we reached the quay, trotting alongside the mechanized baggage cart that bore our belongings and a sulky, flinching Colin, even before we left the gunmetal shadows of the station, we knew we were in the immense presence of water. Light danced its water dance on the metal roof of the baggage shed; we heard, instead of the blat of automobiles, the chugging and splashing of water traffic; we felt on our skin the slightly sticky slipcover of salt air; we smelled—a stronger, darker note under the complex rank exhalation of Venice in the summer—the sea.

We had been talking worriedly, while we waited for our baggage, of what to do about Colin. Venice, with its hundreds of tiny high-arched bridges, its twisting, narrow *calles*, its solid throngs of summer tourists and absence of automobile transport, is no place for the handicapped. Colin insisted he could walk, leaning on Sam and Joe, but his forehead was sheened with cold sweat, and his face was pinched and shrunken under its gold-leaf tan. Pain had aged and enfeebled him, and I thought that this, the first real helplessness of his remembered life, had frightened him. He said almost nothing and shook off Maria's worried fingers. I knew he was going to be difficult to help. Perhaps we could tip our boatman heavily to help carry him to our hotel in the Campo La Fenice. It was, Sam said, about a five-minute walk from the San Marco landing stage if we took the Number One vaporetto, the one we'd planned to take. Sam and Ada both said it was by far the best and cheapest way to see the Grand Canal for the first time. It was the worst sort of folly, they said, to hire a gondola for a trip from the train station to San Marco.

"You'd have to skip dinner for the rest of your trip," Sam said. "They're the modern Italian equivalent of highway robbery."

I could not imagine that Sam and Ada Forrest worried unduly about money, but it was nice of them to think of Maria and Colin's newlywed budget. Or, for that matter, our academic one. Trinity paid its department heads handsomely, but we were not, I knew, in the Forrests' bracket. Far from it.

Ada whispered something to Sam and he nodded, and she went in search of a telephone and came back in a few minutes smiling.

"The Europa and Regina is making up the living room of our suite into a bedroom for Sam and me," she said. "It's directly on the Canal Grande, no walking at all. And they're sending the launch for us. This way Colin and Maria can have our bedroom where we can look after them, and Yolie can take their room at the Fenice. I'm sure the one they found for her last night is a broom closet. This will be better all the way round. That is, if you lovebirds don't mind sharing a bath. It won't be bad; Sam takes very few."

Sam grinned evilly at her.

"Oh, God, we can't take your bedroom, Ada." Colin groaned. "You didn't come to Venice to share a bathroom and wait on me. Where would Sam paint Cat?"

"The rooms are absolutely huge," she said. "Even the bedrooms have sitting areas, and everything overlooks the canal. The light is lovely. Sam can set up his easel by one of the windows and we'll still have enough room for a ball. I'm not going to take no for an answer on this, darling. You simply cannot manage the Fenice right now. You can lie on the chaise by the window and see all the Venice that's worth seeing, and order gorgeous things from room service, and by the time we leave you'll be able to walk much better. You'll be all ready for Florence. It's the only thing that makes sense."

"I hate the fuck out of this," Colin said.

"What a perfectly gracious thing to say to Ada," Maria said tightly. Her skirt and blouse were badly crumpled, and there were yellowish circles under her dark eyes. I thought of the minuscule bunks on the overnight train and suspected that the second night of Maria Gerard's married life had not been what she might have wished it to be. She had doubtlessly slept in her clothes, if she had slept at all. I imagined that she sat up all night, wedged into the lower bunk with Colin's injured foot propped in her lap, trying to buffer him against the sways and jostles of the train. At the very best, she might have dozed a little. No transcendent flying, racketing love for her, as there had been for Joe and me. I did not blame her for the irritation in her husky voice. Colin injured and helpless did not, for some reason, elicit compassion.

"It's OK," Ada said, smiling her little cat's smile. She wore sea-green cotton today, in a pattern of polished swirls; it seemed to catch and throw back the sea stipple on the shed's ceiling. Her hair was tied high off her slender neck, and the green fabric turned her eyes the color of ice in arctic seas. Everything about Ada Forrest was cool on this thick morning.

"Well," Yolanda Whitney said cheerfully, "I accept the offer of your old room at the Fenice, because I know the kind of 'emergency accommodation' they keep vacant, so you've got no choice. Don't be a butt, Colin. Give your bride a break. The Europa's got the best view in Venice, and they'll look after you like you're Michael Jackson. You wouldn't do half that well at the dear old Fenice."

Maria smiled at her gratefully, and Sam gave her a small hug.

"Come on," he said to Colin. "For you I'll bathe once a day. Rest of the time you won't know we're there. Souls of discretion, we'll be."

"Better do it, sport," Joe said. "You don't want to get on the bad side of these ladies."

"There's no way we can afford that hotel," Colin said obdurately. "It was one of the ones we looked at when we planned the trip. Christ, we couldn't even manage one night—"

"The room is courtesy of us," Ada said. "Consider it a wedding present. After all, it's already arranged; it isn't costing anyone anything."

"No. You've done too much for us. From now on I pay my way," Colin said, and I thought it might actually be possible to dislike him if this side of him presented itself very often. But of course it didn't; I had never seen it in all the years I had known him on the Mountain. Pain and disappointment, that's what it was. Not the Colin I knew at all.

"Colin," Ada said patiently, but with a very slight edge in her voice, "we are paying nothing for either room. The suite is gratis because Sam is . . . because Sam is Sam Forrest. We have stayed there often before, and the manager is an old friend. He owns one of Sam's earliest Italian works. I don't like to make a thing of this, but if it will ease your Yankee conscience I will tell you it is a matter of some pride to our friend, having Sam Forrest stay at his hotel. We would feel churlish trying to pay him for our accommodations; we stopped trying long ago. So you are not putting anyone out and you owe no one anything, and here is the hotel launch. Let's by all means get into it and get you settled and get a decent breakfast. I think we'll all feel better then."

I was liking her more and more.

"Then thank you, Sam and Ada," Colin mumbled, not meeting their eyes. "Thank you again."

He did not say anything else as the boatman and Sam and Joe propped him tenderly in the smart hotel launch, and he did not speak for the entire length of the Grand Canal. For once I could not fault him. One's first view of it, coming out of the shadowy cave of the baggage shed on a mist-pearled early morning, literally stops the breath. We were well away and passing slowly between lacy Gothic loggias and striped mooring poles, past small, secret canals winding into shadows and who knew what else, past the fairy-tale palazzi in their stained dress of soft, crumbling red and blue and pink and gold and white, past blade-prowed gondolas and barges and blundering vaporetti and sleek, low-rumbling private motor craft, before anyone said anything at all.

"Oh, my," I said softly, on an indrawn breath. "Oh, my goodness. . . ."

Venice remains to me now what it was that first morning: a city shimmering in midair, somewhere between sky and water. Atlantis risen. It is all movement and mirrors, illusion, mist, radiance, dapple and dance and diffusion. I never knew where I was in Venice, and I never knew with certainty which was the real city, the city of stone and flesh, and which the watery twin. The people I met in the dark *calles* were, I fancied, more often than not ghosts, and I am quite sure that many of the ghosts of Venice I took for real people, and nodded as we passed, and was nodded to in turn. Its opalescent beauty remains for me phantasmagorical and sucking, death at the bottom of it all, life at the bottom of the death. Who knows which Venice is real, or if any of it is? It dances in the air of its lagoon; it decays in the dark green of its water, it dies and is reborn hourly as the fantastic light changes. It is rich with treasures that were born elsewhere, with the plunder of a hundred kings and centuries; it seems to own none of itself but clings to each new eye and heart that is drawn down the great artery to its own heart as if to fashion for itself more sustaining flesh. I loved it; almost to my last day there, I did.

I truly believe Joe hated it. I still am not quite sure why. I think I know: Venice robs you of yourself and hands you back changed. But I still am not sure. It could be that it was because I loved it. We began to change in earnest, Joe and I, on that first slow ride down the Canal Grande. Or perhaps it was simply that we began to become . . . us.

Just before we passed under the Rialto Bridge we met a procession of black gondolas, trimmed sparingly with gold and moving infinitely slowly. Dark-clad men and women with black scarves and shawls over their heads followed in their gondolas the lead one, where a coffin and an oblong of flowers reposed alone except for the gondolier. A funeral; of course it was. How strange, I thought, to go to your last rest on water, as you had come from that first one. It seemed fitting, somehow natural. Our boatman took off his livery cap, and Ada Forrest made a discreet sign of the cross. Sam shook his red head in something like disgust. Joe gazed at the procession raptly. I knew what he would say before he said it.

"Death in Venice," he said. "Perfect. Thomas Mann couldn't have done better; are you sure you didn't set it up for us, Sam?"

"Glad you like it," Sam said. "But it's none of my doing. I'd just chunk the poor bastard into the canal, like they do the dogs and cats. Thomas Mann obviously never had to pay for a funeral flotilla; these gondolas will set the family back whatever inheritance Uncle Aldo or whoever left. They *will* do it, though. I never heard of anybody going to San Michele permanently in a vaporetto."

"Where's San Michele?" Yolanda asked. She had her thick
chestnut hair loose today on her shoulders, even though the gray
stillness was already oppressive, and wore a low-cut yellow cotton dress and sandals. I thought she was looking prettier and
younger each day I spent with her. Her eyes were clear; she had
obviously stuck to the mineral water she still carried with her.

"The funeral island," Sam said. "The cemetery island. It's
where them as can afford it have crypts, and them as can't go
into a common grave after twelve years. Proper field of bones, it
is; like they grow death there. Doesn't matter who you are,
either; if you don't pay you don't stay. Twelve years and zip."

"God," Joe said. "That's barbaric. Why? What about the
English and Americans who're buried here? Aren't there quite a
few? Didn't Ezra Pound die here, and . . . somebody else, I forget
who? Do they dump the foreigners too?"

"Nope. There's a separate Protestant section that doesn't get
the heave-ho unless there's *Acqua alta*—high water. Then, of
course, everybody floats right on out. The reason for the twelve
years is that there simply isn't enough land on San Michele, or
anywhere else in Venice, to hold the dead of all those centuries.
There's a separate Isle of Bones out past Torcello if San Michele
isn't Gothic enough for you."

"Who else is there that we'd know?" Maria said, fascinated.

"Well, Wagner and Browning and Diaghilev, for starters.
There's something nice about Diaghilev, in the Orthodox Church
section. For as long as anybody remembers there's been a ballet
slipper left on his grave, with flowers in it. When the old one
finally rots, a new one appears. Nobody seems to know who
brings them."

"What a lovely thing," I said, the enchantment growing. "To
go across the lagoon in a gondola to your grave, to have someone leave a ballet slipper on it. No wonder you hear so much
about death and beauty in the same breath here."

It seemed to me that every small canal we passed was
arched over with high, curved bridges. Venice seemed to be

strung with them, like spiderwebs of lacy stone. The sight of them made me uneasy. I felt gooseflesh on my bare arms and rubbed them with my hands, even as the sun broke free of the mist and hung in the sky like the white thumb print of a moon.

Joe saw my gesture.

"Bridges, bridges everywhere," he said lightly. "Cat will go out of her skull."

Anger bit me like a stinging insect. I did not answer, but Sam did.

"Well, there's this little saint, Saint Zita, I think," he said. "She's the patron saint of those who must cross bridges. I'll get Cat one of her medals as soon as we land. She and Saint Zita will waltz right over every bridge in Venice."

He looked levelly at Joe. He wore dark sunglasses this morning, and I could not see the piercing blue eyes. He reminded me of a hawk in its hunting hood, thin blade of nose and slash of mouth, coppery face. The earring shone dully. The ponytail was shoved up under the straw hat; it gave him a different look altogether. Florence; I thought he looked far more a piece of Florence than this aqueous, ephemeral place. Savonarola's Florence.

Joe looked straight back at him. "You do that," he said. And then, "Christ, look at that! Jesus! Does every toilet in Venice flush right into the Grand Canal?"

I looked, then looked quickly away. At the mouth of a tiny canal the bloated body of a small black-and-white dog bobbed among a cluster of what could only be human excrement. The sleek, evil head of a water rat bobbed in the midst of it, nibbling. A powerful stench followed the sight by a breath.

"Well, you know, Joe, death and beauty," Sam Forrest drawled. "You said it yourself. Oscar Wilde said riding in a gondola was like riding in a coffin through a sewer. I'd think you of all people would dig it. You know, Gothic decay? Faulkner?"

"Faulkner didn't shit in his water," Joe said tightly. I

thought dismally that things were not going to go well for us in Venice.

"How do you know?" Sam said, smiling murderously, as only Southerners really seem to know how to do. I thought he was angry with Joe for his remark about me and the bridges; the thought pleased me obscurely but troubled me, too. I did not want these two men circling around me stiff-legged, like male dogs.

"Where in Venice did Thomas Mann die? I mean, his character?" I said quickly to Joe.

"On the Lido. A beach. Outside the lagoon, I think," Joe said, diverted. "It's one of the places I'm going to take you, Cat. I've always wanted to see it."

"I can tell you right now you won't like it," Sam said equably. "It's wall to wall with hotels and condos, and the beach is so full of fat bellies in bikinis and tiny tots peeing in the water it might as well be Coney Island. Looks a lot like it, too. You'd have a hard time finding any kind of literary death there, except maybe sunstroke. But don't let me discourage you."

"I won't," Joe said in his school voice. "It has not escaped my notice that we always end up going to the places you want to go, but you by no means discourage me. Cat and I are going this afternoon."

"Joe, I'm sitting—" I began, and bit my tongue. "But I do want to see it. If you'll wait until tomorrow morning—"

"I'm going today," he said. "You come or not, as you wish."

But in the end he did not go that afternoon. By the time we had decanted Colin and Maria onto the private landing platform of the Europa and Regina, followed by Sam and Ada and the luggage, the sky had darkened again, and by the time we had followed Yolanda through the maze of *calles* and alleyways back to the Campo San Fantin and the Campo La Fenice, just beyond it, and found the small, pretty, vine-grown Fenice et des Artistes Hotel, great warm spatters of rain had begun to fall. So Ada Forrest, carrying a huge Europa and Regina umbrella, called that afternoon for Joe and Yolanda and they went off to the Accademia, and I waited, stung and lonely, for Sam to come and fetch me to go and sit for him again, this time in the fabled light of Venice.

"I was going to give you lunch in our room at the hotel," Sam said, herding me through the bumping throngs in the Campo La Fenice under a huge hotel umbrella identical to the one Ada had brought; I wondered if the Europa kept a closetful of them. "But I think we'll stop in at Florian's and get a bite. When I left, the sounds coming from the newlyweds' room were not exactly conducive to dining. I've heard a lot in my day, but I don't think I've ever heard anything quite like that."

"Is his leg bad, do you think?" I said, and then realized what he meant and said, "Shit."

He laughed. "If it was, he wasn't feeling it then. It's probably broken in six places by now. I always heard, back home, about the catamounts screaming in the swamp, though nobody I knew ever heard one. But I think I did this morning. Good thing I wasn't trying to paint you. I'd have ended up jumping your bones. That little gal is going to get us all thrown out of there."

I felt the red heat start up my neck from my chest. I thought of them, the two of them, naked in the rain light on a great canopied bed, thrashing, screaming out their joy. I thought of last night, on the train. I thought of Sam's long, deft hands. . . .

I trotted with him under the umbrella, up and down again, and only when we were past it realized that I had crossed a bridge surrounded on all sides by people and not felt the fear. I grinned, half in exasperation and half in triumph. It was dark and close under the umbrella, and I could see little of Venice but lovely peeling walls—and legs. Thousands of legs and feet, hurrying in the rain. It seemed as if we walked a long time, the warm, musky smell of him thick in my nostrils, and finally I said, "Where is Florian's?"

"Here," he said, and led me between two pillars in a long dark portico of some sort, and lifted the umbrella from us, and we were in the Piazza San Marco. Saint Mark's Square.

I did what I had become accustomed to doing when overwhelmed in Italy: I pressed my fist to my mouth and whispered, "Oh, God," and started to cry. I felt the tears rise, flood my eyes, cling to my bottom lashes—and then, instead, I laughed. It was a kind of hiccup, a reflux of pure joy. The Piazza San Marco was, and is, the kind of space that elicits joy. Even in the rain. Even inundated with the worst of its tourist floods, in July at lunchtime. Even when the man you have loved always is angry at you, and has gone away with two pretty women who are the absolute antithesis of you. Even then.

We walked along the covered gallery on the right, my eyes refusing to embrace the great baroque-domed Basilica and the Campanile and Doge's Palace but sweeping them, averting, then coming back, as if in flirtation. I could not seem to stare squarely at them. Later, later, I would come here and simply sit and let them register, but not now; it was too much. The stones of the piazza glistened in the rain, but there were still knots of tourists grouped about it, flinging food to the flocks of pigeons whose wings made a continual dry, snapping noise in the thick air, and everywhere cameras aimed, clicked; minicams whirred. The hundreds of small chairs and tables that forged out into the glorious space like promontories were empty, though, and old waiters in black, white-aproned, were folding some of them and taking them inside. Sam turned me through a door and into a vast, dim space of dark paneling and apple-green walls and smoky old mirrors. We found a tiny table and sat down on gilded chairs. The room was not crowded but contrived to feel, to me, thronged with people, most of whom were staring at us.

Sam took off the disreputable, damp-splotched hat and raked his fingers through his rowdy, steel-wool hair. In the mirror opposite I saw a red giant, disheveled, barbaric, and a thin woman with eyes like black pools and damp, fair hair pasted in circlets on her cheeks. A waif of a woman, a mendicant. Was that us? Surely they would put us out of this elegant place. Here came the waiter to do it now. . . .

"*Buon giorno*, Signor Forrest," the fine-featured old man said. He might have been one of the Doges, he had the black eyes and the proud prow of chin and nose. "You'll be lunching? Signora." And he nodded to me.

"*Buon giorno*," Sam said pleasantly. "Yes, we will. Let's start with a Bellini for the signora and a gin for me. Then we'll decide."

The old Doge nodded and went away, and I looked up at Sam.

"Not here too," I said.

He laughed. It was like firing a cannon in a small chapel. Heads turned; I heard one or two voices whispering, "Forrest. The painter. You know."

"Who's she? Not his wife."

"I don't know."

"I had my Venetian period several years ago," he said. "We spent a lot of time here. Everybody comes to Florian's several times a day, and since none of the waiters ever seem to quit or die or get fired, a few of them remember me. I tip well. And I always came inside. Most people sit outside."

The Bellini came and was ambrosial. We ordered two more drinks.

"I don't remember seeing anything of yours from Venice," I said. "Where are they?"

"I didn't show them," Sam said. "I guess I worked here off and on for a year and a half; we had an apartment at the Europa. I thought the light was the most glorious stuff I had ever seen; I thought I was going to be the one to really show the world what Venetian light is about. Forget Titian and Tintoretto and Constable and Sargent and Whistler. Sam Forrest's Venice was going to be hotter than catshit. But I couldn't paint it. Never could get it. Whatever I painted by Venetian light turned into nineteenth-century German postcards. I finally realized that what I'm about is solidity. Planes, angles, lines, splashes, masses—*globs*, as Ada says. I can't catch the diffuse, oblique stuff. It makes an ass of me, and I of it. Most of the work from that time is in a warehouse in Rome."

"Do you mind?"

"Naw. Tell you the truth, I've never cared that much for Venice. Something here makes me want to circle the wagons and hunker down. Besides, I think this time may be different. I've got a good feeling about this portrait of you. I think you and I together may crack this damned fool's-gold light."

I said nothing, feeling shy and pleased.

We ate a delicate soup of creamed mussels with saffron and a plate of tiny fried spider crabs, and drank white wine. Florian's, Sam told me, was the oldest café in Italy; it and its rival across the piazza, Quadri, had once been spoils of war. During the Austrian occupation of 1814–16, Quadri became a favorite of the Austrians, and most Venetians shunned it and patronized Florian's. Many old Venetian families still held to the practice.

"Ada likes Quadri," he said, grinning. "But then Ada likes all things Germanic. Ada would like to be a Hapsburg. Sometimes, when we were here, we'd have breakfast at the same time in different camps and wave spitefully at each other. I never could abide the Germans, and she can't resist them. The old boot-in-the-face thing."

"The way you talk about Ada is shameful," I said, only half teasing. "She keeps your slothful life spinning like a top. What on earth would you do without her? What would any of us have done, on this trip? She's been kindness itself."

"I know," he said. "I ought to lay off her. You're right; I truly could not exist without Ada. I'd dissolve in a pool of sheer entropy in a week. She runs my life like a Swiss watch; she's decorative as hell and good company to boot. She rarely bores me. I hate the kind of man who calls a woman a good sport, but she really is. I can't think who else would put up with me."

"You make her sound like a camp counselor," I said. "What's in all of this Sam Forresthood for Ada?"

He grinned widely, the grin of a red wolf.

"Mrs. Sam Forresthood," he said.

"You arrogant ass," I said, laughing. "Maybe you're lucky to be Mr. Ada Forrest."

"Maybe," he said. "You ready to go do some painting? Damn this rain. It never rains in Venice in July."

Ada and Sam Forrest's suite at the Europa and Regina was all she had said it would be. The little alleyway that had led off toward the hotel's plain, small campo from the main route to the piazza had been dark and empty and glistening in the after-lunch lull, and the campo itself deserted, and the entrance unprepossessing. But inside, the hotel had the thick-carpeted, wax-shining amplitude of all good private spaces everywhere, and the second-floor foyer that opened into the Forrests' two great rooms was large, with dully shining tile and a fine old chandelier. Beyond it, the sitting room that was now the Forrests' bedroom, by virtue of the austere white-draped bed that had been moved into an alcove, was enormous. Dark antique furniture sat like islands on the expanse of gleaming Italian tile, and deep jewel-toned oriental rugs shone in the rain-gloom. The windows and French doors that led onto the terrace overlooking the Grand Canal were open, and sheer white curtains billowed back into the room, looking like blown mist. The walls and high ceilings were white. Everything danced with the reflected light from the canal; it was like being underwater. The room was awash in flowers in floor pots and tubs, in bouquets, in single crystal bud vases. A great basket of fruit and cheese, still ribboned and cellophaned, sat on a coffee table before a long sofa.

"Lord," I said. "There must be something to this Sam Forresthood business."

"Ada has a way with concierges," he said. "There was champagne, too, but I took it in to the newlyweds before I left to pick you up. Hoping, to tell you the truth, that it would knock them out for a spell. Want some fruit? Peel you a grape?"

"No, thanks," I said, feeling suddenly shy about being in a hotel bedroom with Sam Forrest, even this most un-boudoirish one. The bed in which, presumably, he and Ada would sleep was undisturbed and piled high with pillows, its hangings drawn around it like mosquito netting. It was possible to think of it as just another massive piece of furniture. Almost.

"Let me go check on Romeo and Juliet," he said, vanishing into the bathroom that joined the rooms. In a moment he returned, grinning.

"Asleep. The spoon position. Great possibilities for the handicapped."

Sam had his easel set up in front of one of the windows and had moved a big overstuffed armchair opposite it for me. The block of canvas that sat on the easel was not large, perhaps sixteen inches square. His pastels and a scurrilous-looking palette sat on a gilt table he had drawn up beside the easel. A thick monogrammed hotel towel covered everything.

"Would it be impossibly bourgeois of me to wonder if oil paint comes out of hotel towels, or do you just steal them?" I said.

"I don't worry about them anymore," he said, holding a brush in his teeth while he fiddled with the blowing curtain at the window. "The first time the manager raised a stink Ada told him he could probably make a fortune selling them as Sam Forrest originals. I don't know if he did, or does, but he hasn't hassled me anymore. Shit. This was right the first time. I think I like the light diffused through the curtain. Sit over there and let's see what it does to your face."

"May I look at your view first? It's apt to be the only time I see the Grand Canal out a hotel window."

We went onto the terrace, and I leaned my forearms on the padded cushion the hotel had placed on the balcony railing for just such pursuits and drank in the panorama of afternoon on the ancient fabled waterway. Just across, seemingly so close that you could see into its windows, a great white dome glowed in the shifting mist. It sat just at the point where the Grand Canal widened out into the basin of St. Mark and dominated the entire sweep of water and land. Its façade was baroque, a bulbous flower of grandness among all the lacy pointed arches and linear façades.

"What is it?" I asked.

"Santa Maria della Salute," Sam said, still around the mouthful of brush. "The plague church. Built in the seventeenth century as a little thank-you to Mary, who's said to have stopped an outbreak of plague. Not, however, before about a third of the city corked off. Come on back in, Cat, I don't want to miss this light; the rain and fog lifting is doing nice stuff. Pull your blouse down off your shoulders and lean your head back some—"

"Sam . . . "

He walked over to me and gave my sleeveless scoop-necked blouse a good yank off my shoulders, laid a length of fine, silky linen across them, and draped it. His face was very close to mine, and his hands were warm on my bare skin, but both eyes and hands were totally absorbed in their business; I felt I might have been anyone, a mannequin. I was grateful for his absorption. I hoped he did not notice the flush spreading over my chest and up my neck. My face felt very hot. It was not until the session was over that I realized he had draped me with one of Ada Forrest's nightgowns. At least, I presumed it to be Ada's.

He painted in silence for a while, whistling soundlessly between his teeth, stepping back and staring, moving forward again to slash a line here or there, stepping back again. The third or fourth of the malodorous Italian cigarettes he smoked was just sizzling itself out in a pool of thick umber paint on his palette when I said plaintively, "Can I move?"

He shook his head, as if coming out of water, and laid down the brush.

"Sorry," he said, rescuing the cigarette. "Actually, you can move whenever you want to. This is more interpretive than literal. But go on and stretch. Want something to drink?"

"Maybe some mineral water."

He gave me some from a bottle on the bar set up on a beautiful old painted console and poured himself a tumbler of raw gin. He drank it without ice, as I had seen him do before.

"I didn't like what Joe said to you this morning, about the bridges," he said abruptly. "I think it was a prick's thing to say. I wondered why you took it."

I was surprised and disoriented.

"I . . . because all it meant was he was feeling out of sorts with himself, feeling that he was—oh, losing himself, not knowing who he was or who I was," I said. "You know how it is with Venice."

"Tell me how it is with Venice," he said, looking at me.

"I know I'm not telling you anything you don't know, as many times as you've been here," I said. "And I don't want you to think I don't like it. I absolutely love it. It casts a spell. But there's something, Sam. Something . . . it isn't the bridges, Joe knows that. It's that . . . nothing is what it seems. You sense it instantly. And maybe nobody is who they seem, either, at least not while they're here. That's what he was feeling. He just picked up on the bridges because . . . "

"Because he saw a chance to humiliate his wife a little in front of a select group of her friends?"

"No. Not at all. Nobody else knows about the bridge; Joe doesn't know I . . . I didn't tell him I'd told you about it. He wouldn't have told anybody himself."

"I would not take any bets on that, Miz Compton Gaillard," Sam said. "You ready to get back to work?"

"What are you saying? That he's told somebody?"

"I'm saying my dear wife has a way of getting the most astonishing things out of people and sharing them with others," he said, grinning. "Can you tip your head back a little more? You have a nice arch to your neck."

"You're absolutely wrong if you think he told Ada or anybody else."

I tipped my head back, looking up at the ceiling. He was silent, working fast.

"How did you meet Ada?" I said presently.

"I literally picked her up on the Spanish Steps," he said. "It was the middle sixties and I'd just come to Rome to paint and find myself and all that shit, and I'd had one New York show with good reviews and was fuller of shit than a Christmas goose, and I'd been through every girl who switched her pretty ass up and down the Spanish Steps. Painted some of them and went to bed with all of them. And then one day there she was, in her little black miniskirt and high heels and white gloves, for God's sake, and with her hair the color of a raven's wing except for one white streak, carrying a big bunch of iris she'd just bought. There was a crowd of greasers three deep around her, and she was trying to get through them and go on up the steps, and I waded in there and got her by the arm and took her to the Hassler to tea. That's what she wanted, tea. She'd just come up from some fly-specked little village outside Naples and found a job as a secretary to an importer of men's hats ... this when JFK had made hats obsolete all over the world. She'd never been away from home. First I took her to bed, and then I painted her, and then I painted her some more, and by that time I was beginning to realize how much smoother my life ran with her around so ... I married her. On the whole, I haven't been sorry. She truly does think I'm an authentic genius, you know. And she has a way of making other people think that way. She's been the best investment I ever made, over the years. Ada ... enables. She makes a great many things possible."

"Do you love her?"

"I don't not love her," Sam Forrest said. "It's not a thing I think about much anymore. I need her, I guess. Isn't it the same thing?"

"Robert Frost said something I've always liked about only

when love and need are one," I said, not liking the life, the world, of Sam and Ada Forrest that I extrapolated from his words.

"Do you love Joe?" he said.

"Well, of course I do," I said. "I love him very much."

"But you don't need him."

"That more than anything," I said.

"No, you don't. But you don't know you don't, yet. I think he knows it, though. Or he wouldn't need to remind you of your fears, of what cripples you. What do you do at home, Cat? How do you spend your days? What did you study in school?"

"Art history," I said. "And I was good at it. I was set to be a research assistant to the head of the department at Trinity. I could have taught anywhere after that."

"If you could have left your mountain. But of course, you couldn't, and then you had your blind child, and then when she was launched, you had your garden and you had Joe's career—"

"You make it sound like I've never done anything for myself," I said, angry. "But I've had a wonderful life. I've had just what I wanted. We live a good life, Joe and I, a beautiful one."

"And has he encouraged you to leave this beautiful life? Has he wanted anything all your own for you?"

"He's wanted what I wanted. What we have, that's what we've wanted."

"Are you happy, Cat?"

"Yes," I said fiercely. "I'm very, very happy," and began to cry.

He put down his brush and came over and held me against him, very gently. He rested his chin on my head. I smelled gin and sweat and paint: Sam.

"I want you to have something of your own, Cat, so he can't do that to you again, that with the bridges—what he did this morning. I didn't mean to make you cry. I have a shit-awful habit of poking my nose into things that don't and never will concern me. You're a lovely woman and I want a lot for you. That's all.

Go home. This is enough for now. Put on something pretty. We'll take you to Harry's, you and Joe and Yolie. I was saving it for the last night, but maybe we all need it more now."

"You don't have to," I said, sniffling, but not moving out of his arms.

"Yeah, I do," Sam said.

At seven o'clock that evening, Yolanda Whitney and I walked from the Fenice to Harry's Bar on the Calle Vallaresso. Joe had said he would meet us there a little later; he had come in very late from his afternoon with Yolanda and Ada at the Accademia and wanted a nap and a bath. The rain had stopped and the heat was back with us, and he was flushed with it, and so voluble that I thought perhaps he might have a touch of fever, or heatstroke. But he felt cool to my touch, and brushed off my fretting with a swift kiss on the forehead and a pat on the behind, and then collapsed full length on the bed.

"Go on with Yolie at seven," he mumbled. "She came back early, said she had an appointment. I think she has a boyfriend here. Ada and I had a drink afterward at the most marvelous place, a workingman's bar, a thousand miles back in real Venice. I'll take you before we leave; it's not the kind of place tourists go. I'll see you at Harry's by eight. You won't be ready to eat before then, anyway."

"All right," I said, standing in the doorway of our darkened bedroom looking at him. He lay with his back to me. He was naked to the waist, and the darker-gold whorls at the crown of his head stirred in the wind from the sluggish ceiling fan. His smooth torso was misted over with sweat. I felt hot too, in my black sleeveless silk. After the two dresses that had vanished with Joe's luggage, it was the most formal thing I had brought, and somehow I felt like dressing up a little tonight. But now it seemed too much. My pantyhose were already damp. I turned away to go out the door. I would have a drink in the lobby while I waited for Yolanda.

"Cat?"

"Yes?"

"How'd the painting go this afternoon? I almost forgot."

His voice was thick with sleep.

"Fine," I said, and shut the door.

Yolanda came down into the little garden, where I was sipping white wine, at a quarter to seven. She looked crisp and young, in yellow linen and citrine earrings that almost brushed her tanned shoulders, and she smelled wonderfully of something both flowery and bitter at the same time, like Venice itself. She kissed me on both cheeks and I returned the gesture, and all of a sudden we grinned at each other like school friends, or cousins. Two pretty, if not so young, women, all dressed up and alone in Venice, with somewhere wonderful to go. Not for the first time I thought it might have been fun to grow up in a large family, to have a sister.

"Where's Joe?" she said, taking a bite of one of the little sandwiches I'd ordered and then not wanted.

"Sleeping off the Titians and the Tintorettos and whatever Ada fed him at some marvelous, authentic little workingman's bar that surpasses all the wonders of the Accademia," I said. I probably sounded spiteful and jealous, and then I knew somehow she would not think so or, if she did, would understand. I had a clear and powerful thought: *She is on my side.* But I did not know in what. I laughed aloud, and she did too.

"Well, she takes a bit of sleeping off, does Ada. But a perfect hostess. You must admit that. The veritable Perle Mesta of Venice."

We walked out into the swirl of pedestrian traffic in the campo and were immediately swallowed up in the street life of evening Venice. On every street corner, from every doorway, men young and old called after us, made as if to follow us, kissed their fingertips and made gestures I was just as glad I did not understand, trotted along behind us baying and snorting and howling. I don't know why I had not noticed this sort of attention earlier; I had been warned, back on the Mountain, that being blond and fair I would attract a great deal of amorous adulation in Italy. But it had not really happened before tonight. Of course, I had mostly been in groups, and moreover in groups that included Joe and Colin and Sam Forrest. I did not think many Italian men would be eager to contend with a great, shambling red pirate with a ponytail.

At first it was funny, and Yolanda took my arm and told me to ignore and enjoy it, and we laughed and shook our heads and the would-be suitors retreated, holding hands to mock-stricken breasts. But one group of three dark, older, unsmiling men did not seem so theatrically amusing and persisted in following closely behind us. We were almost to Harry's when I thought I felt a hand brush my buttocks, and I reddened and quickened my step, and then Yolanda whirled and spat something furiously at the group and I knew she had been fondled too.

One of the men said something equally low and fast back at her, and she planted her small high-heeled pumps apart and put her hands on her hips and shouted, *"Va a farti frattere, stronzo! Va fan culo! Mis lasci in pace! Chiamo la polizia!"*

When the men did not retreat, she smiled a slow sly smile and put her arm around me and squeezed. Then she kissed me on the mouth. Loudly.

The men wheeled abruptly and slunk away, muttering in disgust.

"What was all that about?" I said, laughing a little, but with my heart pounding faster than I liked. I wanted to wipe my mouth with the back of my hand but did not.

"Well, one of them grabbed my ass, and I told him to keep his filthy hands to himself, and he intimated that we were prostitutes and could expect no better, and I told him to go fuck himself and leave us alone or I would call the police. And then I indicated that we were lesbians. That always works when nothing else does. It's funny; you'd think there was nothing too depraved for Venice, but the idea of lesbians absolutely revolts Italian men. A direct disparagement of their manhood, I think. They all suffer from *gallismo*. Roosterism."

I laughed so hard I bent at the waist, holding my arms across my stomach. She began to laugh too. We were still standing there, just outside Harry's famous bar, laughing helplessly and holding on to each other, when Sam and Ada and Maria found us.

"It must be good," Ada Forrest said, smiling. She wore black, as I did, but managed, I thought, to look more the *contessa* than the *prostituta*.

Sam simply shoved his hands into his blazer pockets, rocked back and forth in the filthy, sockless running shoes that seemed to be his only footwear, and grinned affectionately at us. Even Maria smiled; I say even, because otherwise she was the picture of misery. Her face was pale and her nose and eyes were red and swollen as if she had been crying.

"Yolie has just saved us from a fate worse than death," I gasped, and told them about the exchange. By the time I reached the bit about the lesbians, Maria was laughing along with the rest of us. When the others went ahead into Harry's, I hung back and put my arm around her.

"What is it, sweetie?" I said. "Colin feeling bad? You feeling just a little bit housebound?"

"We had an awful fight," she said in a low, rapid voice. "I said I'd like to go out with you all just this once, just to see Harry's, because I've heard so much about it, Hemingway and all, and I'd come home real early and bring him back something wonderful, and stay in with him the entire rest of the time we're here, and he blew up at me. He said by all means to go; he'd see if he could tap out a message to room service with his cane, and I said not to be silly, I'd get something for him before I left, and he said it had been his impression that I'd said something recently about in sickness and in health, and I said I just wanted to go to

Harry's Bar for one damn hour and what was the matter with him, and he said maybe his mother had been right all along! Oh, Cat . . . that hurt! That really hurt!"

She began to cry again, and I found a tissue and wiped her face and gave her my compact and lipstick.

"Dearest love, it's just a fight. Your first; now you don't have to worry about having it later. It's like getting the first scratch on a new car. He's angry because he can't move around and feels foolish because he knows he brought it on himself, and it probably still hurts, and he's bored, and he wants to see Venice too. And it's hot. And he knows he's keeping you from seeing everything you wanted to see on your honeymoon, and that makes him even madder. He loves you and he thinks he's spoiled things for you and that makes him mean."

"You'd think it would make him just the opposite. He's never been . . . mean before. But that thing about his mother—"

"He's lost control. It's different for men than for us when that happens, I think," I said. I saw all at once that this was true. Wasn't it what Corinne had been saying? I needed to think about this. . . .

"You think so really?"

"I know so really," I said, giving her a little hug.

When we went upstairs to join the others at the big table by the window overlooking the Grand Canal, she was smiling again.

Sam Forrest's lips shaped the word *Thanks* to me, silently. I smiled and made the small OK circle with thumb and forefinger. Around us, early diners stopped their talking and sipping and stared, and the dark-suited, distinguished man who had been talking with Sam stood erect and frowned ever so slightly.

Sam leaned toward me and said, in a low voice, "Cat, obviously no one else is going to tell you, so I will. A joke's a joke, but enough is enough. In Italy, when you do that, you're calling someone an asshole. It's what the sign means: asshole. If you really want to be effective, you follow it by hissing, '*Stronzo!*' You

have, my darling girl, called half of Italy an asshole by now, and
I for one do not want to have to fight Signor Cipriani or some
other equally distinguished personage for you."

The blood actually drained from my face, and I thought for
a moment I might faint. Joe. Joe knew. Why had Joe not told me?
Why had he simply laughed . . . and not told me?

"I truly didn't know," I whispered, tears starting in my
eyes.

"Of course you didn't," Ada Forrest said, and patted my
arm. "Joe should have told you by now."

"Wonder why he wouldn't," Sam said equably.

"Wonder why who wouldn't what?"

Joe came up to the table, looking rested and scrubbed and
handsome in his newly cleaned blazer and chinos and the soft
green shirt he'd bought in Rome.

"We were just wondering why you didn't want to tell me
what it meant when I made that adorable little circle sign," I
said. "The one that means asshole."

He laughed.

"I know, I should have. But you were so cute, Cat; you're
such a . . . a lady, I guess, and there you were, the madonna of
the Mountain, calling all those people—well. I'm sorry. Christ.
You didn't do it again, did you?"

"Only to Sam," I said.

"Oh, well." Joe grinned at Sam conspiratorially. Sam was
studying the wine list. He did not look up.

"Let me recommend the risotto *primavera*," Ada Forrest
said. "It is absolutely superb."

It was. The entire dinner was wonderful. You think of
Harry's, perhaps, as a tourist place, but the upstairs dining room
served some of the best food we had in Italy, and the service was
silken and impeccable. The other diners were quiet and attractive, and somewhere between the risotto and the veal chop I for-
gave Joe and slid into the light, lovely fabric of the night. The
only jarring note was a small child, a little English boy of per-

haps seven, with a perfectly tailored, miniature Eton jacket and a chipmunk overbite, who kept playing to his fair, cool mother and eyeing his even fairer, chillier father with the metallic eye of a budding Oedipus. His voice was that shrill, upper-class British tremolo that grates abominably and can pierce concrete and steel, and he kept piping things like, "Doddy is being naughty tonight, isn't he, Mummy? Doddy isn't at all nice to us." And, "It's too bad Doddy is too big to sit in Mummy's lap because I'll bet he wants to, but only I can do that," and he climbed into his mother's ample lap, resting his cheek against her considerable sunburnt cleavage. His father, face frozen into neutrality, did not lift his eyes from his *fritto misto*, and his mother only brushed the thick hair off the boy's avid face and said in nearly the same little trill, "Sit down and be a little man, Derek, darling, do. Doddy isn't going to want to take us anywhere nice again if you can't behave."

"Doddy would love to take the little bastard out beyond Torcello somewhere and drown him," Sam said under his breath. "Mummy probably gets more from little Derek darling than she does from Doddy. On the whole, my sympathies are in Doddy's camp entirely. Christ, the English upper class and their little tots. See what you missed, Yolie? That could be you, pushing some horny little bugger off you while your old man read up on terns."

Yolanda lifted her head and looked squarely at Sam.

"How fortunate for me that I missed it all," she said. I looked at her; what was in her voice? Did anyone else hear it? Did I imagine it? Sam dropped his eyes, and everyone else went on eating.

You are really halfway out of your mind tonight, I said to myself. This place will have you singing with the mermaids if you don't get a grip on yourself.

It was quite late when we finished dinner, and on the way back toward the Campo La Fenice Sam stopped at a flower kiosk and bought bouquets for me, Ada, Yolanda, and Maria. Small nosegays, really, picked that morning and past their prime. But they were pretty, and it felt a very fine thing, to walk slowly through the nighttime alleyways of Venice carrying flowers.

At the apex of one of the high-arched little bridges over a tiny canal, back in the dark quiet maze of tiny *calles* that bordered the campos of San Fantin and La Fenice, we stopped and leaned on the railing and looked down. Around us, on other streets, we could hear conversation and foot traffic and see lights, but this particularly tiny bridge and the canal beneath it were very quiet. One or two lone lights shone, high up in old windows, but they gave little illumination, only pinpricks in the thick velvet darkness. Below us the water was green and black, swirling. We could hear it slapping at stones of doorways. It was like being in a dream, vivid and palpable, but without ambient sound. Mist hung in the curves and bends of the canal and crawled up doorways. None of us spoke.

"Look," Yolie whispered, and around a curve in the canal came a large silent gondola, and behind it another. We could hear the gondoliers singing softly then, sounding bored and ready to go home: "O Sole Mio." An American Italian song, I thought, Neapolitan, a tourist song. It did not belong in this dark oriental fairy tale.

There were three couples in each gondola. All women. All late-middle-aged stout women with "done" American hair and print drip-dry traveling dresses. They sat quietly, hands folded, looking half rapt and half scared. Widows, I thought. Widows from some nice service club or Sunday school class in the Midwest, come to Venice in safe numbers, lost in black-green water, being sung to by bored men who would laugh at them when they decanted them, finally, at their budget hotel near the train station.

Still, in the utter quiet and near darkness, the scene had an enchantment about it. I hoped the women felt it, too. It was all, really, that they would take home with them from La Serenissima. The Serene City.

"Give me your flowers," Sam whispered, and I handed them to him, and he made a little sound as the second gondola drifted directly under us. The women looked up.

"*Bellissima*," Sam called down softly, and threw the flowers into the lap of one of the women. She caught it, her mouth open in a perfect O.

"Thank you," she called from under the bridge as the gondola vanished. Then it reappeared. We stood for a moment longer, looking after them. They were talking softly, excitedly, among themselves and looking back and waving. I wondered if they had recognized Sam but thought probably they had not. It was enough this way. They would retell this story for years: about the night in Venice when flowers fell from a dark bridge into their gondola.

"That was a lovely thing to do," I said.

"It really was, darling," Ada Forrest said, and took Sam's arm.

"It was," Joe said. "I bet it was the first time anybody gave her flowers since the mister passed."

He put his arm around me lightly, and I looked down into the green water and saw us all there, my crowd, my community, my husband, me. I would have been hard pressed, at that moment, to say which of us was real.

CHAPTER NINE

W E MET AT FLORIAN'S THE NEXT MORNING for cappuccino and brioche and to decide what to do with ourselves. Somehow we had all contrived to avoid the subject last night; no one seemed to want to break the beautiful, fragile skin of the scene on the bridge. And I think we all knew there would be discord this morning. The heat that the mist and rain had held at bay had finally straggled in from Rome, and even before nine the humidity was stunning, a palpable thing. Neither Joe nor I had slept well. I had lain awake very late and felt and heard him tossing. When we finally woke, heavy and damp and slow, we did no more than exchange our ritual morning conversation. Neither of us mentioned the Lido, but it hung between us, white and burning as if we were already there. I knew he was not going to give it up. And I knew I simply could not go.

There was a message for us when we went past the desk, from Yolanda: *Have some crafty business over on Burano. See you for lunch and, if not, for dinner. Leave message where. XXX, Yolie.*

"What's on Burano in the way of crafts that would interest Yolie?" I said to Sam and Ada, who were waiting at a table outside Florian's. I almost wanted to shake them both: Sam looked as roaringly vital as ever in the shredded cutoffs and shirttail-flapping blue denim, the dreadful hat riding high on his red forehead, and Ada, in her trademark cotton gauze, looked like a woman carved of ice. No tossing in damp sheets for them; the Regina and Europa had efficient air-conditioning hidden behind its billowing white drapes.

"Lacemaking," Ada said. "Almost every woman on the island does it, and it's exquisite. There are seven stitches in Burano and Venetian point lace, and each woman specializes in one, so every piece gets passed around until it's finished. A tablecloth center will take about a month. I can't imagine Yolie trying to get her viewers to make lace, though. It takes years to learn. Whole generations of young girls ruin their eyesight doing it—"

She broke off and looked at Sam, who was laughing.

"I imagine Yolie's trying her hand more at making whoopee than lace," he said. "The simple fishermen of Burano are notably potent and ardent. An American woman with a nice solid ass and no squint could get laid by eleven, have the best *vongole* in the lagoon for lunch, and be back in time for tea."

"If you mean she's going over there to pick up a man, you should be ashamed of yourself," I said to Sam. "You should have seen her last night when those three creeps came on to us outside Harry's. They're probably halfway to Rome by now."

"Yolie wants to be the one to choose," Sam said. "Don't worry about her, Cat. She's been cruising ever since we've known her. She's smart and careful; nothing's going to happen to her and she won't catch anything. Yolie has more condoms in her wallet than I did when I was fifteen. She just likes to screw. Nothing wrong with that."

I didn't know what to say, so I said nothing.

"I'll say there isn't," Joe said. "Speaking of which, have the newlyweds patched it up? I gathered there was trouble in Tahiti last night."

"Gauging from the sounds coming from behind the nuptial door, I'd say they have," Sam said. "Lord God, I hope they wear the edge off before long. I don't know how much more I can take."

"You didn't hear a thing. You were asleep before your head hit the pillow last night," Ada said, smiling reprovingly at him. So, I thought, they didn't make love. And banished the thought almost before it formed. But it seemed to me suddenly, sitting there in the thick morning heat of Venice, that everybody in this entire lagoon seemed to be screwing everybody else all the time.

"Well, I wish Yolie had told me she was going," Ada said. "I wanted to get Maria and Colin a piece of lace, perhaps a tablecloth. It's much less expensive on Burano than here. Maybe we could go ourselves; would you like to see it, Cat? The little town is very picturesque, and the seafood is really wonderful."

I thought of the squinting children, the near-blinded girls.

"I hoped maybe to take a look at Saint Mark's this morning, Ada," I said. "It's the one thing I don't want to miss, and it seems awfully hot for much else."

"I," Joe said pleasantly, "am going to the Lido. Whoever wants to come with me, meet me at the landing stage in an hour."

He did not look at me.

"Then you shall surely fry," Ada said, smiling, "but I'll come with you. Our hotel launch will take us for free. Come by for me, and we'll leave from there. Cat? Sam?"

"This morning's my date with Saint Lucy," Sam said. "Cat, if you want to come along, I'll trot you through Saint Mark's when we're done. I warn you, Saint Lucy lives in an utterly undistinguished church at the end of the most execrable street in Venice, but I make it a point to drop in on the little lady whenever I'm here."

"Who's Saint Lucy?" I said. I could not imagine Sam, with his scalding contempt for the Catholic Church, visiting any saint at all.

"Saint Lucy was a young lady of Syracuse who, when an unwelcome suitor praised her beautiful eyes, plucked them right out rather than tempt him further. The Venetian Crusaders liberated her body from Constantinople and brought her here, and her mortal remains lie in state above the donations box in the Church of San Geremia, which has never had anything to do with her at all. She had her own church here for a while, but the railroad authorities kicked her out of that in the mid-nineteenth century. Her sight was miraculously restored, and she's become the patron saint of eyesight and, by virtue of truly Venetian logic, artists. I guess she's my only superstition. The cash box has a prayer written on it: *Saint Lucy, protect my eyes.* I always toss her a wad of lire. Can't hurt."

"Is it really her?" I said. "I mean, is it her . . . bones or what?"

"Well, she's pretty desiccated, but yep, it's her," Sam said, his wolf's grin widening. "Come on. I'll show you."

I was about to say that perhaps I'd go on over to the Lido with Joe and Ada after all when Ada said, "Sam, really. Cat doesn't want to go look at Saint Lucy. Don't press her. It would have to be painful."

"Why?" Sam said. I thought he was honestly puzzled.

"Oh, for goodness' sake. Because of her daughter. Really, darling, sometimes your sensitivity rather misses the mark." There was a trace of real annoyance in Ada's voice.

"Oh, God, I'm sorry, Cat," Sam said swiftly. "I just didn't think. Let me show you Saint Mark's. I'll do Saint Lucy tomorrow—"

"Don't be silly," I said. "I'd love to see her. I'm not sensitive about Lacey's blindness, Ada; she's gotten us all way past that."

"Too bad saints can't work retroactively," Joe said. "Maybe

we could pool our lire and lift the curse off Lacey in utero, as it were. Or the German measles, or whatever."

I felt myself go still and cold. "Nobody ever really knew what caused it, Joe," I said. "You know that. There was no evidence I had German measles. Sometimes you just ... don't know."

"I once thought it was that fear of yours that marked her somehow," he said, as pleasantly as he might be saying it was a fine day. "Cat was afraid of almost everything back then, when she was pregnant with Lacey. Of course, I know logically that couldn't be. But sometimes it would be nice to have the kind of faith that believed miracles were possible. Or could find reasons for things. Don't you think?"

And he smiled around at us, the warm white smile made whiter by the deepening tan of his face and the sun-bleaching of his mustache, and I felt run through with the pain of his words—and a following freezing anger.

"Well, I'm not afraid anymore," I said. "Not of anything. Let's get going, Sam. I'll meet you in the Europa lobby in ten minutes. I want to get a sun hat."

I got up and walked away across the sunny stones of the piazza of Saint Mark. Already the flocks of tourists and pigeons were gathering. Behind me, Joe called, "Cat?"

"No," I said, and walked on.

Sam and I had been walking for a few minutes in silence, elbowing our way through the listless, heat-clotted crowds moving like a great, slow tide toward the Rialto Bridge, when he said, "It's because I'm painting you, isn't it? He wasn't taking potshots at you when we first met. It started with the painting. What does he think, that I'm screwing you on the side? We should stop right now."

"No," I said. "We're not going to stop the painting. Not unless you want to for a real reason. Like being finished, or deciding it isn't working. It started when he lost his clothes, or—

I don't know, Sam, it started when Italy got out of control and he couldn't make it work right. Joe's always been on top of his world. Always. He was punishing me today because I wouldn't go to the Lido with him. I've never not done what Joe wanted to do before. It isn't that I obey him; it's that we've always wanted the same things. But now, over here . . . it's like we were identical twins, who'd always been told we were just alike and part of the same flesh, and then we woke up one day and found we were very separate people. We're surprised and hurt and angry. I'm really very mad at him, because what he said hurt a lot, but I also know he didn't mean it. And he knows beyond any doubt that you're not . . . screwing me on the side. So let's drop it."

"Consider it dropped," Sam said. "But he'd be wise not to be so sure of you. If he thinks other men don't think about that when they look at you, he's out of his mind."

I felt heat in my face and chest and low down, in the pit of my stomach. I pulled the brim of the sun hat I'd bought down over my face. On my right in a tiny shop, one of many crammed into an arcade, I saw an array of medals, dusty on black velvet. I thought they were religious ones; I recognized Saint Mark's winged lion and the disenfranchised but still popular Saint Christopher.

"You promised me a bridge-crossing medal," I said. "Here's your chance."

"So I did," he said, and went in and conducted an earnest, crooning conversation in ridiculous Alabama-accented Italian with the shopkeeper, an old woman so bent she looked like a dwarf. I thought of the terrible child dwarf in Daphne du Maurier's *Don't Look Now* and pulled at Sam's arm in instinctive revulsion, but the thin woman turned to me with a smile so purely sweet and benevolent that I smiled back.

"Santa Zita," she said, and proffered a small dimly stamped oblong medal on a pewter-colored chain. I could make out no particular features at all on the medal, but I smiled back at her and said, "*Grazie*." Sam pressed lire into her hands and lifted off my hat and dropped the chain over my head. The medal fell into the small hollow between my damp breasts, just out of sight under the neck of my blouse. It felt icy cold there, and heavy, and somehow wonderful.

The old woman patted my arm.

"*Sicuro*," she said. "Safe."

"Yes. *Si. Grazie*," I said and, to Sam, "Bring on the bridges."

"I think we'll get the vaporetto at the Rialto," he said. "It's just too damned hot and crowded to walk anymore. I wish I could offer you the Europa's launch, but I don't think it goes anywhere near the Lista. And besides, Ada has most appropriately turned it into Cleopatra's barge for the duration of her stay."

"Does that make Joe Mark Antony?" I said, and began to laugh. We were still laughing when the Number One vaporetto wallowed up to the landing stage and we got on for the ride to the Campo San Geremia. I don't know why. It was not particularly funny.

Sam was right about the Lista di Spagna and the church of San Geremia. The street was a carnival affair, a haven for day-trippers who would go no farther into Venice than this tawdry midway, and the church had little to recommend it but the tattered little mummy behind the altar and a beautiful old campanile, twelfth century, Sam said, and one of the oldest left in the city. Still, I was glad I had come, glad to leave my lire for Saint Lucy, glad in some profound interior way that felt oddly and irrationally like the paying of a very old debt.

"I think," I said to Sam, getting on the vaporetto for the trip back to San Marco and the splendors of the waiting Basilica, "that I might have made an amazingly good Catholic. The Graham Greene kind."

"God forbid," he said, but he asked for no explanation and I gave him none.

After the Lista di Spagna and San Geremia, the typical dogtrot Sam Forrest tour of San Marco and the Palazzo Ducale was like being shaken inside a kaleidoscope of gold and gem-stones and satin and light. I had no sense that this great republic had ever had serious concourse with reality; nothing with this sort of wealth and fantasy in its national treasury was truly of earth. Air, perhaps; water, certainly. But hardly of the earth. Even its totems were fantastical creatures: winged lions, dragons, uni-corns, chimeras, mermaids, serpents, sea monsters. It did not seem to matter so much, when you were in the midst of it, that most of the literal and figurative jewels of Venice were booty, spoils, plunder from a dozen cultures and civilizations. Here they had found their true spiritual home, halfway between water and sky.

"What did you like best?" Sam said, as we trotted toward the Europa and Regina, where we had agreed to meet Joe and Ada for lunch. We were late, and I could barely keep up with his long stride.

"Oh, the horses," I said. "I loved the horses. They were—well, you know, I think lovable is the word. Like good carousel horses, that like giving pleasure."

We went through the dark cave of the Europa's lobby, I pausing in front of a mirror like a deep, wavy pool to push the wet strands of hair off my forehead and bite my lips, Scarlett style, and then we went out onto one of the terraces that fronted the white glitter of the Grand Canal. It was so bright, after the dimness of the lobby, that for a moment I could not see, and then I did see them. Joe and Ada sat under an umbrella at the far cor-ner of the terrace, their heads together, talking without smiles, and I thought, It was a bad morning. He's disappointed with the Lido and angry with himself for insisting.

I don't know how I knew it, but I did.

When we got closer, I saw that his face and arms and the V of his open shirt were scarlet with sunburn, and even Ada For-rest's seemingly impervious white satin skin was washed with plum color. She had pulled her white gauze peasant blouse off her shoulders and tied up her silvery hair, and I looked at Sam and winced silently. It was the sort of sunburn that spoke of serious pain later. Ada did not seem to notice it; she talked quickly and earnestly. Soothing. Smoothing.

Sam did not return my look. He was staring without expression at his wife. At her shoulders, to be exact. I looked again. On the backs of her upper arms, just above the line of the white blouse, were the distinct white prints of fingers, just fading from her burnt skin. Fingers that had pressed and held. I knew they could not have been her own.

"Miss a lot if you're late to lunch in Venice," Sam said.

We ate cold soup in near silence. It was not a day for lunching alfresco; even under the umbrella in that choice corner of the Europa's terrace, the heat was as palpably present as an unwanted guest. There was no wind, and the glare off the Grand Canal smote the eyes like tiny glittering knives. I could think of little to say that I knew would not anger Joe. Everything that came to mind smacked of I-told-you-so. I spooned up soup that I did not want and did not look at Ada's bare arms, though the fingerprints had long since faded. I thought, though, that it would be a long time before those white stigmata faded from my mind. On the Mountain I would have teased Joe about it and gotten a soft, laughing, perfectly natural explanation. I could not do that here. I knew the unexplained fingerprints would slide into the stew of festering strangeness that seemed to be overlaying us like amber.

We should not have come, I thought. Not to Venice, and probably not to Italy.

When the waiter took away the soup plates and brought the cold lobster, Joe seemed to make an effort to shake off his mood. He smiled at me, a thin, stretched smile, and said, "You were right to pass on the Lido, Cat. It was godawful. Wall-to-wall people, and not a decent stretch of beach to swim from unless you paid a fortune to rent a beach hut at one of the hotels. The water at the public beaches is a sewer, and the Grand Hotel des Bains is an old whore. From now on I'll trust your instincts."

"But you got a lot of sun," I said. "You must have finally found a good spot to swim. Lord, Ada, I hope you've got something to put on your back and shoulders."

Joe made a small disgusted sound, and Ada laughed ruefully.

"We got the sun walking from the vaporetto stop over to the beach. It took twenty minutes. We couldn't get a taxi, and the hotels won't send a car for you unless you're staying there. I'd forgotten about that. I'm afraid the Lido fiasco is as much my fault as anybody's. I should have checked about the hotels and the taxis. I've never gone over in July before."

"It's none of your doing," Joe said. "It's all mine. God, the traffic! And the Germans. I think they deport German felons to the Lido in July."

I couldn't resist it.

"I thought Aschenbach was a German," I said.

He looked at me with his light eyes. The laughter that would have crinkled them back at Trinity was not there.

"Thomas Mann evidently knew a better class of German," he said.

"And even that one died," Sam said equably, attacking his lobster with gusto. "Was it plague or sunstroke?"

"General stupidity, I think," Joe said. His school voice was back. I knew he loved *Death in Venice* and taught it in some of his small seminars as an allegory of the corruption and death of art when the world comes in upon it. I wondered if Sam Forrest had read it or merely heard of it; I wondered what he made of it if he had. He was as much in the world as any artist I could think of, but unlike Aschenbach's his art seemed to surge and boom with health and vitality. The thought struck me that perhaps Sam should not stay too long in Venice. Maybe none of us should.

"You know," I said, "I wonder if maybe we shouldn't just

pack up the newlyweds and go on over to Florence tomorrow. We'd only lose one day of Venice, and in this heat I can't imagine anyone doing any serious sightseeing. It's bound to be cooler in the hills. Or whoever wanted to stay on could come with Yolie in her car. I just think Joe and Ada ought to stay out of the sun, get up into the hills—"

"Aren't you having a good time in Venice, Cat?" Joe said.

"I was," I said, looking straight at him. He of all people should know whether or not I was having a good time; he, who could read me like a long-loved book. "I was, until today."

He flushed under the sunburn, and I knew he was remembering what he had said at breakfast, about my fear and Lacey's blindness. I knew, too, that he was sorry, and was probably thinking of a way to let me know without apologizing before other people. But he would not apologize now.

"Too bad," he said. "Maybe you ought to go on ahead; I'm sure the bride and groom will be happy to see another set of walls. Maybe Sam will drive you, or Yolie. But Ada and I are meeting some people for lunch tomorrow that I'd like to know, so I'll be staying."

We all looked at him. Ada and I? He flushed again.

"Actually, we're all invited," Ada said, looking from Sam to me. "I thought I remembered that David and Verna Cardigan were going to be here sometime in July, so I called the Gritti, and they're there and have asked us all to lunch tomorrow. I accepted because I thought you'd like to see her again, darling"—she smiled at Sam—"and because he said he'd like to finance a new show for you in London if you've got something going. I said I thought you did, or would have, soon."

She turned to me.

"David and Verna Cardigan. Lord and Lady Cardigan, if you insist, though they certainly don't. Passionate Sam Forrest collectors and investors; he painted Verna years ago and David liked it so much he gave Sam one of the most successful shows he ever had, in London, with the portrait as a centerpiece. I told him Sam was painting you, and they're dying to meet the original of the new Forrest. As I told you, there are very few in the world. Verna's is my favorite of Sam's portraits, but of course I haven't seen yours yet, and I'll bet you haven't either. Nobody sees them till they're finished. So ... of course we won't bully you if you really do want to go on to Florence, but I wish you'd stay and meet them. They're really very nice. And you know, I thought how unusual it would be, to have you and Yolie and Verna all together, three Sam Forrest portrait women, in the flesh. The English papers would just love it. Of course Sam isn't going to let me call them, but it would be extraordinary, just the same."

I looked at Sam, who grinned and said, "Extraordinary is right," and then at Joe. Joe smiled at me; I thought he had to force it, but it *was* a smile, so I smiled back.

"You could dine out on it for years on the Mountain, Cat," he said, and I knew he wanted very much for me to stay and meet Lord and Lady Cardigan, and be exclaimed over by them as the centerpiece of Sam's new London show, and would not be overly aggrieved if the English press did indeed get word of it.

Who on earth are we turning into, Joe? I thought, and said, "Of course, then. It was nice of them to ask us. I just thought the two of you looked so sunburned and uncomfortable—"

"I'll send Joe home with a jar of some wonderful stuff I get in Rome that will take the fire right out of him," Ada said. "That and a nap will do it. I plan to spend all afternoon at a very discreet little salon off the Campo San Angelo. There's a little girl there who will work all kinds of magic on me. There won't be a trace of red when we have lunch with the Cardigans. Or tonight, for that matter. Sam and I are going to take you and Joe and Yolie, if anybody can find her, to that little place Joe and I had lunch yesterday. What did you call it, Joe? The underbelly of Venice? It's not that, by a long shot, but it does have an interesting atmosphere, one you haven't seen before, Cat, and the food is wonderful. We'll have to eat early; it closes at eight. But we can find something fun to do after. Maybe Vino Vino, back in your neck of the woods near the Fenice."

"Well," I said. "Looks like we're all set."

"Looks like it," Sam said.

Soon afterward we left the terrace, Sam and I to go upstairs for another painting session, Joe to go back to the hotel and restore himself with sleep and Ada's unguent, Ada to her secret spa. I was nearly limp with exhaustion by then. I could not quite think why. Nothing had happened, really, at that luncheon under the umbrella by the Canal Grande, and yet, in some subterranean manner, a great deal had.

When we got to Sam and Ada's suite we opened the far bathroom door very quietly and looked in on Colin and Maria. They lay loosely entwined on the great tester bed, fast asleep, a light plissé coverlet drawn up over them. The air-conditioner hummed full blast, and the ceiling fan spun heavily. The bedside radio purred light rock into the big dim room, and a room service tray on a gilt console held the remains of lunch, with three empty wine bottles. Sam closed the far door and locked the other one, which led into his and Ada's room.

"I'd say they'd made up and are out for the count," he said. "They should resurface sometime before midnight."

I went to my chair and sat down. He moved to his position behind the easel and uncovered the painting and stood for a moment, staring at it. He picked up a brush, then put it down and went and stood for a moment before the French doors, looking out into the blazing canal. His hands were shoved into his pockets, and he rocked back and forth on the big running shoes. The ponytail switched back and forth across the broad, sweat-stained back of his work shirt. I felt the prowling tension in him from where I sat.

"Is something wrong?" I asked. "With the light, or something?"

"No. I mean, yes, the light's too bright, but I can fix that. It's not anything, except that—Cat, please don't think there's anything ... going on ... between Ada and Joe. There isn't. I can promise you I would know if there were."

"I didn't think that," I said, but I thought, That's what *you* were thinking, isn't it? Or at least wondering. "They're together so much, is all," I said. "And he's been so annoyed with me, or whatever it is that's eating him. I didn't mean to imply that Ada would—"

"Ada might," he said, not turning back to me. But I could hear the smile in his voice. "Ada in fact has, upon occasion. But this is not one of them. I know her like I know myself; I know when she's being helpful and when she's ... interested. What she's doing now is trying to keep Joe occupied while you're sitting for me. It's very important to Ada that I should be painting again. She gets distinctly nervous when I hit a long dry spell. So you can rest easy on that score, unless you think Joe has the hots for her."

"I don't think he has the hots for her, as you so elegantly put it," I snapped. "But I think he may think he does. Joe and I haven't ever ... there's never been anybody else for either of us, not since we met. And everything's so strange now, and he's thrown with her so much, and she's so very beautiful. I guess I really don't know what I think."

"You ain't exactly chopped liver, kid," Sam said, turning around and picking up his brush. "He's crazy about you; a fool could see that. He wouldn't be so angry at you if he wasn't. But he needs to clean up his act. He'd be a fool to drive you away."

"I don't think he could do that. . . ."

"Any of us can drive anyone else of us away, Cat," he said. "It doesn't do to take people for granted."

"It seems to me you take Ada for granted a good bit of the time," I said.

"On the contrary," he said. "I may not show it, but I am aware at all times of what Ada wants and needs. They are not always the same thing, but I am never unaware of them. Have you and Joe really never had anybody else?"

"No," I said. "We really never have. I mean, I never have ever, and he hasn't since we met. I guess I don't really know about before then, for him. Is that really so very strange? You sound as though you think we ought to be in the *Guinness Book of Records*."

He laughed softly.

"In my world, you ought. No, I was just thinking . . . there's a quality about you, something in your face. It hasn't been there in the other women I've painted, or wanted to paint. I don't think innocence is the right word, but there's something . . . like a new snowfall. Essentially still untouched. I was wondering why I was so drawn to that at this point in my life."

I did not like the direction in which this conversation was sliding.

"Maybe you're looking for a clean slate. Maybe you need to turn over a new leaf. Maybe it's easier to paint . . . untouched faces. Less annoying character to have to fool with."

"Don't get prickly with me," he said, beginning to paint. "I didn't say you lacked character. And you're not easier to paint. I think . . . you're the hardest portrait I ever tried."

I sat silent for a time then. He painted furiously, restlessly, paced about, changed to a palette knife, worked fast with that. At some point I closed my eyes and leaned my head against the chair's back. I hadn't meant to, but I felt myself drifting away, drifting. I was simply so tired. . . .

I'm not sure what time the sounds began. I know that when they disturbed my light sleep, or whatever it was, the stabbing white had gone out of the light, and the water stipple on the ceiling was slower. I lifted my head, my neck stiff, and cocked it to one side, listening. I had never heard anything like the sounds before, and yet I knew them. . . .

Sam had stopped painting and stood still, looking toward the closed bathroom doors.

"What on earth?" I said, turning toward the escalating sounds, and then I knew. Thrust and thump, thrust and thump, the quickening creak of springs, a high, thin keening, a lower moaning that grew and grew, sharp, muffled words—yes, yes, yes, *my God yes!*—a kind of dark crooning, a long hoarse cry, a pure high scream that rose and rose and rose and finally choked sharply off, as if cut by a knife. And then silence.

I had heard it all before: in a small dark room in a tiny house on a mountain half a world away, in the back of an old car, and, one last time, in the back seat of a car on the verge of a bridge swinging high over a rocky creek.

I put my hands over my ears and shut my eyes and rocked myself back and forth in the chair. After a moment, Sam came over and gently pulled my hands away.

"Why does that frighten you so?"

He was leaning closely over me. I could not look up at him.

"That's how it sounded . . . that's what they were doing, that's how they sounded. My parents. I remember hearing that all the time until I was five. That's how it sounded on the night they . . . the night they . . . "

"But doing it doesn't frighten you, Cat. I don't understand. I mean, you and Joe, you do that . . . don't you?"

"Yes," I said, thinking I was going to cry again. I was very weary of crying. "We do that. We do that all the time. But that sound . . . I don't make that sound . . . "

"What sound do you make, Cat?" he said. His voice was so low that I could hardly hear it. I could feel his breath on my face, though.

"None," I whispered. "I don't make any sound. I never have. I can't. I try, I make the motions, but no sound comes . . . Joe calls it the silent death. . . ."

"Because if you make a sound, you can't hear danger coming. That's it, isn't it? If you make the noise of love, that love will kill you?"

"Yes."

He put his arms around me and pulled me to my feet. He bent his head down to mine, and I lifted my mouth up to his, and he kissed me, long and sweetly and softly, and then not softly anymore. Hard, warm, hot—his hands moved down my back and around and up to my breasts and then all over me, and I gave him back touch for touch, eyes still closed, blinded, breath-spent. Strange, his hands were so large, his mouth so hard without the softening brush of a mustache. His body was so very big. I could not get all of him into my arms, as I could Joe. Strange, strange. . . .

When he finally took his arms away he was breathing as though he had been running, hard, and I could only stand staring at him, gasping like a fish pulled onto land. If I had not held to the back of the chair, I think my legs would have collapsed me onto the floor.

"Cat," Sam said hoarsely, "I promise you now that before you leave Italy you will make a very joyful noise, and it will be with me, and it will be a very far thing from killing you. But not now."

"This shouldn't have happened," I whispered. "I didn't mean for this to happen. We can't . . . we can't be together anymore. The painting will have to stop."

"The painting can't stop," he said, and he smiled at me, a very sweet smile, a normal Sam smile. "But I promise you, too, that I won't touch you again until you ask me. And Cat, you will ask."

"I'll sit for you, if I have your promise," I said. "But not for a day or two. We need some time off, both of us. And Sam, I will not ask."

"Oh, yes," he said, "you will."

When I got back to the Fenice, there was a note from Joe saying he and Ada and Yolanda had gone on to Do Spade, in San Polo, and for me to ask Sam to bring me. *Don't come alone,* Joe wrote, *you'll never find it. You can't handle it alone. Sam knows where it is. Come with him.*

In a pig's ass I will, I said to myself, still shaking slightly, still running sweat, still feeling the imprint of Sam's hands on my body and my own arms hard around him. In a pig's ass will I ask him. And I went up to Joe's and my room, as dim and neat now as if no one had ever been in it, and stripped off my clothes and took a very long shower. And then I dressed and went downstairs and asked the desk clerk to draw me a map to Do Spade, in San Polo.

He was the one I liked, a slim, blue-eyed young man who looked like an American college student doing his summer abroad, except that his English, though good, was formal and heavily accented. He had heard Joe call me Cat, and now referred to me, shyly and with a smile to show that he meant no disrespect, as Signora Gatta. When I asked for Do Spade, he looked at me in surprise.

"Signora Gatta goes prowling tonight," he said. "Are you sure it is Do Spade that you want?"

"I'm sure. Can I walk it from here?"

"You can walk it in—oh, perhaps twenty minutes or so," he said slowly, "but I wish that you would not. It is *oscuro* . . . hard to find. There is no sign, and it is not the best part of Venice for signoras. Not even *gatti*. You do not go alone?"

"No," I lied briskly. "I'm meeting someone who'll go with me, but I wanted to be sure of it. I've heard it's very good, very . . . real Venice."

"What is the real Venice?" he said. "Do Spade, it is a place for the—what? The porters and merchants around the Rialto. A local place for workers. They are good men, most, but they are not used to seeing pretty *gatti* coming alone."

"Thank you for being concerned, Alvise, but I won't be alone." I smiled, and took the map he had drawn, and went out into the last of the afternoon sunlight in the Campo Fenice. All at once I wished we were meeting there, at the Taverna; it looked gay and friendly in the slanting light, as familiar to me, now, as home. My place.

And then my skin prickled and my heart gave the profound, half-forgotten wringing twist that meant the fear had woken in its kennel and put its head out. I stopped, stood still for a moment. Then I turned and went back into the Fenice.

"Forgot something." I smiled brilliantly at Alvise, and ran up the stairs rather than waiting for the elderly elevator, and rummaged in my bag until I found the nearly full vial of Valium, and took two. Then I picked up Sam's little pewter medal from the dressing table and dropped it over my head. Saint Zita came to rest once more, heavily, coldly, between my breasts. It made an oval lump under my striped jersey, but I did not care. It was as comforting as . . . a touch.

"*Sicuro*," I whispered to myself in the mirror. "Safe."

And this time I strode swiftly and purposefully through the campo and into the maze of small alleys that would take me to the Teatro Rossini, in the Campo Manin, the first of the landmarks Alvise's map told me to look for. I did not look back until I knew that the Campo La Fenice was lost to me. Then I slowed and looked about me.

The tiny *calle* in which I walked looked identical to the ones around the Fenice and San Fantin and the ones Sam and I had passed through on the way to San Geremia. Miniature arched bridges, winding green canals, peeling soft red and blue and pink walls leaning close overhead, tiny *campielli* opening out for seemingly no reason at all, the inevitable covered wellhead centering each. Some of the alleys led nowhere, and some seemed to lead back to where—I thought—I had just walked. There were people all around me, but few carried cameras; I was not of them anymore. I had read something Henry James had written about "a narrow canal in the heart of the city—a patch of green water and a surface of pink wall . . . a great shabby façade of Gothic windows and balconies—balconies on which dirty clothes hang and under which a cavernous-looking doorway opens from a low flight of slimy watersteps. It is very hot and still, the canal has a queer smell, and the whole place is enchanting."

Yes. It was enchanting. It was not the Venice I had seen so

far, but it was still Venice, and enchanting indeed in the dying light. Enchanting in the old, original sense of the word: a place of magic, sorcery, incantation, witchery. A place that changed its shape and nature and with it, yours: enchanting. The hair on the back of my damp neck prickled. I nodded stiffly to most of the people I passed, and some nodded back but others only stared, stared at the leggy blond American woman with the haircut of a boy, wandering alone through their *calles* and over their bridges. Several groups of men called after me, and one or two made as if to follow me, but I glared at them as Yolanda had taught me, and they faded away. Only their laughter followed me.

Where was the Campo Manin, the Teatro Rossini? I stopped in a tiny, silent *campiello* and studied Alvise's map. It was empty, barren, hot, and dim, but there was something in the shadows around the blank, closed doorsteps, shapes shifting, moving . . . cats. I looked harder. Many cats, slipping through the shadows, watching me, crouching patiently before bowls that had been put out for them. Not precisely feral, then, if not house pets, either: these cats were lean and wary but not starved. There were many bowls. The people of this other Venice cared for them, they were kind, they would not—had I been about to think it?—harm me.

Just around this corner and over a bridge should be the Campo Manin, and here it was. Not thronged with tourists and dinner-goers, as the campos nearer San Marco were, but full of people strolling, talking, carrying bundles, sitting at scuffed plastic tables outside tiny *caffès*. Neighborhood people. Home people. I took a deep breath and felt my heart slow. The map worked. Next, beyond another warren of *calles* and canals, the Fondaco di Tedeschi, where the main post office was, hard by the Rialto Bridge. I had been there, with Sam. My spoor was still on it.

And after that, simply across the Rialto straight down the Ruga degli Orefici to the Ruga Vecchio San Giovanni, and I would see the sign of the little Do Mori bar, and if I walked straight past it, there would be the few tables and chairs that belonged to Do Spade. It had no sign, but they would be there waiting for me. Joe and Yolanda and Ada and Sam.

I could do this.

I smiled at everyone around me, my heart beating high with success and only the scuttled remnants of the fear, and sailed out of the Campo Manin and back into the heart of this other Venice.

And into the dark. It was a dark that was more than the sudden dying of the light, which happens on the eastern rim of lands that touch the seas. East: I had forgotten just how very far east we were here. But it was more than that. It was a darkness of places where people have, for centuries, kept to their houses after nightfall, and those houses were high and close together and with only narrow slashes of windows, so that there was no light from them, only oblongs of lesser darkness. It was a darkness of old water, that moved in and out each day over doorsteps and around foundations and sometimes, in the winter *acqua alta*, over campos and courtyards, and always under the bridges, old themselves. Old water, green and silent and always moving; wherever I went on the old, glistening cobbled alleys and *calles*, over the countless high bridges, I heard it, moving with me. The dark water of Venice, that night, was like the surf of my own blood. My footsteps rang over and around it, and finally with it. Blood and water, running together. Up and over this bridge and that, down this alley and that, into this dead, lunar campo and that, back out, into another *calle*, over another bridge. . . .

Where was the post office, the Rialto Bridge, the lights, the people of Venice? I could hear them, off on other streets, always just out of sight; I could see, not light but the diffusion in the sky, thickening now with fog, where light shone below. But I could not find any of it.

I was lost.

I was lost. All right, stop and take a deep breath and hold Alvise's scrawled map up to the pale night-light in the little greengrocer's, long closed now. Breathe in and out, slowly. And again. You are not lost. No one is lost in Venice; how can one be lost on a small island? Who said that to be lost in Venice is to be found? There are people all around you; you can hear their voices. Go to one of the places where they are and ask the way. Some one will point you there.

Don't be afraid.

I am afraid. I am lost and my heart is going to stop, it will attack me; no one will find me; the wrong people will find me; someone is going to find me and hurt me. I must be very quiet. I must hear it coming.

I stood beside the tiny light in the closed shop and leaned against the stone wall. I breathed in and out, in and out, as Corinne had taught me, and presently I looked again at the map. I could see so clearly the route one must take to the Fondaco di Tedeschi: so simple. But I had missed it somehow, and now I did not know how to get back on one of the map's penciled streets because I did not know where I was.

I heard footsteps, several of them, brisk and firm and confident; they seemed just one *calle* over. There must be a bridge down this alley; there was always a bridge. If I crossed it I would find the walkers, and I would walk with them, or just behind them, as if I was going where they were. It must be to some place of lights and people. The steps were so sure. . . .

I hurried down the alley and found the bridge and crossed it and ran straight into them—four men who did not look like husbands and fathers going home to dinner or to a bar or a video arcade. Not at all. They stopped, a quartet of darkness, across the street, barring my way.

"*Scusi*," I said, and my voice trembled. "Where is the . . . *dove il* . . . I need to find the post office. . . ."

They smiled. They smiled and looked at one another, and then at me, and began to make that simpleminded crooning I had thought was so funny when I first heard it with Yolanda. The kissing of fingertips, the motions in the air with the hands, and the guttural words that I did not understand but knew in my cold blood. And they began to walk toward me, very slowly.

"I want you to tell me where the post office is this instant," I said, in a high, silly voice. "If you don't I will call the police."

Call the police because four men will not tell you where the post office is?

I had the absurd notion that I would simply sit down on the cobbles and laugh like a madwoman, but then I said, "Oh, never mind, I'll find it myself," and turned, and walked very fast back down the way I had come, to the steps that led up the little bridge. Behind me I could hear them coming fast, almost running.

I began to run. I ran over the bridge and down the other side, and down a winding *calle* beside still another canal, and ahead, sensed space, an opening. I ran for it as hard as I could, without pretense and without hope. I knew I could not outrun them.

I reached the opening: another dark campo, this time with a small plain church in it, and a covered wellhead, and dark houses all around, but nothing else. Dead end. No way out. I turned to the men behind me.

"*Va a farti frattere, stronzi!*" I screamed. "*Va fan culo!*" I went at them with my fingers curved into claws, my eyes screwed shut, and my mouth wide open. I must have seemed a madwoman. Far up, in two or three of the houses, pale lights bloomed. The men stopped, backed up, muttered among themselves, turned around, and sauntered out of the campo, laughing. They did not look back. I went over and sat down on the steps of the little church. Soon the lights in the houses went off again.

I sat there for what seemed a very long time. I did not look about me or consult my map. I only sat there. I had no idea what time it was. Surely, at Do Spade, they had missed me by now. Someone would be looking for me; someone would go back to the Fenice, and Alvise would tell them about the map, and they would begin to retrace it. Perhaps I had only to sit here and they would come for me. When I saw it in my mind, it was Sam Forrest I saw. I saw him come around the corner of the alleyway into the campo, and I heard him say, "For God's sake, Cat, where have you been?"

There was another sound. A thin, wavering, strangling sort of sound, a kind of tiny gagging.

I looked toward it, in the shadow of a big terra-cotta pot with a dead plant of some sort in it, by the door of one of the dark houses. It was a cat. A cat crouched low, its head hanging almost to the cobbles: wheezing, struggling for breath, very sick. The cat was very sick; I knew it was dying. I thought, simply, This is more than anyone should have to bear, and got up to go away from there, to leave the campo, to begin my hopeless journey through the streets again.

And saw the others.

All around the dying cat, other cats were ranged, utterly silent and still, in a circle. Dark, they seemed, and large, and sharply made, sharply carved in the thin light from the foggy sky. They sat or crouched, and they waited. The terrible choking went on, faltered, stopped. Began again. I ran. I thought that if I was still in that campo when the sound finally died, what came after would send me beyond reason forever.

I ran for a long time, and when I had to stop, my sides knife-stitched and my throat aching with spent breath, black motes dancing in front of my eyes, I was at a street corner where a few people were gathered. I heard still others, not far away. I looked and then began to run, a sob of joy in my throat. Just ahead of me, leaning against a gray wall, his head bent down to the person in front of him, was Joe. I could only see his back, a slender, slouching back in his blazer, and the gilt of his hair, but it was Joe; it was there in the way he held his head, the way he put his hands out to the person with him. . . .

I stumbled and nearly fell and caught myself against his shoulder.

"Oh, God, I'm so glad to see you!" I cried, and he turned around.

Lipstick, running crazily up from the long mouth and under the large nose, thick green eye shadow on the drooping eyes, so sad, so sad . . . rouge like plague spots, like pestilence, on coarse-pored cheeks. We stared at each other.

I began to cry and ran past him and around a corner—and was in the elegantly lit, sweetly shadowed Campo La Fenice. There were the dear green vines on the little pillars of my hotel, and there the crowds of well-dressed, strolling people, and there the Teatro Bar, with people like me, people I know, eating and drinking and laughing. And in the midst of them, Sam Forrest, at a table on the fringe of the space, staring straight across the campo at me. Beside him sat Yolanda Whitney. They had been drinking beer, and when they saw me they got up hastily and trotted across the campo, and I stood still and let them come to me.

It was Sam who caught and held me, smoothing back my hair, rocking me gently back and forth, back and forth. And Sam who sat me down and washed the tears and sweat off my face with a napkin dipped in mineral water and listened as I said, "I thought I could find you all, but I got lost. I couldn't . . . I saw a cat die, Sam. And . . . I think some others ate it. . . ."

His face twisted and he said, fiercely, "Goddamn them for going off and leaving you. And damn you, Cat, for not calling me. We've been looking for you for two hours. . . ."

"Joe," I said. I was amazed at how, now, my voice was cool and even. "Is Joe here?"

It was Yolanda who spoke then. She put her arms around me and said, "They're waiting at Vino Vino. They thought you might think to go there. We . . . Sam and I . . . went out looking. Don't worry about them. I'm sure as hell not going to. Right now I'm taking you up and putting you straight to bed. Sam can go tell them you're safe. If he wants to."

"I may," he said, "and then again, I may not. Sleep well, Cat lady. See you at lunch tomorrow with their fucking lord and ladyships. Ah, sweet Jesus."

He kissed me on the cheek and shambled off toward San Marco. Yolanda led me into the Fenice, her arm firm and warm around me, and up to our dark room, and shucked me out of my clothes and pulled the coverlet up. She did not turn on the light, but she started the ceiling fan.

"Sleep late," she said. "And then, about ten, you and I are going to have a long breakfast and then go shopping and bleed Joe Gaillard's American Express card bone dry. Don't even think we're not."

"Thanks, Yolie," I whispered, and wanted to say more, but sleep and the fan's wash took me down like an undertow. I have no idea when Joe came in. I did not stir until after nine the next morning, and by then he was gone again.

CHAPTER TEN

THERE WAS A NOTE. I picked it up from amid the clutter on the bureau top. Perhaps Joe and I would simply go on communicating via notes for the rest of the trip.

Have gone over to the hotel with Ada to help her and Maria get Colin up and dressed. He insists on coming to lunch. See you there. By the way, where were you last night? We waited and waited. Love, J.

We waited and waited. Love, J. I crumpled the note up and threw it into the wastebasket.

"What's this *we* stuff, paleface?" I said aloud, and then snapped my lips shut as I felt tears well and sting feebly. No more tears. I was not going to cry anymore. In any case, I did not think there were many more tears left. There seemed to be a vast, cool, dead space inside me. I would operate out of that and go through the remaining days, and then we would go home.

When I thought the word, no picture came.

I showered and dressed, feeling as stiff and frail as if I had been beaten or was in a wreck of some sort. It was still very hot, and the sun had burned most of the color out of the canal and sky. I thought I would have some coffee, and then perhaps a plan for the morning would present itself. It seemed important to have one. It was nearly ten when I went downstairs.

The desk clerk—the day clerk, not Alvise—told me that Signora Whitney was waiting for me in the garden, and I remembered then that Yolanda had said we'd have breakfast and then go shopping. Why not? It would pass the time. And then, when I saw Joe again, there would be people about, and I would not have to ask him the huge thing that hung in the air between us.

Why didn't you look for me last night?

And I would not have to see in his eyes the answer. I could not imagine one that would serve.

Yolie was there at a table, drinking *caffè lungo* and poring over a list of some sort. She was in a white linen blouse, sheer gathered skirt, and sandals, her hair tied up in a ponytail, sunglasses pushed atop her head. She looked about fifteen. Her face was scrubbed and shining, her eyes clear. It struck me she had looked younger and healthier each day we had been with her, after those first two in Rome, and I remembered she had drunk nothing stronger than mineral water since then. Rome had obviously been an aberration, a kink of some sort. Tension and anger over the dropped program, the despair of a woman making her way alone in a fast, hard profession. She looked as appealing and wholesome this morning as she did on her television programs, and I liked her a great deal more than I had ever thought I might.

She looked up and smiled, and I smiled back. It was a stiff, small smile, but it made me feel a little better. I could function, then.

"Ready to do some serious Joe Gaillard bashing?" she said.

"You mean shopping?"

I busied myself with the menu so I would not have to look at her. I did not want to talk about last night; what happened was too large and intense for chatter. It felt shameful, as if I had done something so irrevocable and embarrassing that everyone would remember it about me forever after, even though they might not wish to. Maybe it was like that to be a drunk.

"Shopping, dishing, bitching, whichever way you like," she said, pouring coffee for me. "He was an asshole last night, and so was Ada. I told him so too. And I'm going to tell her when I see her."

"You saw him this morning?"

"I sat out here until he came by on his way to go help Ada with Colin, as he so carefully explained his errand of mercy. And I asked him as nicely as you please how you were this morning, and he said he didn't know; you were dead to the world when he got in last night, and he hadn't wanted to wake you. So I let him have it."

"Lord, Yolie, what did you say?"

"That you'd gotten lost way back in that section over near the Rialto where nobody in their right mind goes after dark, and practically walked yourself to death trying the find the restaurant, and a bunch of greasers cornered you and nearly raped you, and you ran into all kinds of other gruesome things, and what in hell did he think he was doing, sitting over there drinking wine with Ada Forrest while you were lost in Venice and Sam and I were out of our minds trying to find you? And that I wouldn't leave my worst enemy to try and find that damned bar by themselves and it had been my impression that you were his wife, not his enemy, though lately you couldn't prove it by any of us. And—"

"Oh, God," I breathed. "You didn't. Oh, Yolie, I was going to handle it. I . . . there was no real harm done."

"No?" she said. "You were shaking and crying and white as a sheet—I thought you were going to faint—but there was no harm done? Cat, listen, it may be none of my business, but it's pretty obvious that you . . . that there's some sort of emotional thing going on with you, or has been. You handle it well, but I've seen the little tremors in the hands, and the sweats, and the pills in your bag. I know the signs. I've been there myself. I think you're much better, and you may be nearly well, but you don't let someone who's fragile, who's . . . healing . . . go into that kind of jeopardy. Not knowingly. And he can't say he didn't know."

"Well, he didn't know I was going to try to do it by myself," I said. "He said in his note for me to call Sam and go with him."

My own words sounded reasonable to me, calm and sane. Perhaps I had overreacted; maybe he had not, after all, been careless with me.

"But you didn't."

"No. I fooled around until it was so late I knew he'd have left himself, and . . . well, really, I wanted to see if I could do it. It seemed simple, and it was still light. I thought an idiot could do it, and I was tired of always being—unable to do things by myself. I'm not a child and I'm not stupid. But I couldn't do it. I guess . . . I'm not ready yet. Maybe I'm not going to be. I feel like such a coward!"

She leaned over and put her hand over mine.

"Listen," she said. "I know what you've had is agoraphobia. And I know you've been in therapy and gotten strong enough to come all the way over here, after not being able even to leave your town for your entire life. You think that's cowardly? You think what you did to those creeps last night was cowardly? Christ, Cat, you turned around and stood up to them, and ran them right out of that campo, and told them to go fuck themselves to boot. As Winston Churchill said, 'Some chicken!'"

We stared at each other, and then we began to laugh. The awfulness of the night before took a sly, sliding skew in my mind and became darkly funny, a thing to remember and laugh about later, a story to tell and retell for many years. I wanted to reach across the table and hug her, gather up the sleek brown solidarity of her in my arms and squeeze as hard as I could.

"You taught me everything I know," I said. "Thanks for more than you'll probably ever dream. What did Joe say when you told him?"

"He said he was sorry, he had no idea," Yolanda said. "And to give him his due, I think he really was. He was quite shaken. He was going to go back up and see about you, but I told him no dice, to hand over his Amex card and go ahead and minister to the newlyweds. And to take you somewhere wonderful tonight all by yourselves, and start treating you like you deserve, and let Sam take his own damned wife to dinner. He said he would."

I felt dizzy. I could not imagine anyone talking to Joe like that. It was not that his presence forbade it, it was simply that he had never done anything to prompt such words. It seemed impossible that it would come up. He had never been anything but cherishing to me.

But we had, I thought, been in a place for some days now where the old rules simply did not hold. Suddenly I wanted to run, literally run, over to the Europa and Regina and take my husband by the arm and pull him out of there and take him home. Just . . . take him home.

"Why couldn't Sam help Ada and Maria with Colin?" I said, and heard my own peevishness in my ears.

"He was going over to Torcello this morning," Yolie said. "He goes at least once every time they come to Venice. Nothing stops him. If Ada couldn't have gotten Joe, she'd just have had to work it out. It's not as cold-blooded as it sounds; he knows she could manage."

"What's on Torcello?" I said.

"I'm not sure. It's a kind of pilgrimage, or something. I know he has a friend over there, an artist, and he takes Sam over to San Francesco del Deserto in his boat. There's an old Franciscan monastery there, and it's very peaceful and beautiful, full of birds and cypresses and wonderful plants, a kind of botanical specimen garden. But that's all there is. Maybe eight or nine monks at most. He's told me that he goes but not why, and I don't think he ever takes anybody with him. I think Sam has a place in every city, a kind of bolt-hole, a retreat, that he goes when things get messy or complicated or overwhelming. Especially if he's painting or is about to start one of his frenzies of work. He's absolutely singleminded about not letting anything get in the way of that. So he has places he retreats to. It's my bet, too, that he didn't want to mess with Joe and Ada this morning. He was really steamed at both of them last night for leaving you."

I felt myself redden.

"I absolutely hate being the cause of . . . turmoil. Discord," I said. "I wish he didn't feel he had to hide from all this. I wish nobody felt they had to *handle* me. I'm tired of it."

"Sam doesn't feel he *has* to do anything," Yolanda said. "He does what he wants. That's the only thing I hope you'll remember about him, Cat. Sam does what he wants to do. And needs to do."

"That sounds pretty cold-blooded," I said. "Like he's arrogant or uncaring or something. But he's not; he's as caring a man as I've ever met. And why do you say you hope I'll remember it?"

I was tired, suddenly, of skating around things. If she wanted to tell me something about Sam Forrest, let her do it. If she thought anything about me and Sam Forrest, let me hear it.

"There are people like us and everybody else," she said slowly, "and there are people like Sam. There are . . . geniuses, I guess. They aren't like other people. Some things have gotten left out. You might not notice it for a long time; they're usually warmer and more charming than anybody else you'll ever meet. But eventually you'll see that the things most people value just . . . aren't there. Some of them, anyway. What they have instead is that enormous force, that focus, that energy, that sheer *talent*. It's enough, as long as you know. But some people . . . vulnerable people, gentle people . . . always seem to get hurt around them. That's what I wanted you to remember."

"Are you trying to tell me something else, Yolie?" I said. My face burned.

"Nope," she said. "Just that. Come on. You ready to shop till we drop?"

I got up and followed her slowly out of the garden of the Fenice et des Artistes and into the little campo beyond it, toward San Marco. The heat was a weight that pressed down on me, and I felt as though I were moving along the bottom of the sea, slowed and dreamy and surreal. It did not matter. It was not worth pursuing. Who knew what she meant? Hadn't we decided, Joe and I, that she had been in love with him once and might still be? I did not want to know what her purpose was in talking so of Sam Forrest, and I was going to let it slip from my mind like a thick ribbon of oil, sliding into the sea around us. I liked her and I felt better and it was my last day in Venice. Enough.

As we crossed the great piazza from the dark shade of the loggias around it, heading for the shops, I thought of something.

"When did Joe tell you I had agoraphobia?" I said. "I don't mind your knowing; it's true. I'm just a little surprised that he'd tell you."

"He didn't," she said. "Ada did. Way back in Rome."

I said nothing, only walked beside her in the white brightness, the air full of the wind of wings around us. She knew, then. Ada Forrest knew of my crippling fear, and still she let my husband go with her to Do Spade without me.

And if she knew, who told her, Sam or Joe?

I did not know which prospect bothered me more. So I let them both go, too, go with the other dark ribbon curling into the blue water, and followed Yolie on in brightness.

We did, indeed, shop until we dropped. By noon our arms were laden with packages, clouds of tissue, beautiful marbleized papers tied with string and ribbons. I, who disliked shopping and seldom fancied, on first glance, anything I saw in shops and stores around the Mountain, fell in love with nearly everything I saw that morning. I was literally drunk on things. I have a good eye, I think, for quality, but that morning all the spoils and baubles of Venice enchanted me, and Yolanda had to steer me away from the dross and toward the gold. I would have bought indiscriminately. As it was, we found treasures and bought enough of them so I would, I knew, literally gag when the bills came in on the Mountain, next month. But it did not seem to me that that would ever happen, and so we foraged on.

I bought a beautiful lace tablecloth and napkins for Maria and Colin, and goblets and pitchers and other glass fantasies for people on the Mountain and for Joe and me and had them sent, and I bought a glorious silk paisley ascot for Sam, laughing to think of it over his matted red chest, and perfume in an exquisite crystal decanter for Ada, and a scarf like sun on butterfly wings for Yolie, and a dress of a silvery green for myself, a simple column of silk that looked like poured green honey on me, strange and lovely. I thought I would wear it to our royal lunch. In a shop far back on the other side of the piazza, one that advertised itself as an outfitter for English gentlemen, I snatched up things for Joe I would never on earth have bought for him in America: shirts of Sea Island cotton so fine they felt and draped like tissue silk, ascots, a gorgeous off-white silk slub jacket that was as light as voile, a black silk T-shirt, a panama hat with a black ribbon band. And a soft, silvery Mandarina Duck bag to carry them all home in.

"Charge it, please," I said, over and over, in the thick, dreaming voice of a drunk ordering one more round, and clerks who looked like dukes and duchesses smiled and said, "*Si, signora,*" and hastened off to wrap my purchases in gold and silver.

"You are," Yolanda said as we ambled back toward the Fenice with our arms heaped high, sweating and sated, "as apt a pupil as I've ever had. I could have you in bankruptcy court in a week."

"You can't take it with you," I said.

When I got back to our room, staggering under my load of plunder, Joe was there, stretched out on the bed with his arms crossed behind his head, sipping wine. He looked at me, not quite smiling.

"Hey," he said. "I was afraid I'd missed you. And I'm not

going to do that again. Come here and give me a kiss and tell me you shoplifted all that. And then I'll start telling you how shitty I feel about last night. It's going to take a long time."

I dumped the packages on the bed and ran around to his side and dove onto the bed and on top of him, pinning him down.

"I'm so glad to see you," I said.

We lay there lazily until well after one, the thumping overhead fan cooling our damp naked bodies, our legs loosely entwined. I felt distanced from everything around me except Joe; I knew we must and undoubtedly would talk soon, but I was reluctant to speak. It was enough simply to be. There had been little of simplicity in our lives in the past week, and I was fiercely reluctant to let it go now. We had not spoken since we made love.

"We probably ought to get up," Joe said finally, leaning over to bite my shoulder gently. "I'm not sure how permissible it is to be late for a lunch with royalty."

"They're not royalty," I said, tracing the sharp crag of his hipbone with my fingertips. "He's not even a real lord. It's a lifetime peerage. He got it for being such an enthusiastic supporter of the arts in Britain, which means he dropped a wad or two to sponsor people like Sam Forrest. He's a Scot from Glasgow who made his first billion in plastics and she's German: East German, actually. An actress, or was. He met her when she was nineteen; she'd just gotten to London and was beginning to get little parts here and there. She was sort of a cause célèbre, I gather; she'd come over the wall when she was sixteen. Literally over it, on her hands and knees. She's supposed to still have scars from the barbed wire on her legs and hands. I think she was a great beauty. He's much older."

"Where on earth did you hear all that?" he said, stretching hugely. I could hear the bones of his spine and hips and knees pop, in sequence. I smiled. It was a sound I always associated with Joe.

"Yolie. She told me this morning. She said Sam was determined to paint her before he even met her. He'd heard about her and was just knocked out with her courage. It was Ada who arranged a meeting, when she and Sam were in London not long after they married. He asked Verna if he could paint her before an hour was up, Yolie said, and the rest is . . . you know."

"History. It's a good thing she was a beauty; what would he have done if she'd been plainer than knockwurst?"

"Painted her anyway, I imagine. Yolie says he was so smitten with the idea of her that he couldn't have seen her plain. He painted her as a Valkyrie, you know. With the spear and the fire and all. It sounds like the worst of the German romantics—Hitler weeping at Wagner—but Yolie says it's stunning. It's in that horribly chic little expressionist gallery near the Tate. Only on loan from Lord Cardigan, though. His name is Orkney, by the way."

He began to laugh.

"Jesus. As in Isles? Sir Orkney Cardigan. What does she call him, Ork?"

"She calls him David, fool. Orkney is a middle name or something. Wait'll you hear what he calls *her*."

"My breath is bated."

"Dump. For dumpling. Yolie says she'd put up with it too, for four billion dollars—but only for that."

"There's little our fair Yolanda doesn't know, is there?" he said. "Or tell."

I knew from the carefully neutral tone of his voice that Yolanda's scolding this morning had nettled him. Joe hates being lectured.

"I brought you a surprise," I said. "Some surprises, rather. They're in those biggest boxes over there. You can take them back if you hate them, but you need clothes so badly, and these are perfect for Italy. You don't have to wear them again until we come back."

He got up and opened the boxes and lifted out the things I'd bought that morning, smiling quizzically as he held them up, one by one. The blinds were slatted against the blinding glare outside, and light fell in stripes across the long, angular length of him. I thought again what a beautiful body he had still, and how wonderful it felt under my hands. The thought flashed quick and bright, like a flashbulb, of another body: thick, powerful, damp with sweat. I shook it away. I rolled off the bed and hurried over to the hatbox on the chaise, and pulled out the pale panama fedora and clapped it on his head.

"Voilà! Instant Italian. Oh, Joe, you look just like a young, skinny Marcello Mastroianni!"

He walked, still naked, to the pier glass in the corner and looked at himself. He cocked his head this way and that and pulled the hat low over his eyes. He turned to me, grinning.

"It's ridiculous. Who wears this stuff?"

But I could tell he liked himself in the hat. He did not take it off.

"People who lunch with Lord and Lady Cardigan on the Gritti terrace, or whatever," I said.

"I'd be booed off the Mountain."

"Who cares? You're not on the Mountain now. Wear it to lunch, will you? Just for me?"

"Just for you, I'll wear it all," he said. Then he came over and took both my hands and sat me down on the edge of the bed and sat himself, facing me.

"Yolie gave me holy hell this morning," he said, "and she should have. I had no idea you'd been through such a bad time last night; I'm sorry, baby. I thought you'd just decided not to come. I truly didn't think you'd try it alone, but that's no excuse. I've left you by yourself way too much on this trip. I'm not going to do it again. You've done wonderfully well over here, so well I forget what you've come through, how bad it was for you all those years. Shit, I haven't even told you, have I? That I'm proud of you? But you're not up to things like last night, and I'm not going to let you go it alone again. I'm going to take much better care of you. If you'll forgive me?"

They were the words I'd wanted to hear, and they should have made me feel like Cat with Joe again, cherished and safe. Instead, I bristled inside, very slightly.

"I did OK by myself, considering," I said. "Did Yolie tell you I ran off a bunch of thugs who were going to rape me or worse in some deserted little campo? Went at them with my nails and told them to go fuck themselves?"

He laughed and hugged me to him briefly. The hat tipped off his head and tumbled onto the floor, and he got up and retrieved it.

"You probably insulted the very life out of a bunch of good blue-collar husbands and fathers on their way home from a little bocce," he said. "My God, Cat, I'd love to have seen that! My good little kitten, her tail all fuzzed up and spitting, yelling Italian dirty words at the butcher and the baker and the glassmaker."

"They were going to hurt me, Joe," I said.

"Oh, honey—"

"They were. You weren't there. I know they were."

"Well, they shan't get a chance, because I'm not going to let you go off by yourself again," he said soothingly, and began to collect his luncheon outfit from among the things I'd bought him. I sat for a little space of time, looking at the naked back of him, feeling inexplicably out of sorts, and then I got up and showered and dressed.

He wore the hat with his beloved chinos, the black silk T-shirt, the creamy jacket with the sleeves rolled up, and a red ascot. He rolled another of the ascots thin and tied it around his waist. He had had his good Brooks Brothers loafers polished to a dull shine, and he wore them without socks. His ankles were slender and tanned and strong. He looked, literally, like no one I'd ever seen before, theatrical and foreign and incredibly handsome, film-star handsome. His face had darkened from the days in the fierce sun of Italy, and his mustache was lighter, spun gilt against his face. His teeth flashed. You could not see the blue eyes under the brim of the hat.

"My Lord," I said. "Marcello Mastroianni in *Miami Vice*. Just look at you! You'll be beating women off you in the streets."

He studied himself again in the mirror, laughed, and turned to me.

"That's a great dress," he said. "Did you get it today? Turn around and let me see."

I turned slowly before him, like a mannequin.

"It only needs one more thing," he said, grinning at me.

"What?"

"Take your bra off, Cat. You don't need it anyway. That dress was made to kind of slide over little nipples."

"Joe!"

"Will you try it? For me? If I can wear all this stuff to please you, can't you just shuck a bra you never did need to please me?"

"I'd feel like a call girl," I said, my face hot. "What on earth do you think you're doing, pimping for me? I'm not going to lunch with Lord and Lady whoever and half of Venice with my tits showing!"

"You can get away with it precisely because you look like a Florentine angel and not a call girl," he said. "Very few women could, but you can. Come on, Cat. Dare you."

"This is absolutely perverted," I said. "You'd hide your face if any woman we know on the Mountain came to lunch with her tits hanging out. Me especially."

"As you say, we're not on the Mountain now," he said. "I just thought since I was going to go native, you might like to try."

I went into the bathroom and took off my bra and smoothed the silver-green jersey dress down over my body and looked at myself in the mirror. He was right. The silky stuff of the dress just skimmed my nipples and hips and stomach, like a tunic; the effect was insouciant and erotic, in a careless sort of way, and very young. I took off the earrings and pearls I'd put on with it, and stripped off the pantyhose, and slid my feet back into the cobwebby high heeled sandals I'd bought that morning. That was right, just dress and shoes and skin. I went back out into the bedroom and stood there, hipshot, while he examined me.

"Wow," he said softly. "I think maybe you better go put your underwear back on. You didn't take off your panties too, did you?"

"Jesus, Joe! Of course not! But I'm damned well not going to put the bra back on. You started this, you can live with it. Come on, we're late already."

We were. By the time we reached the Gritti terrace the others had gathered under one of the ubiquitous market umbrellas. This table, like the one at Sam and Ada's hotel, occupied a choice situation in the corner of the vast floating structure, separated from the glitter of the Grand Canal only by large pots of flowering trees and shrubs. It was, I thought, stepping onto the slightly heaving floor, like being on a giant raft; it felt oddly festive, gay, and carefree.

"Like Huck and Tom, running away on the river," I said to Joe as he took my arm to steady me.

"Well," he said, "here goes nothing," and we walked over to join our party.

Sam and Ada sat together, something I had never seen them do, with their backs to the dancing canal, Sam in the disreputable blazer and a sweat-splotched shirt and blue jeans, the plantation hat resting almost on the tip of his nose. Ada wore a red linen sheath that bared her incandescent shoulders and an enormous red straw hat that left only her sunglasses, her red mouth, and the loose fall of the silver hair on her neck showing. It was a spectacular effect. I saw eyes all over the terrace go to the group again and again, though whether drawn by Ada or by Sam Forrest I could not tell. I remembered anew that his face was internationally known by those who followed the art and celebrity scene, but then I thought that even if you did not know who he was, you would have to look at him. He drew the eye like a wild animal, or wildfire. He stood when we approached, looked Joe and me both up and down, and grinned.

"Holy shit," he drawled. "We have been visited by the *haut monde*, no two ways about it."

I thought his eyes stayed a bit longer on me, and blushed, and put on my dark sunglasses. From behind their comforting shade, I saw him nod, very slightly.

To their right, on a padded wooden bench that ran along the railing on that side of the terrace, Maria Gerard sat, and beside her, his leg stretched out full length on the bench, Colin Gerard half sat, half lay. He was noticeably thinner, and his golden tan had gone mustard-yellow and was flaking over his high cheekbones, but he was smiling widely, and there was color in his face, two hectic circles of it on each cheek, like theatrical makeup. It should have made him look healthier, but somehow it did not. I thought he did not look well at all. His hair was lank and needed cutting, and there were deep saffron circles under his eyes. All at once I was worried about him, quite worried. He looked as if he had been literally eaten away by the pain of his injury.

And Maria. Maria was a pasty shadow of the buxom, joyous young woman whose marriage we had celebrated not a week earlier. She, too, had lost her high color and the shine that had sat upon her like the bloom on a grape. Her unruly dark hair had been dragged straight back and tied low on the neck, like a European peasant woman's, and she had not bothered to put on lipstick. Or perhaps, I thought, watching her chew distractedly on her lower lip, she had eaten it off. Maria had never been one to make herself up, but she did wear lipstick. Without it she looked sallow and used; in a black knit dress and black shoes and stockings that I had not seen before, she seemed to me a foreshadowing of the middle-aged woman she might, with ill

luck, become. Even as she looked up to greet us, she glanced
obliquely at Colin. Worried, I thought. She's worried too. We
really ought to get him to a doctor.

Yolanda was not present.

Across from Maria and Colin, on Sam and Ada's right, sat
the two people we had come to meet. Even without introduc-
tions, you would have known Verna Cardigan for what she was:
an Eastern European woman of once-great beauty, now enormously wealthy. Lord Cardigan, beside her, could have been any
frail old man taking the sun like an ancient turtle at any grand
European hotel. It was Verna who was unmistakably herself and
no one else.

She was not beautiful now, but she was monumentally
handsome, and I thought perhaps that was all she had ever been.
But in her first youth she must have been truly spectacular. There
was something about her, even now at fifty or thereabouts, that
was monumental, like a pagan colossus. Like ... yes, like Sam
Forrest. Lord, I thought, what a matched pair they must have
been in those early London days, when he was painting her. I
wondered if he had kissed her too, on an afternoon of dancing
light, and what had come after that. I looked around the table
smiling a polite, social smile while I waited to be introduced,
thinking there were indeed three Sam Forrest portraits on this
deck over the water of Venice, and wondering if he had kissed us
all, and more.

I had gone a long way yesterday, I thought, a long distance,
measured in more than miles. I did not think I would come
entirely back from it.

"Hello," I said, walking over to Verna Cardigan and putting
out my hand. "I'm Catherine Gaillard. It was lovely of you to ask
us to join you."

"Yes," she said in a deep, cigarette-rasped voice. "I wanted
to meet you. So you are Sam's Cat. His eye has not left him,
I see."

She tilted her head and looked at me intently and smiled.

Her teeth were long and square, slightly yellowed with nicotine, and her lipstick was a startling candy pink, thick and chalky, the kind we had worn in the seventies. Her eyes were hidden behind huge dark glasses, but crinkles fanned out from their corners when she smiled. Her chin was large and square, her nose was aquiline, and her forehead was high and slightly domed. She wore her straw-blond hair in a chin-length straight bob. It fell over one eye like Marlene Dietrich's had. Her skin was olive, sallow with old tan and leathery, and she wore no makeup that I could see except the lipstick. She was lined like fine old glove leather, and there were creases in her face and neck and jowls, and there was no hint that she cared at all. She took off the glasses, and her eyes were the strange dark-lashed yellow of a wolf's. This woman was a Valkyrie, without doubt. Sam's vision had been true.

"This is my husband, David, who has also been so anxious to meet you," she said. "He thinks perhaps Sam needs a tiny little kick from the muse and hoped you would administer it. See, David, she is lovely. He has not done anyone like her before. I think there will be a new show soon, yes?"

She just missed saying, *Ja*, and I could hear the millenniums of undiluted Aryan German in her voice. Her simple surety, the sense of self, was almost frightening. Well, it was what they had always had, wasn't it, those purest of Germans?

David, Lord Cardigan, held up a tiny face like a monkey's, or a very old papier-mâché mask, and smiled with his thin lips pressed together. He did not wear sunglasses, and his eyes were almost colorless, opaque and milky. But I thought they had been blue, and his hair sandy, like a proper Scot's. Remnants of it were pasted over his mottled skull like strands of seaweed. He had liver spots and tissue-paper wrinkles, and the closed-mouth smile somehow held great charm. It was impossible not to smile back.

"Lovely, yes," he said in a cracked, chiming voice. "A Botticelli in her green, like she has just come in with the spring. *La*

Primavera. Or were you thinking della Francesa, Sam? There is that too."

"Bernini, perhaps," Ada said, smiling her red smile.

The Cardigans were silent, studying me, and then they smiled and nodded together.

"One can't see it at first, but then ... oh, yes. Quite stunning," said Verna Cardigan.

"I shall lobby very hard to finance this show, Sam," Lord Cardigan piped.

Sam grinned lazily.

"I think she'd prefer you thought of her as Cat Gaillard," he said. "Wouldn't you, Cat?"

"That would be nice," I said. I was intrigued with the Cardigans, but I was childishly annoyed too. I did not like being studied and cataloged, and I did not wish to be dismissed as simply Sam Forrest's new painting. I could not have said why I cared what Lord and Lady Cardigan thought of me; they were so obviously the people I had thought I would meet in his orbit when we first came to Rome, the international artsy set. And I surely would not see them again after today. But I did care.

"Of course," David Cardigan said. "Of course you are a woman in your own right, my dear, and no doubt a gifted one; all of Sam's portraits are of distinguished women. Verna, and our dear Yolanda, and Ada, such a manager and hostess she is. What is your area of expertise? Don't tell me you race motorcars."

"She takes exquisite care of me," Joe said, stepping forward and bending over Verna Cardigan's large, shapely hand. Diamonds flashed massively in the sun. I looked at him incredulously; surely he was not going to kiss her hand?

"She's a great gardener," Sam said. "Her garden is famous all over the place back home. And an art historian."

"Then you will love Florence," Verna Cardigan said. "The wonderful art, and the Boboli Gardens, and of course the gardens in Fiesole, and the Medici villa at Poggio, and I Tatti, though I think that is private now.... Well, and so this is Professor Joe. Mm-hmm. What a wonderful hat. I think I will take it home with me, and you with it."

She cocked her head and deepened her smile, and diamonds and precious stones flashed all over her: at her ears, throat, wrists, on her fingers. I thought meanly that if Joe planned on kissing her flesh, he'd have to hunt for a bare spot.

I smiled gratefully at Sam and mouthed, Thank you, and Joe laughed and dropped Verna's hand in her lap and said, "Ready when you are, Lady Cardigan," and shook Lord Cardigan's hand firmly.

"I'm delighted to meet you, sir. Thank you for having us to lunch."

"It is entirely my pleasure," Lord Cardigan said, and then, to the group at large, "Don't you think we might have a wee nip more, now that everyone's here? Except Yolanda. Where is that lass?"

It's like he forgets he's a Scot, and then remembers and throws in a Highlandism or two, I thought. He's really more European than any of us.

"Hell, yes, let's have several more wee nips," Sam said. "Yolie asked me to give you her profound regrets. She had sudden and urgent business over on Burano. This is a working holiday for her, you know."

I laughed aloud, and Lord Cardigan raised his wizened paw for the waiter, and the afternoon flowed on.

It's odd about times like that luncheon, when strangers come together in a strange place to do such intimate things as eating and drinking together. There is no context for them, and so, like amoebas, they form their own, make their own shapes by simply flowing in to fill the natural hollows and emptinesses. People behave in ways that are as strange to them and those who know them as if they were actors. Perhaps it's because the other strangers present have no conception of them, and they are free, for once, to choose their roles. On that swaying, dipping, dreamlike raft terrace, under that relentless sun, amid that dancing glitter of foul green water, we became, for that small capsule of time, other people entirely.

Ada became a child, a pretty one, winsome and giggling. She touched people lightly with her long fingers; she patted knees and let her hands linger on other hands, and clapped them together in glee and said over and over, "Tell Verna and David about that, Sam," and "Oh, Joe, do tell everybody what you said on the Lido!"

. And under her capricious urging, Joe did indeed tell what he had said on the Lido, making of it something wry and drawling and understated, so very English I half expected him to say at the end of each sentence, "Don'tcha know?" He was English all afternoon. He sat there under the shade of the umbrella, lounging gracefully, his bare ankle crossed on his knee, the hat riding low over one blue eye, and tossed off Lesley Howard one-liners until I thought Colin and Maria at least, who knew him so well, would jeer him off the terrace. For myself, I would wait until we got back to the Fenice and could read his mood better, but then I planned to tease him unmercifully. It was what I would have done at home, on the Mountain.

But Colin did not jeer him. Colin became the other half of this fedoraed, sockless English county duet and fed lines back to him, Cary Grant playing Brat Farrar, or maybe Michael Redgrave, just back in his shot-up Spitfire, wisecracking as he bled to death in the cockpit with his damp-eyed, stiff-lipped crew.

They were so utterly alien to me, and yet really so attractive and funny, that I could only sit and stare and drink. We all did that. Lord Cardigan kept the drinks coming and Joe and Colin kept the Empire bit going and I sat and drank and drank and drank, and did not get drunk, only more and more paralyzed. Sometime about the third Bellini, I realized that Joe and Colin were being who they were at home, on the Mountain, only carrying it to the ultimate, logical degree. Or they were being who they would love to be and dared not: British to the core. Upper-class, Oxbridgian, donnish, foppish, utterly English. It was what

Trinity was all about: training you to be British and then insisting instead that you be Southern. It must be a great relief to Joe and Colin finally to come out of the closet. They never would have dared to, at home.

I licked peach nectar off my lips and realized I would forget this startling insight as soon as I sobered up a little and, on the main, was glad.

Maria became waspish, a Sicilian fishwife. She tossed her head, pouted, shook her foot, spilled wine down the front of her dowdy black dress, whined and carped and once or twice shouted shrilly at Colin.

"Look at him, jumping around over there, showing off and acting like Sir Laurence Olivier," she said to the group at large. "He hasn't moved in three days without moaning and groaning, and God forbid I should want to put my head out of the room for three seconds. He's in such pain we can't even go down to the dining room, but all of a sudden he's ready to run the four-forty. Colin! For God's sake, sit down and quit posing! If you sprain something else I'm not going to wait on you another second!"

"Easy, old girl," Colin drawled, winking at Joe and Lord Cardigan. "Don't get your knickers in an uproar."

They laughed heartily, the three of them. Maria's brown eyes filled with tears, and she took a deep breath to shout something I knew she would regret. I didn't blame her; I wanted to smack Colin myself. There was nothing of the golden boy about him now.

I reached over and took her arm.

"Don't, love," I said softly. "It's something in the air, and it's going to have to wear off, like malaria. If you can be noble about it now you can lord it over him for the rest of his natural life."

She looked at me. I did not know this woman.

"Sometimes I hate him," she said. She did not bother to lower her voice.

Sam became utterly silent, a sphinx. He did not say another

word until we had eaten our lunch, he who dominated every gathering with his good-natured roars, his drawling, mercilessly funny patter, the sheer, physical fact of him. He pulled the hat farther down over his face, until his eyes were utterly obscured, and sank his chin onto his chest, and slumped motionless in the sun. Perhaps he slept.

I thought of Yolanda's words that morning: "Sam has a place in every city that he goes when things get messy or complicated or overwhelming." Perhaps he had places inside himself he went, too, when things did not please him and he could not retreat physically. Perhaps he was there now. I did not blame him, but the thought made me feel oddly lonely.

After we had finished lunch, the waiter brought espresso and coffee and we lingered on. I was hot and depleted and inert, and longed for a nap in a dim room, and Maria and Sam were silent. But still Joe and Colin nattered on, and David and Verna Cardigan still applauded and encouraged them.

"You two, you are wonderful," Verna Cardigan said. "I'll take you both home with me. Joe, would you really trust your Cat to Sam?" Her tight linen dress had ridden up over her knees, and I could see, then, the cross-hatching of tiny white scars on them, dead white against the dingy tan. Well, so what if she was a genuine heroine? Heroines could behave as smackably as anyone else. I hoped Sam was listening.

It's me he's painting now, lady, I thought. You don't like that, do you?

"Cat's a big girl," Joe said, smiling his new, slow white smile at Verna Cardigan. "She does what she pleases. The painting seems to be doing her a world of good."

"Ah, ha! Sam is good, all right!" Lady Cardigan cried archly.

"Dump, you're being a bad girl now," Lord Cardigan said fondly. "I can't take you anywhere these days."

"I think," I said, putting aside my coffee and beginning to

rise, "that we've kept Lord and Lady Cardigan out in this sun far too long. It's surely time everyone had a rest."

There were protests, but Maria rose too, and Sam came out from under his hat, got to his feet, and stretched. Just at that moment, a scurry and puff of wind found its way under the umbrella, set the napkins aswirl, died away, and gusted again, stronger. Then it began to blow in earnest. It was steady and dry, and felt absolutely wonderful. Around the terrace, people shifted and stretched and seemed to revive.

"That feels heavenly," I said, holding my bare arms out to the wind. It seemed to dry the perspiration off them in seconds.

"Sirocco. Comes across from Africa," Sam said. "It may feel good now, but wait a day or two. We'll probably all have killed one another. The Sicilians call it the murder wind. It's supposed to drive people to bodily mayhem."

"I'll worry about that tomorrow," I said. "Right now I love it."

Lord Cardigan produced a small camera from somewhere.

"Must have a wee photo or two, to remember this fine day by," he said. "I want to have the first photo of Catherine Gaillard, before she becomes immortal."

I shook my head, laughing, but he insisted, and so I let him snap me, and then me and Sam, and then all of us together.

"This'll show up in the authorized biography of Sam Forrest someday," Joe said. I knew he meant it, and loved being in it.

"Now," David Cardigan said, "somebody take one with me in it. Joe, how about it?"

"Yes, do," Verna Cardigan cried. "You look like a photographer for Le Monde or Town and Country. The famous photojournalist, snapping our picture."

Joe grinned and got up and took the camera and squinted into it.

"Turn around and face the water," he said. "It's not going to come out with your backs to the sun."

He walked around us, lining us up, squinting judicially,

stepping back, arranging us again. I thought he was fully into his new role as photographer to the famous. Joe had seen *Blowup* four times.

"Come in closer together," he said, his eye pressed to the viewer. "I can't get you all in. No, it's still not enough. Wait a minute—"

He stepped backward, once and then twice.

"Joe!" I shouted.

He waved at me to be quiet, stepped back again, and went straight down into the Grand Canal. For an instant, only his hat bobbed on the oily water. I gasped, unable to say a word. No one else did, either. Only when Joe shot up out of the water, his eyes closed, spitting and flailing, did anyone move or speak.

"Oh, God, darling!" I cried, and started for him.

Sam Forrest began to laugh.

It did not help at all that it was Sam's great bare arms that fished Joe out of the water as if he had been a child.

Not at all.

Much later that afternoon, just at dusk, Joe and I sat at a small table outside Florian's, having a *caffè granita*. The air was cool and dry, like wine after the sluggish stew of the past few days. The sirocco blew and blew. The great piazza was full of people, strolling, drinking, eating. The light was clear and blue-edged. A few tables over, the small string quartet was sawing away.

"I did it my way," they tremoloed, and then segued into "Those little-town blues . . . "

"Napoleon called it the finest drawing room in Europe," I said to Joe.

"He should know," Joe said.

He was very quiet. He had been quiet since he came out of his long hot shower in our room. He had scrubbed himself until he was raw and red, and I thought once that I had heard him vomiting. But I had said nothing. On our way home, trudging the endless alleyways, people regarding him curiously as he squelched along, I had said, "Darling, it matters less than nothing," and he had said, in a low, hopeless voice, "Cat, please. Just don't talk." So I had not.

I had slept for a while, and I thought he had. Around six he'd said, "Get dressed. I promised you dinner out, and dinner out, you shall have."

"We don't have to. I'd truly just as soon get something here—"

"No," he said. "I want to. Just us. We'll have a drink at Florian's and then just walk somewhere and find something we like and stop."

And so we had come out into the twilight of our last night in Venice, he in shorts because he had nothing else dry, I in pants and a striped shirt. He had given the chinos to the hotel valet to wash and press but had told them simply to keep the rest of the things.

"They won't dry in time," he said to the valet, but I knew he did not want to see them again.

He seemed calm, abstracted, not really upset, but some essential fire had been drowned in that thick green water. I knew he hated the thought of it; filthy, he had called it. Full of excrement and dead things. My heart hurt with pity for him.

I touched his hand.

"We really should get you a typhoid shot or something," I said.

"Ada knows a doctor in Florence; she said she'd call him when we got there," he said dispiritedly. "She thinks he'll probably come to the hotel."

"I'm surprised she didn't just pull out a hypodermic with the proper antidote and tell you to drop trou right there on the Gritti terrace," I said meanly. Ada would, of course, know a doctor in Florence who would come to the hotel.

Joe laughed, unwillingly, and I felt better.

"I'm sorry you didn't get to see Saint Mark's and all," I said.

"I'm not," he said. "I'm sick of Venice. Nothing is what it seems. They even stole their saint."

"Joe," I said suddenly, "do you want to go home? We could. We could fly from Florence to Rome and then straight home."

He picked up my hand and traced the lines in my palm with his forefinger. Then he looked up at me.

"Do you?"

"Maybe so," I said. "It wouldn't be a disgrace. Maybe all this is just . . . not us. Maybe what we are is what we are at home; maybe that's our best talent. It's an honorable way to live; it's a wonderful way to live. So what if it isn't Sam's way, or Ada's? They couldn't live our way."

"I love you, Cat," he said, so softly I almost did not hear him.

"I love you too."

Then he raised his head and looked past me, and something came into his face, a hectic, glittering thing, and I turned and followed his gaze and saw Sam and Ada Forrest coming across the piazza toward us, with David and Verna Cardigan in tow. I saw it go in his eyes, knew the instant I lost him.

"Speak of the devil and he shall appear," Joe shouted genially, rising from his seat. "Sit ye doon, lasses and laddies. Name your poison."

CHAPTER ELEVEN

H E CAUGHT A COLD. OF COURSE HE DID. Joe, who plays tennis on the Mountain in January without his warm-up suit, who dashes all over the Trinity campus during cold spring rains in a sodden, flapping gown without an umbrella, caught a virulent cold from the waters of the Canal Grande and was very sick from it and other things all the way to, and nearly through, Florence. I was quite worried about him for a while, and I think the doctor Ada Forrest knew in Florence, who did indeed come to the hotel, was too.

"The water of Venice is bad," he said, and gave Joe injections for many things, among them hepatitis, tetanus, and something "for the *febbre* . . . the fever."

I heard the coughing start the night before we left, a dry, tight sound that I recognized, with dread, from his infrequent respiratory illnesses and Lacey's frequent childhood ones. I got up and gave him aspirin and found him shivering and turned off the overhead fan. As I was getting back into bed, he said from beneath the muffling covers, "Could you close the windows? The wind hurts my skin."

I lay there for the rest of the night, running sweat and thinking that if we had gone back to the hotel after dinner and summoned a doctor, as Ada and I had wanted to do, instead of going on to Harry's Bar with Sam and the Cardigans, as Joe had insisted upon, we might have forestalled some of what I knew lay ahead. Joe seldom gets sick, but when he does, it is a baroque sickness, florid and full-blown. If he had had medication and a long night's rest, instead of many Bellinis and a great deal of food and many brandies after that, long into the night, we might have been spared this. But somehow I did not really believe it. The bile that boiled in Joe that night was as much the byproduct of his crushed and humiliated spirit as of the canal water. It was going to come out no matter what. He spent his last night in Venice trying to atone, with drinks and food and cleverness, for the foolishness that had plunged him into the water. And he was brilliantly funny and handsome and utterly charming to Lord and Lady Cardigan alike. I truly believe that by the time we finally parted in the Piazza San Marco they had quite forgotten the mishap, and he had forgiven them for witnessing it.

I did not think he would ever forgive the rest of us. Especially Sam. Not for laughing—I could hear that damned braying laugh underwater—and not for rescuing him.

I called Ada Forrest early the next morning and told her he was ill and I thought we should get a doctor.

"I'll be right there," she said, and hung up before I could dissuade her. Joe still slept heavily, tossing and coughing, wet with sweat but shivering. I ordered coffee and was sitting at the desk, sipping it and trying to think what to do, when she tapped softly at the door. I let her in, tiptoeing so he would not waken, and she put her finger to her lips and went silently over to the bed and looked down at him. As if he sensed her presence there, he started and woke.

"Not too good, hmmm?" she said, putting her long fingers on his forehead.

"Not too bad," he said, struggling to sit up. "Christ, I must look like ten miles of bad road. What are you doing here, Ada? Have I died? Is this heaven?"

"A long way from that," she said, smiling. "You have a dreadful cold. We're thinking about getting a doctor for you and maybe staying over another day. It'll be a lot easier traveling tomorrow when you feel better."

"I don't want to stay in Venice," he said fretfully. "I want to get out of this damned . . . miasma . . . and get up into the hills. Do you know any doctors here?"

"No, but the Europa will know a good one. I'm sure he would come."

"Absolutely not," Joe said, getting up out of bed and stumping on tottering legs into the bathroom. He slammed the door, but we could hear him clearly. "I'm going to Florence this morning whether anybody else does or not."

She rolled her pale eyes theatrically at me, one woman to another, a testament to the monumental and eternal obstinacy of men. It was a comforting gesture, for some reason, and I grinned, even though I was very worried and annoyed at his pigheadedness. I was annoyed at her too, obscurely, even while I was grateful. If she had not come so early, Joe would have finally let me talk him into staying in bed and having a doctor. I knew he would. He was grandstanding for Ada Forrest.

I wondered if she got up early to put on her makeup or simply slept in it. Even at this hour, after little sleep, she looked flawlessly put together and polished, silvery hair sleeked straight back and lacquered, red mouth fresh, crisp white shirt tucked into linen pants, soft Italian flats on her narrow feet. She was perfectly dressed for a day of motor travel. She's got a ticket to ride, does Ada, I thought.

"Your wish is our command," she called to Joe through the bathroom door.

And so we set out for Florence, the six of us and Yolanda Whitney, in a caravan of two cars, pinned to the flat, straight road by the relentless sun of the Veneto, buffeted all the way by the sirocco out of Africa. The murder wind.

Ada arranged us.

"There must be someone who knows the road in each car," she said, as the Europa and Regina's launch wallowed along the Grand Canal toward the Hertz agency at the station. Joe sat dumbly, his face blank and thick with misery, on the back bench seat next to Colin, whose foot was buffered with pillows. Sam half stood, half sat, his face under the hat brim turned toward the beautiful stained palazzos we passed. He said little; it was impossible to tell what he was thinking. Gone away inside himself again. This heaving procession of illness and mayhem must be overwhelming to him. He had thought to come with us simply to relax and paint. What a great bother we've been to the Forrests, I thought bleakly.

"I will go with Colin and Maria in the station wagon, and Joe will come with us," Ada said. "That way there will be room for Colin and Joe both to stretch out, and Maria and I can take turns with the car. I can dose the patients too." She smiled. "I have the first-aid kit.

"Sam will go with Yolie and Cat," she went on. "He's a terrible driver, but he knows the roads like the back of his hand, and he's a formidable presence, just in case."

She smiled at him. He gave her a slight, mocking bow.

"I ordered box lunches for us because there's really not a decent place to eat between here and Florence. We can stop somewhere and picnic. We'll need to stretch, anyway. They look wonderful; cold chicken and brioches, and cheeses and a little salad, and lots of wine."

"You think of everything," Maria said. "What would we have done without you on this trip?"

She looked as if she had not slept in days. When had she lost so much weight? I thought she and Colin both looked as if they were dwindling away. The hills, I thought. We need to get up into the hills. The wind blew and blew. It did not seem to cool this morning as it had done the afternoon before. It parched you, tightened your face into a mask, picked at your hair with its fingers, sang in your ears. A dry sirocco, Sam had said when we boarded the launch. No rain in it.

"Thank God for that," I said.

But by noon I would have welcomed the rain. Our battered Opel compact had no air-conditioning, and the wind that buffeted us through the open windows was as hot as the breath of a blast furnace. Moreover, the car's radio fell out on the feet of the passenger in front whenever the glove compartment was opened, dangling by red plastic wires, and there was a rhythmic grinding deep in the car's bowels that spoke of hopeless stalling in some lunar sun-parched mountain pass farther on. The glare from the road was blinding, and though we were not yet on the Autostrada, cars whipped by us on the left at such high speeds that they left the Opel rocking in their wake. Yolanda drove steadily and well, but she did not talk much, and Sam, in the back seat, was fathoms deep in his sketchbook. I could hear the furious scribble, mile after mile. Once, when I looked back to say something to him, he was so utterly absorbed that I turned back without opening my mouth. Sweat ran down his face and his shirt was wet, but I didn't think he noticed. I wondered what he was sketching. Not, surely, the back of my head. Ahead of us, the neat silver-blue station wagon swam steadily on, wavering like a minnow in the undulations of heat from the road.

Hot. Dear God, it was hot!

We moved onto the Autostrada. The Veneto, the flat, humid plain that is Venice's home region, is cupped loosely between the Italian Alps and the Appenines. On a clear day I suppose it is possible to see both ranges; Yolie says so. But on this day we could make out only the Appenines, seemingly so far away as to be unattainable, lying cloudlike on the southern horizon in a strange, colorless, opaque radiance. I spent a long time staring at them, wondering why they were so hard to see. The immediate landscape off A13, the Autostrada, was bleached in pale sun. But all around us, the horizon was nebulous, ghostlike, wavering. Presently Yolie noticed my puzzlement and said, "The *afa*. Back home we call it smog. We're in a bowl; nothing much gets out. You've got exhaust fumes, all the factories and chicken processing plants, all the insecticides, everybody's b.o. and garlic breath . . . it's all here. It can't go anywhere. Add the humidity to it and it's like living on Three Mile Island. I wouldn't live in the Veneto for a million dollars. But on the other side of the mountains it'll be cool and clear as a bell."

I found my breath sticking in my chest for a time after that, but soon even the impulse to breathe shallowly faded, and I laid my head back against the seat and wiped sweat off my face and neck and looked at the mountains. Please, I thought dully, over and over. Please. Let us get to the mountains. Just let us get there. . . .

Just outside Ferrara, Ada flashed her turn light and gestured toward a wide place on the freeway verge, where a clump of willows spoke of water of some sort and there was what I took to be a rest area. One or two other cars were parked near it, but at first I saw no people. There seemed to be shade, though. Yolanda pulled in behind the station wagon and we got out stiffly into the monstrous heat, to have our lunch.

There was water, a small fetid trickle of it in a concrete drainage ditch, but it was enough to spawn a canopy of sheltering willows, and under these, along the banks, tufts of grass struggled to grow in hard-packed earth. Down at one end of the area a few picnic tables were occupied by families, and there were wire trash containers, largely ignored, set about, and a bunkerlike concrete structure labeled GABINETTI. Ada indicated a place at the other end, with no tables but deeper shade and a thicker growth of grass, and she and Maria and Sam set about unloading hampers and a cooler and blankets and a picnic cloth. I would not have been surprised to see flowers in a Venetian glass vase, but none appeared. Yolanda spread the road map out on the steaming hood of the Opel, and I went to see about Joe.

He lay stretched out on the back seat of the wagon, his head resting on a small traveling pillow, covered lightly with one of Ada's beautiful shawls. The wagon was air-conditioned, and the lingering chill of it puckered my wet skin. Joe's eyes were shut, but he opened them when I opened the back door. Despite the chill, his face was flushed, and when I laid my hand on his forehead it was damp and hot. The crease of his neck was damp, too. He was shivering slightly.

"Hey," he croaked. "Are we there?"

"No. Lunch stop. Want some cold chicken and wine?"

"Christ, no. Nothing. Except maybe some Pellegrino over ice. Ada's got some of both. How far are we? I've got to get to a doctor. This feels like more than a cold."

"Not too far." But I knew we had many miles to go yet, hours. "Let me bring you just a little something," I said. "You haven't eaten since last night. That can't help. And I have some aspirin in my purse—"

"No. I don't want anything. Ada's got some stuff that makes me feel a little better. Would you get her for me?"

"Joe, I can—"

"Cat, don't hover, *please*. I can't handle it. Would you just call Ada?"

I turned and walked away, shutting the door carefully behind me. My face burned, and there was a hard, painful lump in my throat.

"Joe would like to see you," I said to Ada Forrest. "He wants some more of whatever you're giving him, and some mineral water over ice. I think he looks awful. I wonder if maybe we shouldn't try to find a doctor somewhere. What's the next big town, Bologna?"

She got up smoothly from the grass where she was kneeling, setting out lunches and wine.

"Oh, he'll be fine until we get into Florence," she said. "I'm giving him antibiotics along with aspirin. It might not hurt to sponge him off a little with ice water, though. I'll be right back."

"Ada," I said, "I appreciate it, but I can sponge him off. You go ahead and give him your magic bullet, but after that I will sponge him off."

She smiled and inclined her head.

"There's a clean washcloth in that plastic bag inside the cooler," she said. "And some ice water in the thermos. I'll be back in a minute."

And she went off across the matted ghost of grass, lithe and silent-footed in her soft moccasins, her back straight and her shirt unsplotched. I stared at the earth, embarrassment humming in my ears. I had sounded like a jealous fishwife.

Maria and Colin and Yolanda looked at one another and then away. Sam stuck a lazy finger into his glass and flicked a spray of cold white wine at me. It felt wonderful on my hot face.

"Come sit down and leave the succoring to the Angel of Mercy," he said, grinning evilly. "She's in seventh heaven and he's plumb out of it. Everybody wins."

"He looks pretty sick to me," I said, as neutrally as I could.

"This drive is no picnic," Colin said faintly. He was lying on the grass with his head in Maria's lap, his eyes closed, bandaged foot extended. She was holding a wineglass for him to sip from and looking down at him with no expression at all.

"Poor baby," Yolanda said, not looking up from her map.

"Looks like a job for the Misericordia," Sam drawled in an unctuous announcer's voice. Yolanda giggled.

"What's the Misericordia?" I said, more to divert attention from myself than from interest.

"Probably the oldest public ambulance service in the world. Started in Florence. Members wear robes and hoods with slits, so nobody can recognize who's who, and they carry the dead and dying to hospitals, free of charge. Volunteers can be garbagemen or royalty; everybody's sworn to anonymity. They go in procession, absolutely silent, with the red cross of mercy banner at their head. They wear black now, but in the Middle Ages it was red. Red robes, for the red death. That's what they used to call the plague. A bell tolls—or, nowadays, a phone rings—and all over Florence men get up from whatever they're doing and just leave without a word. And pretty soon you see them, coming down the street. I saw them right after the flood, in 'sixty-six. It was pretty impressive, all that water and darkness, and these guys all in black, with the red cross going before them, without a sound."

"What were you doing here during the flood?" Maria asked.

"Helping mop up, like everybody else."

I thought of it, solemn ranks of red going two by two down tortuous, narrow old medieval streets, torches flickering, gowns brushing cobbles, otherwise silence. . . .

"I think I'd absolutely die of terror if I were hurt and looked up and saw that coming at me," I said.

Sam looked at me with interest.

"Why?"

"I don't know. It would be like the very angels of death coming for you, two by two, the splashes of red like blood and the hoods like executioners, and the damp glistening on the old gray stones, and just . . . silence. . . ."

He stared at me. His eyes seemed to be turned inward.

"Yeah," he said slowly. "I can see that. Yeah."

"I think," Yolanda said, "that I smell the imminent birth of a painting."

"Might not make a bad one at that," Sam said. He looked past us, seeing . . . what? Nothing we could see.

I felt oddly gratified, but somehow uneasy too. What was it he saw, when his eyes went away from you like that?

Ada came back.

"He's feeling some better and doesn't want to be sponged off," she said. "I think he's gone to sleep. But I believe I'll just take Yolie's car and run back to that telephone we passed—it's hardly a mile—and call on ahead for the doctor to meet us at the hotel. It'll save time, and he can look at Colin's ankle at the same time. It's hurting him more than it should by now."

Colin murmured something and closed his eyes. I thought I might have heard Maria snort, very softly, but I was not sure.

"Let me go with you; you shouldn't have to do all this by yourself," I said.

"No, eat your lunch. Yolie's probably going to make you drive some now, unless she's lost her mind and asked Sam, and you'll need some food in you. It's a haul on in to Florence. I can rest. Maria's taking over for me."

She got up and Yolanda tossed her the keys, and she got into the Opel and slid it smartly out into the stream of traffic booming by. I did not think she even looked back. The thought of driving in that hurtling maelstrom made me almost physically sick.

The food the Europa and Regina had packed was very good. Even in the heat the cold, sweet chicken and crisp salad and icy wine tasted wonderful. We had almost finished when Ada came back.

"Have any luck?" Sam said.

"He'll be there when we get in," she said, smoothing her silver hair back. "And listen, everybody, see what you think about this: I know you four"—she nodded at me and Colin and Maria—"are staying at the Croce di Malta. Now, I have absolutely nothing against it; it's a quirky, wonderful old hotel, but it's right on a main artery from the station into the heart of the city, and it has no air-conditioning and no window glass, only shutters. The noise is going to be hideous, and the heat and grit and dust worse, and nobody will get any rest. So I called our hotel, the Villa Carol, up in the hills just above Oltarno, and they've found rooms for you. Signor Guiducci there knows Sam too, from way back. We always stay there. It's very old and lovely and small, and has a garden and a pool and wonderful unobtrusive service, and it's going to be fifteen degrees cooler. I promise Signor Guiducci will make his rates comparable, and they have a jitney to take you into Florence, free, whenever you want to go. I really think everybody will be much better off up there, but of course if you think—"

"I think you're an angel," Colin said. "I accept. I accept for us all. Let's go there this instant."

She looked at me, smiling obliquely.

"Cat?"

"Of course. We'd be truly grateful," I said. How could I not? She was right. The Villa Carol would be infinitely better for Joe.

"It'll be easier for you and Sam too," she said. "For the painting."

"Yes."

I opened the door of the station wagon on the way back to our car and leaned in and brushed Joe's cheek with my lips. He felt much cooler but did not stir.

"See you in Florence," I whispered.

When I got back to the Opel, Yolie was back in the driver's seat, and Sam was in the front passenger seat beside her.

"It's my turn," I said, my heart pounding rapidly. "Fair's fair."

"It is, and that's what I'm being," she said. "I know you were up with Joe all night, and I like to drive. If I get tired I'll enlist Sam. How much worse can he be than everybody else on the road?"

"Try me and see," Sam said agreeably. He looked back at me. "Everything OK?"

"I think so. He seems cooler, and he's sleeping."

"I meant with you," he said.

"Oh, sure," I said. "Everything's fine."

But it wasn't. I was worried about Joe, and his abruptness had hurt my feelings badly, and I hated his growing dependence on Ada and my seeming inability to help him or even engage him, and I did not want to stay in Ada Forrest's villa in the hills, with garden and swimming pool and perfect unobtrusive service. I wanted us to be by ourselves, Joe and me, if we still could. And there was something, something about Sam. . . .

We had driven almost an hour, into and through the steely haze around Bologna, before I let myself put a name to the feeling. I was disappointed at his preoccupation, hurt and diminished by the distance he had put between us. Whatever the cause of his abstraction, I had to admit I missed the prickling tension, the almost tactile connection, that had grown between us since we met. Missed the prospect of whatever his kiss had promised. . . .

The realization appalled me, and I stretched out as best I could on the Opel's back seat and tried to sleep. Ahead of us, not seeming to be closer, still half drowned in frizzling gray heat, the mountains shimmered.

Please, let us get up there, into the mountains. . . .

If we can just get to the mountains. . . .

For a long time I lay awake, feeling the swaying motion of the road under my head and crossed arms, hearing the rush of the big Lancias and Mercedes-Benzes and BMWs around us, feeling the monotonous vibration of the Opel, feeling hot wind on my face and arms. I thought desolately that I would never sleep, but finally I drifted into that kind of half-drowsing, half-waking state you reach when you try to sleep in a car, when the road noise gets louder and louder in your ears, and then fades away, and then hums in again. I don't know how long I lay there, drifting and snapping back, drifting and snapping. At one point, I thought I heard Yolanda and Sam talking in the front seat.

". . . do it again," I thought she said. "How can you?"

"It's really working now," he replied, or I thought he did.

"I hope to God it's worth it," Yolanda's voice said, blending into the singsong of the tires and the road under my cheek.

What's worth it? I remember wanting to say, and thought I would sit and see if we were any nearer to the spectral succor of the mountains. Oh, the mountains. . . .

But then the road roar grew louder in my ears, and the drone of their voices faded, and when I woke up we were through the Appenines, and through Florence, and pulling into the gates of the Villa Carol, which were of stone so old they were blunted and burnished like satin, and topped with winged bronze lions that looked just as old, and Sam was saying, "Wake up, Cat. Christ, you look like you've been whupped through hell with a buzzard gut."

Ada's doctor, a slender, pale Florentine with rimless wire spectacles whom she called Giampolo, was waiting in the cool tapestry-hung lobby of the Villa Carol when we got there. He had taken the liberty, he said, of checking us in; Carlo Guiducci was an old friend. We could go straight up to our rooms, and he would come with us and see to the two American gentlemen. The porter would bring our luggage. Then he really had to run; Leonora had guests coming. He knew Sam and Ada would understand.

"Perfectly," Ada said, rising to kiss him on both cheeks. He went ahead up the curving stair with his worn medical bag in his hand. She followed. The rest of us came up in an ornate scrolled-iron elevator with a liveried attendant. It creaked and shimmied and seemed to take forever.

The Villa Carol remains one of the loveliest places I have ever seen. It is a three-story Romanesque structure with pale honey-colored stucco walls and the ubiquitous red-tiled roof of Florence, tall, wide, green-shuttered windows, and a graceful curving staircase. It was built, Ada said, in the late fifteenth century. It sits in a cool green park planted with the formal green-black cypresses I so love, full of secret grottoes and small gardens and fountains, broken statuary, stone paths bordered with herbs and flowers, and a long covered loggia flanking a glittering blue pool. The rooms on one side and the back overlook the pool and a terrace with umbrella tables and chairs. The air is fresh and sweet, the scent of sun-warmed flowers and basil and thyme drifts everywhere, bees hum in the picking gardens. The whole affair overlooks Florence from its hill. I still do not know why I disliked it on sight, except to think, It will make a lovely setting for Ada.

Ada's Giampolo was waiting for Joe and me in a large tiled room with luminous faded frescoes on the wall, a tall, narrow canopied bed piled high with white cutwork pillows, dark old armoires and chairs and a desk, and a sitting area in an alcove with a small sofa and a chaise. A velvet-padded window seat overlooked the gardens and pool, and a small balcony off the French doors held wrought-iron chairs and a tiny table. It was a wonderful room; its cool dimness reached out for me as I followed Joe into it. How lovely it would be to have a bath and sink into that tall Viking ship of a bed. I could tell from the doorway that it had feather mattresses piled one upon another.

It also looked as though it would hold only one person comfortably. Italians, I thought sourly, especially the wellborn ones, must be accustomed to sleeping on their backs, side by side in decorous repose, like effigies on a tomb. I foresaw either a roll-away bed for me or three nights spent on the small alcove couch.

The doctor listened to Joe's heart and took his temperature and blood pressure, heard his story, pronounced his judgment on the water of Venice, and gave him several injections. He also left a vial of pills.

"As much rest and sleep as possible," he said. "I will telephone in the morning."

"Thank you," I said.

"It is nothing."

Colin was not so lucky. The impassive doctor poked and prodded, clicked his tongue, shook his head, and pronounced the ankle fractured instead of sprained.

"It should have been seen to immediately and set in a cast," he said disapprovingly. "No wonder he has the pain. I would not be surprised if there was damage."

He left with Colin and Maria in the back seat of his large

black Lancia, saying he would drop him off at the small hospital near Bellosguardo, where he had privileges. His colleagues there would set the ankle and give Colin medication for the pain. He would be well taken care of. "This time" hung in the air.

"It is no trouble," he said to a grateful, trembling Maria. "I live nearby. Perhaps Ada and Sam will call for him?"

And so Colin went and was ministered unto, and came back in perhaps an hour properly cast and medicated, saying the pain was better already. Joe had been dosed and put to bed and was sleeping, and I sat with Sam and Ada in the garden near the pool, sipping whiskey and trying to absorb the profound, expensive peace of the Tuscan twilight. Maria had remained with Colin. Yolanda was staying at a small pensione in Oltarno, where she always stayed in Florence. She knew the proprietors well, she said, and was eager to see them again.

"I'll join you for dinner once or twice, and maybe we'll do some gardens, Cat," she had said, sliding the Opel away from the Villa Carol's portico. "But I really do want to see Freddo and Cari. They're family by now. And they say they have a surprise for me."

She grinned and was gone.

"I wonder what the surprise is," I said after she had gone, more to fill the void of quiet that had fallen than from real curiosity.

"I wonder who it is," Sam said.

"You have a wicked mind," Ada said. "Now what we must all do is simply be still and rest."

It was what we did for nearly the entire remainder of our stay. We rested.

Or rather, Ada and Maria and I rested. Joe slept. All through the first and second day he slept heavily, waked to eat blindly and have a quick shower, then slept again. I sat with him the first morning, but after that I was driven from the room by sheer ennui and the fear of waking him. I staked out a table and bench at the end of the garden, shaded by a thickly vined arbor, and sat there in the forenoons, had my lunch there alone or with Maria and Ada by the pool, sat for Sam in the afternoons, had dinner with Joe, and sat silently in the alcove or on the balcony, trying to read, until bedtime. I slept, badly, on the sofa in the alcove. Somehow I did not want to ask for a rollaway bed, not in this seat of some unremembered Florentine noble. I felt suspended in amber, stopped in time. I was restless but did not want to take the jitney into Florence. I did not know what I wanted and could seem to make no move to break the spell of the slow, sunny days in the Villa Carol. I was waiting, I thought, but I did not know for what.

Maria spent mornings and evenings with Colin, but she swam and sunned in the afternoon with Ada, and after the first day Colin joined them by the pool. You could see that the pain was gone. Even with the cumbersome cast and the crutches, he moved nearly as lithely as he had before, and I often heard his voice in the afternoon, as I sat on the chair Sam had set up for me by the windows in his and Ada's room, crowing and teasing, full of strength and his old untouched, easy foolishness. When I glanced out the window I saw them, Colin and Maria browning in the sun, glistening with sun oil and droplets of water, laughing as they had laughed by the pool at the Hilton in Rome. Colin, I thought, was himself again, but Maria was not. She was happy again, once more the sensuous Latin creature she had been when we got to Rome, and yet not quite the same. There was something older about her now, entirely a woman, the girl all gone.

You will have to grow up to her quickly, Colin, I thought, surprising myself. Or you will lose her.

Ada oiled herself and lay under the sun on a lounge or swam lazily in the turquoise water. It was not crowded because the Villa Carol kept only twenty or so guests at a time, and during the day most of them were in Florence. The ones who were at poolside looked often at Ada Forrest, alabaster in her black bikini and her scarlet mouth. After luncheon she disappeared. I do not know where she went; not to her room. Sam and I were there.

He was painting furiously now, largely silently. He was as withdrawn as he had been on the trip from Venice, but there was a new electricity about him. He fairly crackled with it. Oh, he talked with me, and joked, as he had before, but I did not think his heart was fully in it, and we did not talk deeply again, or long, as we had before. He worked on my portrait in the afternoons; I do not know what he worked on in the mornings, but I knew he was laboring at something. Ada said so, and I could see the piles of sketches and tissue overlays scattered all over the room, along with his clothes. He was losing the flush of sun he had gotten in Venice, and there were strain marks around his blue eyes and his mobile mouth, and the coppery freckles stood out more masklike than ever. His Brillo brush of hair was wild, uncombed, and badly in need of cutting. He could also have used a bath. He looked like a man possessed.

On the second afternoon I got up to go and give Joe his three o'clock pill, as I had done on the first day. I heard Ada calling me and looked out at the pool. She was waving up at me.

"Don't stop," she called. "I'll go up and give him his medicine. It's on the bedside table, isn't it?"

"Yes," I called back. "But it won't take me long."

"Go on with the portrait. Don't break the momentum. I'll sit with him for a while. I need to get out of this sun, anyway."

"Let her," Sam muttered from behind his easel. He had a brush between his teeth and was working with a palette knife, slashing hard and rhythmically.

"Sam, I'm the one who should be taking care of him," I said.

"Any idiot can give a man a pill," he said. "Only you can sit for this portrait. Come on, Cat. We're getting near the end. It's going to be just goddamned wonderful."

I sat back down. He had not commented on the portrait before.

"I'm anxious to see it," I said. "It's going to be interesting to see how you see me."

I was fishing and knew it. I wanted the old effortless understanding between us back, the sense of specialness, the total weight of his attention. I wanted it on me, not on the woman of the canvas.

"How I see you is not the point," he said. "How I see you would probably scare the shit out of you or embarrass you. This painting is about something else that's in you. Something that the paint sees, and the canvas, and the brush. Sometimes it doesn't have a goddamned thing to do with the way I see."

"Well, what do you think? Two more days, three?"

"Can't tell. I'll probably wind it up in Siena. Well before we go on from there. What is it, you getting tired or bored? God, you must be."

"No," I said. "Really, I'm not. But I haven't seen anything at all of Florence yet."

"Well, you didn't really come to Italy to see the sights, did you?" he said. I could hear the knife scurry on and then stop. I thought he was listening to his own words and for mine.

"How do you mean?"

"I mean, you came to be with the newlyweds and all that. I think. Maybe it wasn't what I meant."

"I guess you're right," I said in a low voice. "I didn't really come to Italy to see the sights."

He was still for a moment and then resumed his work. After a few minutes, I knew he was lost to me again.

Toward the end of the session, when the light was slanting lower and I was tiring, a great mass of silver-white cloud, like back-lit alabaster, sailed over the sun, and the light in the room turned odd and luminous.

"God, that's wonderful!" he cried. "Hold that, just like that. God, please let that cloud stay. . . ."

He worked frantically, humming to himself, muttering tonelessly under his breath, jumping back from the canvas, lunging forward again. He paced about, fiddling with the shutters, touching me abstractedly in small pats, moving my neck and arms and head with swift, light fingers. He dove at the canvas again, painted some more, darted out to touch my hair, close my lids with his thumb. I sat very still, let him move me about like a doll, my breath high and shallow in my throat.

He bent and kissed me lightly and softly on the mouth and then sprinted back to the easel. I did not think he was even aware of doing it, but then he put his head around the canvas.

"Did I really do that?" he asked.

"You did. Who did you think I was?"

"I knew who you were," he said. "I always know that."

"You couldn't have proved it by that piddling little kiss," I said, wishing that I could bite off my tongue.

He walked slowly over to me and stood there, his hands on his hips.

"You asking, Cat?"

"No. . . ."

"You don't want to put it off too long," he said, and went back to work.

Just then the sun came flaming out from behind the marble cloud, and after a few more minutes we stopped for the day.

That night Joe coughed dryly and monotonously until nearly dawn. I took the pillows from the sofa and a blanket and slept on the balcony.

Joe was still asleep when I started down to breakfast the next morning, but when I touched his face it was cool and dry, and it seemed to me that his breathing was deeper and fuller than it had been for several days. Just as I was pulling the door shut behind me, he called sleepily, "Cat? Where you going?"

I went back into the room.

"Down to breakfast. I thought you were asleep. How do you feel?"

"I think I'm better," he said. He stretched, long and hard.

"God, every muscle in my body is sore. Are you coming back up?"

"I will if you want me to. But I thought not; you coughed all night long. Maybe you ought to sleep some more."

"Well, maybe I will. But first I'm going to take a long shower and shave. I can smell and taste me. And then I'm going to order some breakfast. Real breakfast, not a goddamned *caffè lungo* and a hard roll. *Then* I'll sleep a little more. Maybe I'll get up for lunch; will you have it with me?"

"Of course," I said, smoothing back the lank hair on his forehead. It looked darker, sunless. His face was pale and gold-stubbled. "But let's have it up here. Maybe, if you feel like it, you can come down for dinner. You don't want to push too hard with the drive to Siena coming up tomorrow. Meanwhile, I'll ask them to bring you something breakfasty to eat."

"I'm sorry about this," he said, looking up at me. "I don't even remember getting here; I'm going to miss Florence completely. Have you seen even a scrap of it?"

"I think I might go down this morning," I said. "Maria said she wanted to do a fast lap around the Uffizi. I haven't missed it, Joe. I've seen the entire city spread out below us every day and every night, and to tell you the truth, it's been good to just stop for a day or two. Everybody was tired. This way we'll be fresh for Tuscany. We can always come back to Florence; Ada says this isn't the time to see it anyway. It's wall-to-wall students and tour buses now. And hot."

"How's Ada?" he said. "The last thing I really remember is Ada stuffing pills down my throat in the back seat of the car. How's everybody? How's Colin? How's the portrait coming?"

"It's getting down to the wire," I said. "Sam says it should be done by the time we leave Siena. Everybody's fine. Colin's ankle was fractured, not sprained. It's in a cast and he feels much better. Yolie I don't know about. She's staying somewhere in the old section with a boy toy presented to her by her loving land-lords. Or that's what Sam says, anyway. She'll meet us here in the morning. You haven't missed much."

"I've missed you," he said, and drew my hand to his mouth and kissed the palm.

"I've missed you too," I said, my eyes filling.

Everyone was at breakfast on the terrace except Sam. Ada said he was working on the portrait's background.

"It's no use even trying to talk to him when he's this close to finishing," she said. "I don't envy you, Cat. I'll just have them toss some raw meat in to him. I plan to stay well out of his way all day."

"Want to come with us to the Uffizi?"

"Oh, no," Colin said. "She's promised to play seven-card stud with me this morning. If I can't go down to Florence, at least I can win all Ada's money."

"Don't be piggy, baby," Maria said indulgently. "Ada's done nothing but hang around here and dose sick people for two days. Give her a break. Maybe she'd like a breather from the halt and the lame."

"It's not a lot of fun to be stuck up here while everybody else is off seeing Florence," he said sulkily. He was in plaid madras shorts this morning, with a freshly ironed oxford shirt and a scuffed Topsider on his bare brown foot. His face and arms and legs gleamed red-gold with fresh sun, his chiseled face was flushed bronze, and his hair gleamed. Except for the cast ankle, he was as perfect as one of the statues we would see in the Loggia dei Lanzi this morning. He seemed untouched by pain or much else, new-minted. The thought slunk guiltily through my mind that at home, on the Mountain, he would have seemed a young god, immortal. Here, in this rich old country, he seemed merely barely finished.

Do be careful, Colin and Maria, I thought. You really should go home.

"I don't mind staying; I want to," Ada Forrest said. She wore white slacks and a pale peach T-shirt almost the color of her skin and looked like a piece of fruit at the absolute shimmering zenith of its ripeness. "I hate Florence in the summer. I'll stay and pass out the morning medications. Doesn't Joe get a pill about midmorning?"

"He can take it himself," I said. "He's much better. I'm going to send him up breakfast and then he's going back to sleep, and will probably have dinner with us. Don't bother, Ada."

"It's no bother," she said.

The Villa Carol's smart van dropped us, at Maria's request, at the Oltarno entrance to the Ponte Vecchio, and we walked across it slowly, past the dim, fabulous small jewelry shops on either side, like Aladdin's caves, past the vendors and portrait artists and sidewalk performers. It was like going to a circus, a medieval one. We were caught fast in the slow-swimming shoals of tourists and Florentines. The bridge smelled of dust and close-packed people and the good, fishy, river-water stink of the Arno below, and simply of great, dry, shadowy age. I felt a prickle of the old bridge fear, a warning curl, like a subterranean growl from a waking dog, and I walked lightly and breathed shallowly, waiting to see what the fear would become. I took Maria's arm, more out of a need for the feel of familiar flesh than to steady either of us. But the fear remained at a low simmer, giving a kind of preternatural seeing to my eyes, a clarity to the teeming dimness of the bridge. I remembered reading somewhere that in times of stress, the pupil dilates so that as much light as possible will be let in, so that nothing dangerous will remain unseen. It served me well on the Ponte Vecchio. I believe I saw things that morning, details, bits of richness, that perhaps the others did not. After a few minutes I began to revel in it. I still remember that walk.

"It's really wonderful, isn't it?" I said gratefully to Maria.

"It is," she breathed. "It's incredible. I'm so glad we got away."

I thought she had been going to add "by ourselves," but she did not.

I stopped at a shop and bought things: a signet ring for Joe that I knew he would not wear on the Mountain, a pair of lovely, austere, dull-silver candlesticks for Corinne, a heavy gold cuff bracelet with bas-relief lions and unicorns on it for Lacey. She would love the matte satin feel of it, and the fine detail of the animals, and it would look beautiful on her slender arm. I had a sudden sharp vision of her standing just here, as I knew she had stood three summers ago. She would have smelled the smells, tasted the dust and river thickness, heard the complex symphony of sounds, felt the cobbles beneath her feet and the presence of many people all around her. There was little she would have missed. She would have perceived the bridge in a crystal wholeness that few sighted people did. The thought made me suddenly and fiercely glad. I missed her, in that instant, as you miss a newly amputated limb.

For the first time, I know that you are truly not handicapped, my darling, I said to her silently, across the enormous gulf of miles. I wish I had known that from the beginning. It would have been much easier on you.

We dodged through the traffic hurtling along the embankment and walked diagonally across the Piazza Pesce into the Uffizi Gallery and into a world made of flesh and shadow and light. It literally stopped the breath.

We were totally silent as we walked through the great crowded salons. Few other people spoke, either.

It was the most unrelievedly sensuous two hours I have ever spent. I knew that many, perhaps most, of the paintings here had a religious genesis, either Christian or pagan, but it was the sheer, living presence of naked flesh that took my breath. I thought that if I had been in an actual place among so much nakedness, among even so much ideally beautiful nakedness, the impact would not have been the same. It was the insight, the vision of all those long-dead eyes that brought this flesh so powerfully, so particularly, so—to me—erotically alive. This was, I realized perhaps for the first time, what the artist's eye was. It was pure focus; it was a funnel, a powerful prism, that shut out all extranei and gave to the subject its staggering immediacy.

Flesh in these paintings was flesh you felt on your own, with nothing between: a baby's sweet pliant flesh, as in the early madonnas of Cimabue, Duccio, and Giotto. The warm, damp flesh of the young and unearthly, as in the ripe, pearled Botticellis, the *Primavera* and the *Birth of Venus*. The overtly and rankly female flesh of di Credi's Venus. The pale, secular flesh of the Medici portraits, the frankly and skin-prickingly erotic self-explored flesh of Titian's *Venus of Urbino*. The bursting, palpable flesh of Michelangelo's *Holy Family*. My skin crawled, cried out for touch. We did not speak until we were out of the Uffizi.

"Wow," Maria said. "I wonder how many babies have been conceived after a trip to the Uffizi?"

"I wonder how much of the exalted Stendhal syndrome was just an extreme case of horniness?" I replied. "Although I doubt you're supposed to react this way. Or admit it, rather. Do you think there's something wrong with us?"

"Nothing"—Maria smiled creamily—"that a nice, long nap back at the Villa Carol wouldn't cure. My God, Cat, you're actually blushing."

"I am not." I laughed but knew that I was.

I wondered what she would have thought if I had said, Whose room at the Villa Carol?

We had thought to linger among the sculptures in the Loggia dei Lanzi, but we had lost time in the gallery, and the driver was meeting us up in the Piazza della Signoria at noon. It was eleven now, and we were both powerfully thirsty. So we hurried through it toward one of the outdoor *caffès*. Even so, it was inescapably more of the same: flesh, naked and palpable, somehow even more so than the paintings. This was secret flesh bared to the air and sun of the world, flesh that could be touched, that cried out to be handled. Bandinrelli's bulbous *Hercules*, that Cellini had compared to "an old sack of melons." Ammanati's *Neptune Fountain*, that the sculptor himself piously declared later to be an incitement to licentiousness. Giambologna's *Rape of the Sabine Women*, leaving no doubt at all as to who was doing what to whom. Donatello's impassive and somehow profoundly corrupt *Judith and Holofernes*, nearby.

And Michelangelo's *David*. Even when we sat down at last for *caffè granita*, our eyes went to the *David*, again and again.

"It's no wonder the Medici coat of arms has balls on it," Maria said, sitting in deep shade but stretching her legs out to the sun. They were brown now, sleek, newly shaved and lotioned. Her toes, in sandals, were bare and polished.

I laughed. "You seem to have noticed everything."

"How could you not? There are balls everywhere in Florence. Every guild sign and palace and church and shield and escutcheon in this place has balls on it. Not, of course, to mention every statue. Didn't you have that course on Florentine iconography in Art History?"

"No. We were still violently Episcopal in my day."

"You just want to reach up there and bounce that little bundle in your hand, don't you?" she said, looking up at the *David*.

"Do," I said, feeling my chest redden. "I'll enjoy explaining to Colin why you're in the Firenze pokey."

We sipped our drinks in silence. Then she said, "Do you feel as if you're changing, Cat? Over here?"

"How do you mean?" I did not want to talk about this.

"You. You and Joe. Me. Colin. I feel like I'm on some runaway train or something, and everything that's familiar to me is receding at the speed of light. I feel terribly out of control."

It was so exactly how I had felt in Italy that I wanted to grasp her hand in relief, babble, pour it out. But I sensed that she was reaching for reassurance, the young woman to the older one. Almost daughter to mother. I wished I could have said, as she needed, Everything will be all right. You're imagining things. But I could not. She *was* changing, had changed, before our eyes. I did not think she was in control. I knew I was not.

"I think foreign travel does change things," I said slowly and carefully. "I think anything that's so profoundly different alters your view of the world. But I don't think it changes people into someone they've never been before. I think rather that it adds to them. You're you, only more so."

I could tell by her face that she did not believe me; it was not what she meant. I did not blame her. I didn't believe it either.

I reached over and put my hand on hers.

"Sweetie, go easy on yourself. Go easy on Colin. Look at what's happening; you're still so very young, both of you. You're not who you're ultimately going to be. You'll change a dozen times in your lives. You've just gotten married and you've just come to Europe for the first time, and he's been seriously hurt a long way from home, and you've been thrown with people you don't know, people who live very differently from the way you have. No wonder things feel strange. How could they not? We should have let you come alone, Joe and I, and I think Ada and Sam should have butted out too. You've had no chance at all to get to know each other."

"We had those years back home to do that," she said doubtfully, but I could tell she was thinking about it.

"Not as married people, not as a formal couple. It's different."

"But you and Joe have changed—" she said, and fell silent.

I felt my breath go high and thin.

"Not dramatically, I didn't mean that," she said hastily. "Not in any bad way. You're just not the same over here as you were back home. *You* seem . . . more solitary than I ever thought you were, more adventurous. You'd never have gone off by yourself at home like you did in Venice, or at least I guess you wouldn't have . . . we really never saw you except with Joe. It's a nice difference. It's not just you; he's different too. Of course, he's been sick, too. . . . I'm babbling." She fell silent.

"You are. It's the heat. Drink up."

"The only one who hasn't changed is Colin," she said in a low voice. She looked up at me under her lashes. I knew we were at the heart of it.

"He hasn't had much chance to," I said lightly. "He hasn't

seen anything since he got married but the inside of hote
rooms."

I wasn't going any further with this.

But her face cleared, and she said, "He really hasn't, has
he?" and I knew I would not have to.

We finished our drinks and looked around for the van
driver, but did not see the smart maroon livery among the
throngs in the piazza.

"What do you think of Ada?" Maria said.

I will not do this, I thought.

"I think we'd still be sitting on the curb in Rome, trying to
get to Venice, if it hadn't been for her," I said.

"She isn't what I thought she'd be," Maria said. "She's not
like the others I know in Mother's family. We're such a loud-
mouthed tribe, the Italian half. We argue and yell and cry and
make scenes. She's out of another place entirely. An Italian Step-
ford wife or something. Only a million times smarter. I'm grateful to her down to the soles of my feet, don't think I'm not, but
somehow I wish she'd go home and let us do it by ourselves
now, just the four of us. It's like she has this big agenda, but
nobody knows what it is."

"Sam would be like a beetle on its back if she went home," I
said lightly. This lumpy, unworldly child missed nothing.

"I wish she'd take him with her," Maria said with sudden
vehemence. "He's charming and a genius and I know I'm lucky
to have him in the family, but he . . . he sucks all the air of a room
when he's in it."

"He does, doesn't he?" I smiled.

"Does it bother you—you know, when he's painting? When
you're alone with him?"

Her cheeks reddened, and she looked down at her glass. I
felt light-headed. It was obvious she thought there was something between Sam and me, or could be.

"No," I said. "He's very easy to be with. Totally absorbed in
what he's doing."

"He certainly doesn't pay much attention to Ada," Maria said. "It must be hard for her. She doesn't seem to have anything much of her own. She must miss that. I wonder how she makes up for it."

I saw, suddenly, where this was going. I held up my hand for the waiter and at the same time saw the van driver standing at the edge of the piazza, scanning the crowd. I stood and waved.

"Over here," I cried.

On our way back to the villa we spoke only of paintings and statuary and of the things we had bought on the Ponte Vecchio. I knew we would not have this conversation again. I would see to it.

When I got to our room, I softened my steps and eased the door open, in case Joe was sleeping. But he was not. He stood at the French doors onto the balcony, his back to the room, in only his pajama bottoms. The rush from the overhead fan stirred his hair, which I could tell was newly washed even in the dimness, even from where I stood. It lifted and fell silkily with the wind. His narrow torso looked pale and thinner, so that his ribs made shadowy stripes against the skin. He was looking straight out into the garden, over the pool.

Ada Forrest stood in the circle of his left arm. Her head was tipped toward him, and the silver hair, loose today, fell against his shoulder. She was, I thought, not so tall as I was. When I stood there my head was level with his nose. Hers reached only to his chin. I thought at first that she too was naked to the waist, but it was only the pale peach jersey that she wore. They did not move, and I did not. I did not breathe, either.

Then Joe bent his head down to her, and she lifted hers, and he kissed her. I moved then. The air around me rang and shivered as if there had been a huge silent concussion in the empty hallway, a blast. I ran on tiptoes through it and up the staircase at the end of the hallway to Sam and Ada's room and knocked on the door.

Sam answered it in a ratty blue terry-cloth robe, wet all over, barefoot. He blinked at me in the dimness.

"What's the matter?"

"Nothing, I just forgot my key and I . . . there's nobody in the room. I thought you might walk down to lunch with me, if you're going, but you don't usually, do you? It was a stupid idea; I'll just get the clerk to let me in. . . ."

He pulled me into the room and sat me down on an alcove sofa identical to mine except that it was covered with strewn clothing and sheets of an Italian newspaper and the remains of his breakfast on a room-service tray. He dumped the clothes on the floor to make a place for me.

"What's the matter, really? Are you sick?"

"No, I swear I'm not. I ran up the stairs, is all. And it's hotter than hell, and I didn't have any breakfast, and Maria and I went to the Uffizi, and it was crowded as all get out—"

"Ah," he said. "Stendhal. Let's order some lunch up here and have some wine with it, and you can sit for a while, if you will, and then I'll let you go take a nap till dinner. We're going to eat in the garden. Yolie's coming. I gather from her tone of voice her rooster has flown the coop."

"Oh, I'm sorry," I said, and clamped my mouth shut. I knew if I talked anymore I would begin to cry. Poor Yolie. Her man had gone. She must feel as if she had a cold sword blade through her very guts. I did.

He phoned down for lunch, one hip resting on the desk, staring at me as he talked. The room was full of crumpled paper from his sketch block, as it had been the day before, and the rich, pungent smell of fresh oil paint hung thick in the air. His palette was uncovered. He had been working on my portrait. As Ada had said.

I concentrated fiercely on talking lightly and normally and eating my lunch and drinking the wine that came with it. I thought I did it well. I felt totally removed from this room, from this place; I felt as if I watched myself from behind a pane of glass. My ears still rang, and my lips felt numb, but all in all I thought I did very well indeed. I could even laugh at Sam's foolishness. I could even make some small teasing sallies myself. But it was better when he was quiet, when he worked. When he did, with the same restless, prowling intensity as the past two days, I could lay my head back against the seat and close my eyes. Then it felt as if I were floating in a bubble, far above the earth.

He worked in silence for a long time, and I drifted in my bubble, thinking only that I would find some way to keep it around me, intact, and that way I would get through the night, and the day after it, and the days after that. Perhaps I could even keep it whole across the Atlantic and up the Mountain.

After that, I could not see.

I think I must have dozed, because when Sam said, "Well, look who's back in the land of the living," I started violently and shot to my feet, heart pounding in my ears. His voice had seemed to boom in the air like cannon shot.

He stood on the balcony looking down at the pool, and I went to look too. Maria and Colin and Joe sat in chairs at the umbrella table where our group always sat, sipping drinks and laughing at Ada, who was doing a sinuous, absurd little dance on the burning terra-cotta of the pool apron. She wore her black bikini and had her silver mane pulled over her face, and a scarlet hibiscus thrust between her teeth. She should have looked ridiculous, but she looked exotic and wonderful and all but naked, a pagan eater of red flesh. Joe called something to her through cupped hands, and she laughed and tossed her hair back and rushed at him and planted a long kiss square on his mouth and went back to her dancing. Colin and Maria laughed and cheered and clapped.

"That should make him all well," Sam said laconically, and then turned and looked at me.

"Is that what's bothering you? Your distinguished husband and my charming wife?" I shook my head, but he said, "I believe it is."

"No."

"I hope not. It means less than zero. I mean really less tha
nothing. Ada does that. Some women shop and some do volun-
teer work; Ada kisses men. Each according to their talents."

My husband doesn't kiss women, I thought. Or didn't. And
this kiss is not like that other one.

Aloud, I said lightly, "I don't mind. Why should I? Joe's
wife kisses Ada's husband. Or had you forgotten?"

"Not hardly," Sam said, looking at me without smiling.
"Not so's you'd notice."

"Maybe," I said, the ringing in my ears escalating until it
seemed to roar in my head, "Ada's husband ought to do it again.
Just to make sure he remembers how."

He stepped back into the room and opened his arms to me
and I went into them, and raised my face, and closed my eyes.
When he kissed me this time, when his mouth moved to my
throat and then to my breast, when he pulled me so hard into
the curve of his body that I could feel the heat of him through
his clothes and through mine, I did not pull away. I pressed him
against me so tightly I could feel my nails go into his flesh
through the shirt. Explain that to Ada, I thought dizzily. Something deep inside me, which had been clenched and chilled ever
since we got to Italy, heated and softened and opened. I heard
a sound start in my throat. Against my breast, his mouth
answered me.

The phone rang.

I froze. He did not move either.

"Let it ring," he murmured hoarsely.

But the moment was gone, broken. Finally he moved away
from me and went to the desk and picked the phone up, pushing
the wiry tangle of copper hair off his neck. I stood looking out
into the garden, seeing but not registering that Ada was back in
her chair and everyone was talking normally now. Presently I
felt, rather than saw, Sam behind me.

"Yolie, wanting to know what time," he said. His voice was

⌐ thick and hoarse. "She's a regular ballbreaker, is Yolie. Well, ⌐at. Saved by the bell. Unless you were asking?"

I turned to him and put my hands on his shoulders and smiled. Somehow things were better now. I could not have said why, except that the savage, shocking pain was gone. I felt equal to anything.

"Not yet," I said. "Not quite yet."

"Ask soon, Cat."

"I will," I said. "I will."

The session was over and we both knew it. I gathered up my packages and started to the door. I did not care, now, whether Joe was in our room or not. I could handle it either way. I had a formidable weapon. I could effect it with one word: now.

He walked with me to the door.

"I forgot to ask you," he said. "What did you see? What did you like best?"

I started to laugh.

"Balls," I said. "I saw balls."

I was still laughing as I reached the staircase. Behind me, I heard him start to laugh, too.

Our last dinner in Florence did not quite jell. The food was wonderful, and we drank a great deal of wine before and during dinner and had brandy and grappa after, but there was still a lingering feeling of unease and disorder. I could have accounted for it if I thought Joe knew I had seen him with Ada in our room, but I knew he had not. And I knew I was handling myself flawlessly. You can always tell when you are doing something well.

Joe had been asleep when I got back to our room, and I had bathed and changed into the green dress I had bought in Venice and gone down to the little library off the lounge to read until dinnertime. He did not appear until we were all seated at the table on the loggia, in the vine-shrouded arbor where I had sometimes sat during the days. In the flickering light from the hurricanes he looked very thin, and there were still shadows under his blue eyes, but his narrow face was washed with new color, and the silky fall of his hair seemed lighter, sun-bleached. There was a kind of interior hum about him, a motor running softly and strongly somewhere inside. It was the way he had been with me in the early days of our marriage, when he and I both had known that we would soon make love. I felt a kind of weary, bitchy amusement when he sat down next to me and slipped his arm around me. His hand slid back and forth on my bare back, under the dress. Now, at the evening's end, his fingers traced my shoulder blades and ran lightly up and down my spine. Save it, bubba, I know who lit that fire, I thought. I smiled at him.

"You look good," he said into my ear. "You really look pretty tonight, Cat. You must have had an awfully good time at the museum this morning."

I turned my face into his neck and bit his earlobe delicately and quite hard. I felt him flinch slightly.

"Fabulous," I said. "Maria and I saw more naked balls than at a marine boot camp. Marble, of course."

"Did you, now," Joe said. Across the table, Sam laughed. I looked at him. I had not done that much this evening. Our eyes met and held, and I turned away.

"What a pity they were marble," Yolanda said.

"Isn't it," Maria said from across the table.

There were round pink spots on her cheekbones, and her eyes glittered. Beside her, Colin tossed back brandy and did not look at her. He had said little all evening; Maria had chattered.

They've had another fight, I thought. We are not going to survive this trip. None of us are.

Yolanda was drinking quite a bit, for the first time that I knew of since that awful night in Rome when Joe had physically carried her into the Hassler. She was not at all drunk now, though, simply quieter than usual, and somehow very sharply focused. Her face had a full, suffused look to it, and her mouth seemed swollen, and there was an unmistakable fading hickey on her neck. When she had first appeared at the table, Sam had grinned at her and said, "Christ, Yolie, you look like you been rode hard and put up wet."

"I have," she said, grinning fiercely back at him. "Don't you wish it had been you?" To the rest of us, she said, "I've missed you guys. What's been going on in Eden?"

"Sam is nearly done with Cat," Ada said, smiling across the table at me, shimmering in silky white. "And Colin is in a cast but out of pain, and Joe is much better. Maria and Cat went to the Uffizi this morning. Other than that, we've been very quiet. We've stayed pretty close to home."

"Sounds like a veritable barrel of monkeys," Yolie said. "In case you were thinking of asking, I've stuck pretty close to home, too, at least until this morning, at which time the lovely and talented young Cosimo got his feelings hurt and went home to his mama. She's going to get the shock of her life. He's definitely wind-broke, as Sam would say."

"I bet he is," Sam said.

Every one of us at this table is in some kind of state over sex, I thought suddenly. I am so goddamned sick of sex and innuendo and nuance I could vomit.

At the end of the meal, when we were sitting and drinking grappa, putting off getting up and going to our rooms, Joe said, "I did a smart thing. I went off and left all our travelers' checks in the safe at the Fenice. You guys are going to have to pay up till we get to Siena."

For some reason it infuriated me.

"Damn it, Joe," I said tightly. "When did you discover that wondrous feat?"

"When I got up to take a bath this morning."

He looked at me in slight confusion. His brows puckered in annoyance; I was not generally sarcastic with Joe.

"I wish you'd told me. American Express is right past the

Ponte Vecchio, on the Via Guicciardini. Maria and I were there."

"You were already gone, Cat," he said coolly. "It doesn't matter. There's bound to be an office in Siena."

He looked at Ada and raised his eyebrows questioningly.

"There is," she said "It's up near the big banks. I know exactly where. I'd be glad to run down tomorrow afternoon and get them for you. You ought not stand in line for hours, and it usually takes that in a small office like Siena."

"I can get them," he said. "I feel fine now. Really."

"Maybe we could all go get them," I said.

"I have an even better idea," Yolie said. "Cat, why don't you stay behind for another day and get them here in the morning, and then we can see some gardens and maybe the Pitti tomorrow afternoon, and I'll show you my Florence. You can have half of my bed; it's absolutely huge, and I promise they'll change the sheets. We'll drive over to Siena the next morning and meet the others. It's only forty miles."

"Well, you know, maybe I might," I said slowly. I thought of a slow, sunny day, full of gardens and secret old streets and a long dinner in some tiny dark restaurant in a lost part of the city, and laughter. Easiness and laughter.

Joe put his hand on my shoulder.

"I don't think that's a good idea at all," he said. "I don't think Cat can handle that by herself."

I turned to look at him. He stared impassively back at me.

"Yes, I can," I said.

"Cat, I want to do about another hour tomorrow afternoon," Sam said. "We're getting awfully close now."

I looked at him across the table. In the candlelight his face, too, looked closed, almost unknown. The anger flared again, surprising me.

"Sam, really," Ada said. "Cat needs some time to herself. You've had sole custody of her almost every afternoon."

"I really need her now," he said.

'No, you don't," Yolanda said briskly. "You're spoiled. ..at's one day? Cat hasn't had much time just for herself this .rip."

"Do what you like, of course," Joe said distantly. He moved his hand from my shoulder. "Ada can get us settled in."

There was a silence around the table. I could feel it rippling, like water when you have tossed something heavy into it. I looked across at Yolanda in the wavering light and smiled. She smiled back.

"Let's do it," I said.

CHAPTER TWELVE

THEY LEFT EARLY THE NEXT MORNING FOR SIENA, Ada at the wheel, Maria beside her, Sam alone on the middle seat, already opening his sketchbook, Joe and Colin on the back seat.

"Sick bay," Sam said as they climbed into the back. Joe looked at him sharply, but Sam only grinned benignly and said to me, "You can still change your mind, Cat. No telling what you're going to miss."

"That's as good an argument as I ever heard for staying," I said. "Be careful, you all. We'll see you tomorrow around lunchtime. Wait for us."

Joe looked at me through the open window. He seemed much better; rest and the new coat of tan made him look himself again. He had been fast asleep when I came out of the bathroom the night before, and was nearly dressed when I woke this morning. We had said little, but that had been pleasant. I was relieved. I knew he had been genuinely angry at me last night about stay-

ing over. I wasn't sure why. It was hard to read Joe's anger in this
place. It was hard to read my own.

I knew he was still annoyed at me, though. He gave my
cheek only a swift, glancing kiss when he got into the car.

"Be very careful," he said. "I still don't like this."

I put my hand lightly over his.

"It's only a day," I said.

I watched the station wagon out of sight down the curving
drive and then went out into the garden and sat down to wait for
Yolanda. It was early yet for the other guests, and I had the terrace and the pool to myself. The sun had not yet climbed over
the line of cypresses at the far edge of the garden, and the pool
was perfectly still, a mirror giving back terra-cotta urns and
flowers, the sentinel fingers of the cypresses, the sky still
brushed with fingers of pink cloud, but blue high up in its vault.
There was no sound except birdsong and occasionally, from the
road far below, the cicada buzzing of *motorini*. I took a deep
breath and inhaled thyme and the sweet scent of drying grass
clippings and, from somewhere nearby, the rich smell of fresh
strong coffee. I stretched my arms and legs as far as they would
go and closed my eyes and smiled. I was alone in Italy for almost
the first time. Alone in a place not the Mountain for only the second time in my life. The first time, in Venice, I had been sick with
fear, ravaged by it. Here I was so happy as to be almost giddy.

A waiter came and I ordered a pot of coffee and two cups. I
was nearly through my first one when Yolanda came out
through the French doors and toward me. She had her hair in
one fat, glossy braid down her back and wore a peasant blouse
pulled down on her brown shoulders and an ankle-brushing
skirt of a vivid print. The skirt had a slit far up her sleek thigh,
though, I noticed with amusement, and she had on espadrilles
that tied at the ankle. She looked like a peasant painting from the
Mezzogiorno, perhaps by Mantegna, lush, high-spirited, very
young. I had never known anyone whose looks could change as
swiftly as hers: worn, jaded, almost old when she had been

excessive or was sad; bursting with youth and health when all was well with her. It struck me that I had no idea how old she was. She could have been any age from the mid-thirties to the mid-forties, depending on when one saw her. I knew she had still been a student when Sam had painted her, but I did not know exactly when that had been.

"*Buon giorno*," she said, slipping into the opposite chair and taking a deep gulp of the coffee. "Ready for Mother Whitney's Magical Mystery Tour? You look like Madeleine this morning."

I looked down at the navy shirtdress I had traveled in. It was light, cool, impervious to dirt and wrinkles, and, with its white-piped sailor collar, it did indeed look like the uniform of a French convent school. Especially beside Yolanda's gypsy cotton. I grimaced.

"I could slit the skirt to my waist and leave the top three buttons unbuttoned. Then I'd look like Madeleine on a bender."

"Don't bother. It's a good combination, the sacred and the profane. You can get us into churches and abbeys, and I can get guys for us. It works out perfectly."

I laughed aloud, joy rising like a geyser in my throat. The day opened out before me, as rich and dense with possibility and magic as if I were a child on her first away-from-home adventure. In a way that was true. I had never, I realized, done precisely this before: gone off on my own with a friend for a spur-of-the-moment totally unplanned lark. Lark. The word sounded in my ears as if it would taste wonderful on the tongue, round and rich like a bonbon.

"Lark," I said aloud, rolling it in my mouth. "We are going to have a lark."

She grinned at me.

"Bet your fanny. Where's your luggage?"

"Don't have any. I put a fresh set of underwear and a toothbrush in my bag. We aren't going anywhere fancy, are we?"

"Nope," she said, laughing and getting up from her chair. "In fact, you're probably overdressed for where we're going. I do like a gal who can just throw in a pair of panties and go."

"Then let's," I said.

I threw a wad of lire down on the table and we went out through the lobby to the Opel, arm in arm, like school friends in the brightening day.

We did not, after all, go out into the countryside to look at gardens. When Yolie dropped me off at American Express on the Via Guicciardini, just shy of the Ponte Vecchio on the Oltarno side, the line was out the door. Although it was early, the sun was climbing and the sky whitening with heat, and the throng inside the narrow office was already restless and uncomfortable. People were fanning and rolling up sleeves, unbuttoning shirts, and craning around to see what was holding up their line. There were four work stations open, and each one seemed to me to be hopelessly stalled, clogged with God knew what effluvia of away-from-home strife. Most of the whining, imploring, and then angry voices were American. Most of the curt, indifferent ones were Italian.

Goddammit it, Joe, this is not at all funny. I wish I'd let you mop up your own mess in Siena, I thought, as ten o'clock turned into eleven, and then crawled toward noon. By twelve there were still four people ahead of me. Each of them held enough *documenti* to precipitate individual international monetary crises. None of the other lines looked any better. Sweat ran down my back and soaked my bra, and the hair at my nape and temples was sopping. You'd think American Express would have caught on by now that six out of twelve months in Florence were hot.

Yolie wandered in every now and then, looked over the situation, and drifted back out, to browse along the Ponte Vecchio or to run and move the car from the space she'd found nearby to the big public lot in the Piazza del Carmine. She stayed with me after that.

"It's right near the place I'm taking you for dinner," she said, "and it's just a minute or two from the hotel. After you're done here maybe we can walk around Oltarno, see the Boboli and the Pitti if you'd like, and get some lunch. Or the way this is going, we'll do lunch first and then the tour. I think the country villas are out."

"I'm so sorry," I said. "I should have let Joe go on and do this in Siena. It's a rotten substitute for breezes and scenery."

Yolie stretched her arms high up over her head and arched her back and let her head tip back until the braid brushed her waist. Her brown breasts made as if to escape the white cotton blouse. She let her arms fall and settled back beside me, weight resting heavily on one leg, hand on hip. She looked around the room, scanning the crowd slowly and fully.

"Scenery's not so bad in here," she said.

I saw her eye had fallen on a young man standing at the end of the line beside us. He looked to be college age or a bit older, a tanned, dark-pelted, hulking young man with peeling sunburn on his nose and the thick arms and big hands of a linebacker. He did not seem to be with anyone in the crowd, as the other young men and women generally were; was not thumbing impatiently through papers or fidgeting or craning his neck to see if his line was moving. You could tell he was hot; his white T-shirt was wet, and the dark mat of his chest hair showed through it, but he did not fan himself or pull the shirt away from his body. He simply stood there, like a statue or a tree or perhaps a placid, sun-stunned bull. Waiting his turn. Looking back at Yolanda.

Yolanda smiled and the boy smiled back. He did not drop his gaze or avert his head, as most strangers will when they inadvertently smile at another stranger in a public place. He simply looked at her, all of her, from her feet to her face, and smiled. It was a smile to match the rest of him, thick and slow and somehow battering. Her smile did not falter either, and she did not look away. Volumes of things that I thought were best left unsaid passed between them in the humid air. I thought I could almost smell her.

"Yolie, really," I said under my breath, and the line in front of me moved up, and I saw that I was next after the man ahead.

She broke the look and turned back to me, letting the smile trail behind her like a thrown net.

"You're right," she said lazily. "By the time he gets his business done I'll be out of the mood. Pity. That was U.S. Grade A Prime."

She did not lower her voice. Someone behind us laughed. My face burned. My turn came at last, and I got the duplicate checks I had come for, and we made our way through the crowd to the door. As we went out into the sweet, blinding air, she looked back and blew the hulking young man a kiss.

"You'll be lucky if he doesn't batter the door down tonight," I said.

"I'll be lucky if he does."

"You are really incorrigible, you know it?"

"Not really. Just still horny. I didn't get the motor turned off before Cosimo the Beautiful cut for home."

"Well, take a deep breath or a cold shower or something, and let's get some lunch. My treat. Pick somewhere wonderful. It's the least I can do after botching up your whole morning."

"It was yours too," she said equably. "I don't mind. I'll see gardens and villas for the next five days, in Tuscany. I won't be back here for at least a year, though. I'd much rather spend this last day in my neck of the woods. It's the best part of Florence, even though there's nary a villa or a swimming pool in the lot of it."

"Thank God," I said. "Come on. Let's walk."

We walked in the deep, still heat to the Borgo San Jacopo, turned left, and made our way through streets so narrow and closely overhung with houses and shops that it was like walking through a tunnel. The light here was a permanent half-light, pierced by shafts of pale sun. Dust motes danced in them. The yellow-walled old houses glowed, sulfurlike. Yolie was right; I had not seen this Florence before. It was a distinct neighborhood, a village; the sense of lives being led, work being done all around you, was intense. People walked the narrow cobbled streets, went in and out of shops with baskets and string bags, called to one another, dodged the marauding autos and *vesparini* that roared by so closely their clothing billowed in the wind. Shopkeepers set their wares out; tourists and housewives examined them critically; children shrieked and scuffled; impassive teenagers with boom boxes and earphones leaned on their Vespas or the doorways of the old shops, or on each other, their eyes hooded with contempt and coolness, many hundreds of thousands of lire worth of supple dark leather on their bodies. Old men sat in the sun in small street *caffès* and argued or played board games.

One street over, the village disappeared abruptly and gave way to extravagant palazzi and dim, rich antique shops whose artful windows frankly intimidated me. I saw few people in them, and those few were so relentlessly austere and dark-clad I could not tell if they were customers or dealers.

"If I had a billion dollars I'd still be afraid to go in one of those shops and buy anything," I said to Yolie. "I'm sure they'd show me out for not having the right thing to wear."

"Probably," she said. "Salespeople in Florence are the rudest in the world. They'd like you to think they're aristocracy just helping out a friend for the day. I don't see how they ever sell anything. But Americans buy that stuff by the ton. I think Texans buy the most. Dallas women don't seem to know when they're being snubbed."

"How do you know all this stuff?"

"It's my business to know stuff." She grinned at me. "In my line of work, the more you know, the safer you are. Stuff is power."

"It must be awfully tiring," I said, meaning it. "To be always keeping your antennae up."

"You don't know. That's why I love coming to Italy; Florence especially. This part of it, anyway. Down here nobody cares what you know or don't know. This neighborhood is about see-

ing and tasting and feeling. It's not as eerie as Venice or as overpowering as Rome, and it's not as relentlessly rustic as Tuscany.
It's still a city, but you can let yourself slump here. And it's good
grazing, if you know what I mean. You can meet interesting men
without having to fight them off until you find one you don't
want to fight off. You couldn't do that much of anywhere else in
Italy. Forget the Mezzogiorno; you'd be black and blue or raped
or worse in two hours if you went trolling like you can in
Oltarno."

I looked at her as we ambled across the Borgo Tegolalo
toward the Piazza Santo Spirito. She was as round and sleek and
sinuous as a relaxed cat in the warm, close gloom.

"Aren't you ever afraid something will happen to you?" I
said.

"Nope. I'm street smart and I've got great instincts. I wrote
the book on safe sex. I'm more afraid something won't."

It crossed my mind that she might really be pathological in
some way: a nymphomaniac, if anyone still used that sad, innu-
endo-sodden old word. But then I thought not. She was too successful; had carved out too lofty and seamless a career for herself
to be driven by pathology. What she had achieved undoubtedly
had taken enormous drive and singlemindedness and determination, as well as talent. I put it out of my mind, partly because it
was enough, on this burnished day, to take her as the funny and
endearing companion that she was and partly because coming
into the piazza from the dusky tangle of streets was like coming
into a burst of pure light after a long dull time in the dark.

At one end of the tree-lined oblong Brunelleschi's great
Romanesque church sat, austere and classical, a remote and
beautiful white-carved sentinel presiding over benches full of
old people taking the sun, tangles of children playing ball, and
umbrella carts full of used clothing and stray flowers left from
the morning's market. In the center of the piazza lay an oblong
defined by more old trees, and in its center a fountain's lazy play
caught the sun in a dazzle of refracted rainbows. More children

splashed and screamed here, and mothers and nannies chatted, half watching them. All around the piazza more shuttered, anonymous *palazzi* stood, alternating with shops, a *latteria*, and a *gelateria*. Some were half shuttered by the ubiquitous corrugated metal shades that meant the long lunchtime siesta was getting under way, but others were open, and business in them was brisk.

Yolie steered me toward a trattoria at the opposite end from the church. A few umbrella tables had been set out, and most of these were empty.

"Manno has the best *tribollita* in Oltarno," she said, sinking into one of the chairs. I followed, gratefully.

"Is that the entrails of something, or do I want to know?"

"It's bean soup. Did you think I was going to make you eat intestines? Though that's pretty much what they did around here, or at least in San Frediano, where I'm staying. It was where the tripe makers worked. They boiled it up in huge vats and then delivered it early in the mornings all over the city, in wheelbarrows. You can still get the best *trippa alla fiorentina* around here. Maybe we'll try some tonight."

"Just don't tell me beforehand," I said. "Bean soup sounds fine. God, I'll bet it smelled something fierce around here back then."

"Probably not a lot worse than it does now, at least first thing in the morning," she said. "It's a bad place for drugs, and before the street cleaners get here the smell of vomit and God knows what else is potent. You have to step over syringes, sometimes, and worse."

"Lord, is it dangerous? It must be. This beautiful place seems a million miles from that kind of thing," I said, looking around at the peaceful piazza in the sun that was just now beginning to slant westward.

"For some reason it never has seemed dangerous to me," Yolie said. "Sad, maybe, and wasteful—all those poor thin furtive kids, most of them foreigners, a good many of them

American, squatting on the church steps and smoking and snorting and shooting up and sneaking around behind the trees to
fuck. I come here late at night sometimes because the way they
light the church is just so fantastic, like a set for *Tosca* or something. There are always police and, for some reason, soldiers.
Nobody has ever bothered me. Florence just isn't the place for
that."

Manno came then, exclaiming over Yolie, kissing her
cheeks, bending over my hand to kiss it. He sent a carafe of
chilled white wine like a wind off a mountain, and we drank it
and another one before we ordered. When the bean soup came
we fell upon it like starving foundlings, mopping the remains
with Manno's thick crusted bread, and then had two or three
glasses of *vin santo*. I had never thought I liked sweet wine, but
this was wonderful, with just enough of an afterburn not to be
cloying on the tongue.

It was quite late now. The heat was draining slowly out of
the day, and a small, teasing dry wind made its way through the
maze of streets into the square. It lifted the hair off the back of
my neck and riffled the lace-edged ruffles of Yolie's blouse. She
stretched and looked at me.

"Do you really want to go to the Pitti and the Boboli? It'll be
light for a long time. . . ."

"What I really want to do is never move again," I said.
"Let's sit awhile and then go take a nap before dinner and tell
everybody we went."

"I think we're sisters who got separated at birth," Yolanda
said. "Well, so tell me where you're going from Siena. The usual
lap around Chianti-shire? There are some wonderful gardens,
though a lot of them aren't the old Italian ones anymore. English,
mainly."

"I'm not really sure," I said. "Maria and Colin planned Tuscany originally, but I think Ada has edited it. San Gimignano, I
know, and Montepulciano and Pienza. Colin wanted to go over

to Perugia and Assisi, but Ada is lobbying for the coast. I know we'll go back to Rome by way of Orvieto."

"Ada must have a new bikini." Yolie grinned.

"Probably. They have some friends who have a place somewhere around Elba. I'm hoping Colin wins. I really don't want to stay with anyone we don't know. It's hard enough—"

I had been going to say, for no reason that I could think of, "getting to know each other," but thought how it would sound, and said instead, "moving the ill and the maimed around in hotels."

She looked at me keenly but said nothing. She was, I knew, going back to Rome from Siena, to sign her new contract and collect her crafts research from the Hassler, and then to New York. I thought suddenly that I would miss her a great deal.

"Will you be glad to get home?" I said.

She smiled.

"New York isn't home."

"Where is?"

"Nowhere, really. I have a tiny apartment in New York, and a share of a little place up the Hudson Valley. But I spend so much time traveling. The show is shot in LA, and I'm there for two or three months at a time. I always thought home might turn out to be here. Florence."

I thought about that, thought how strange it would be to say "home" and mean this small wedge of Oltarno. How strange her life was, without a center, a core. How strange it would be not to have that. A small pulse of anxiety began to beat in my throat at the very thought of it. But maybe her center was in herself. That would be something else entirely; that would be real strength, real power, not to need home.

"Why here?" I said.

"Because there's more of everything that appeals to me here than anywhere else in the world." She smiled, and the smile left no doubt as to what she meant.

"Did you ever think about getting married again, settling down?" I said. It did not seem awkward, now, to ask her.

"Not in a very long time. Not since I learned how to be alone. Not when there's so much good young stuff strutting around. And the nice thing is, when one gets his feelings hurt and flounces home to Mamma, like my dear late lamented, there's always another one right behind him. I don't kid myself that I'm always going to be young, but I'll probably always be rich, and that will help immensely."

I laughed helplessly. Her words were hopelessly cynical, of course, even corrupt, and I would have hated them from almost anyone else. But she sat there so easily, so bright-eyed and apple-cheeked, fitting so well and feeling so fine in her tight skin, grinning with such frank enjoyment, that you could only laugh. At the same time, I wondered what sort of wife she would have made to someone other than the bird-watching British anchorman, what sort of mother. I realized she probably considered my focus provincial in the extreme, but I had no other. The wonder was that we did not antagonize each other, the very worldly and the unworldly. But we did not. This had been a lovely day. I thought she thought so too.

"What about you, what will you do when you get home?" she said.

"Oh, I'll . . ."

I paused. In my mind's eye I saw my beautiful stone house on the Steep; saw the bright air-flown rooms and the overflowing garden, dreaming in the sun of full summer, burning with the wildfire of autumn. I saw our sky-hung bedroom, Joe's and mine, and the kitchen, the house's warm heart.

But I did not see anyone in it. I could not find myself there. I could not see Joe.

"I'll tackle the garden," I said firmly. "It's going to look like a jungle. It'll take a week or so to get things cleaned and put away, and then Joe will have to think about classes this fall, and we'll see everybody, maybe have a dinner party and make every-body look at our slides. And Lacey will be coming home between semesters for two or three weeks, and that will be heaven."

"And after that?"

"After that we'll just live, like we always do. Not everybody has your kind of gypsy life, Yolie, wonderful as it is. We've always lived very quietly. We will again."

"Will you really? I wonder if you can," she said seriously. "Do you have any idea of the commotion that portrait is going to attract, when Sam finally puts the new show together? You'll have every newspaper and art magazine in the world calling you."

"I doubt that," I said, unsettled by the idea. I had not thought that far ahead. "Anyway, how do you know there'll be a new show? And if there is, surely it will be a year or two away?"

"Oh, there'll be a new show," she said. "You could no more stop it now than you could stop Niagara. But you're right not to worry about it. It shouldn't change your life. . . ."

Her voice trailed off, and I wondered suddenly if her life had been changed, substantially altered, by having been one of Sam's subjects. Joe and I had thought at the beginning that she had been in love with him and perhaps still was, but I had long since discounted that. Their relationship was simply too casual, too uncharged, so much the camaraderie of old friends. Surely you could not bear to spend the time she had spent this trip in the presence of someone you loved but who did not love you. It would be too painful. Yolie's whole focus was immovably fixed on pain's polar opposite.

We left the Piazza Santo Spirito and walked slowly back to her small hotel off the Borgo San Frediano. We went by way of the Via dell' Ardiglioni, down the narrow street where Filippo Lippi was born in 1406. The street did not seem to me wide enough to admit automobiles, and indeed, in the shadow of the tall, leaning old houses, the fifteenth century seemed all around us. The noises of modern Florence were so dim they did not intrude. When Yolie pointed out Lippi's house, number thirty, she was whispering.

We crossed the Piazza del Carmine, lying partly in the shadow of the church of Santa Maria del Carmine, past the car park where the dusty Opel sulked in the late sun. I grinned at it, a familiar if sullen piece of this strange old landscape. We turned into the Borgo Frediano and down the little street, really an alley, that led to her hotel. It was tiny and narrow, five stories tall, painted the same stained yellow as the houses around it; the lobby was actually a dark hall that spoke of tomato sauce and a general contempt for deodorant and held a rusty little cage elevator. The Centrale, it was called.

"Well, it's central to the neighborhood, I guess," Yolie said, when I smiled at the name. We were wallowing our way up in the elevator.

She manned the creaking old controls expertly, shimmying it to a stop only inches before the top floor.

"This part of San Frediano is full of working-class people," she said. "They used to be the rag pickers and the tanners and the tripe boilers, and they like to think they're great characters still, tough as alley cats, colorful as hell. They all act like they're in a bad fifties movie: film noir. But they're decent people, most of them, really pussycats. Once they know you, they're family. They've smartened the neighborhood up a lot since I've been coming here. There are all kinds of shops and bistros and quaintsy little places opening, and we're beginning to get the more adventurous tourists in here. They've got places you can buy underwear that would make Frederick's of Hollywood look like Laura Ashley. You in the market for some crotchless panties? I get all mine here."

"I think I'll pass," I said. "Oh, this is charming."

The elevator let us out in a bright tiled lounge filled with plants, comfortable if slightly spavined old chairs and sofas, and small tables and chairs. Many of these were occupied by people drinking coffee or wine, and most of them called out to Yolanda. Beyond the lounge was a roof garden teeming with flowers and plants, where a few more people sat at tables drinking and admiring the view of jumbled red-tiled roofs and the dome of San Frediano, and beyond it the slate-gray Arno and the tower of Ognissanti on the far bank. There was a forest of telephone wires and television aerials, and a spidery tangle of clotheslines almost as far as the eye could see, but somehow they seemed festive and endearing, a stage set. The unapologetic, slightly raffish charm of the Centrale gathered you in like strong, slightly sweaty arms. I felt peace flood me and sighed gratefully.

Yolie's room was large and high-ceilinged and starkly furnished with a huge dark bed, freshly made up in white but strewn with clothes. There was an armoire big enough to sleep in, a table and chair by the French doors that led out onto the roof, and a spidery bureau. The noise from the street below was horrendous, but it did not bother me. It was, after all, the evening rush hour. Later, I thought, it would be quiet; it would be like sleeping in the prow of a ship, high over the Arno. Yolie put her head out of the door and yelled something in rapid Italian to someone called Butti, and I went into the tiny white bathroom and ran a bath in the huge claw-footed old tub and climbed in. Presently she brought me a glass of good red wine, so stoutly acidic it made my tongue pucker, and I lay swishing tepid water around me and sipping it and thinking nothing at all except that I was happy. When I came out of the bath, wrapped in a huge, thin old bath sheet, she was stretched out on the bed sipping wine from a fresh bottle. The empty one sat on the table beside her. A packed suitcase and a pair of overflowing Vuitton totes stood beside the door into the hall.

"You're all ready," I said.

"I am ready for absolutely anything."

We sat out on the roof terrace garden for a bit, finishing the second bottle of wine. Night was falling fast; the rose and gold light that had lain over Oltarno and the river was turning dusky blue. A thin shaving of a white moon rose just over the tower of Ognissanti, seemingly pinned there by the spire. Below us, the street roar had abated a little, but I could still hear spatterings of conversations over the grind of the autos and *motorini*. The noise did not intrude, though.

"Want some more wine?" Yolie said presently, regarding the empty bottle. We were both slumped far down in our chairs, resting our feet on the low parapet around the roof.

"No. I'll be drunk as a goat. I thought you'd given it up, anyway."

"The hard stuff, not wine. Wine never did bother me, for some reason."

I looked sidewise at her. She must be right. There were spots of vivid pink on her cheeks, but her eyes were clear and her smile and voice steady. She looked pretty and relaxed in the dusk, and younger than ever.

"What I am," I said, "is ravenous. I could eat a cow."

"Maybe we will. Have you had *bistecca alla fiorentina* yet? Steak from locally grown cattle brushed with olive oil and pepper and grilled? It's wonderful."

"I didn't mean literally," I said. "I didn't come to Italy to eat steak. What are some other specialties besides steak and tripe?"

"Wild hare, boar meat, larks, thrush—"

"And I thought the Tuscans were supposed to be the most civilized of the Italians. Could we just go get some spaghetti or something?"

We went down in the woozy elevator and turned left, walking deeper into the alley that led off the Borgo San Frediano. Half a block down we turned left again, into a passageway so narrow and dark I did not at first recognize it as a street. Here the cobbles gleamed with a greasy moisture that you felt never entirely dried, for surely no sun or wind could penetrate. The rooftops leaned so closely together overhead that you could have stepped easily from one to another, and the closed doors were of thick, damp, dark wood. There seemed no street life here. There seemed no life of any sort.

"Are you sure this is right?" I said, realizing only after I had spoken that I was whispering.

"I'm sure. I come here all the time. It's safe. It's just dark."

I stumbled behind her in the gloom, tripping on the slick, uneven cobbles. Presently she stopped. I did too, but I saw nothing.

"Here," Yolie said, and disappeared down a narrow, winding flight of stone stairs so dark I had not seen them. I plunged down behind her, unwilling to be left alone in that black alley for even a moment. I stood behind her in utter darkness, hearing a deep metallic clang, and realized she was banging on a door with a brass knocker. I could see neither.

The door opened then, and light spilled out into the stairwell, and we went inside.

Afterward I could never remember the name of the restaurant, and I still cannot. Perhaps Yolie never told me, or perhaps it did not have a name. It seemed the kind of place that would not, except to be called after the owner. I met him almost immediately, or someone I took to be the owner: a squat, thick bear of a man who came to hug Yolie and grunt at me. She called him Taddo, or Tadeo, but she never did tell me who he was. I heard no other names that night, either. Yolie seemed to know many of the people who sat and stood in the shadows, drinking and dancing and kissing and perhaps other things, and even eating, a few of them. But she called none of them by name. I couldn't have heard, anyway. The din was too loud.

It was a cellar of some sort. The walls were a stained stucco that had once been white, and the back one was actually dug out of dirt and stone, the old earth of this place. There were paintings or posters scattered about on the curving walls, but the smoke was so thick and the paintings themselves so grimed that I could not tell what they were. Groups of people loomed up out of the murk like ships out of a heavy fog; they were all intertwined with each other in Bosch-like knots, and everyone seemed to be young. Heavy-metal rock reverberated in the cavelike space, from a hidden record player or tape deck, I thought. There was no room for a live band. We pushed through the throng. Hands reached out to touch Yolie: tweak her cheeks, slide across her shoulders perilously close to her breasts, cup her buttocks under the skirt. They were familiar touches in every way; she knew all of them and jibed at them in Italian as she passed. Comments whose tone, if not content, I recognized followed me as I plowed along behind her, but no one touched me.

Taddo had kept a table for us in the very back, against the earth and rock wall, and we slid into chairs. It was quieter here, and there was a good view, if you could call it that, of the entire long room and the stand-up bar that bisected the far wall halfway down. This was three deep with young men. All of them turned to look at us, slow, nearly insolent looks that were like fingers on flesh. Yolie stared back at them, her eyes measuring their flesh as they had done ours, her head cocked. Then she blew a kiss to the crowd, calling out something guttural to them, and they all laughed and turned back to their drinks.

"What did you tell them?" I asked brightly. I was almost frightened of this place. I had seen nothing like it before.

"To go beat their own meat; I'd seen them all before and we weren't buying. Tonight."

"God, you didn't—"

"Not in those words, no. But I do know them all. I come here a lot. Besides having the best pasta in Florence, it's a veritable supermarket."

I felt a curl of distaste, just the faintest plume. Enough was enough. I was tiring of her obsession with young men. I wanted to eat a leisurely dinner and get a good night's sleep and be on the road to Siena early. I found I missed Joe quite a lot. It struck me suddenly that this would be the first night I had ever spent away from him, except for his rare trips out of town for Trinity.

I looked at the bar full of young men and around the room again. Except for two or three couples dancing in the middle of the room, and one or two who seemed to be kissing in dead earnest at tables at the other end, I saw no other women. Almost everyone in this place was male.

"It's a supermarket, all right," I said. "Where are all the women?"

"Oh, they come and go," she said. "Mostly they're upstairs right now."

It dawned on me.

"My God, Yolie, this is a . . . a *bordello!*"

"Probably more of an old-fashioned 'ho'house," she said, grinning sidewise at me. "Don't worry. Your virtue is safe with me. I established a long time ago that I don't work here. I just shop. Where better? And like I said, the pasta really is the best I've ever had."

A waiter appeared with three bottles of wine. He poured out for Yolie and me, into thick, chipped glasses. She tasted and made a grimace of pleasure and nodded, and asked what pasta the house had tonight.

"*Salsiccia di cinghiale,*" he said.

"*Due,*" Yolie said. "*Più tardi.*"

He nodded and went away, and she motioned for me to taste the wine. I did. It was powerful, raw and thick. It warmed me all the way down.

"Well," she said, lifting her glass and clicking it to mine, "to your night in a Florentine whorehouse. You can dine out on it for years."

I drained my glass and she refilled it. Suddenly all the sinister darkness, the dampness, seemed to drain out of the place and the night. It *would* make a wonderful story, I thought. I knew I would tell it again and again on the Mountain. It was the sort of thing Trinity loved. Joe would laugh each time and be secretly

envious that it had not happened to him. Sooner or later the
story would be transmuted so it had. No matter. I would tell it
tomorrow night, at dinner, in Siena.

Sam would love this night, I thought. I laughed aloud.

"Feeling better?" Yolie said, smiling at me across the table.
She was on her third glass of wine.

"I am," I said. "I must have looked like Little Nell."

"Nope. You look good, in fact, Cat. You look like a different
woman from the one I first met in Rome."

I thought about that meeting. It was she who was a different woman now, not I.

"Do I? I don't feel different," I said.

"Oh, I'll bet you do, if you think about it," she said.

We finished the first bottle of wine and started on the second. That one was nearly half gone before she spoke again.

"How's the portrait coming?"

"Nearly done," I said. "Sam says he'll probably finish it in
Siena."

"Ah. And you haven't seen it yet?"

"Nobody has."

She laughed. "Ada has. You can bet your bottom."

"She says not," I said.

"That doesn't mean anything. Ada says what needs to be
said. It's why she's aboard. She's seen it, all right. She's peeked if
he hasn't shown it to her. It wouldn't be hard. He doesn't hide
his work."

I looked at her more closely. Were the bright eyes just a bit
too bright; was her mouth a bit stiff, her words just the slightest
bit slurred? I couldn't tell. My own face was flushed and my lips
felt larger than they should, and a little numb. I should stop with
the wine right now, I thought, but I did not. I drank another
glass. We were near the bottom of the second bottle, now.

"You don't like Ada, do you?" I said.

"No. You don't either. Women never do."

"Why don't you?" I said. My own words felt thick. I

thought I should cut this conversation off right now, but I didn't want to.

"No," Yolie said owlishly, "you first. Why don't you? Is she fucking Joe?"

"God! No!" I cried. I was profoundly shocked. At the bar, heads turned to look at us.

She was silent, looking at me, smiling slightly. I felt my face flame.

"Ah," she said softly.

"No," I said again. "She's not fucking him. I don't think. But she's kissing him. Or vice versa, or both. I saw them yesterday, at lunch. Oh, what do I know? She could be; they've had enough time. . . ."

"Well, then, are you fucking Sam?"

Through the Chianti haze I felt a clear, sharp rush of anger.

"I certainly am not! Why would you think I'd . . . do that?"

"He does that when he's doing portraits," Yolie said matter-of-factly, reaching for the last bottle. She spilled a little on the rough wooden tabletop and touched her finger to it and licked it. Then she looked at me.

"No reflection on you. It's just that you've spent all that time together, and you do seem terribly vulnerable. You did from the first. That excites Sam. Not even a few kisses, Cat? Not even tempted? He's irresistible when the dam starts to break. I know."

"I don't like the way this is going, Yolie," I said, with as much dignity as I could muster, around my thick tongue.

"Ah," she said. "So there *has* been a little slap-and-tickle. Thank God. I was afraid he was losing it this time, and you were approaching sainthood. Well, then, you really can't blame Joe too much, can you?"

"It's not at all the same thing! Not at all!"

"Oh?"

"No. I didn't kiss Sam in the first place; he kissed me. And I told him when he did that it couldn't go any further."

"But you kept sitting," she said. "*Did* it go any further?"

I fell silent. It had, of course. At my request. But only because Joe . . .

I felt tears start in my eyes. She put her hand over mine, on the tabletop.

"Americans behave badly in Italy, Cat. All of us, in one way or another. You ought to stop it now, though, before it gets past the kissing. It will, sooner or later. Sooner, probably, if he's nearly done with the portrait. He'll hurt you."

"Maybe I'll hurt him," I said pettishly.

"Oh, Cat, you can't. I wish you could. There's nothing there to hurt. You know, when I first met him, I kept waiting to see his dark side. Every genius has one, you know: the wild rages, the romantic drunkenness, the black despair, whatever. It's part of the mystique, it comes with the territory. It lends humanity to all that . . . extraordinariness."

She stumbled on the word, badly. But she went on.

"But Sam doesn't have a dark side. The other side of him is just this flat, pure plane of focus and energy; it all goes into the work. It's one slick, straight, hard, shiny surface. You couldn't chip it with dynamite. There's no way to hurt him."

I was angry now, really angry.

"You make him sound inhuman. He's not. He's the most human man I've ever met. If you don't know that, you never really knew him."

She stared at me, squinting a little, as if to focus on my face.

"You planning on fucking him? If you are, you better hurry. You've only got between now and the instant he finishes that painting. After that you're history."

I started to get up out of my chair. She put her hand out and grasped my wrist. Her grip was strong.

"Stay," she said. "I need to tell you something about Ada and Sam. It's for your own good, Cat. It really is."

I sat back down, slowly, more because I realized I was not sure how to get back to the hotel than to hear what she would say. But I was curious too.

"Did you fuck him, Yolie?" I said, and thought simply to myself, I don't think I've ever used that word to anybody but Joe in my life before tonight, and now I'm scattering it like grass seed.

Yolie grinned widely.

"Did I ever. From the first day. All over the place. In taxis. In doorways. On the Janiculum in broad daylight. In his studio; he had a room somewhere in Trastevere, a great, huge, shabby space with nothing in it but a table and a chair and an easel, and these wonderful, heavy old brocade drapes across a whole wall. We did it on the chair and the table and managed to rip the drapes right off the wall. His landlady ran him out for that. Of course, he was a lot younger then, and I was still in college. . . ."

Her voice trailed off, and the smile softened. Her eyes were focused a long way away.

"You were in love with him, weren't you?" I said quietly.

"Oh, yes. And for that time, he was in love with me. He doesn't fake that. He wouldn't bother. But the minute the painting was done, even before the paint was dry, it was over. I became a sort of pet, one of Sam Forrest's girls, a family member. He keeps us, you know. It took me years to get over him."

You're not over him yet, I thought. Aloud, I said, "Where was Ada all this time?"

"Who knows? Shopping. Or bending over with her eye to the keyhole. Anywhere. Nowhere. I used to worry about Ada. She was terribly good to me; I really didn't want to hurt her. But later I came to see that she encouraged the whole thing. It was she who suggested the portrait, she who asked me to stay with them. She threw us together, literally."

"That's sick. It really is," I said, my voice trembling.

"Hang on," Yolie said, putting a hand on my arm and getting up from her chair. "I have to go pee. I really do. I'll be right back. Don't go, OK, Cat?"

"I won't," I said.

I sat looking down at the tabletop. It's all spoiled, I thought.

Nothing will be the same after this; it can't be. She's wrong about
Sam, of course, but I wish I'd never heard that stuff. I wish I'd
gone on to Siena with them. . . .

I wondered if I could get her to eat when she came back, eat
and sober up, so that we wouldn't have to talk of it anymore. Or
even better, just to go back to the room and go to sleep. Then I
looked up, in the direction in which she had gone, and I saw her,
standing in the doorway to the toilet, holding herself upright
with one hand. The other was on her hip. She was looking at a
young man who stood at the bar. I had not seen him before; he
was tall and slender and very pale in the gloom, and his glossy
blue-black hair grew down over his forehead in a point, like a
medieval jester's cap. He stood sideways to the bar, so that he
was in profile to me, and he was looking straight at Yolanda
across the smoky room. His nose was a crag, a jut, a beak, his
mouth red and thin. He was smiling slightly, and his hand rested
lightly, casually, on an enormous erection. It strained his pants,
stood out like the prow of a Viking ship. I saw his eyes drop to it
and go back to Yolanda's face. Her eyes followed his, and held
the taut cloth, and then climbed his body to his face. She smiled
in return.

I knew we would not be leaving.

She wobbled unsteadily back to our table and sat down,
still smiling at the young man. Then she turned to me.

"New boy on the block," she said.

"Listen. Why don't we take out our food and go back to the
room?" I said cheerfully. "We've both had too much wine."

"No. You listen. It's important."

She was serious now. I knew she was going to say what she
felt she had to, no matter what I said or did. Well, then, I would
listen, hear her out. Then, perhaps, she would agree to leave.

"Shoot," I said.

"Well, first, Ada wasn't a secretary when he met her on the
Spanish Steps," Yolie said. "She was a prostitute. Young, alone,
and far from home, gorgeous, scared to death, and turning tricks

like a house afire on the Spanish Steps because she couldn't afford an apartment. He was young and stupid and he wanted to paint her and he did, and while he was doing it he fell in love with her. For his pains she gave him the clap. Gonorrhea. God knows how long she'd had it. For some reason he didn't show symptoms, not at first anyway. By the time he did, and got to a doctor, the damage was done. He's been sterile ever since. Later he became impotent for long periods of time. He's always blamed her for that, though the doctors told him it didn't have anything to do with the disease. She's sterile too, of course. She had a hysterectomy not long afterward.

"I think they stayed together simply because she willed it. Her will is incredible, a real force of nature. She literally made herself over into the Ada you see now, glamorous, serene, confident, capable of running his life and his work like nobody else ever could. He's the painter he is today because of her. When the impotence started, he also started to get long dry spells when he just couldn't paint. There was just nothing there. Impotent in every way. She cured the first one by getting Verna Cardigan to sit for him. He fell in love with Verna, got it up in all ways, and had the first really great show of his life. When I met him at the embassy party and he brought me home to Ada, he was in the middle of another drought. I cured that for him, courtesy of Ada. The fertile spell I started outlasted me for years, but he'd been dry for a long time until this summer. Until you came along. I don't have to tell you how simple Ada has made it for Sam to paint you; she's literally taken charge of Joe so you could be alone with Sam. I've watched her do it. She knows I have. She'd have done anything to get him back on track, including kiss your husband or fuck him if she needed to. They were getting low on money and Sam wasn't getting many calls from the art magazines anymore. This new show will probably set them up for life."

I stared at her.

"I'm not saying he doesn't really feel something for you,"

Yolie said. "But you need to know that when he's finished your portrait he's shot his wad. No more nookie. No more Cat, unless you want to be a house pet. I've often wondered if Ada doesn't miss it. Who knows? Maybe she goes outside. Maybe she gets all she needs from his subjects' men. Maybe she doesn't need anything at all, except to be Mrs. Sam Forrest. Sam thinks that."

"How do you know this? Did he tell you?" I could barely whisper. My ears rang and my head pounded.

"No. She did. Much later, over sherry at Doney's, as cool as a cucumber."

"Why?"

"Who knows?" Yolie said. "I don't. I don't know who she is, or what. If she thought telling me would 'cure' me of Sam, she was right."

Rage shook me.

"No, she wasn't! You're not anywhere near over him! If you were, you'd never bother to tell me this; you're jealous; you want me to stop—"

I stopped, breath rasping in my throat, hearing my own words over the babble of the bar as if listening to a stranger. A mad stranger. I wanted to get up and run from the place, but I did not think my legs would hold me up. He was not like that, he could not be; none of this was true. She had made it up, had asked me to stay over so she could tell me this monstrousness, stop my being with him. I remembered my first impression of her, drunk and belligerent, by the pool in Rome. Across the table she looked like that now. Drunk, anyway. Her face was slack and unfocused. Her lipstick ran up the sides of her mouth.

But there was no malice in her eyes, and no anger. She looked at me for a long space of time with something akin to pity, and then she shrugged.

She turned her head toward the bar and made words with her mouth, without a noise. Slowly she pulled the elasticized neck of the peasant blouse down off her shoulders and bared one large brown breast, and touched it with the tips of her fingers.

She smiled. Behind me, the bar exploded in noise: catcalls, smacking of lips, laughter.

The rage nearly choked me. I scrambled to my feet.

"I'm not going to stay here and watch this," I said furiously. "I'm not going to listen to any more of this crap!"

"Where you going, Cat?"

She was still looking at the young man at the bar and smiling. She made a kiss with her mouth.

"Back to the room. Anywhere. This is disgusting."

She shrugged, broke eye contact with the young man, and fished the room key out of her purse. She handed it to me.

"I think I'll stay awhile," she said. "Let yourself in. Go on to sleep. Don't worry, I'll be good as gold tomorrow. You'll see. Put it right out of your head."

For a moment I did not move.

"Go on. You'll be safe on the street. I won't be long. This should only take a few minutes. . . ."

I took the key and turned and walked out of the restaurant. As I passed the young man, I saw he had started across the room toward her, bearing the erection before him like a battle standard.

At the door, I heard her call, "Cat?" and stopped and looked back. The boy was at the table now, leaning over her. Over his shoulder, she smiled broadly at me.

"You better fuck him fast!"

She laughed. I ran out of the bar and up the steps, turned right, turned right again, and was at the entrance to the Centrale before I drew another deep breath. When I reached the room I did not even turn on the light. I grabbed a half-forgotten vial of the sleeping pills Corinne had sent with me to Italy out of my purse, swallowed two with tap water, shucked off my clothes, and crawled naked into the huge white bed. From the street below the snarl and spit of traffic went on unabated, but I did not hear it. I was asleep practically before my head touched the pillow.

* * *

I woke with the start of the early rush hour the next morning and sat up groggily, tasting last night's wine and the pills. Yolanda was not there, and the other side of the bed had not been slept in. I found a note, though, stuck on the bathroom mirror with a Band-Aid:

Have decided to stay over awhile. Key to car is on chest under your purse. Car is in the parking lot in the Piazza del Carmine; you saw it yesterday. Right out of the hotel, first left, you'll see it. Map on back of note. Take the car and drive on to Siena, and tell everybody I'll catch up to them, or maybe I'll call. Love, Y.

I sat down heavily on the bathroom floor.

"I can't drive to Siena by myself," I whispered aloud. I looked back down at the note. There was a postscript.

Yes, you can! it read.

I dropped my head down on my drawn-up knees and put my hands over my face. The fear boiled up like a volcano erupting, pure and terrible, stronger than it had ever been on the Mountain or anywhere else. I began to cry and to rock myself.

"Help me, Sam," I whispered, rocking, rocking. "Help me, Joe."

Then: "I want my mother!"

The fear rose into my mouth and filled my eyes, ran out to the ends of my fingers. It seemed to explode inside my head, in a huge, white, soundless burst. I felt the reverberations in my chest, in my legs, in my teeth. Then it drained away and icy anger flowed in behind it like an avalanche. I shook with it, briefly, and then it steadied down into a silvery shimmer, a cold, all-sustaining flame.

I got up and dressed and got the Opel from the lot in the Piazza del Carmine and drove to Siena.

CHAPTER THIRTEEN

~~~~~~

Y OLANDA SENT ME THE OLD WAY. It took much longer because of
 the narrow, twisting roads. Often I had to slow almost to a
stop to grope my way around a particularly sharp hairpin
switchback, and once I spent nearly an hour behind an ancient
jury-rigged truck laden with farm machinery so old it looked like
a rust pile. Passing was next to impossible. At first, shimmering
with anger and the brassy foretaste of triumph, I raged inwardly
at her, adding this impossible route to the litany of her sins that
sang in my head. But soon I saw she had literally given me the
gift of Tuscany. I would have missed it on the Autostrada, in the
hot, howling wash of the huge cars and trucks.

I came to Siena via the Chiantigiana, the eighteenth-century
wine route from Florence. I picked it up at the Piazza Ferruci, following Yolie's scrawled but surprisingly clear directions from
the Piazza del Carmine, hands and teeth clenched so hard that
the muscles there would ache for days after. I do not think I drew

a deep, full breath until halfway there. Anger is a superb agent of focus; I was so angry when I got into the car that I saw, as if in a tunnel, only the streets and landmarks she had indicated on her map. The shrieking maelstrom of traffic around me in Oltarno might as well not have existed. I laid the map on the seat beside me and turned where it said to turn, exited where it said to exit, and saw with great and simple surprise that I was indeed in the Piazza Ferruci. It is always a matter of wonderment to me when maps work.

From there I picked up SS222 and bowled smoothly out of Florence following the promised blue signs to Greve and Siena. After Grassina, the countryside opened up and the entire panorama of Tuscany lay before me, hill after dusky blue-green hill, sweeping in rounded waves south to the horizon. I saw them clearly for the first time then, the *cittì di colli:* the little cities on the hills. They crowned the soft peaks like cubes of pale brown sugar, red-roofed, cypress-guarded. Their thick towers reached into the sky, already bluer here than in Florence or anywhere else in Italy I had seen. Each town was separate unto itself and its hill; each was the same as the next and yet profoundly not the same. Each was surrounded with a great surf of cultivated land, land in patchworks of green and gold and dusty pink, up to the very walls of the towns. Around these, and around the lone farms and villas that I saw on the nearer crags, the black cypresses stood tall and the elegant umbrella pines leaned close.

"Oh," I said aloud, into the warm wind that flowed into the Opel's window, bringing soft dusty earth and a dry sweetness like straw in the sun. "Oh!"

Just past a great baroque villa I saw the sign that said I was entering the Chianti Classico wine region. Just past that, the road took a spectacular turn and swept down toward Greve. I saw the first of the great sunflower fields there.

Somehow I had not read or heard about them. I saw with the comforting sense of meeting old friends the low, tumbled

vines and the silvery gray groves of the olive trees, and the dense
emerald of the cornfields, even the pale gold of the fields of
sedge. But nothing had prepared me for the sunflowers. They
were incredible, fantastic, impressionists' fantasies: flaming Van
Gogh suns with hearts of pure red-orange fire. Acres of them
swept away from the road, miles of them. Lava pouring down
the slopes, settling in the tender, womanlike curves of the val-
leys, bisected by narrow road ribbons of black-green cypress. I
stopped the car for the first time since the Piazza del Carmine
and laid my head on the steering wheel and wept.

I knew the tears came from several places, several levels
inside me. The top level was the pure, drowned shock of beauty,
classic Stendhal. I cried with joy for the sunflowers. But there
were other, deeper levels: Joe's betrayal lay there, and the sly
ugliness of the story Yolanda had told me the night before, and
the sheer repugnance of her behavior with the young man in the
trattoria. Confusion and loss were there too, and the exhaustion
of the long days of travel and the bleeding sense of myself leak-
ing away, along with almost everything else that was familiar to
me. Deep, abiding anger at Yolanda was there; I knew that
would not leave me. Loneliness for Joe was there, simple and
childlike. Loneliness for Sam Forrest, not at all simple, not at all
childlike. And above all, triumph was there. Mastery. Exultation
that was so fierce I could only weep with it. I was actually doing
this thing, making this drive, alone and with competence. In
another hour or so I would have done it. At that moment there
was virtually nothing in the world I could imagine that I could
not do.

I wept because I had never felt such strength before.

I wept because I was no longer afraid and knew I never
would be again, not with the great old fear. Not ever again with
that.

I wiped my eyes on the heel of my palm and put the Opel
into gear and drove on. I passed small cars coming in the opposite direction, saw farmers and herdsmen in the fields, families

walking along the road. I waved to all of them, and they all waved back. Handsome; they were handsome people. I saw many blondes. On that transcendent morning I thought them the most extraordinary people on earth, natural heirs to the enigmatic Etruscans whose playful, beautiful art I so loved. I felt a kind of kinship with them. I thought I understood why they chose to stay here on these old hills, to go into the cities outside Tuscany only with reluctance. Sam had told me that Tuscans suffered almost to a man from *campanilisimo*, intense loyalty to their own bell towers. I had laughed, but it made great good sense to me now. This spasmed old earth was safe. I felt the safety deep in my bones, humming up out of the very earth, pouring into me through the droning tires of the Opel. Other parts of Tuscany and Umbria might be—were, in fact—wild and inhospitable, but here, in the Chianti, there was a thick and indestructible felting of permanence over the bones of the earth. The old towns did not change. They were whole; they were not aggregates. They had been born whole, planned whole. Nothing was piecemeal, left to change. Each town had a purpose: to protect, to nurture. Each mile of earth had one: to bear fruit, to sustain. And the sheer beauty of the countryside was as much a part of the towns as their brick and mortar. I remembered reading, before we had come, that an early Tuscan pope had built a palace around a view, the first time in European architecture anyone had thought to do that.

I turned left at Casteilina, into the very green heart of the Chianti district, passed through Radda and Gaiole, and swept down upon Siena on SS408. By the time I reached the small road that veered off into the hills just above Siena, where Yolie's map said the Villa di Falconi should be, I was thrumming like a tuning fork with a kind of crazy rapture. As the road climbed, I began to sing; I sang "La Marseillaise" and "We Shall Overcome," and "Waltzing Matilda." I finished "Waltzing Matilda" at the top of my lungs just as I swerved the car in between the stone gateposts of the Villa di Falconi and skidded it to a stop, spurting gravel.

It was a big, sprawling, honey-colored stucco building, more rustic by far than the Villa Carol, rougher, not nearly so old. I thought it might have been built in the last century, perhaps for a prosperous farmer and his family; it had that look of utilitarian sturdiness, of fruitful use. Weather had softened its walls and bleached its roof tiles, and the dark wood framing its deep-cut windows and the massive open front door had gone silver. No nobility here, I thought with satisfaction. Just generations of living in harmony with the rhythms of the seasons and the earth. Before it lay a semicircle of raked gravel, and to each side I could see hedges and fruit trees and gardens formally laid out, bisected by brick paths and studded at intervals with huge terra-cotta pots of lemon trees and roses and hibiscus. Stone benches were set about, though at this hour of high sun no one rested on them; I saw no one else about in the gardens. The soft, warm wind smelled wonderful: I identified roses and perhaps gardenias; light curls of lemon balm and thyme and basil and other things pungent and peppery spoke of a serious herb garden somewhere close by. I would love exploring this garden, I thought. I would love spending hours dreaming here in the sun, an old wall warm against my back. I had thought I did not want to be sequestered outside yet another city in yet another of Ada Forrest's villas-with-pool, but the Villa di Falconi was different. It put its arms about you when you first entered, like a stout farm mother.

I'll bet somebody told her that Saint Catherine was born here, or something, I thought, and got out of the car and walked toward the villa. Behind it a thick tangle of trees and vegetation lay dark and cool and secret, and I could tell that the earth behind fell sharply away. Stepping-stone paths led away into the thickets and groves on either side. I went a short way down one and saw that there was, indeed, a vast gulf of space just beyond the small forest. In a clearing between the shouldering cypresses

I could just see, far across a gullied red valley on a lower hill, the pale jumble of Siena spilling downhill. The top of the great taffy-colored Torre del Mangia reached into the sky, blue as the sea now with the sun of early afternoon.

I shut my eyes and held my face up to the sun, felt its sweet weight on my eyelids and cheekbones and lips, smiled enormously, and went back up the path and into the lobby.

Inside, I was momentarily blinded by the cool darkness. Then a small flagged lobby came into focus, and beyond it a great lounge dominated by a stone fireplace, blackened and empty, that I could easily have stood erect in. I thought of winter nights, and wind, and roaring flames; it reminded me powerfully, for just a moment, of the Mountain. Deep, comfortably sagging sofas and leather chairs were set about it, and small tables, and little islands of rugs dotted the polished wood floor. At the other end was a bar with stools and tables and chairs and a great television set on its own table; it had the look of a suburban American rumpus room in the 1950s and was empty. A battered grand piano sat nearby. The long wall was all French doors giving upon a wide terrace with more chairs and tables. The terrace looked into empty blue space, the tops of the trees below just bobbing over the low stone wall that bound it. One or two people sat there, chatting and drinking, but the overall impression was of cool, clean emptiness and expectant waiting. I thought most of the guests would be at lunch, or having their siestas, and turned to the small windowed cubicle in the lobby. A powerfully built man with a jet-black crewcut and bluish jowls sat behind the open window, working at a computer.

"*Buon giorno,*" I said, and he lifted his head and looked at me out of eyes the color of arctic ice, a strange opaque green.

"*Si, signora?*"

"*Mi chiamo Caterina Gaillard,*" I said clearly. "*Mio marito e' qui*—ah, here. Signor Gaillard?"

I had practiced it over and over on the drive: "My name is

Catherine Gaillard," I would say confidently in fluid Italian. "My husband is here, Mr. Gaillard. Where may I find him?"

But I could remember none of the Italian under the steady green gaze. I had never seen a green-eyed Italian. For some reason, it annoyed me.

"I have just come from Florence," I said briskly. It sounded wonderful, even in English, tossed in ever so casually. I have just come from Florence. Alone.

"Oh, yes, Mrs. Gaillard," the man said in perfect English, only slightly accented, and that in something heavy and darkish, not at all Italian. "Your husband and his party are on the pool terrace. I believe they are waiting luncheon for you and the other signora. Is she . . . ?"

He looked over my shoulder, out into the parking lot.

"She has been detained in Florence," I said. "She will not be joining us."

"Ah. Then perhaps I may let her room? I have many people anxious—"

"Please do," I said, my cheeks burning with the implied rebuke. Obviously, people who could not keep their reservations at the Villa di Falconi called well ahead to cancel.

"It was very sudden," I added.

"Yes."

The telephone shrilled, and he turned to answer it.

"Where is the pool terrace?" I said to the back of his head.

"Down the path," he said with his back to me, gesturing toward the door. "You can't miss it."

I stood for a moment, waiting for him to finish, but he broke into a spate of fast guttural German—German, of course—that sounded as if it would go on for a while.

"Scratch one tip, bubba," I said under my breath, and went back out into the garden. I looked at both paths, but neither of them gave me a clue as to what lay at their ends. I shrugged and took the one I had followed a little way earlier.

The old flagstones led through the underbrush on a fairly level plane for a little while, and then down a flight of narrow, moss-slimed stone steps with no railings. After that the path was dirt and fell away steeply. The trees and undergrowth leaned closer, until the sun was nearly shut out, and the light was green and wavering, and the earth smelled of damp, secret places. I heard small scurryings, and once a sharp crashing as if something quite heavy was running away through the brush, and stopped for a moment. What had I heard about Tuscan wildlife? Snakes, of course, and squirrels and such, but ... what else? Boar, I remembered. They eat a lot of boar in Tuscany. But surely a boar would make a great, blundering crash.

I went on a few steps, but more slowly. Surely no pool terrace lay down this path. I put my head around a great clump of rhododendron and saw a small clearing, a natural glade, where shafts of sunlight fell in clear amber layers upon bare, packed earth, and a little wind stirred. In the center of the glade stood a ramshackle shed affair that looked as if it might hold garden tools; beyond it, a great ravine, or gully, yawned. I could not see the bottom of it. It was narrow, though; it was spanned by a swinging rope bridge that looked centuries old. My heart gave a queasy lurch, and I turned away to go back the way I came. When I did, I saw the falcon.

It sat on a perch in a tall cylindrical cage made of rusted iron, at the far side of the glade. The cage reached from the floor of the glade into the bottom branches of the small tree that arched over it. The door was bound shut with a leather thong, but in any case the falcon could not have gotten free. It was fastened to the perch by a slender leash affair of leather that encircled one yellow foot like a manacle. The falcon was the size of a large crow, feathered in sleek slate gray, barred and spotted on its cream breast. It had a black head, like a leather executioner's hood, that curved under its white chin like sideburns. The yellow beak was powerful and curved, and the claws were steellike, terrible. The bird looked at me impassively with the cold yellow eyes of an executioner. It looked totally wild there in the green gloom, even in the cage; nothing about it spoke of captivity, of being broken to the hand of man. But it was captive. It could not have spread its long wings if it had wanted to. The cage was too narrow.

For some reason my chest burned with sorrow, and my throat ached. I went nearer to the cage and put my finger lightly on one of the rusted bars. The yellow eyes followed me, but the falcon did not move.

"You're very beautiful, aren't you?" I said softly. "Who do you belong to? Who takes care of you?"

The falcon lifted its wings very slightly and stirred on the perch, then settled back into itself. It did not move again. I stood staring at it for a long time, thinking nothing at all, simply bathing myself in its wildness. There was a metal cup of brackish water affixed to the cage beside the perch, but I saw no sign of food. I looked back into the cold sulfur eyes and turned away. Obscure guilt and pain pierced me like an arrow.

When I reached the garden again I was almost running.

As I neared the bottom of the other path—this one flagged all the way, and raked and mowed, and guarded by stout wooden handrails—I heard the light sound of voices and laughter, and splashing, and began to run again. I felt my lips begin to tremble with laughter of my own, seeming perilously near to tears. I heard Sam's rich tenor and Ada's light, tinkling laugh.

I heard Joe, laughing.

I slowed my steps and smoothed my hair and bit my lips to redden them and walked around the last curve in the path, and there they were, in wrought-iron chairs around a white-clothed table, at the far end of an oval pool.

For a moment I stood still, simply looking at them. Sam sat at the head of the table, telling a story. He was making intricate patterns in the air with his big freckled hands, and the sun dappling through the leaves laid flaming copper pennies in his wiry hair. The awful planter's hat lay on the ground beside him. He

wore a striped jersey over the bikini I had seen him in at the pool
in Rome, and some trick of the light made his eyes flame and
spark blue, even from a distance. I felt my mouth curve up.
Hello, Sam, I said silently.

Ada sat beside him in a short red terry robe, another red
towel wrapped around her narrow head. Her eyes were shielded
by her big black glasses, and she was laughing. The sound was
like flutes.

On the other side of her, Joe leaned forward to say something back to Sam. He too was laughing, and his blond hair fell
down over his eyes. I could tell it was damp. He wore his blue
oxford-cloth shirt over his bathing trunks, and his bare feet were
brown. So were his long legs and his forearms, brown with a
haze of gold hair over them. For some reason, his strong wrists
and forearms brought the lump back into my throat.

Sam looked up as if I had called his name and saw me. For
just an instant we were both perfectly still, looking into each
other's eyes, and then he rose to his feet, singing loudly. "There
she is . . . Miss America!" Joe and Ada turned, too, and got to
their feet. Joe grinned and started toward me.

I ran across the pool's apron and hugged him hard, burying
my face in his shirt. It smelled of sun lotion and Joe, warm.

He kissed me lightly and walked me back to the table, his
arm around my shoulders. Sam reached over and hugged me,
and Ada gave me her light kiss, cheek and cheek again, smelling
of her accustomed green, slightly bitter scent.

"We'd about given you all up," Joe said, pulling out a chair
for me on the other side of the table and settling down beside
me. "Did you have a good time? Where's Yolie?"

"Yolie had an appointment in Samarra or something," I
said, grinning around at them. "She decided to stay on in Florence."

I watched it sink in around the table.

"Who drove you over here?" Joe said, honestly puzzled.

"Nobody," I said, trying not to let the grin stretch my

mouth like a jack-o'-lantern's. "I brought the car on over. I don't think she's coming."

There was a moment of silence, and then Sam said, "Did you, by God."

I looked across at him. He was not exactly smiling, but his mouth was curved a little.

He watched me intently, his head slightly to one side. Then he said, "I believe you did. Way to go, Cat!"

"You did? Did you really?" Joe could not seem to take in what I had said.

"I really did," I replied, watching the import of my trip fill his eyes and face. He smiled at me, slowly and tentatively at first, and then broadly. It was a delighted smile, but a little wary, too, almost shy. I had not seen a smile of Joe's precisely like it since the earliest days of our courtship. It made him look absurdly young.

"Well, Cat," he said. "Well, old kitten. God bless you."

He leaned over and gave me another kiss. I touched the side of his face and leaned back in my chair.

Across from me, beside Sam, Ada gave me a long, measuring look. Then she turned her head to Sam. The look that passed between them was long, too, and opaque; I could not read it. Then she looked back at me and smiled her three-cornered little cat's smile.

"Cat, dear, I think this calls for champagne," she said, and looked around.

As if summoned by a whistle that only dogs and waiters can hear, a young man in black pants and bow tie and a starched white shirt appeared at her side. Ada said something to him in soft, rapid Italian, and he nodded and made a little bow and went away.

"Now," Ada said. "Tell us all about it. Tell about last night, and how you happened to get stuck driving over here by yourself—oh, Yolie, *really*; Sam, you're going to have to talk to her again. Tell how it was on the drive."

Suddenly I was tired. Tired to the very marrow of my bones and as light-headed with triumph as if I had already had champagne, a lot of it. I found that I did not want to talk about the drive; I only wanted the moment when they knew I had done it and I had had that. And I certainly did not want to talk about the night before. Here, in the warm sun of this sweet place, in the old silence, cupped in the hands of the sheltering hills, last night seemed tawdry beyond belief, Yolie herself tawdry, what she had told me both tawdry and simply and forever unbelievable. I knew I would not tell them about it. Joe, maybe, later and in little detail. But never Sam and Ada. Never Colin and Maria.

"Ada, you wouldn't believe how uninteresting it all was," I said. "I promise, there's just not anything to tell. Maybe, later, when we run completely out of things to talk about and are all glaring at each other. Right now I'd much rather hear what you all did last night and this morning. Did you eat dinner somewhere wonderful? Have you been into Siena yet? Where are Colin and Maria?"

"In reverse order," Sam said, still looking at me intently, "Colin and Maria are in their room, finishing up last night's fight. Or maybe starting on a fresh one. Or, if we're extremely blessed, screwing and making it all up. You should know soon; they're right next to you. If there's silence, you can assume there has not been a cessation of hostilities. If, on the other hand, you hear a screech like the beginning of a Sioux scalping party—"

"Sam," Ada said mildly. He grinned.

"OK. Yes, we did eat somewhere nice last night, but not as nice as we're going to tonight. We've saved the best for you. It'll be your victory dinner. Maybe another kind of celebration, too. And yes, Ada and Joe and Maria went into Siena this morning, to shop. I worked on the portrait's background. Colin, I believe, meditated in his room."

"What did you buy?" I said to Joe. "Is Siena wonderful? I can't wait to see it."

"It really is," he said. "Very dark and severe, very . . . what?

Medieval. They never did get around to acknowledging the Renaissance. I saved most of the good stuff for you. Ada and Maria used me shamelessly as a beast of burden, staggering up all those steep old streets under loads of chattel—"

"Most of which was yours," Ada said. "Cat, you simply will not believe what this man of yours bought."

"What?" I looked from her to Joe. She began to laugh.

"Well, aside from a complete set of tableware—"

"Dishes?" I said, looking at Joe. Would he really have bought dishes without me present?

"If you don't like them, I'll take them back," he said. "But they're really beautiful. Kind of blue and yellow and white, very rough, very . . . natural. Ada says it's one of the oldest Siennese patterns. I thought they'd look great in the kitchen."

"I can't wait to see them," I said, smiling tentatively. My kitchen at home on the Mountain is green and cream and terra-cotta.

"But wait, that's not all." Ada giggled. "He bought a holy-water font!"

"A what?"

"A little white ceramic wall font, for a private home, you know. Yellow and blue glaze with delicate scrollwork. It's really very pretty. But a holy-water font! Joe! He seems so . . . "

". . . very Anglican," I said, beginning to laugh too. "So very like Mr. Chips. I know. I can just see it, the Rector of Justin, with his own holy-water font. We'll have to hide it in a little niche when people come, like a priest's hole."

Joe looked at us, Ada and me, sitting in the sunlight, laughing, and began to laugh himself. In a moment we were all near hysterics. We laughed a long time.

"I thought it was, you know, to hold keys and stuff," he said, and we were off again, helplessly. This time we did not stop until the young waiter, smiling at our foolishness, brought the champagne.

We drank a lot of it that afternoon, three bottles, and had

more wine with our lunch. We laughed some more, and talked of very little that mattered, and lingered there beside the pool until the light began to slant low through the trees and the little breeze stiffened into a small cool wind. Finally Ada stretched and made as if to get up.

"I believe I'll go up," she said. "I'm really pretty tired. You three stay."

I looked at her. I had never heard Ada admit tiredness. But her voice was fragile, and she did indeed look tired, somehow slackened, emptied out. I wondered if she was coming down with Joe's cold, just briefly, and then put the thought away.

"Please go on," I said. "We've all but worn you to a shred this trip. Take a long nap."

Sam glanced up at her. There was the look again, long, unreadable.

"Do," he said. "You've earned it."

"You coming?"

"In a minute. I won't disturb you, though," he said. "I'm going to do a little more on the portrait. Let's meet in the bar about six-thirty. Maybe I'll have a surprise for everybody."

"What?" I said.

"Well, now," he said, looking at me with his big copper head cocked. The hat rode low on his nose once more. "It wouldn't be a surprise if I told you, would it?"

We all got up, then, and went back up the path to the villa, and up the curving staircase to our rooms. Joe's and mine was on one end of the top floor and looked straight out across the valley to Siena on its hill below us. In the late sun it seemed to float on radiant air, a mirage, a vision.

"This is beautiful," I said. "I think this is my favorite place so far."

The room was large, carved out of heavy white plaster like a peasant barn, plain, but washed with air and light. There were no curtains, only shutters, and the rich smells of the garden floated in to us. The bathroom, though, was luxurious, all warm bronze marble and chrome, with piles of thick white towels and a whirlpool. Its window, too, looked out over the valley and the town beyond. Pots of geraniums sat about, and cakes of rosy, transparent glycerine bath soaps. All of a sudden I wanted a long hot bath more than anything I could think of.

When I came out of the bathroom, wrapped in one of the great towels, Joe was lying on his back on one side of the bed, looking at me. His face was serious.

"Are you sure you're OK?" he said. "It's just what I most wanted not to happen, you to be left alone to get yourself over here. She's a damned menace, Yolanda is. I'm angry as hell at her. I know there's more to it than you're saying—"

"I'm perfectly all right," I said. "It was good for me. Can't you tell?"

"I guess I can't. I'm not sure you can, either. Christ, Cat, you've only been off by yourself once since we got married—I mean when Corinne wasn't monitoring you—in Venice, and look what happened. It nearly destroyed you."

I sat down on the other side of the bed and looked across at him. "It wasn't Venice or being alone that nearly destroyed me," I said carefully. It seemed very important that he understand what I was saying. "It was the *fear* of those things that did the damage. Joe. The *fear* of being alone, the *fear* of being lost, the *fear* of those things . . . there was nothing dangerous but my own fear. There never has been. And Joe . . . that's gone. The fear's gone."

He looked at me for a long time. He did not speak. His eyes did, though.

How can we live without your fear? they said.

However we must, I said back to him with mine. Because I will not live with it again.

Presently, and still without speaking, he reached over and squeezed my hand and turned over and went to sleep. I lay for a long time looking at his back, at the line of his ribs under the brown skin, at the double cowlick at the crown of his head.

I wish you had not kissed her, I thought. Maybe I have no right to wish that, but I do. Or at least, I wish I had not seen it. I don't know how much it changes things.

In a little while I, too, fell into a light sleep, but it did not last long, and it did not seem to relax me. When I awoke, all at once and fully alert, I was still humming all over with the odd, fine vibration that had ridden with me from Florence. It was not anger, though that was still there, far down below, the cold anger at Yolanda. And it was not all the exultation of the vanquishing of the fear. It felt like something else entirely, a breath-held thing, a kind of waiting. It felt like champagne in my veins.

I tried to lie still but could not, and I did not want to wake Joe yet. I got up and dressed quietly, pulling out the white linen that Sam had favored when I sat for him. I had had it laundered and ironed in Florence, and some unknown hands had ironed it to crisp, silky perfection. It felt wonderful against my body. I slipped into sandals and tiptoed to the door, closed it softly behind me, and went downstairs.

I turned into the lounge, toward the bar, but I did not see any of us there. While we napped it had been colonized by a group of American men, and they were sitting and standing around the piano, singing loudly while one of them pounded on it. There could be no doubt at all that they were American. They were around Joe's and Sam's age, I thought, perhaps just a bit younger, and most of them wore what Joe and his peers on the Mountain call a "full Cleveland": white belts and white buck oxfords, plaid pants, polo shirts in pastel colors. It was not a compliment when Joe said it.

There were seven or eight of them, and they were all sunburnt across their cheeks and noses. They were Southerners; their accents were thick and slow, slightly slurred now by what I assumed to be quite a lot of bourbon. Two empty amber bottles and one half-full one stood on the round table they had staked out, and most held half-full glasses in their hands. They were just bawling out the last lines of "Go Alabama, Crimson Tide," when

I came down, and they finished it as I stood in the doorway, yelling in unison, *"Roll, Tide!"* This was followed by a series of yipping yelps and a long, eerie cry I thought might be the Alabama version of a Rebel yell. We had one on the Mountain, but it was rarely used except at football games and fraternity parties, and in any case it did not sound like this. One or two of them beat on the piano with the flat of their hands. The piano player struck up "Dixie," and they joined in. I turned to go, but one of them saw me.

"Whoooeeee!" he shouted. "Wait up, here! Who is this muffin come puttin' her head in our door?"

The song broke off and they all turned to grin at me. One of them began "The Sweetheart of Sigma Chi," and they all took it up, advancing toward me as they sang. I took a step to flee, but one of them caught me by the upper arm, and in an instant they had surrounded me.

I stood there, face flaming, half laughing, half angry, as they serenaded me. I could smell the gusts of bourbon. I was not afraid, but I felt crowded and cornered and embarrassed. They were so grossly out of context here that they were almost obscene. But they were in high good humor, and I knew they meant me no harm. I let them finish the song and then said, smiling, "I'm very flattered, but I have to go now. My husband is waiting for me."

They set up another chorus of yips at my accent.

"Could tell by lookin' at her she was a Dixie belle, couldn't y'all?" bawled the one holding me by the arm. "What's yo' name, sweetheart? Where y'all from?"

The accent was exaggerated theatrically. I had to laugh. They were so like the fraternity boys at Trinity on house-party weekends, rowdy and ridiculous, even ill-mannered, but essentially sweet, somehow very young, even with their paunches and thinning hair and the fine lines around their eyes.

"I'm Cat Gaillard from Montview, Tennessee, and I really do have to go now," I said. "Please go on with your singing."

There were more howls of glee, more slappings of the piano. One of them said, "We are the 1964 pledge class of Delta Kappa Epsilon, University of Alabama, at your service, Miz Cat Gaillard, honey. Part of it, anyhow. We had a suite at the Deke house together for four of the best years of our lives. Our esteemed president here, Mr. Reggie Haynes, Esquire, of Talladega and now Birmingham, won him a trip to Italy sellin' Ford automobiles and asked us all to join him for a little *re*union, just us Dekes, no ladies allowed. I 'spec we'd make an exception for you, though!"

"*Deke! Deke! Deke!*" they bayed. I tried to tug my arm away, but my captor did not let go. Then he did, looking over my shoulder.

Sam Forrest stood behind me, very close, looking mildly at them. He wore the blue blazer and wrinkled seersucker slacks and a white T-shirt stained with the faded stigmata of red wine, sandals and no socks, and the filthy plantation hat. It shaded his eyes, but I caught a glint of flame blue from the shadows, and the gold earring flashed in the gloom. The ponytail exploded from under the hat like a burst of Brillo. I felt a spurt of laughter start up in my chest. He must have looked like something escaped from an itinerant Italian circus, towering there in the dim lounge.

He reached out and gently unhooked my arm from the grasp of the Full Cleveland Deke, who let it go in silence.

"Y'all will perhaps excuse the lady," he said in a slow, soft drawl that sounded not at all like his normal voice. It was flat and polite in the extreme, and somehow had murder in it.

"Sure," muttered my captor, stepping back a little. "No offense. We just heard the accent and it reminded us of home. Pretty lady, one of us in a strange country, you know. No offense."

"None taken." I smiled at him, wanting suddenly to ease his embarrassment, assuage his humiliation before his group. They were all quiet.

"Sam, this is the 1964 Deke pledge class from 'Bama. You might know some of them."

"You go to 'Bama too?" one of them said tentatively. "You in a lodge there?"

"I was way before your time," Sam said affably. "Well. You guys go on with your party. My wife and I are due somewhere."

He turned me with his hand on my shoulder and walked me out into the lobby. Behind me I heard subdued mutterings, and then, in a moment, the piano started up again, and they began to sing. I heard the clink of glass on glass and knew the remaining bourbon was making the rounds.

"You really are a *stronzo*," I said, half laughing, half scowling up at him. "'My wife and I are due somewhere,' indeed. What did you think they were going to do, sing me to death? That was no match."

"I'm not real fond of my countrymen in groups," he said cheerfully. "They get loud and grabby and so goddamned down home it makes me think I'm back in the Phi Delt party room, throwing up after a football game on some little gal's new suede shoes. I went to considerable trouble to get away from that. Now they're importing it."

"Well, you probably did me out of a drink, so why don't you buy me one on the terrace?" I said. "Joe'll be down in a little. I feel like bourbon, I think."

"You can take the girl out of the South, but you can't—blah, blah, blah," Sam said. "Find us a seat. I'll ask the manager to see if he can scare us up a waiter."

"OK. Oh . . . wait. I want to ask him something myself," I said, and went with him up to the little window.

The green-eyed man nodded to us. His jaw was even bluer now, in the twilight.

"Signora?"

"I wanted to ask you about the falcon," I said. "I took the wrong path this afternoon and blundered into his cage. Is he yours? Do you ever let him out? He's a beautiful thing."

"He is a she," the man said, and smiled. It changed his face into something else entirely, an approachable face. "She is a peregrine, a fairly young one. She is a hunting falcon. I trained her myself. She belongs to the owner, but he is very old now and lives in Florence and does not often come here. So I have taken her over. Her name is Guinevere. She is the third Guinevere since I have been here; there have always been falcons at the Falconi: hence our name, you see. This was a hunting lodge in the last century, and they hunted the peregrines here. She is a good hunter, but she has not got a very good temper."

He held up his arm so that the cuff of his jacket fell away, and I saw a line of small, round white scars there, like a flight of distant birds.

"She *pecked* you?" I said incredulously. I thought of that cruel beak.

"No, these are from her feet. We do not call the feet of the raptors claws. With her feet she impales and grasps her prey; the foot is very strong. Only then does she eat them. It is my fault. I flew her once without my arm guard. She had not tried to impale me before. She is very smart. She knew I was without the guard."

"When do you hunt her?" Sam said. His blue eyes were intent, and there was a half-smile on his mouth. I knew he was taken with the idea of the falcon. I thought, not for the first time, that he had a falcon's face himself.

"Oh, I do not hunt her when there are people about," the manager said. "She is unstable, and I cannot be responsible. And then she frightens people. She has a very, what do you say— eerie call. It sounds quite inhuman out over the valley. High and thin and ghostly: *We-chew! We-chew! We-chew!* Not like a bird at all. I hunt her very early in the mornings, before there is anyone about."

"What does she take?" Sam said.

"Oh, rodents, big insects. Other birds. A rabbit, sometimes."

I thought of it, the bird, very high up, a shadow flying

silently on the old red hills, and then the cry, and the swoop, and the thin squeal of the victim, impaled. I shivered.

"It sounds very medieval," I said. "I can just see her, out there over that old valley and that old town. It must be as if time had stopped in the Middle Ages."

"Just so," the manager said. "They have hunted falcons in Siena since there was a city. I feel very much its oldness when I hunt her."

"What do you feed her?" I asked.

"Nothing. She must stay lean for the hunt, a little hungry."

I felt again the swell of pity I had felt when I first found the beautiful captive bird.

"Does she ever try to get away . . . just not come back?" I said.

"Oh, no. She does not know about flying free. She has never flown unless it was to return to the arm. For her it is a part of flight, like the patterns."

"Patterns?"

"They make patterns out over the hills and gullies. It seems to be a natural thing for a falcon; in the wild they will do it. They divide up their range in patterns and fly them, looking down. I think it makes things clearer and simpler for them."

"By God, I'd like to see that," Sam said.

"I wish I could invite you to join us one morning, but I dare not," the manager said. "I cannot tell what she would do. I cannot take the responsibility."

"I quite understand," Sam said. We walked away, he looking off into the distance where the last sun glinted off the towers of Siena. I knew he was with the falcon in his head, up there in the thin blue air, riding the thermals in her ancient patterns. It made me want to hug him suddenly, as I would a child. I wanted to give him the gift of the falcon's flight.

We went out onto the terrace beyond the lounge, nodding to the Alabama Dekes, who lifted their glasses to us as we passed. They began to sing once more after we had gone. Joe and

Colin and Maria were there, at a big table at one end. The other tables were vacant.

"Did you see the tableful of Full Clevelands?" Joe said, grinning, as we slid into our seats. He was drinking bourbon. Colin and Maria sat side by side, bright social smiles painted on their faces. So they had not patched up their quarrel yet. They sipped wine and did not look at each other.

"Sure did. They were just fixing to drag Cat off to their tent when I stepped in and saved her," Sam said. "What is it with the bourbon? Cat said she wanted it, too; y'all on some kind of psychic wave length?"

"They say it happens to people who've been married a long time," Maria said brightly, and then flushed. I could not imagine why and felt only a sort of fatigue. I did not want to spend any more time trying to decipher nuances and minister to frazzled brides.

"They put a move on you, Cat?" Joe said with amusement. "Good ol' home boys, they are. Introduced themselves, and tried to give me the grip, and invited me to join them later in what I gather will be a kind of Siennese nooky search. After dinner, of course. Kept asking me where a guy was supposed to get any in a town that didn't have any places to park. They're going across Italy in an RV, I believe. Their leader told me it had leopard print upholstery and a big mattress in back. See what you missed?"

"Be still, my heart," I said.

"Christ," Colin said virtuously. "The proverbial ugly Americans. You all can castrate me if I turn out like that in twenty years."

Maria looked at him levelly and Joe and Sam laughed. He looked so young and scrubbed and handsome in his blazer and lightweight gray flannels, one leg cut to accommodate his cast. So totally American. It took only a small leap of imagination to clothe him in years and pounds and disappointments. He would look, I thought, not unlike the Alabama Dekes, if he had bad luck.

The waiter brought a bottle of bourbon and ice, and Sam poured drinks for himself and Joe and me. We clinked glasses and tipped our tumblers to Colin and Maria's stemmed ones, and Sam said, "To beginnings and endings."

"What's beginning?" I said. "What's ending?"

"I don't know about the beginnings," he said. "I kind of thought you did. After driving over here by yourself, I mean. A whole new Cat, maybe. But the ending is the ending of the painting. I decided this afternoon it was finished. No more slaving over a hot easel, Cat. I thought I might unveil it for you all before we went to dinner."

"Sam!" I exclaimed. "Is it really? I thought you said—"

"Yeah, but I looked at it once more and realized it really was done. I'll just spoil it if I try to push it further. You game, or would you rather not?"

I was silent. Suddenly I did not want to see the painting. I did not want the days of sitting for him to be over. I was not ready to give them up. To give him up.

"Let's see it, by all means," Joe said. Maria and Colin chimed in. Sam rose and went inside to get the painting. We all sat still, looking at one another.

"Do you realize this is a historic moment?" Maria said. "The unveiling of a new Sam Forrest painting, the centerpiece of the world's next great one-man show? And to think that it's you, Cat; imagine showing it to your children and grandchildren."

"Shit, Maria," Colin said in a low voice, and I saw her remember about Lacey and flinch. I reached over and patted her knee.

"She'll know," I said. "She'll know as well as anyone else. And I fully expect to have grandchildren, all of whom will be mortally embarrassed that their grandmother is grinning off the wall in some museum or collection."

"How does it feel?" she said. "It must be a strange feeling, to know that people all over the world will be looking at you forever."

"I don't guess I've really thought about that," I said slowly. "It doesn't feel any way at all; the famous part of it isn't real to me. I think it's Sam who'll be the talk of the international arty set, not me. Nobody knows the name of people in portraits; they know them by the artist."

"Yeah," Colin said. "Like the Mona Lisa."

Joe said nothing and poured another drink.

"Is this bothering you?" I said.

"No. I'm honored that he chose you. It feels funny, though. I just thought about all the people who'll see it and maybe wonder who you are, or were, and if you had a husband or a boyfriend. I'm going to be Mr. Catherine Gaillard."

"Don't be an ass," I said. "He's not going to title it 'Portrait of Catherine Gaillard.' Artists never do."

"What would he call it, then?"

"I don't know. 'Woman in White Dress,' maybe, or 'Bored Woman Beside Window.' Ask him."

"I will," Joe said.

He drank off his bourbon and poured another, and I held my glass out. My head was beginning to buzz pleasantly. There was a knot of anxiety in the pit of my stomach, though. I wished I had asked Sam not to bring the portrait down. I should have seen it for the first time alone with him.

I drank off the bourbon.

Sam came back with an oblong wrapped in newspaper and tied with string. Ada was not with him.

"Where's Ada?" Joe said.

"Ada has taken one of her sleeping pills and gone to bed," Sam said. "She asked me to give you all her regrets. She'll be out like a light until morning. She was already snoring when I went back up."

"What's the matter?" Joe said, and there was concern in his voice. I did not like hearing it. "She isn't sick, is she?"

I knew without knowing how that he was thinking of his

cold, and I dropped my eyes to the glass in my hand. The anger nipped at me, far down.

"Nah, she does this occasionally, after she's been going on all burners for a while," Sam said. "It's like getting a facial or something, I think. Part of her personal care routine. Her way of dieting. She'll be raring to go in the morning."

"We'll miss her tonight," I said, and Sam grinned at me. I knew he knew I did not mean it. I wondered what else he knew about Ada on this trip, and if he cared. He gave no indication of either.

"Well, then, here we go," he said, and fumbled with the string around the painting.

"Ta-*da!*" Maria sang out.

Suddenly I wanted to get up and run.

Sam propped the painting up on the chair that Ada would have taken and folded his arms and looked at us.

"Behold Cat," he said.

There was a silence, and then two gasps. Then silence again. I lifted my hand to my mouth and found that my lips were parted; only then did I realize that one of the gasps had been mine. I still do not know whose was the other. Maria's, probably.

It was me, no doubt about that. In meticulous brushstrokes overlaid by bold slashes of impasto, my own face, drowned in a diffused white light that you knew somehow was the hot light of afternoon. My own face, head thrown back, eyes shut, mouth open, neck corded with some force that suffused it with pink; he had caught the way I blush from my breasts up to perfection. Just my head and shoulders . . . naked shoulders, sheened as if with sweat, with only a suggestion of wrinkled white linen around them. Just my head, with the hair at my nape and temples dewed like the rest of my flesh, sheened with light and sweat.

Just my head and face, in such a sensual and explicit ecstasy that even as I recognized its genesis, Bernini's Saint Teresa, in the church in Rome, I felt the force of it in my groin, in the pit of my stomach. I looked like the Bernini, there was no doubt of that; his eye had been true.

It also looked like me and no one else, me at the precise moment of climax, me in the act of love. Me, as no one in the world had ever before seen me, except Joe Gaillard.

I could not get my breath. I could not move my eyes from it.

"That's the dress you're wearing tonight, isn't it?" Maria said presently, in a high, silly voice.

Colin cleared his throat. "It's a fine piece of work, Sam," he said judiciously. "Very powerful. Not at all derivative. It transcends style and school. Not really Cat, of course, but very evocative. . . ." His voice trailed off. He looked down at his hands.

I raised my eyes to Sam's face. He was smiling faintly and looking at me inquiringly. I did not think he saw anything at all amiss with the painting. He was merely waiting to see what I thought.

I looked over at Joe. His face was still and very pale. He did not move his eyes from the painting.

"It's modeled on a Bernini statue that we saw in Rome the afternoon you didn't come with us," I said chattily to Joe. "The day you and Colin had the footrace, remember? I wish you'd seen it; it's a remarkable likeness. Sam thought so at the time. Ada did too; I remember that she agreed. . . . It's called *Saint Teresa in Ecstasy*."

I stopped. Finally he moved his eyes to me. They were flat and dark.

"Maybe he can call this one 'Cat in Heat,'" Joe said, and got up and walked away toward the lounge.

I got up and ran after him, my legs rubbery and trembling. I stopped him with my hand on his arm. He turned and looked at me. I will never forget that look. There seemed nothing in it but a vast, cold distaste. He pulled his arm away, but he stood without moving.

"It's a thing he does, Joe," I said. "You know he painted Verna Cardigan as Brünhilde. I know when he first saw me in Rome, he thought of the Saint Teresa. . . . Please don't do this. Please don't spoil things. It's . . . you *know* there wasn't anything—"

"I know," Joe said very clearly, "that he knows how my wife looks when she's getting fucked. That's what I know. And now the entire world is going to know it too. What is it, Cat, you expect me to go to the big opening for it and chomp shrimp on a toothpick and sip wine and say, 'Yes, indeedy, that's my little wife, all right, coming like a house afire'? Sure I will. Sure I will."

"How can you say that? I have never in my life slept with anybody but you! You know that! You *know* that!"

My voice cracked. I couldn't get a deep breath.

Behind me Sam Forrest said, "Take it easy, Joe. Cat doesn't deserve this. If you want to yell at anybody, yell at me. It's exactly the pose of the Saint Teresa; don't go accusing her of anything until you've seen the statue. My God, man, what do you think—"

"How did you know?" Joe spat at him in a voice I did not know, had never heard. He did not look at Sam but at me. "How else could you possibly know?"

"I'm a painter," Sam said. "I paint what I see. She looks for all the world like the Bernini *Teresa;* I saw it when I first saw her, at our place in Rome. I'm sorry if you're upset, but if I were you, I wouldn't go throwing accusations at Cat. She's done nothing wrong. Nothing. She might, in fact, want to ask you about the time *you've* spent with my good wife!"

I went hot all over, felt sick. Please stop this, I thought dully. Everybody please, please stop.

Joe's face went even whiter, but he dropped his eyes from my face. He turned away again and walked into the lounge. Just beyond the doorway he looked back over his shoulder.

"Did you holler, Cat?" he said.

I turned away, blindly, and went back to my seat. I heard

Joe say something to the group of Dekes around the piano, and
heard them laugh and cheer, and when they began to sing again,
his rich tenor rose with them.

"Roll your leg over, oh, roll your leg over," they sang. "Roll
your leg over the man in the moon."

"I think maybe we'll pass on dinner," Maria said in a small
voice. She got up out of her chair and walked from the terrace.
Colin looked at Sam and at me and then lifted his hands and let
them drop, silently, and followed her. His crutches thumped
loudly.

"Well," Sam said presently. "How about another drink,
Saint Catherine of the sorrows?"

"Please," I said, holding out my glass.

We drank our drinks in silence. I clenched mine very hard,
trying to stop the fine trembling that had begun again in my
stomach and now shook every part of me. It was like a tiny
engine; I did not think he could see it, but I could not stop.

I simply could not think of anything to say to him. I thought
I would like to sit here on this terrace, with the Tuscan treetops at
my feet and the little night wind tasting of dust off the pink hills
on my face, until everyone else had gone away and night had
fallen, and I could go back to my room unseen. I knew I must
talk Joe through this, but the effort seemed so monumental it
was ludicrous, as if I had been asked to move a mountain
unaided, empty a sea.

"Not a great night for art fans," Sam said. He was slumped
down in his chair, his long legs extended straight out in front of
him, chewing ice. His eyes seemed very blue in the dusk.

"It's a beautiful painting," I said dully. "It really is. Please
don't think I think it isn't. But it . . . I guess I didn't know you
were going to do that."

"Didn't you?" he said.

I did not reply. Had I not known? I wasn't sure, now.

"I'll go in and talk to him in a minute," he said. "Soon as

those assholes have gone. I can make him see what I was doing, that you and I didn't—well, whatever. I can probably even make him like it, or think he does. I've done it before. Christ, you should have heard David Cardigan when he first saw what I'd done with Verna, and now he thinks he invented the portrait himself."

"What did you do with Verna?" I said.

"Well, one of her tits sort of hangs out," he said. "And they were something to see in those days. Cantilevered, I guess you'd say."

I burst out laughing in spite of myself.

"What on earth am I going to do with you?" I said, near tears. "What am I going to do with him?"

"I don't know about with me. That's up to you. I'm going to go talk to him. Though I really ought to let him twist in the wind awhile. I'm not real fond of what he said to you. You ought not be, either."

"Well, I'm not," I said. "I hate what he said to me. He's never said anything like that before. But Sam, it's been hard on him, this trip. Back home he's . . . I don't know. So totally in charge. So many people look up to him. He's really good at what he does. Over here, every time he turns around, something happens to him. He falls in a canal. You pull him out. You haven't exactly made him look good, you know."

"Goddammit, Cat, I haven't tried to sabotage him," he said, frowning in annoyance. "Most of the time I haven't even been thinking about him. If he feels he's been shown up in Italy, the problem is his. Not mine. Not yours."

"I know," I said.

After the last drink, things did not look so bad. I felt suddenly lazy and loose-jointed, indolent, powerful in an odd and offhand kind of way. I stretched, and rolled my head back until I heard vertebrae crackle, and said, "Well, let's finish this bottle and then we'll both go talk to him. You wrap the painting back up and take it upstairs, and we'll take him somewhere great for dinner and maybe get him a little drunk. It won't seem so bad to him in the morning. Joe doesn't hold grudges."

We finished the inch or so left in the bottle. Sam reached out and touched my cheek with one finger, very lightly. Just that touch. I reached up and put my finger where his had been.

"In a way I'm sorry the painting is done," he said.

"So am I."

"Maybe," he said in a low voice, "I can go back and rework some of it. I'd need you to sit again a few times. . . ."

"Maybe you could," I said. My own voice was husky. I cleared my throat.

"Let's see what happens," Sam said. "Shall we? There's a lot of Tuscany left."

"Let's."

He got up and gave me his hand and pulled me up. Then he dropped my hand and we walked into the bar to talk to Joe. It was full dark now. The lamps in the bar were lit, and a small fire blazed in the huge fireplace, but there was no one there. The Dekes had gone. Joe was gone too.

I looked at Sam and walked rapidly out to the desk. The green-eyed man was not there. A heavy young woman with improbably carmine hair piled up on her head was sorting forms of some sort. She looked up, smiling courteously.

"The gentlemen in the bar, have they left?" I said.

"Yes," she said. Her accent was heavily Italian, the Italian of the South. "They have go to Siena to eat and howell. They gone in the big fan."

"Howell?" I said stupidly.

She grinned and threw her head back and pantomimed a wolf's howl. I could just see the Dekes doing it.

"Ah . . . there was another gentleman with them, another American, tall, blond, wearing a blue jacket. Did he go too?" I said.

She just stared at me. I realized those words could have described any one of the Dekes. I tried again.

"Gaillard. A Mr. Joe Gaillard."

"Ah. Choe. You mizziz Choe? He leave you a note."

I nodded. She handed it to me. It was sealed inside a Villa di Falconi envelope. I opened it.

Going to travel a little with the Dekes, it read. *Maybe I'll see you in the morning. Maybe I'll see you in Rome. Maybe I'll see you in a gallery.*

He had signed it with a large, looping J. The writing and the signature were loose and sloppy. He was drunk, I thought.

"What's up?" Sam said. He was looking at me intently.

"Joe's decided to join the Dekes and see the world," I said, and giggled. The giggle came out more like a hiccup. Perhaps a sob.

"Jesus," he said. "The asshole. Want to go down to Siena and look for them? There are some pretty raunchy spots down there, in the back alleys. Somebody will point them toward one. It shouldn't be any problem finding the RV. There're only one or two public lots where they could park it."

"No," I said. "I don't. What I want to do is go down to Siena or somewhere and have a wonderful dinner and then go somewhere and dance. Or something. Will you take me to dinner?"

"I will," he said. "And to something, too."

"Can you dance, Sam?"

"Like a waltzing hippo. But I can something like there's no tomorrow."

"Then," I said, taking his arm, "let's go something."

"Your call, Cat," he said.

CHAPTER FOURTEEN

WE NEVER DID EAT DINNER. I think I knew when we set out in the Opel that we would not. I had a powerful sense that another woman entirely wore my skin that night, sat in the seat beside Sam Forrest as he drove, barbarously, down the sinuous road to Siena. This woman laughed as he skidded perilously through curves, sprayed gravel on dizzying overhangs; this woman laughed as oncoming cars veered out of the way of the Opel, blatting their horns, their drivers mouthing silent curses and shaking fists. This woman leaned her head far back on the seat, stretched her arms, and arched her back until the linen of her dress threatened to part over her breasts. This woman clung to the arm of the man in the driver's seat, leaned her head over to bite his shoulder none too gently, sang a little, hummed the rest of the way.

This woman had not come to eat dinner.

"What first?" Sam said, when he had rammed the Opel into

a narrow parking place in the lot beside the Cathedral. The rest of the lot was full, but there was no RV there. The old Catherine Gaillard would have gotten out of the car trembling and ashen and asked for dinner, but the woman who had pushed her far back and down danced out, demanding drink.

"I want some more bourbon," I said. "And then maybe some more someplace else. Seedy places, Sam; dark. Can you pub-crawl in Siena? That's what I want to do. And then I want to dance. Then, maybe, we'll eat."

He laughed.

"Not a lot of night life in Siena; it's a clubby place. If folks are going to let it rip, they usually do it in the clubs in their *contrada*. But I'll see what we can do. There are a couple of little places down in the old town that might be seedy enough for you. You up to some walking?"

"I'm up to anything. The question is, are you? I saw you stagger getting out of the car."

"So did you, me proud beauty. Wonder we both aren't crawling. Do you really think you ought to drink any more hard stuff? Wine might be smarter."

I whirled around and put my hands on his shoulders and leaned up into his face.

"This is not a night for wine," I said. And then I twirled away, spinning on one foot so that the skirt of my dress would bell out.

He caught me by the arm and looked down at me, smiling.

"And who have we here tonight?" he said.

"Catherine of Siena," I said. "They're going to talk about her for a long time in this town. You are too."

"I bet," he said, and we plunged none too steadily down into the spiderweb of narrow streets that led into the heart of Siena.

The old part of Siena huddles around the great open fan of the Campo, jumbles of severe Gothic houses and palazzi and shops, their plain brick walls studded by small shuttered windows. They are set so close to the tortuous streets that you must walk there; there seemed that night to be no sidewalks at all. But there were no automobiles either. None could have circumnavigated the streets. They were too narrow and too steep; often they gave up, and simply became flights of shallow stairs, and then were transmuted into streets or alleys again. The houses on either side shouldered into one another, so that it was like walking between high, forbidding walls. The overall feeling, I thought as I lurched along beside Sam, clutching his arm and stumbling on the rough cobbles, was of verticality and darkness. Shops were guarded with corrugated iron. Windows were shuttered, and what little light leaked through was pale and thin. And yet, even in the darkness, Siena seemed to glow. The very stuff of the houses did; they seemed to breathe out pale golds and yellows and reds into the thick night; their tile roofs seemed to burn like embers. There was a huge white moon; we had driven down into the city bathed in its light. But it did not penetrate in here. Roofs leaned too closely over the streets. Nevertheless, Siena lay that night in its own glow.

"It's like being in the heart of a banked fire," I said once.

"Burnt sienna," Sam said. "It's the color of the earth around here. It makes one of the best pigments for painting. I use a lot of it; it's the undercolor for a good bit of your portrait. Most of the houses are built of it. There's a saying; I think it's the motto of one of the districts: 'It's the red of the coral that burns in my heart.'"

"I love that," I said, squeezing his arm and stumbling. He righted me. "I think that will be my motto for tonight." I giggled. "I'm going to be the coral that burns in your heart. Watch out, or I'll burn you up."

"I think you would," he said, and leaned over and kissed the top of my head. I put my arms around his neck and kissed him, fully and deeply, and then broke free of his tightening arms and pulled him on down the alleyway.

"We haven't even crawled one pub yet," I said.

Behind me he made a sound that might have been laughter or a soft groan.

He dogtrotted me down one dark old street and up another; I had no sense at all of where we were. There were people on the street, but not a great many. They all seemed to be heading the same way we were: down. Back and forth, in and out, but always and inexorably down. At last, breathing hard and beginning to feel the spongy deadness of sobriety, I said, "Dammit, Sam, we could just have brought a bottle and sat in the car. Where are we going?"

"Here," he said, and we broke out of the cobweb of alleyways into a great open space, bordered with uplit red towers and graceful Gothic palazzi and houses. It seemed, after the claustrophobic darkness, to be made of light. Lights blazed in the symmetrical structures fringing it; lights picked out the contours and details of the fine towers; light seemed to pour upward from the very stones of the piazza toward the moon, lying just above the great white-tipped bell tower. The Torre del Mangia.

"Oh, God," I breathed, blinking. "It's the Campo, isn't it?"

"It is. Now was that worth the hike, or what?"

"I never saw anything so brazenly dramatic," I said. "It's stunning. It's almost scary. How could you ever relax here? You'd have to sit up straight the whole time."

"This is where people come to relax, though," Sam said. "This is the big civic playpen. Shops and *caffès* and restaurants; in the daytime this is wall-to-wall people. And you should see it during the Palio, the big medieval horse race. It's a circus. We missed it by a week. Watch your step; there may be a few tokens from it still lying around. When your eyes get accustomed you'll see there's plenty going on."

They did, gradually. He was right. There were people walking arm and arm across the great shell-shaped piazza, people sitting in the outdoor *caffès*, people going in and out of doors on the ground floor.

"Are we going to drink here? It's awfully bright," I said.

"We are going to eat first," Sam said. "If I'm going to last out a night of debauchery with Catherine of Siena, I'm going to have to get something on my stomach, or you'll end up having to drive my inert carcass home. And we wouldn't want that."

I scrubbed my face into his upper arm.

"No, we wouldn't," I said.

But in the end we did not. Sam headed for Il Campo, directly on the piazza, but it was hopelessly jammed. A line straggled out the door.

"I thought all doors opened for Sam Forrest," I said. "Don't they know who they just snubbed?"

"All doors open for Ada Forrest," Sam said. "I don't have anywhere near her clout."

We tried a few other restaurants on the square, but all of them were just as mobbed. In the end, Sam led me back into the darkness, into the warren of alleyways behind the Palazzo Pubblico. There, after another seemingly endless stumbling trot through the darkness, we found a tiny hole-in-the-wall of a place where only a few dark-clad men sat silently at tables, drinking.

"Maybe they have sandwiches," Sam said, sinking down at one of the scarred tables in back, beside a rough-cut concrete wall. "Christ, it's like Hitler's bunker."

"They have whiskey," I said, seeing the bottles lined up above the tiny, filthy bar. "That's a good omen."

"We are doomed," Sam said. "On your head be it."

A silent waiter brought a bottle of whiskey and thick, filmed glasses to our table and went away. I don't know what sort it was. It was fiery and raw. I poured us both half a tumbler full and lifted mine to him.

"To *la dolce vita*," I said. "And lots of or something."

"Or something," he repeated solemnly, and we drank.

The evening seemed to dim out then, to soften, flicker, snap back into focus, blur again. We drank the bottle of whiskey and went somewhere else, a dark grotto full of quiet, anonymous people, that might have been the first. We had whiskey there, too. Somewhere in that place, or perhaps the next one, there was a jukebox. I remember dragging Sam to his feet, laughing, and dancing with him in a tiny dark space next to it, surrounded by empty tables with their chairs tipped over them. I think there were still people at the bar, but by then I could not have been sure. I knew I had drunk enough so that the Cat Gaillard I had been earlier that day would be out cold, but this new woman was still on her feet. On her feet, her body pressed hard against Sam Forrest's, her arms around his neck, her face pressed into it. This woman nibbled his neck and kissed his face and held her mouth up to his and was kissed in return. This woman was still swaying there with the big man when the music ended and the dim lights flickered on.

Sam lifted his head and looked down at me owlishly; he shook his head as if he were coming up out of water. I still clung to him, drowning in the feel of his body against mine, smeared and swollen with the kisses. He lifted my chin with his hand.

"I think they want us to leave," he said hoarsely. "What now, Cat?"

"Now," I said, letting my head fall back over his arm and then snapping it up again, "now I'm asking."

He was silent for a moment, and then he said thickly, "You sure? A spite fuck is a sorry thing."

"It ain't spite when it's willing," I said.

"Then let's go home."

But when we reached the dark pavement outside, it was obvious that neither of us could manage the long, black climb back up to the parking lot beside the cathedral. We leaned against each other for a moment, and then he said, "I'm going to get the manager to call us a cab. We'll never find one. We can come back and get the car tomorrow, or get somebody at the hotel to do it."

"There's no tomorrow," I sang. "There's just tonight."

"Hold on," he said, and went back into the bar.

When he came back out, I pulled him into the shadows and
kissed him again. We were still kissing when the taxi driver came
around the corner to fetch us, and we clung tightly to each other
as we stumbled after him to a street where cars were able to navigate, and fell back into each other's arms in the back seat of the
cab when the driver jerked it into motion. By the time it stopped,
on the gravel in front of the darkened Villa di Falconi, there was
nothing in the world for me but sensation and the feel of him,
and the thick smell of his body and breath.

After the taxi left we stood for a moment, looking up at the
sleeping villa. No lights showed, at least on the front. My room
and Joe's was dark. So was Sam and Ada's, on the other end. I
glanced into the parking lot across the road; no RV towered
there. It was the first time that night, I realized murkily, that I
had thought of Joe. The thought did not hold.

The semicircle of gravel gleamed ghostly white in the bright
moonlight. Sam looked down at me.

"It's like standing in a floodlight. We can't stay here. What
did you have in mind, Miss Cat?" he said. His tongue was as
thick as mine.

I hesitated. What *did* I have in mind? Now that I knew I
would make love with him, and soon, where had I thought to set
that love? I did not know.

"I guess my room and yours are out," I said. "And the car is
back down there. What do *you* think?"

He took a deep breath.

"Christ, whatever's closest . . . I'm not going to be able to
wait long."

"I don't know," I said. And then I did.

"This is perfect," I said, taking his hand. "This is absolutely
perfect. This spot was made for us."

I pulled him behind me, around the side of the villa and
down into the tangled vegetation the lay behind it. Three steps in
and we were swallowed by profound blackness.

"My God, Cat, they'll find our skeletons ten years from now," Sam whispered behind me. "We're going to fall and never land."

But I knew we would not. The night and the moonlight seemed to have seeped through my skin into my bloodstream; darkness and wildness bore me up like invisible hands. I felt surreally clear and focused and surefooted, a creature of the night, a wild thing. I was not going to fall, and I would not let him fall.

"Come on," I whispered back to him. "You're safe."

He was. We both were. My feet felt the path through the soles of my shoes; my eyes saw the shapes of trees and shrubs and thorns as if they had been lit for me. I went down the slick, overgrown path as if it had been a floodlit highway, and he followed me, stumbling and grunting and flailing but never falling. By the time we reached the clearing, I was tingling all over with the night and what lay ahead; laughing, manic with it.

"*Voilà*," I said, and stepped into the little glen where the falcon's cage was.

The moonlight was so bright here it seemed solid; you might simply climb it up into the sky, to the cold moon itself. Maybe, I thought raptly, we'll do that. After. After. . . .

"Holy shit," Sam breathed. He looked around the little glen and then walked over to the falcon's cage. We could see her clearly in the white radiance. She sat still in her dully shining gray, looking at us impassively out of her black hood with the yellow headsman's eyes. Sam put a finger into the cage, slowly. She lifted her long wings silently, as far as she could, and snaked her head low, but she did not move from the perch. Slowly, as she had done before, she settled back into herself, still looking at us.

"Holy shit," Sam breathed again, to himself. "I want to paint that."

"Well," I said. "Is this going to do?"

He looked at me, and then around the clearing.

"You mean, in that little shack there?"

"No. I mean right here. On the ground. Under the moon. With her for a witness. Right here, Sam."

He looked at me a little longer, smiling faintly, and then walked over to the shed and jerked the creaking door open.

"I don't want to go in there—"

"No."

He leaned into the shed, and when he straightened back up, he was holding a tattered blanket. He snapped it smartly in the air, and the dust motes rode dizzily up the shafts of moonlight.

"There's a pillow too," he said. "Somebody else has the same idea, or had. You want the pillow?"

Silently, I shook my head. I looked at him.

He spread the blanket out on the floor of the glade and stepped onto it and looked back at me.

"Then come here to me," he said.

I started forward and then stopped.

"Wait," I said. "Wait just a minute. Stay right there. I want to do it this way."

Smiling, he sat down cross-legged on the blanket.

"Like I said, Cat. You don't want to wait too long."

I ran across the glade and ducked into the little shed. It was piled and jumbled and smelled of rotting cloth and dust and something like dusty grain. I felt spiderwebs break across my face, but they did not bother me on this night. On this night I felt nothing but the steady, sweet hum of my own blood and the print of his body still, against mine.

I unbuttoned the white linen and let it fall to my feet. I unhooked my bra and let it fall; I stepped out of my panties, out of my shoes. I closed my eyes for a moment, and then I opened them, and ducked back out of the shed, and stood before him in the moonlight.

It seemed that I stood there a long time before he spoke. The white bath of the moon was almost palpable on my naked body; it was like being touched all over by millions of tiny, prickling fingers. They almost burnt, but I could not tell if it was a cold burning or a hot one. When he still did not speak, I lifted my arms under the weight of the moon and held them over my head and turned around, very slowly.

"Do I look like you thought I would?" I said. My voice was caught deep in my throat.

"I knew how you would look," he said, and his voice caught too. "I knew when I started to paint you. How you would look. How you . . . will be. I have seen you already; I have had you already, a hundred times."

I felt a flicker of flatness, of disappointment. I let my arms fall.

"I hope the original lives up to the image," I said.

"A hundred times over," he breathed. "A thousand times over. God, but you are beautiful! Come, Cat. . . ."

He got up onto his knees and held out his arms to me. He did want me; I saw that he did.

"Wait just once more," I said, a new thought coming into my mind. A fine thought, a wonderful thought. "Wait and watch me. Watch me, Sam!"

"Jesus, Cat!" he said, and then, "OK, I'm watching."

I turned and ran across the glade toward the little hanging bridge. I think he only noticed it then.

"I hope you don't have any therapeutic ideas about fucking on that thing," he said, and there was laughter close under his words.

"No, now watch!"

"I'm watching."

I stopped at the lip of the bridge, took a deep breath, and ran onto it. It dipped and swayed sickeningly, and my heart rose up in my throat, but I did not stop. I let my run take me on out, into the very middle. Then I stopped and looked down.

There was nothing below me but blackness. Nothing on either side. Nothing in the air above me. Here, on this bridge swinging over darkness, the moon's fingers reached only the very tips of the trees that made a canopy over whatever lay below. I stood still and let my hands fall away from the damp ropes on either side that served as the bridge's only guard rails. I closed my eyes. I did not hear water and did not sense earth. The bridge might have spanned some essential chasm that opened straight into the core of the planet.

I stood for quite a little time, listening to the deep, sweet thrum of my blood past its pulse points, thinking of nothing at all except the feeling of the thick night on my naked body. Then I thought of his hands on it, and my blood quickened, and I turned and ran off the bridge again and across the glade to the blanket.

He lay on his side, eyes closed, chest rising and falling serenely.

All of a sudden I was very tired and cold. I knelt beside him and shook him, feeling a little night wind that I had not known was there putting fingers all over me, into secret crevices and folds, into my hair, on my lips.

"Wake up," I whispered, shaking his shoulder. "Sam, wake up!"

"Jus' a minute," he mumbled, not opening his eyes. "Jus' got to rest a minute. Jus' a little while. Then we'll do it. . . ."

"Sam, I'm cold."

"C'mere," he said, eyes still shut, reaching his arms out to me.

I stood for a moment more and then dropped down onto the blanket and fitted myself into his arms. I was very cold. I burrowed close to him, wriggling until the entire length of me was pressed against him. He was very warm. I put my face into the hollow of his neck, and he closed both arms around me and wrapped me to him.

"Rest just a little while," he whispered. The wind of it stirred my hair.

"Just for a minute," I said. I was warm all over now. "Just for a minute."

I closed my eyes. . . .

When I opened them, the glade was ashen with the gray that comes just before sunrise, and he was gone.

I sat up, blinking around the glade. He had laid his blue jacket over me, and I held it close. There was cold dew in the glade now. Everything seemed damp and cold and empty. Perhaps he had gone into the shed, or over the bridge.

But I knew he had not. The very air around me was empty of him. If he had been close, I would have known. I lay back down on the blanket and pulled the jacket closer around me, and curled up into a small ball on my side, and closed my eyes again.

I do not think I lay there long, but I seemed to hear many words. No pictures came with them, but the words were as clear as if the people who said them lay next to me.

"Americans behave badly in Italy, Cat. All of us, in one way or another," Yolanda said.

And, "It's all one slick, straight, hard, shiny surface. You couldn't chip it with dynamite."

And, "I don't have to tell you how simple Ada has made it for Sam to paint you; she's literally taken charge of Joe so you could be alone with Sam. I've watched her do it."

And, from some earlier place, "Your vulnerability. That excites Sam."

But I had not been vulnerable last night.

And he had not, after all, made love to me.

"You better fuck him fast, Cat," Yolanda had called to me from the table of the restaurant in Florence.

I had, it seemed, waited too long. He had already made his love, and that was to the woman on the canvas. The woman in his arms last night had been the image.

Oh, yes, there would be a new show soon. He was burning with it, throbbing with it.

I had thought the burning was for me.

I lay with my face pressed to the old earth of the hill and knew I was not safe and never would be. And it did not matter.

Presently I got to my feet, still clutching the jacket around

me, and looked again around the clearing. He had folded my
dress neatly and laid it at the edge of the blanket with my shoes
and underwear. I put them all on and smoothed the dress and
my wild hair. Across from me the falcon stirred her great wings
silently and cocked her head. But she made no sound.

I went across the glade and opened the door to her cage. I
reached in and loosened the leather tie. Then I stepped back and
looked at her.

"Go on," I whispered. "Go. No more cages for you. No
more."

But she shrank back against the bars on the far side and did
not move.

"I don't blame you," I said. "It's not what it's cracked up to
be out here."

I started out of the glade, and then stopped, and turned,
and went onto the bridge again, to the very middle, and looked
down. The bridge itself lay in the thin first light, but whatever
lay below was still in darkness. I balled the blue jacket up and
held it out over the rope railing and let it fall. I heard it tumbling
through vegetation, but I did not hear it hit. Then I went back
and through the glade and up the path toward the Villa di Falconi. I did not fasten the door to the peregrine's cage when I
went.

When I came out onto the gravel semicircle, it was full light,
though still very early. A gardener pushed a wheelbarrow along
a brick path on the far side of the garden, and an elderly man
came out of the villa dressed in a warm-up suit and jogging
shoes and began to trot down the drive toward the road to Siena,
nodding to me as he went. But no one spoke. I thought that, in
my white dress, I might have looked like an apparition sprung
from the woods in the chilly dawn, but not one, now, with the
power to frighten.

There was no one about in the lobby, but from somewhere
just out of sight I heard the chink of china, and smelled coffee
brewing. The manager's window was shuttered. I stopped on

the polished wooden floor just as a pool of sun spilled over the line of the eastern trees outside, letting its fragile warmth touch me. I stood still under it for a moment, as you might under a warm shower. Then I turned and went softly up the stairs.

All the doors on my floor were shut, and there was no sound. I do not know what I had thought to hear. At my own door I stopped, and reached into the pocket of my dress for my key, but then saw that the door stood slightly ajar. I pushed it open and went in, feeling absolutely nothing except a great, simple desire for sleep.

Joe sat on the far side of the big bed, his head turned toward the open window that commanded the distant skyline of Siena. He still wore the oxford shirt and chinos he had worn last night, but he was tieless, and the shirt was as wrinkled as if he had picked it out of the dirty clothes hamper. His hair fell over his eyes, and even from the doorway I could see the glint of stubble on his jaw. He held the telephone in his hand. He was not using it, simply holding it.

He turned slowly to face me, and I saw that his eyes were sunken in the blue hollows where they retreat when he has had no sleep, and his face was dirty, actually striped with dirt. He took a deep breath and let it out in a long, shuddering sigh. His lips moved, but he said nothing, and then he said, "Cat. Where have you been?"

His voice was old. Thin and weak, cracked, old.

I shook my head, looking at him.

"I've been out all night looking for you," he said in his old, old voice. "You weren't here last night when I got back, and I couldn't raise anybody in Sam and Ada's room, and Colin and Maria didn't know where you were, and the manager didn't. And the car was gone. I went back down to Siena looking for you. I looked in every restaurant and bar and joint and hole in the wall and back alley I could find; I had a cabdriver with me, and he looked too. I was going out into the hills around here this morning. I've just talked to the police. They wanted me to come in and sign some stuff. Some *documenti*."

Incredibly, he smiled, but it did not hold. His mouth began to shake and he closed it. He got up and walked to the window and put his hands on the sill, as if to rest his weight there. With his back to me, still in the old eggshell voice, he said, "They've gone, you know. Sam and Ada. Colin and Maria. Gone back to Rome in the station wagon. I saw them as I was coming back in this morning."

He stopped and I nodded, as if he could see me. Of course they had gone. I had known that back in the glade. He was not anywhere in the air of this place. Ada would get some rest now. Her job was over; his was just beginning. That was what the look that had passed between them at lunch yesterday had said. He had even said it aloud to her: "You've earned it."

I still did not speak. I looked at Joe's back.

"Cat," he said finally. "You and Forrest. Did you . . . ?"

"No," I said. "No, we never did."

He did not move, but his shoulders slumped.

Then he put his hands up to his face and rubbed his eyes, and I saw that the right hand was wrapped in white, white spotted with red. His handkerchief, I thought. I went a little way into the room, near enough to see that the hand was swollen, the flesh pouching redly around the sides of the tight cloth.

"What did you do to your hand?" I said. It was my own voice; how strange.

He still did not turn.

"I knocked him down," he said.

"You knocked Sam Forrest down?"

"I asked him where you were. He wouldn't tell me. He said it was for you to decide if you wanted to tell me or not. And . . . I knocked him down."

His voice sounded queer and stifled; I had the wild thought that he might be laughing.

"Wow," I said. It sounded precisely as stupid as it was, but I could think of nothing else to say.

He did laugh, then. He put his face back down into his hands and laughed and laughed; his shoulders shook with it. And then he took a deep, strangled breath, and I knew he was crying, not laughing. Crying in a terrible and total way I had never heard before; crying and trying not to.

"Please don't," I said softly. "Please don't."

"I thought you had gone," he said. He could hardly speak. "I thought you had just . . . gone. I'd have died if you had, Cat. I wouldn't blame you, but I'd have died."

I went around the bed and put my hands on the back of his shoulders and steered him to the bed. The sobbing did not stop, and I did not look up into his face. I did not think he would want me to do that. I sat him down on the bed and pulled the covers back.

"Let's sleep," I said. "That's what we both need, more than anything. Come on, slip in here. We'll both sleep. After that we'll talk."

He said nothing more, but he did slide into the bed and under the covers. Still in his pants and shirt, he rolled over onto his side, as he did when he slept at home, away from me. I pulled the covers up around his chin. I could still hear his breath, still catching, still uncontrolled, as I went to the window and closed the shutters. He did not sob again, but he still did not breathe well.

I slid out of my dress and shoes and crept into the other side of the bed. I lay looking up at the ceiling. Small bars of sun, going from white to yellow now, danced there, cast up through the shutters. They were hypnotic. I don't know how long I watched them. I could not seem to capture a thought, so I simply lay, watching sun flickers.

After a long time Joe said, "What will happen now?"

He did not turn to me.

"I don't know," I said.

Another pause, then: "Can we go home?"

"Whenever you like."

"No . . . I mean, *can* we? Can we go home again?"

As I had on that morning in Florence, on the terrace by the pool with Yolanda—had it only been two mornings ago?—I thought of the stone house on the lip of the Steep. I saw it again as I had then: saw the bright rooms washed by the thin, clear air of the Mountain, one by one; saw my garden with all its flowers blooming; saw scrubbed counters and kitchen flagstones, shining softly; saw sofas indented by years of our bodies, pillows that held the imprint of our heads, newly vacuumed rugs that still held the tracks of our feet.

I did not see us, though. Joe and I were not there. But then I looked again, and there were our shadows. The two of us, shadow Cat and shadow Joe, close together in the sun of the living room, in the sun of the kitchen. We were there, then. We were still there. I just could not see us.

"I think so," I said.

He did not say any more. But in a moment he reached over his shoulder with the bound hand and laid it on my hip, and I covered it very lightly with mine. I left it there, listening to his breathing. Pretty soon it slowed and deepened, and his hand slackened and slid from under mine. Joe has always gone softly down into sleep.

I felt my own sleep coming toward me then, felt the shape of it out there, white and deep and vast as a glacier. With my thoughts I reached out toward it, wanting that great, softly hissing whiteness, wanting just that.

Before it reached me I heard the falcon. I knew instantly what it was, that primal unearthly cry, high in the air over the villa.

"*We-chew,*" she called. "*We-chew, we-chew.*"

I lay listening, eyes closed, mouth curved in a smile. I heard her as she made her old immutable patterns, wove them into the high, thin blue air, back and forth, back and forth. The call receded and came back. Receded and came back. I lay waiting.

Finally it did not come back. I listened as it climbed up into the vault of the morning one last time, and then it faded and faded and finally vanished. I could not hear it anymore.

But I thought that if I got up and went to the window and leaned out and looked up, perhaps I might see her, just for a moment, just for a heartbeat, a speck against the sun that was only now brushing the tops of the city below us on the hill.

Warner now offers an exciting range of quality titles by both established and new authors. All of the books in this series are available from:
Little, Brown and Company (UK) Limited,
P.O. Box 11,
Falmouth,
Cornwall TR10 9EN.

Alternatively you may fax your order to the above address. Fax No. 0326 376423.

Payments can be made as follows: Cheque, postal order (payable to Little, Brown and Company) or by credit cards, Visa/Access. Do not send cash or currency. UK customers: and B.F.P.O.: please send a cheque or postal order (no currency) and allow £1.00 for postage and packing for the first book, plus 50p for the second book, plus 30p for each additional book up to a maximum charge of £3.00 (7 books plus).

Overseas customers including Ireland, please allow £2.00 for postage and packing for the first book, plus £1.00 for the second book, plus 50p for each additional book.

NAME (Block Letters) ....

ADDRESS...

....

☐ I enclose my remittance for _____

☐ I wish to pay by Access/Visa Card

Number ⬚⬚⬚⬚⬚⬚⬚⬚⬚⬚⬚⬚⬚⬚⬚⬚

Card Expiry Date ⬚⬚⬚⬚